The Protector Of Esparia

Lisa M. Wilson

Other Books by Dragon Scale Publishing

The Dragon's Champion series by Sam Ferguson

The Netherworld Gate Series by Sam Ferguson

The Exile by Eric Buffington (Coming Soon)

Dimwater's Dragon by Sam Ferguson

Jonathan Haymaker by Sam Ferguson

DEDICATION

To my children who are my biggest supports.

Prologue

The sounds of clashing swords and the cries of men dying were closer now. Gayleena stared down at the newborn infant she held in her arms. "Sleep on little one," she whispered. "I wish I had your peace." She swallowed hard, trying to slow her racing pulse and undo the twisted knot in her stomach.

"Blasted hair!" Larone's outburst caused the baby to jump, her little hands flying into the air. "When this is over I'm going to shave it all off."

Gayleena glanced over to where Larone crouched. A well-worn stellar map was spread out in front of him, its ragged edges curled upward from the polished marble floor. He swiped at the long silver hair that fell in disarray around his face. Sorrow swept through her. The stately man should have been safely tucked away at the university, not here enchanting a pathway from one star to another halfway across the map. He looked anything but stately now; his robes of office exchanged for armor and a sword replacing the writing brush. His lips moved silently while he traced and retraced the astral course with his finger.

"Shave it? Would he really?" A lad, no longer a child, not yet a man, whispered at Gayleena's side.

"No, Haesom," she soothed. The innocent query momentarily lessened her anxiety. "He's feeling the pressure."

"Uncle Anton and I have finished setting up. Can I hold her?" The boy reached for the baby. Without a word, she slid the tiny form into his arms.

All furniture had been pushed against the walls of the spacious room and an immense, flat stone now lay in its center. A fist-sized crater in the middle of this stone held a blue, oval shaped crystal. A vein of fine amber sand rimmed the crater's perimeter. Another encircled the stone.

Anton, large and imposing, leaned against one of two marble pillars that flanked the chamber's closed doors. His normally ruddy face was drained of all color. His frizzy hair lay matted against his head and neck. With one hand he repeatedly tossed upward then caught a small vial of green liquid. The other hand gripped the hilt of his drawn sword.

Gayleena closed her eyes. She forced her breathing to remain even. They were trapped. Her two uncles and her two, sweet children because of her…because she was too weak to run. Only Larone's healing magic had stopped the bloody hemorrhage caused by the birthing. Then Anton had burst in with forewarning, just ahead of the attacking army. Graesion, her beloved, never had the chance to hold their new little Shallenon. In her heart Gayleena feared he was dead, yet the hope of a miracle still flickered in the back of her mind. If only reinforcements could arrive in time. Time...it had become their greatest enemy. Had Graesion bought them enough time? Would her uncle's desperate plan save the children? They should have killed Segal when they had the chance, but it was too late now. Too late for...

"I have imprinted the course on the map." Larone's comment pulled Gayleena from her thoughts. "Are you ready, Anton?"

"Yep," the big man pulled upright from the pillar and sheathed his weapon. "The persite's sittin' in the stone." His booming voice seemed out of place in the somber room. The baby twitched in Haesom's embrace.

"Here." Larone handed the map, now folded into a small, tight square to the big man, then crossed to Gayleena's side. "I am sorry, my dear. I wish there were some other way." He leaned down and kissed her on the forehead. "We will find the means of bringing you back, I promise."

"So, this place where we're going is safe, right? You're certain? I only have a sword and dagger to protect them." Haesom said. He handed his sister back to Gayleena.

"Safer than it is here, my boy—that I will guarantee," Larone answered. "It is our sister world, apart in physical distance, but joined together in the Transmirian Sea. After two millennia the passage is still intact, so the choice was clear."

Gayleena looked from one uncle to the other. "You've both worked so hard these last two days."

"The portal's ready to open," Anton's deep bass cut in. He had placed the folded map into the hole in the stone next to the blue crystal. "Just in time, too. N'before you go askin--yes, I'm sure I got everythin' right. Sure enough to bet the lives of the people I value most in this world. Now come 'ere boy." Anton held his arms wide. "It's time for good-bye." Haesom rushed to the embrace.

With a boom, the tall chamber door crashed open. A bloodied soldier charged in. "Protector....Graesion... is dead," he panted. "We hold...the hall...but not for long."

Gayleena felt the blood drain from her face. The hoped for miracle died with this news.

"If my father is dead, then I will stay." Haesom stepped away from his uncle.

"No!" Gayleena gasped.

"Mama," Haesom's voice was soft, but firm. "The people will need me. You have to leave...have to save Shallenon. With papa gone, I'm the last Protector."

"But, you're only thirteen."

"I'll be fourteen in a week."

"If you live that long!"

"Gayleena," Larone broke in, "we can save him. He can run and he can fight. After you leave, Anton and I are going to the lower tunnels. If we hurry, with those left, we can protect Haesom. But you and the baby…there is no possible way."

Haesom went to his mother and put his arm around her waist. "Papa trained me, and I'm as good as any soldier."

Gayleena's tears fell in bitter frustration. Her enemy had won, time had finally run out. "Haesom…Haesom." Her mouth formed the words, but no sound gave them voice.

"I know what I'm doing, Mama. I understand."

Anton opened the vial he had been holding. While pouring the green liquid over the map and blue crystal, he chanted. "By the voice of T'Aalin, through the Expanse of Gonta, I call on the powers of Bree, to open this passage, through the winds of Malana, I call the Transmirian key. By the voice of T'Aalin, through the Expanse of Gonta…"

Larone's tenor joined Anton's bass, but his words wove a different spell. "The threads of love through blood generations keep us close though we be apart. Of one family, of one mind, of one spirit, of one heart." The two brothers harmonized their voices in a melodic blend. Never faltering, Larone reached out and touched first Gayleena and then the baby. An almost imperceptible shock ran through Gayleena's body.

The crystal melted into the green fluid, filling the crater to overflowing. The folded map burst into white flame, its heat sparking the amber sand. Each grain popped in the fire, releasing thin yellow vapors shooting upward to the ceiling. Plumes of white and blue smoke spiraled around the yellow wisps, momentarily hanging in the air above the stone. Abruptly Anton's bass voice dropped further in pitch and Larone's was silenced. The three smokes slowly swirled in a clock-wise motion, their distinctive colors blending together, changing to ebony. Round and round the darkened mixture went, picking up speed and expanding outward like the churning of a giant whirlpool. A low-pitched whoosh hissed from the spinning air, increasing in volume and intensity.

Anton, continuing his chant, backed out of the way, for within seconds the massive, black pool of churning air filled half the room. Larone, his unruly hair whipping around his head, stood next to Gayleena, his arms wrapped protectively around Haesom.

"I love you!" Gayleena cried above the tumult. She ran a hand through her son's red hair, gave him one last kiss, then clutching the newborn child to her chest, bolted into the heart of the swirling tempest.

CHAPTER 1

Dreams

"Hey, Dad, I'm home," Jessica called when she entered the brightly lit house. She knew he was still awake, reading one of his many medical journals or researching a new procedure on the internet. He never went to bed, no matter how late, until she was safely home. She found it endearing yet highly irritating.

"How did things go?' he called from the den. "Will the cat make it?"

"It was a dog, and yeah, I think so." She began her nightly routine of shutting down the house. Kitchen door locked, cupboards closed and lights switched off. Television powered down, lamps extinguished, and window draperies closed. She bolted the front door. "Did you go downstairs while I was gone? Anything down there I need to worry about?"

"Nope. Haven't budged since you left." Porch lights out, hall lights dimmed and cell phones plugged in. She paused at the den and stuck her head through the open door. "I really hate these late night emergencies. Doc needs to hire another assistant."

Her father smiled up from his computer terminal. "Welcome to my world."

"You can have it. I told you, this is only for the summer. Much as I love animals, my heart belongs to the lab." She yawned. "Cutting edge research is eight to five, not twenty-four seven."

"Not for first year bio majors, however, your point is well taken. Sleep good, Jess."

"Don't forget the lights when you're done." She tapped the switch for emphasis, blew him a kiss then headed for her upstairs bedroom. "Note to self…check the den lights in the morning."

* * *

A chilling gust roused Jessica from her sleep. She caught her breath at the unexpected cold. When she opened her eyes, blades of slender grass came into focus. It took a moment for the foliage to register and when it did, she flinched; for it was not a sweet herbal scent that filled her nostrils

4

but the distinctive stench of blood. Another gust brought smoke. Fire!? She pushed to a sitting position.

Gone were the warm comforter, the soft bed, and her familiar room. Enough starlight filtered down through fissures in the clouds for her to see she rested on a grassy knoll. Behind her, several buildings smoldered orange-red. A few massive beams still stood here and there, like skeletal fingers rising upward from glowing ashes. A partial moon, uncovered by the rising winds, momentarily bathed the landscape in its platinum light. Jessica gasped. Armor-clad bodies lay strewn throughout the surrounding field. Several were so close that details of their fresh slaughter were easily distinguished. Far away, the clashing of steel and the howls of men in agony drifted on the breeze.

"Addex! No!" A man's plea startled Jessica. "Spare my family. Daenon hasn't ordered their deaths."

Only a few yards away knelt a man, his hands tied behind him. Light from at least a dozen torches reflected off blood oozing through a wound in his scalp. The sticky liquid matted his shoulder-length red hair. A second man, his face partially concealed under a metal helmet, loomed over him, his right arm raised in a striking position. He held a sword in the elevated hand.

Without seeing his face, Jessica knew the unfortunate prisoner. "Haesom," she breathed. She knew this man and his home that lay in ruins behind her. For ten years, since the night of her mother's funeral, she had dreamed about him and his family. They had always been good dreams, filled with magical animals, wondrous places and kind, gentle people. Her dreams, though not frequent, came often enough to fill a void in her heart, for Haesom looked remarkably like her mother.

Behind captor and captive stood a battery of soldiers, some held the torches while others detained a woman and two teenage boys. Jessica felt sick. *Not the boys*, she thought. She had come to love them; their antics always making her laugh. She had dubbed them Big and Little Red, for their hair was the same fiery color as their dad's. Bound by thick ropes, the grim-faced youths stood silent, staring down at their kneeling father. Their mother, her blond hair disheveled around her shoulders, stood rigidly beside them. She looked straight ahead, her thin, ashen face devoid of expression.

"Please, Addex," Haesom begged again, "let my family live. They've done you no harm." The passion in his voice stirred Jessica, but Addex appeared unmoved.

The pounding of horse's hooves brought a momentary reprieve for the condemned man. From the direction of the burned out buildings, a rider galloped up the hill. One of the torchbearers approached and whispered in Addex's ear. The executioner lowered his weapon and turned

5

to face the newcomer.

The black clad soldiers sprinted apart; one narrowly escaping the horse's hooves. The rider pulled to an abrupt halt in front of the kneeling prisoner. "Where is it, Haesom?" he demanded, jumping from his mount. "Where is the Sword of Judgment?"

The kneeling man squared his shoulders. "That is one prize you'll never have."

For a moment the rider fingered a shiny metal hoop hanging from one of his ears then he began to pace. The light from the torches danced off his polished armor at every sharp turn. With his constant motion and the firelights flickering in the wind, Jessica was unable to get a good look at his shadow-filled face.

The woman's lips twitched upward into a tiny smile. She looked to her doomed husband and slowly shook her head. The movement seemed to have caught the interrogator's attention.

"What about your wife and children?" his hand flicked in the lady's direction. "You know you're already dead, but give me the sword and I swear I'll spare their lives."

Jessica's blood pressure spiked. He had lied. She saw the lie leave his mouth and coil around him, a wispy gray tendril. Big Red cried out. "Father, no!" From behind, a soldier slugged him for his bravery and he fell, face first, to the earth.

"Listen to me, cousin," the tempter baited, his voice low and smooth. "I can show mercy to your family. Give up the weapon and give them life."

Time ticked by in heavy silence, until at last Haesom shook his head. "I know you all too well, Daenon. You have never honored your word. As soon as you have what you want you'll murder us all. Keeping the Sword of Judgment safe will be this family's final act as High Protectors."

Daenon growled. "You and your pathetic duty! It's a piece of metal! Would you condemn your loved ones for bits of gold and steel?"

"If that were all it was, you wouldn't want it so desperately. We both know its power. No, Daenon, you will *never* have that prize."

Daenon stopped his pacing. He raised an arm and backhanded Haesom across the face. "Kill them all, Addex. Rid me of the House of Saylon."

"No!" Jessica screamed. Her dream had become a nightmare. No one moved; no one appeared to have heard her. She tried to run, wanting to intervene, but her limbs would not respond.

"Let the Protectors die," the cold, emotionless voice of Addex cut Jessica's soul like a knife. Her eyes darted over the group. All were riveted on Addex as he slowly raised his sword arm, all except Little Red. He stared directly at Jessica. Their gazes locked and for a brief instant the corners of his mouth went up in a slight, sad smile. "Goody-bye", he silently mouthed to her and a single tear slid down his face.

Jessica sat straight-up in her bed. Her breath came in short, deep gasps. She pushed her hair out of her face and used her sheet to wipe the tears that streamed down both cheeks. Anger, astonishment, and sadness rolled through her like waves in a churning ocean. She had always let her dreams unfold by themselves, never trying to direct their outcomes, but this one time she had tried, tried so very hard and yet she could not control the ending. She was certain Little Red had actually seen her. Never before had anyone seemed aware of her watchful presence. Overwhelming sadness filled her entire being.

A soft meow and a wet lick at her hand brought a measure of relief. "Sneakers." She reached for the animal and stroked his soft fur. Sneakers meowed again and rubbed his head against her hand. His strong purr calmed her, brought her thoughts back into focus. "I…I'm okay," she said to the tabby, and releasing him, snuggled back under her comforter The clock on her nightstand read 3:00 am.

Jessica tossed and turned. Sleep came in snatches that were measured in minutes by the bedside clock…3:15…3:25…3:42. Even her comfortable bed felt hard and uninviting, as if she were lying on a concrete floor. "This is ridiculous." She rolled over to peek, for the fourth time, at the glowing readout, but it was obscured.

Smoke? Smoke! Smoke so thick it obscured everything. Her heart jumped and she instinctively scrambled to her feet. "Dad!" She took three steps toward the door before realizing it was not there. Nothing was there. For the second time that night, her room had vanished. She waved her hand through the white, enveloping cloud. No, this wasn't smoke. Thin, moisture-less vapor swirled in every direction, shrouding the world around her. The air held no humidity, which should have been present with a watery mist. There were no choking fumes that would have come with fire. This odd haze held neither cold nor warmth. No smell. No taste. So light and gentle, if she closed her eyes her other senses would detect nothing.

The only illumination came from her very person, a weak glow, giving a few feet of visibility. This phenomenon did not surprise her. After all, she reasoned, dreams have many odd elements and certainly, for a second time that night, she was dreaming. Slowly, she turned a full circle, trying to peer through the fog, but nothing opened to her view. Even her feet and the firmness on which she stood evaded scrutiny. Once again, she passed her hand through the mist.

With the sensation of being in a sealed tomb, Jessica stood in the pervasive silence. Unsure of the passage of time and with no change in her environment, she finally decided to move. Unable to see the ground through the fog, her first step was tentative. When nothing happened, she took a second step and inched herself forward. She did not travel very far before catching the low vibration of voices. Turning toward the sounds, she carefully continued on.

A strange urgency to hear the conversation propelled her. However, with each step that brought her nearer, the haze thickened. It became oppressive. Sadness swept over her. As if in slow motion, she pushed her way through the sorrow-laden fog. She trudged onward, fighting back grief. The effort was exhausting. With three more strenuous steps she could finally make out their words and she fell to her knees.

"They are dead sir, every one of them," a gravel-voiced man moaned. "Even the boys were murdered. I arrived too late with my warning. I watched the soldiers drag each body to the kitchen well and throw it in. From my hiding place I recognized all four." A sob escaped him. "All is lost now...lost. It's only a matter of time before he searches for you. He will destroy everything and everyone who dares oppose him." Despair filled the man's voice and Jessica felt pity pierce through her own heartache.

"No, Quirt." the other man corrected. "All is not lost." Deep and resonating, this voice inspired trust.

"But, with Haesom's death, and his family, there's no one left."

"We have one chance."

"Wh...What?"

"Not all the Saylon's are dead." The heavy sorrow eased just a little.

Jessica inched a little closer to where she thought the men were. She tried to see the speakers, but the thick mist prevented her.

"It...It's so hard to believe! I heard rumors, foolish whispers, but..."

"Believe it, old friend. Graesion's family was not killed, but sent far away."

"Where? Why didn't the Lady return? Segal's been dead for over fifty years?"

"Only recently has Anton found the means for a return journey. This is ancient magic, volatile and dangerous."

"An heir of Graesion's lives." Jessica strained to hear Quirt's whisper. "What if he refuses to help us, to take his rightful place?" Despair crept into his voice again. "The danger...Protector Haesom had an entire army and defeat still came. Does he know his heritage?"

"I do not know that answer. As with all Protectors, this one too will have to choose whether or not to take the position and all that goes with it. Undoubtedly by now," there was a slight pause, "the successor has discovered some unique gifts, but not a full understanding of their true value, higher skills will need developing at Ramadine."

"Do you think Daenon suspects?" At the mention of this name, hate replaced Jessica's sorrow.

"No, and this is our greatest advantage. If he thought for one moment another Protector existed, he would be relentless in his search.

Family is nothing to him. My nephew even wants my head."

There was a deep, tired sigh. "Quirt, it has been a long day and you have traveled far to bring me this sad news. You must get some rest, for tomorrow I am sending you on another mission." The tone of his voice became firmer. "This fight we will win, so do not be discouraged. Now, I must contact Anton. We have much to do, and our time is short."

The glow around Jessica dimmed. In the distance, the rumble of a faint, familiar purr caught her attention. *Sneakers.* Gradually, the purr grew louder and sharper, bringing with it a pervasive weariness. Jessica could no longer sit upright and she lay down. Closing her eyes, she settled into a deep slumber.

* * *

The morning sun streamed through the bedroom window. Jessica sat up and rubbed her face. She shuddered. The dreams from the night before came flooding back. Surely they were brought on by the grisly surgery she had helped with at the veterinarian's office, she reasoned. Yes, that made sense.

Hopping out of bed, she ran to the window. The morning sky was a rich shade of blue sprinkled with high wispy clouds. She slid the glass pane open. A warm breeze blew in, bringing with it the smell of lavender from the flower bed below.

Pulling on a creamy yellow robe, she noticed her mother's picture frame on the floor beside the dresser, photo side down. "Sneakers!" she scolded. Gently she turned it over, hoping that the glass was not broken. Haesom's face stared up at her. She froze. The resemblance between this dreamed up friend and her mom was uncanny. She blinked several times. As she did, Haesom's image faded and her mother's came into focus. With a shaking hand, she put the frame back on the dresser, then hurried from the room.

Jessica bounded down the stairs. In the kitchen she found her dad seated in his usual place at the glass table. Clean-shaven and dressed in a brown suit with matching tie, he appeared completely immersed in the morning paper, the Spokane Spokesman-Review. Knowing the sound of her feet on the tile floor would bring him out of his inner world, she threw her weight into each step. A smile twitched at the corners of his mouth and his gray eyes lit up.

"Good morning, Dad." She kissed him on the cheek, her long, red hair sweeping across the top of his head.

"Good morning, Jess. It's a big day today."

"Yeah, I can't believe it's here. After twelve looong years, I'm actually graduating." She reached for a sack of bagels on the counter.

9

"I thought you'd sleep in today; after that late night surgery."

"No, I'm supposed to meet Melissa and run in an hour. I also had a pretty disturbing dream last night so it's definitely time to get up."

"Really?" John lowered his paper. "How disturbing?"

"Well, I've told you about that family I dream about periodically; the one where the dad looks a lot like mom."

He nodded. "The Saylon's. The relatives on your mom's side that your subconscious dreamed up."

"Yeah....well...they died last night. Murdered, or assassinated. There were bodies all over and blood and guts...it was awful."

She tore off a piece of blueberry bagel and popped it into her mouth.

"Dreams are funny things, Jess. Maybe that surgery affected you more than you thought."

"That's what I figured." She considered telling him about the mist dream and seeing Haesom's face in her mom's photo, but decided against it. He would only worry. Turning back to the counter, she grabbed a small glass from the cupboard above. "Now remember, graduation begins at five. I have to go early, so you," she shook the glass at him for emphasis, "need to be home by four for pictures."

"Yes, yes." He turned back to the paper.

With the glass in one hand and bagel in the other, she sat down beside him. "Well, I took a few precautions. I talked to your secretary yesterday."

He looked up. "You did what?"

"Let's face it. Punctuality isn't your strong point. She promised to keep the major headaches off your desk until tomorrow. All you have going today are some interviews or something."

Sighing, he refolded the paper. "Okay, I get the message." Leaning over, he kissed Jessica on her forehead. He gave his tie one last straightening, then clipped on his I.D. tag. *Dr. John Ernshaw, MD; Director Medical Services.*

Jessica observed her father tenderly. "You know, Dad, you really are in great shape for a guy your age. If you'd let your hair grow out a little...no one would ever guess you were almost fifty."

"Almost fifty!" he rolled his eyes. "Don't make me old before my time! Forty-seven isn't fifty...and what about my hair? I happen to like my military cut." His slight staccato laugh made Jessica grin.

"You've been out two years, Colonel, live a little."

"I'll think about it." He pulled his car keys from his pant's pocket, gave her a wink and walked out the side door.

Jessica bolted after him. "'Thinking about it' always means 'no'", she hollered from the doorstep. "Just be on time tonight."

"Always, Jess. Always."

After finishing her breakfast, Jessica cleared the table and tidied up the kitchen. While she was wiping off the table, the side door opened and a sweet-faced woman in her late sixties walked in. Here stood the reason the kitchen, as well as the rest of the house, preserved its good order. The owner of Barts Professional Cleaners had just come to pay a visit.

Sophia Bartlowski reminded Jessica of a Christmas picture she had seen of Mrs. Claus, short and pleasantly plump. She removed a worn straw hat from her snowy white head, then placed it, along with a bulging purse, on the granite counter top.

With a warm smile on her face, Sophia turned to her young friend and chirped with a slight polish accent, "Good morning, Jessie dear." She slid one arm around the girl's waist and gave her an affectionate squeeze. "Is your father gone already? He works such long hours."

"Yeah, he's gone and I warned him to come home early." Jessica rinsed the dishcloth under the tap and placed it on the counter. "How come you're here and not one of your maids? It's not cleaning day it it?"

"I wanted to see you myself. Tonight's the big night. We'll all be there. Rachel's been counting the days. My granddaughter's very excited about being your roommate this fall."

"What would I do without Rach? You have no idea how I'm looking forward to the 'U'."

Sophia smiled, a twinkle of mischief in her brown eyes. "Since you'll be off on your own, how about a cooking lesson this morning?"

"Oooh, no." Jessica gave a hearty laugh. "So that's why your're here. Good try, Sophia, but you know how that stovetop hates me. So does the blender, the mixer, and the oven, but I think the microwave and I get along okay."

"I had to try. I promised your Grandma Gaylee I'd make an effort to teach you more than just noodle soup."

"But I like noodle soup."

Sophia chuckled. "I think while I'm here I'll tackle that front room closet for you. It's quiet at home today and I need a project."

"Well, okay. But be careful. The closet isn't a priority."

"Yes, I know, but my home's in good order and your closet's been bothering me since Christmas."

A soft meow caught Jessica's attention. Sneakers sat patiently by the kitchen door. "No, you can't bring me a mouse today. You know I hate those things, but thanks anyway." She opened the door and the big tomcat bounded outside.

The sound of Sophia humming an old polish tune drifted into the kitchen. It was a happy sound that made Jessica smile. She glanced at the calendar next to the kitchen phone. The gladness faded when she read the current date. Ten years ago on Saturday. One trip to the grocery store and their lives changed forever. Maybe that was why she had dreamed of death.

"Oh, Mom, I miss you so much," she whispered. Now she had only her father and her grandmother left. Thank goodness for Sophia and family. She left the kitchen and walked down the hall toward the stairs.

At the end of the hall, in the front entryway, Sophia was busily cleaning out the coat closet. Jessica paused. "What's Jacob doing today?" she asked.

"Hubby's off to a small remodeling job." Sophia frowned at a stray glove in her hand.

"I'm glad he's better."

"So am I. I don't know what we would have done without your father." She smiled at finding the glove's mate. "He never sent us a bill. I can never do enough to repay him for his kindness."

Jessica smiled. "That's exactly how we feel about you. I feel spoiled with your maid service keeping the house so clean. And wow! From what Grandma says, I could be speaking Polish right now."

"Escaping without Gaylee would have been like leaving my sister. I've decided to have a big party in August, to celebrate our fortieth year here in the United States."

"I love parties. If you need help planning, just let me know." The grandfather clock next to the closet chimed. "Oh, no! Is it eight already?!" Jessica glanced at the timepiece.

"School?"

"No, my run! Melissa and Clarice are going to kill me if I'm late again."

"Like father, like daughter."

12

CHAPTER 2

Plans

Jessica plodded up the driveway and shuffled through the kitchen door. 8 am was late for a run, but her friends wanted to sleep late and everyone forgot how hot June mornings could get. After two hours in the morning heat, she was dog-tired. She went straight to the sink, turned on the cold water, and leaned under the faucet to take a drink. She felt her muscles screaming for a cool shower and then fifteen minutes of relaxation in the built-in sauna downstairs. Strains of Elvis Presley came from the stereo system in the living room.

"I'm back," she called as she headed for the basement stairs.

Sophia poked her head into the hall. "Hello dear. I've just finished the closet. Did you have a nice run?"

"Yeah, I did and now it's sauna time."

Sophia frowned. "You be careful. You know I don't trust that hot box. Someone's going to get hurt in there."

Once downstairs, Jessica flipped on the heat to the dry sauna before slipping into the bathroom next to it. Shower finished and towel in place, she filled a plastic pitcher with water. Balancing the pitcher while clutching the towel, she glanced at the sauna thermometer before entering. It read one hundred sixteen.

The initial blast of dry heat eradicated the lingering muscle tension that the shower failed to relieve. She poured a little water from the pitcher onto the hot stones, then sat on the two-man bench opposite the heating unit to watch the water droplets dance and sizzle across the rocks before exploding in bursts of steam energy. After sprinkling on more water, she stretched out and lazily gazed at the mist curling up to the ceiling. The first few wisps vaporized into the warm air. However, within a few moments the wisps condensed into puffs, then the puffs swelled, like marshmallows roasting over warm coals. Amazed, she stood up and reached out to touch the small clouds. A tiny spark flashed from her finger tip. The clouds exploded. Hundreds of pea sized balls shot around the room. They doubled in size then doubled again and again. A billowy fog quickly filled the closet sized room. No longer moist, it swirled thicker and thicker around her. Within moments it obscured the cedar walls.

In the thickening mist all external light faded, but her body glowed, emanating enough light to see a few feet in each direction. "Unbelievable!" she muttered. *But last night was just a dream!*

A low vibration, directly behind her, filtered through the haze. Turning, she felt for the sauna bench and walls, but they were no longer there. She took a few steps. There was nothing to hinder her movement, so she hurried toward the sound. Two men were speaking. Like the night before, she felt an overwhelming urgency to listen to the conversation. .

"Larone, I've got it! It's all so simple now." A man boomed in a baritone that was obviously unaccustomed to whispering.

"You have finished the calculations already?" Jessica immediately recognized Larone's deep and resonating voice.

"Yep, I have," came the thundering reply. "Alderic's manuscript had the missin' part, the persite factor. I've wasted fifty years goin' over 'n over Tiard's incantations, not knowin' that white persite was the other Transmirian key. Alderic's writings fit like a puzzle with Tiard's. I needed both together. Blue sends ya off and white brings ya back. Did ya know these guys were brothers?"

"No." There was a gentle laugh. "How appropriate, that two brothers unravel their work. There is so much more here, now that we understand their dual writing...but that is for another day. Tell me what you have learned."

"Normally spirals are tiny; poppin' up from time to time. They're pressure outlets for the Transmirian Sea. For instance, when ya lay somethin' down and it just disappears...No one took it, it isn't misplaced, it's just gone...into thin air. Well, a right turning spiral opened up and sucked the thing in, transforming it into an energy signature floating on the astral plane. That much we knew from Alderic's manuscript. The new information is from Tiard. He writes about left turning spirals. They open up, reanimating the energy, and spit things out, no harm done. Green persite makes the spiral bigger, lots bigger. And a map, enchanted with the right coordinates, gives the spiral a course to follow to where ever we want it to go. You figured that one out, but this confirms it. So, blue persite forces a right handed spiral spin, and white persite forces it left. The right transports one way and the left spin brings ya back." He chuckled, a low rumble that made Jessica smile. "We just got to keep our persite colors straight."

"When you explain it like that, it certainly does seem simple, but Anton, do not minimize your part. Deciphering the writing code was brilliant, and then perfecting the transport system...well, as you said; it has all taken fifty years."

"Yeah. I've pulverized more logs of wood than I'll admit to in testin' this out."

"But everything works now, right?" Concern crept into Larone's tone.

"Yep. The first rabbit I used came back safe and sound, so Varnack volunteered to go next."

"Varnack! You kept that a secret."

"It was a quick trip, but he came back in one piece. Um...he was unconscious for a day or so, but I've adjusted the amount of persite so's the tidal pull won't be as strong." Here Anton paused. "That persite is powerful stuff, 'specially the white. I remember the last time we did this. We just about killed everyone."

"As I recall, we had little time. The Demarian army crashed in moments after we left. Sending them off-world saved their lives."

"Yeah, too bad I didn't understand the persite better. I could've sent them somewhere closer."

"All ended well, Anton...As well as could have been hoped for. Your incantation controlled the persite long enough to create a spiral, while Graesion bought just enough time to test it. What you did was incredible, opening a Transmirian spiral and holding the portal long enough to transport two people through it."

"Well, I... Never...I...Graesion." Anton cleared his throat, "I've thought of him a lot. He was as fine a man as I ever did meet. Too bad we couldn't have sent his boy through too. He'd still be alive." He cleared his throat again, much harder this time.

"Haesom chose to stay, fully understanding the dangers. He was an outstanding Protector, giving the people security and hope, and rebuilding the country after Segal's defeat. He will be revered as one of the finest Protectors Esparia has ever known." Jessica was stunned. Haesom had been someone she'd dreamed up, a subconscious response to her mother's death. These men spoke of him as a real person. But wasn't this also a dream?

"That doogeroot! Segal!" Anton choked out the name. Jessica jumped. "Segal began all this with his lustin' for power 'n his self-appointed godhood."

"Yes, and now the son is more malignant than the father. Daenon's strength grows daily." Jessica felt a cold lump in her stomach. She shivered, but not from cold. "As the news of Protector Haesom's death spreads, the people will start to lose heart. They will rally to us for a time, but without a true heir of the Saylon family to lead them, they may lose their resolution." Larone sounded grim.

"I agree we need a true heir. A power vacuum right now would be disaster, but," Anton faltered, "but have ya considered how the family's goin' to feel? I'd be killin'mad if someone took my kid."

"Of **course** I have! Do you **not** think I have gone over this a hundred times trying to find another way? Another solution? I've weighed the

15

heartache of a few against the welfare of a nation. I feel sick inside, yet I know, nothing doubting, that this is what we must do."

"I'm sorry, Larone. Yeah," he sighed heavily, "this is the only option, I just wish there was some way of giving a warning."

"Yes. It would be nice to lay all the facts out in the open. And, I will still do that. No one will be forced to take on the role of High Protector, but the invitation, with all of its ramifications, must be made in person."

Anton's voice was softer now, "I'll begin working on a return trip, just in case the answer is no. But for now, I've set up the trigger mechanism so's it activates when someone with the right life force touches it. Since I didn't have an exact sample, I set it to any variation of my own. Just family can set it off. We don't need any accidental day-trippers showin' up here."

"Well done."

"I haven't been totally unsuccessful in fifty years of tinkerin'." Talking about his project rekindled the enthusiasm in his voice. "I've been workin' on the fine details, like the size of the spiral. Don't need to fill a whole room. So where do you want the key turned?"

"Someplace away from Daenon's spies. Ramadine is not safe. I cannot explain it, but something is not right here. We need time to better secure the city."

Jessica stood transfixed. This was too crazy. She *must* be hallucinating. Graesion. Did she recognize that name? She wished she could remember.

There was silence. Were the men still there? She took a tentative step forward, her body so tense, that when Larone finally spoke again she jumped half a foot.

"I think the Southern Greenwood, close to Ider Hoffle would be the best location. How long will it take you to go there?"

"Hmmm. Several days to Greenwood, but if I turn a half spiral, I can get there t'day. There's a meadow south of Ider Hoffle where lots of soft moss grows. Enchant me a map and I'll have everythin' in place by midnight."

"Half spiral! You really have been tinkering."

"A weaker spiral goes short distances. Once ya get used to it, it's kinda fun. Do ya want me to stay 'n wait? Someone should be there."

"Agreed, but not you. We do not know when the spiral will be activated. It could be several days and, given the current state of national affairs, your presence here is mandatory. No arguments. Take Varnack with you. He is quite capable of taking care of himself, and other than you, he is the only one I trust as guide and guardian. He can wait as long as necessary. Besides, my dear baby brother," Larone added with a low chuckle, "the sight of you could frighten anyone back into that black portal."

"Jessica…Jessica dear." Sophia's voice came from worlds away. Instantly, the mist stopped swirling and a blast of warm air hit Jessica full in the face. She closed her eyes against the onslaught. When she opened them a moment later, she found herself standing in the small home sauna.

"Jessica, are you still down there? Are you alright?" Sophia called from halfway down the basement stairs.

"Yes, I'm here," Jessica called back. She fumbled to open the sauna door. "I'm fine." No she was not fine. She was losing her mind!

"I've been calling you. Why didn't you answer? Do you need some help?"

"No, I'm fine…really. I was day dreaming…I didn't hear you call." Standing just outside the sauna, Jessica took some deep breaths.

"Are you sure? Do you have that thing turned up too high?"

"No. I…I was just off in a fog."

"Well, all right." Sophia sounded unconvinced. "You're wanted on the telephone."

When Jessica turned the sauna off, Sophia's light footsteps receded back up the stairs. She swiped the perspiration from her face then reached for the telephone on the wall opposite the sauna.

"Hello?"

"Hey, Reddica, it's Mark."

She paused before responding. She hated that nickname and he knew it, but she was too rattled to argue with the friendly tease.

"What's up?"

"I decided to have a party after graduation tonight, my house around nine. What do ya say?"

She was annoyed. This was so typical of Mark, always last minute. In the eleven years they had been friends, she never knew him to plan ahead. "Maybe. I'll have to work it out with my family, but…yeah…I think so."

"Heads up…I've invited Thomas Banks. He's off on a huge summer vacation tomorrow, but I convinced him he couldn't miss my party 'cause you'd be there."

"Whatever. Fine."

"Cool. See ya later."

Jessica had butterflies. She had kept it to herself, but Thomas Banks was someone she had been attracted to for years, though from a distance. She had her group and he had his, and except for her buddy Mark, who was friends with everyone under the sun, the two groups seldom interacted.

For a full minute after hanging up the phone, she leaned against the wall. She had a headache. Was she losing her mind? She groaned. Maybe she should call Grandma. Grandma always had answers. But then it hit her. "I don't have a thing to wear!"

17

Jessica glared at her open closet and the frustration mounted while the minutes ticked by. The normally neat row of clothing was now a jumble of skewed hangers and dangling garments. She had already been through everything twice, and a third pillaging would be needed before a final decision could be reached. Glancing at the thoroughly ransacked chest-of-drawers, she knew Sophia would cringe if she saw the room, but she just had to find something to wear. She couldn't concentrate.

The vision of a kneeling man, with an executioner's sword poised above him, and the faces of his two sons helplessly looking on kept propelling itself into her mind.

The sauna experience, as well as the dream paralleling it from the night before, weighed her down with an almost physical force. She could explain neither how they occurred, nor what they meant, but one thing was clear in her mind…they were very real.

Rubbing her eyes, she tried to rid herself of the memories. "Stop this, Jessica," she commanded out loud. A telephone ring intruded on her thoughts. Snatching up the cordless she answered a little too loudly, "Hello?"

"Happy graduation day, Jess!"

Relief swept through her. "Grandma Gaylee, I'm soooo glad you called." She flopped down on the edge of the bed. "I've been wondering if I should call you. The weirdest things have been happening to me and I think I'm going crazy!"

"Jess, tell me what's going on."

Jessica talked for nearly forty-five minutes. She recounted her two dreams from the night before and her strange experience in the sauna, followed by the phone call from Mark with the party invite and how excited she felt about Thomas Banks being there. She did not leave anything out, for Grandma always seemed to know when she did. At last she ended with, "and Grandma, I just don't know what to wear!"

The silence from the other end of the phone lasted for so long that Jessica wondered if her grandmother was still on the line. "Grandma? Are you there?"

"Yes, dear. I'm…still here," came the slow reply.

"Are you all right?"

"Jessica, there are many things I've never told you about myself." There was another long pause. "I understand the dreams and I can unravel each one. I do have answers for you, but not right now. I need to digest what you've told me. Besides, today is your day and I won't do anything to spoil it. I think we have a little time, so first thing tomorrow morning I'll come over and tell you a fantastic story about devotion to duty, bravery beyond self, and a lust for power that almost destroyed a nation. We'll sort everything out together so don't worry anymore."

"Grandma, you've really got me going. Can't you tell me now?"

"Jess," there was a catch in the woman's voice, "*not now.*"

Jessica knew not to push her grandmother. "Okay," she resigned herself, "but, you really do understand this stuff?"

"Yes, dear, I really do. Everything's going to be alright, I promise."

"You don't think I'm losing my mind?"

Grandma gave a slight laugh. "No. In fact, I know you're not. Now let me help you with that outfit."

* * *

Jessica paced back and forth in the kitchen. Her high-heeled shoes echoed on the tile while her graduation gown swished with every turn. The microwave clock showed another minute had ticked by. "Eight minutes after four. He's late." she complained to Sneakers, stretched out on the cool tile floor. A persistent flutter in her stomach made her feel especially edgy. "Why am I so jumpy?"

Sneakers lifted his head and meowed.

"I know you don't know."

Shifting to his belly, the cat meowed again.

"Yeah, I know I worry too much, but it's more than that. It could be graduation, or even this Thomas thing, but that should make me excited, not...scared." She stopped in front of the large bay window located next to the kitchen door. Only her car, bathed in bright sunlight, was in the driveway. A few rosebuds peaked above the sill from the bushes underneath. Jessica always worried when her father was late. She realized long ago this was a reaction to her mother never returning home, but no matter how hard she tried, she could never stop the anxiety. Finally, her father pulled into the drive.

He dashed from the car, almost before it stopped moving, and ran up the walkway that led to the kitchen. A second later, he flew through the door. Checking the clock on the microwave, he panted, "Not bad, not bad at all. I made it in fifteen minutes." He offered no explanations for his late arrival and Jessica knew not to question him. "You look beautiful, just like your mom." He gave her a huge bear hug.

"Dad," she squeezed him back in relief. "Thanks for trying." She let him go, then grabbed the camera on the table. "Let's go."

Sneakers followed the two out the kitchen door and around to the front yard. When Jessica posed in front of the weeping willow for the first picture, the animal sat at her feet.

"Jess, tell the cat to move."

Looking down at her pet she responded, "He just wants to be in the picture with me."

"Well, this isn't a family photo."

"Sneakers," she called.

The cat stopped grooming. His yellow eyes met her sapphire blue ones.

"Dad says this is not a group opportunity, so will you please go over and sit by him?"

Sneakers looked at John for a few seconds.

"Now, please."

He obediently scampered to John's side.

"As usual, Jess, I'm amazed. You and that cat have quite a relationship. It's uncanny how you two communicate."

After snapping thirty or so frames at various locations around the yard, the fashion shoot ended. Back in the house, Jessica grabbed a small bag with her party clothes.

Picking up her wallet and car key, she headed for the door. "I guess I'm off," she called over her shoulder. "You're getting Grandma, right?"

"Yes, I'm right behind you, just have to grab the video camera."

Jessica's car stood next to her father's. When she opened the door to throw her bag in, she remembered the party.

"Hey," she yelled, "There's a party tonight at Mark's house. It starts around nine. Okay if I go?"

"A party, huh?" He locked the deadbolt behind him. "Sure. Have a great time; just drive carefully."

"Thanks...oh, and Dad," she added.

He paused at his car, parked beside hers.

"Please, please, please...don't leave every light on in the house for me. I'm a big girl now and just need a porch light...not afraid of the dark."

He smiled and nodded.

* * *

Downtown, Jessica found a parking place across from the Opera House where graduation ceremonies were held. As she left the car, a white pickup drove in beside her. Thomas Banks climbed out of the driver's side with his cap and gown tucked under his arm.

Jessica's pulse picked up speed. "Hey, Thomas."

His face flushed a light red, but he smiled. "How's it going?" he replied.

"Fine." Jessica felt awkward. She desperately wanted to say something witty, something to impress him, but her mind was completely blank.

They stood together in silence. Finally, Thomas broke the uneasiness when he cleared his throat, "I guess Mark's having a party tonight."

Relieved, Jessica nodded. "Last minute as usual, but it should be fun."

They started across the parking lot. "Maybe tonight you can show me some of those awesome kicks you did in self-defense class. I never knew a girl could be so intense."

Jessica laughed. "To be honest, I took the class for an easy 'A'. I've studied martial arts since I was five."

Thomas gave a hearty laugh. "Five! No wonder I was constantly being thrown onto my back. My sisters all took dance or piano." They reached the traffic light at the corner and as they waited for it to turn green, Jessica glanced up at the large Opera House Marquee. 'Ferris High School Graduation 5pm'.

"My dad's retired army, and I'm the first girl in a long line of military men. Mark said you're off on a big trip tomorrow." Jessica was vaguely aware they were crossing Spokane Falls Boulevard. Her attention was completely riveted on Thomas.

"My parents have planned this summer vacation for a year. We head to Europe at six tomorrow morning. Mark's party wasn't a high priority, but to be honest...when he said you'd be there...I couldn't say no."

She caught her breath at the unexpected comment and felt her pulse increase. They reached the backstage door. He held it open for her. Most of the three hundred seniors had arrived and were in various groups. The two of them would go their separate ways in a few moments, he to his friends, and she to hers; however, she wanted his company just a little longer.

"Are you ready with your speech? Are you nervous?" she blurted out.

"You should be on the program, not me. I've heard you speak, you're good." Shaking his head, he sighed. "I hate talking in public, but I guess I'm ready."

She placed her hand on his arm. "I know you'll do great."

"Thanks."

"Jessica! Hey Jess, over here!" A pretty blond, already in cap and gown called and waved.

"Looks like you're wanted, Heather's calling." Thomas gestured to a group of girls at the far end of the room. "And there's Mark." He nodded at a group of guys off to his left. "I'll see you later tonight then."

"Yeah, later." Turning away, she strolled toward her friends. She did not know if Thomas watched her leave, but just in case, she wanted to look as regal as possible. She almost succeeded too, but as luck would have it, a trio of boys started a game of keep-away with a graduation cap. Within a few feet of reaching her companions, one of the boys, his eyes on the cap, ran headlong into Jessica, sending her sprawling in a most unregal fashion.

Her wallet and keys went flying as she tried to save her dignity in heels and a dress. She managed to fall, as Heather later told her, gracefully. While she and her friends quickly gathered up her scattered belongings, she stole a glance in Thomas' direction. To her utter horror, he and most of his friends were staring.

CHAPTER 3

The Transmirian Spiral

Twenty minutes after graduation dinner, Jessica pulled up to Mark's house, an older colonial home, located in a nice neighborhood on Spokane's South Hill. Several cars, including Thomas's truck, were parked in a vacant lot beside the home.

Thomas stood on the front lawn next to the makeshift parking lot. She wondered if he'd been out there waiting for her.

"Hey," he called when she opened her car door.

Before she could return the greeting, a black jeep skidded into the last open spot at the end of the lot. The driver was yelling inside the vehicle. His words were unintelligible, but the tone of his voice was unmistakable. Ray, a football player who Jessica intensely disliked, raged at the crying girl beside him.

Thomas, now at Jessica's side, scowled at the scene. "That doesn't look good."

The yelling stopped. "Let's go," he whispered.

Jessica nodded.

They walked over the freshly manicured grass, past the neat rows of planted pansies and petunias, to the front porch. Just before stepping through the open door, Jessica took a quick look back toward the jeep. The occupants were heading toward the house. Ray had a grip on the girl's wrist and she wiped at the smudged mascara under her eyes with her free hand.

The aroma of fresh baked bread permeated the home. A woman carrying a steaming pepperoni pizza nearly collided with Thomas. "Oh Tommy, didn't see you there…and Jessica! Here, take this to the game room, will you?" She held the hot pads out to Thomas.

"No problem Mrs. R." Thomas reached for the burden. "Smells great."

"Mark made me promise to bring one down every half hour, so if you want anything special on it, just let me know."

Jessica followed Thomas downstairs. Music and laughter grew louder with each descending step. A spacious game room, equipped with a foosball table in one corner, an air-hockey table in another, and gaming system in a third came into view. The center of the room had a ping-pong table. Jessica cleared a spot for the hot pizza on a table loaded with cookies, nuts, popcorn and chips. Music played from a portable stereo set up under the refreshments. On the far wall a sliding glass door opened onto a walk-out patio lit by tiki torches. About thirty friends were busily engaged in the various activities as well as dancing on the patio.

"Are you up for a round of air-hockey?" Thomas challenged.

"You're on!" He beat her soundly, three games to one.

"Talking about unfair," Jessica laughed. "I'll bet you practice all the time. I've played air hockey a total of three, maybe four times." They watched a game of foosball for a few minutes and then wandered over to the video games.

"Ahhggg!" the boy playing sighed. "I've had it. This game's impossible."

"Which one is it?" Jessica asked.

"I dunno," he shrugged, "some fantasy adventure. Here, Thomas." He handed the controller over.

"Only one can play this game." Thomas held the controller out to Jessica. "Go ahead; show me what you've got."

"Not me." Jessica held both hands up. "I never got into video games. I have enough addictions with Solitaire on the computer at home. You go for it; let me see a master at work."

Thomas began the game and Jessica settled in beside him on a small couch in front of the television monitor. An armor clad warrior, a sword in one hand and a shield in the other, appeared on the screen. The musical score swelled in volume, base violins and tympanic drums punctuating each step the avatar took. Thomas deftly maneuvered the man through a maze of burning buildings, the sword twisting this way and that, slicing through falling debris. A monster made entirely of flame appeared from behind a stone hedge. The warrior jumped over it, spun around and drove his sword deep into its red-orange heart. It stumbled backwards. Bright, white-hot sparks sprayed in all directions. Trumpets blared when the creature screamed out in pain. The sound pounded in Jessica's head. Cymbals clashed as the monster exploded. The warrior held up his shield against the thermal blast. Waves of stifling heat surged over Jessica. A nearly consumed building, several yards from the warrior, crumbled. Smoke from the charred debris swirled into the air. The distinct smell of smoldering wood filled Jessica's nostrils. Her eyes watered. She closed them and swiped away the involuntary tears.

In an instant, the happy sounds of a room full of people grew silent. Jessica sat on what was left of a demolished marble statue. Shattered white stone lay in piles at her feet. For a moment she was immobilized, stunned by her abrupt change of location. Smoke tainted the air she breathed. The foul stench of charred flesh made her stomach churn. She threw her hand up to cover her nose.

The distinctive smell brought a sickening feeling of familiarity. Barely one hundred feet in front of her was the burned out shell of a once great building. Most of the foundation stones, though blackened by smoke, were in place. Only a few charred beams, still upright in the piles of smoldering ash, remained of the actual structure.

She knew this place. She knew the statue had been of a large bird in flight. She knew the home had been a welcome haven to all who visited there. It had been that way for hundreds of years. It was the home of the protectors, of Haesom, his wife and his two sons. Slowly, Jessica turned. Behind her lay the once manicured lawns of the estate. A devastating scene of armored corpses, some heaped in groups and others singly sprawled on trampled grass, lay in all directions. Light from the setting sun punched through holes in the smoky haze that covered the field and reflected on polished helmets and broken swords. A cracked spear, its point sunk deep into the earth, protruded at an angle next to her.

From across the yard, a lone man stumbled through the mist. Using a sword as his cane, he limped from body to body searching the unresponsive faces. It seemed a slow, arduous process.

"Hello", Jessica called out. The man paused, straightened. He looked to where she was standing, but no emotion registered on his blood smeared face. He went back to his grizzly task, seemingly unaware of her presence. Several thin strips of cloth were tied around his left leg, from the top of the thigh to the end of his calf. They were all that held the slashed muscle together, and threatened to snap with each step he took. He arrived at the first of several corpse piles. Jessica was nearly overcome with pity when he reached for the top corpse and pulled it down.

"AAAAGGGHH!" His anguished cry ripped through the eerie silence. He leaned heavily on his sword. "Dead…all dead. How can I bear it?"

Yes, how could he bear it? This poor soldier…how could she bear to witness it? Why was she back here, to this horrible scene of death and destruction?

A low groan came from a cadaver mound only feet from Jessica. She jumped. The man hobbled to the pile, nearly tripping in his haste. He checked each body for breath before heaving the lifeless form to one side. The fifth one he came to coughed. "Reese! Good Lord, boy! I can't believe you're alive!"

"Barely, Cordon, barely." The young man was ashen white, his breath came is shallow gasps.

"Can you stand?"

"Maybe, just give me a minute." Slowly, some color came back into his face. "Okay…okay, let's try this." With help, the rescued soldier rose to a wobbly stance. "How many survived?"

"Now that I've found you, four."

"Four?" Reece's voice quivered. "We were a thousand!"

"They slaughtered every one left alive. I found the other two, like you, under piles of corpses. I too fell at the head of my men."

"Grandpa?"

The man shook his head.

"The family?"

"I've spent all day searching for survivors. Been over the entire estate and there's no sign of them. A lot of bodies are burned beyond recognition, others mutilated so badly I don't know who they were."

A sob escaped the younger soldier.

"Pull yourself together, boy."

"I failed, Cordon. You assigned me the duty of protecting the family. They were just boys, and a defenseless woman." Cordon nodded, his anguished face reflected Reese's misery.

Jessica fought her own tears. Remembering her dream-or had it been a vision- from the night before, she turned her gaze toward the grassy knoll beyond. Did he search for the family on the hillside? She closed her eyes against the horror she felt, but then she remembered. Quirt reported he saw the bodies being thrown in the kitchen well.

She opened her eyes. The two men were leaving, leaning on each other for support. "The well," she called, "look in the kitchen well!"

The younger man stopped, his abrupt action nearly causing the older one to collapse. "Did you hear that?"

"I heard nothing but the wind," Cordon replied irritably. "Come on. I've got to get to Ramadine, warn Larone. And you're going to Ider Hoffle, tell the elders what happened."

"Look in the kitchen well!" Jessica yelled. She maneuvered around two bodies to get closer to the retreating men. "Do you hear me? The family's in the well!"

Cordon froze, his bad leg in mid-air.

"Tell me you heard that." Reese barely whispered.

"I heard it...a buzzing noise making words in my head."

"The kitchen well? Could the Saylon family be in the well?"

"It's worth a look. That's the one place I haven't searched."

Smoke cloaked their receding forms. Jessica didn't follow after them, she had no desire to see what was in the kitchen well. Instead, she turned her attention to what was left of the great building before her. She walked to the edge of a crumbled partition and gazed into the gutted interior. From deep within the bowels of the burned out building, something called to her. It touched her mind, a whisper, a yearning. She stared downward, past the rubble, past the cinders. A weak light, like the beam from a tiny flashlight, appeared through the darkness. It called again…more insistent…more compelling. It wanted her to reach for it, take it and command it. Justice. Judgment. She reached forward.

"Oh man! This game's impossible! Marko, when are you going to get cheat sheets for this thing?" Thomas's voice jolted Jessica back.

"Only wimps use cheat sheets," Mark retorted.

"Then I guess I'm a wimp."

Jessica combed her fingers through her hair, trying to reorient. She was certain she was losing her mind.

"You're probably not very hungry, having eaten such a late dinner, but let's go look at the food," Thomas suggested, seemingly unaware of Jessica's loss of reality. "My dinner was before graduation and Mrs. R. just brought down another pizza."

"Yeah, yeah…that sounds really great. I could go for a big chunk of chocolate right now. About a pound would be good. "

"You like chocolate, huh?"

"Ooooh, yes. Best stuff in the world."

When they reached the table, most of the goodies were gone, but a fresh pizza still steamed. "Hmmm, no chocolate. Guess I'll settle for pepperoni," Jessica said. "You'd be amazed at how much I can eat. Running cross-country keeps me famished most of the time. I'll bet the girls' cross-country team could out eat the football team any day. I've been to buffets with those runners and even I'm amazed at how much we can all put away." Jessica grabbed two pieces of the homemade pie.

"Drink?" Thomas gestured to a row of sodas.

"Just water. I'm still in training."

He filled two cups from a glass pitcher.

They took their food outside onto the small, well-lit patio. Music came from hidden outdoor speakers. Thomas led the way, weaving through six sets of dancers to reach two empty chairs. A full moon illuminated the clear night sky. Its light shimmered on the four foot high rock wall surrounding the cement pad. A pleasant breeze blew, and the smell of newly mowed grass drifted on the air.

"So, are you going to Europe with your family?" Jessica nibbled on her large slice of pepperoni.

Thomas set his cup down. "Yeah, I'm the youngest, so my mom planned this whole summer adventure: Italy to see a brother in the Navy, Paris to a friend, and of course, Euro Disney." He paused for a bite of his pizza. "I did pretty well in our German classes, so there's Berlin, and finally England for Dad to do some genealogy. We'll be home the week before college starts." He took a long drink of his water.

"Sounds exciting. My summer vacation started today and ends Monday when I go fulltime at the vet clinic."

"Are you going to school this fall?"

"Yep, to the U in Seattle."

"That's where I'm going. In fact, Mark and I are rooming together."

Suddenly college seemed more enticing than ever. She wanted to say something clever, but a large bite of chewy pizza crust stopped her.

On the other side of the patio, a Siamese cat darted out from under some blooming lilac bushes and jumped from the stone retaining wall onto the concrete patio. The feline sprinted across the courtyard, dodging its way around several slow dancing couples. When nearly to the open sliding doors, the animal stopped, twitched its ears and fixed its yellow eyes on Jessica.

"Thomas, look at him." She pointed to the large cat. "What's he up to?"

"What makes you think he's up to something?"

She barely heard him. Her concentration was on the tom. He meowed twice. "Something's wrong," she murmured. "I know this sounds crazy, but a girl's in trouble. There." She pointed to the clump of bushes from where the cat had emerged.

A muffled scream, barely audible above the music, was heard. "Did you hear that?" Jessica asked.

"Yeah, I did." Thomas stood up.

Moments later, tearing out from the bushes, came Ray. He leaped to the patio and collided with two couples while crossing to the game room.

"Something's very wrong," Jessica repeated.

Thomas headed for the bushes with Jessica close behind.

Through the shrubbery, at the base of a large pine tree, lay the crying girl from the jeep. She was curled up in a ball. Streaks of wet mascara ran down her cheeks. The blackened tears mingled with blood that oozed, unchecked, from the side of her mouth.

Jessica knelt next to the hurt girl. She placed her hand on her head and stroked her hair. Thomas helped her to a sitting position, allowing Jessica to cradle her.

"What's your name?" Jessica gently asked.

"Jennifer."

"What happened?" Thomas asked through clenched teeth. His eyes held compassion for the girl, but his mouth was tight, in a grim line.

"Ray's psycho. I've only gone out with him a few times....thinks he owns me. I'm terrified," she sobbed. "I had to do something, I just had to. He flipped out. I tried to run, but..."

Thomas seethed, "Ray crossed a line."

Jessica agreed. "He's probably high."

"You okay if I leave you?"

Jessica nodded, then caught his hand before he turned. "Thomas..."

28

"Don't worry, I'll be careful."

Left to themselves, Jessica helped Jennifer to her feet. They pushed through the bushes and walked around the oblivious dancers to the game room. While they were heading to the bathroom, Mark's mom stopped them.

"What on earth happened?"

"Her date got abusive," Jessica answered.

Sliding her arm around Jennifer's waist, the older woman took charge of the situation. "First of all we need to call the police. No one gets away with this behavior, especially at my house." Having been relieved from duty, Jessica went in search of Thomas.

She found him out on the front lawn talking with Mark. "...temper." Mark said. "Got into lots of fights when we were kids." He shook his head, "I always hoped he'd grow out of it."

"He needs help." Thomas added.

"Hey," Jessica called from the front door. The two young men turned.

"How's Jennifer?" Mark asked.

"Your mom's taking care of her. She's calling the police." Jessica walked over to them and Thomas took her hand in his.

"Yeah. Ray can't get away with crap like this," Mark sighed, "He bolted out of here before Thomas could let us know what happened to stop him. I'm going back in. Oh, by the way Reddica," he called over his shoulder, "that was a sweet fall you took before graduation today."

Jessica winced. Thomas snickered. "Not nice, Mark!" she yelled after him. Looking at Thomas she moaned, "I hoped no one had noticed."

"Well it was a little hard not to, but you were very graceful."

"Thanks a lot, you're about the fifth person to tell me that." Looking around the deserted yard, she asked,

"So Ray got away?"

Thomas nodded. "He was probably drunk before he got here. I saw him peel out of the parking lot just as I made it ouside. I hope he doesn't kill somebody."

"My mom was killed by a drunk driver." She blurted it out without thinking and now she felt embarrassed. Jessica never talked about her mother's death. She talked about her mother all the time, but never about her death. Looking down at her shoes, she rubbed her toe in the grass.

"I'm sorry," Thomas gave her hand a squeeze. "I knew..., but I didn't know how."

"I didn't mean to say anything; I don't normally talk about it." Feeling uncomfortable, she stared out at the deserted street. To her relief, Thomas changed the subject.

"How did you know Jennifer was in trouble back there?"

"I didn't know it was Jennifer in trouble, or exactly what was wrong. I just knew...or rather felt there was a problem."

"Yes, but *how* did you know? Are you clairvoyant or something?"

"Well...um...uh, something like that." How could she tell him the cat had told her the girl was in trouble? Or that it told her exactly where to look? She didn't understand it herself. Seeing a psychiatrist was looking more and more appealing with each passing hour.

He seemed to accept her answer. "Since you're going to the U, and so am I, would it be all right if I look you up in the fall?"

Her mood brightened immediately. "I'd be wounded if you didn't."

A police cruiser pulled up to the home and for the next thirty minutes Thomas, Jessica, Jennifer and Mark's mom gave statements. After the policeman left Mark suggested, "Hey everyone, we've got karaoke."

"Can you sing?" Thomas asked.

"Not really, but if he's got 'I will Survive' then I'll give it a try."

"Have you seen the alien version of that on the internet? It's great when the chandelier smashes her right when she gets to the chorus."

"It's not a chandelier, it's a gigantic disco ball."

"Oh, yeah."

With the karaoke, the party took off again. Even Jennifer, after being tended to by Mark's mom, joined in a group effort and seemed to have a little fun. Part way through an off key rendition of 'Sweet Caroline' by Neil Diamond Thomas's watch alarm went off.

"Twelve-thirty already?" He looked at his watch in disbelief. "I need to go, still gotta pack."

"I'll go too," Jessica said. "It's been a long day and I promised Jennifer I'd give her a ride home."

Mark accompanied the three to the door. "I'm glad you came, Jess. Thomas would never have come if you hadn't have said yes." He turned to Jennifer. "Sorry about Ray. If, uh, you ever need help, you can call me."

"Thanks." Jennifer blushed.

"See ya, Tommy...told you she's hot."

Thomas turned several shades of red, but laughed good-naturedly. "In the fall, Marko." Holding out an arm for each girl, he asked, "Shall we go ladies?"

When the three reached Jessica's car, Thomas first took Jennifer to the passenger side. After helping her in, he walked Jessica to the driver's door. "We should have done this sooner. It's just that school, sports, work...I just..."

"I was pretty busy, too." She rescued him. "I'm looking forward to the fall."

"Yeah. You're..." Their eyes locked for a moment and in that instant, time stood still. The world around Jessica faded to shadowy gray. All she could focus on were Thomas's brown eyes and fleetingly, what lay behind them…Light, a bright white light. It was so bright, it forced her to blink, and with that blink, the moment passed.

…pretty great." Thomas seemed unaware of what had happened.

Jessica felt awkward. Not only had another odd experience just occurred, but this one left her breathless.

Jennifer prompted from inside the car, "Will you hurry up and kiss her so I can go home?"

"Ah my dear Jennifer, one does not kiss the class black belt on the first date," Thomas smiled mischievously. "However…" He kissed Jessica's hand. "See you in the fall," he whispered in her ear, then opened the car door. She climbed in without a word. Jessica last glimpsed him through her rearview mirror as she drove away. She could not wait until September.

Still shaken from her 'bright light' experience, Jessica found it difficult to keep up her end of the conversation with Jennifer. However, she did manage to give one bit of advice before arriving at Jennifer's house. "If you think Ray's going to be more of a pain, call Mark. He offered to help and I think he'd come through." No wispy tendrils had escaped his lips when he spoke, so Jessica knew the proposal was sincere.

She turned up the radio and hummed to the music while making the short trip home. She almost missed turning into the familiar driveway. For the first time that she could remember, the house was not ablaze in lights. A spotlight on the garage and a single porch light at the kitchen door were the only welcoming beacons. She laughed aloud and tried to imagine the agonizing restraint it must have taken for her dad to keep the lights to a minimum.

After parking in her usual spot, she slipped the key ring onto her little finger, grabbed her jean jacket from the car floor, and exited her vehicle. Her wallet and bag were forgotten in the back seat. Leaning against the car, she idly toyed with her keys. She replayed every detail of the last few hours and wondered what it would have felt like if Thomas had actually kissed her. A shiver of excitement shot down her spine. She mechanically slipped her arms into her jean jacket and pulled it closed, hugging her arms in front of her stomach.

At length, she pulled herself back to reality and sauntered up the pathway leading from the driveway to the kitchen door. She pulled the keys off her little finger and automatically poised the house key in her right hand, readying it for the lock. With her left hand, she reached for the brass door knob, preparing to turn it when the lock disengaged, but the instant her fingers touched the metal, a small, white spark shocked her hand. She jumped in surprise. A low rumble came from the other side of the door, faint at first, but grew louder and louder with each passing second. Then the door trembled. Within moments it faded away, dissolved from white to gray, then ebony. Even the porch lamp grew fainter and fainter until it too disappeared. Only the moon, high above, provided light to the changing scene. A cavern, six-feet high and four-feet wide, materialized in the space. The shrill sound of rushing air blasted out, immediately followed by a faraway whistle. The distant sound grew in volume, much like the increasing sound of a train whistle as it approaches the hearer. Within seconds, an iridescent funnel of wildly spinning air, the source of the deafening sound, appeared deep inside the hollow. The rotating cone hurtled forward until it reached the mouth of the opening. Jessica stared in horror, transfixed before the swirling hole. *Run,* her mind yelled, but her muscles froze up. *Run!* This time the order reached her feet, but before they could respond, the spiral achieved full strength and, like a vacuum tube, it pulled her in. She was swept upward, her body shooting forth, headfirst into a shimmering void. Multi-pitched whooshing filled her ears. The phenomenal speed of travel numbed her four extremities. She couldn't move.

This was not possible! What was happening? The internal pressure of the spiral immobilized her entire body. Her arms were pinned to her sides and she could not turn her head. Oxygen filled the darkened chute, but forcing it into her lungs took Herculean strength, and they burned with the effort. She did not know how long this suction tube held her...minutes probably, but each second seemed an eternity. Terror! Confusion! Paralysis! On and on she hurtled. Would this never end? She did not want to die! In desperation she squeezed out the air left in her lungs and screamed, "Daddy!"

Her insides churned, her brain could not focus, and her extremities throbbed with intense pain. Mind numbing fear warped into complete panic seconds before the hole mercifully spit her out. She hit, then skidded and rolled along soft, mossy ground. When she finally came to a stop, her head swam. Breathing came in huge, deep gasps. She could not, must not, pass out. Inhale, exhale. Inhale, exhale. A sound...a footstep. Someone was there. Summoning her last bit of strength, she opened her eyes and barely lifted her head. Two, bright golden-yellow orbs, outlined in thick black stared down at her. Then darkness closed in.

CHAPTER 4

Varnack

The green orb pulsed with power, its glow an ominous warning for any who dared come too near. Two old men cautiously circled the pedestal upon which the golf ball sized sphere rested.

"Wh...what are we going to t...tell him?" The shorter man stammered, his face pale, his eyes wide.

"I don't know," his companion shook his head, "but we'd better come up with something. He'll be here any minute and demand an explanation."

Jessica watched the white-haired gentlemen from high above them. She clearly perceived their every action, heard each breath, and felt every anxious heartbeat. The edges of the small room were shadowed and fuzzy, her focus of attention was immediately around the radiant, emerald ball. Somewhere in the back of her mind she realized she wasn't in her body, only an ethereal sense of spirit. The feeling was extraordinarily liberating. She felt light and free.

The distant sound of pounding footsteps disturbed the silence in the near empty room. Someone rapidly approached. He was agitated. He? Yes, she could sense it; a man's energy.

"What are we going to say?" The short man wrung his hands.

A heavy door crashed open, sending shock waves throughout the chamber. A richly dressed man, complete with polished riding boots and gold fringed cape, strode in. He stopped a few feet from the glowing crystal.

"Well?" he demanded.

"It began glowing ten minutes ago, my Lord," the short man responded.

"We sent for you as soon as it showed life," the other added.

"What caused this power?"

The men hesitated. After a moment, the taller one stepped forward and bowed low. "We honestly don't know, my Lord, but..."

"You don't know?" The Lord's voice was low. Each word crisply articulated. "You didn't trigger the pulsations?"

The short man, his face even whiter than before, shook his head.

"You've had three weeks to understand this thing. Why have you been wasting my time?"

The tallest bowed once more. "The magic contained within the persite has only been harnessed by a few. What little I have read of Alderic's writings refers to blood lines, and even then the ability to tap the power is sporadically inherited."

"Which blood lines?"

"House of Saylon and House of Liedia are specifically mentioned, though I'm certain there are other random individuals capable of…"

The Lord held his hand up for silence. "I've held his ball and though I am Liedian, it remained dead in my hands." He stared at the green light.

"I suspect there is a surge in the Expanse of Gonta, my Lord. This ball is responding to that disturbance."

The Lord nodded. "You," he suddenly pointed to someone in the shadows, "bring me the globe."

A black clothed soldier walked out from the blurry darkness. The uniform seemed familiar. Jessica stretched her memory. He wore the same colors as soldiers on the grassy knoll in her dream, those who held a proud woman and her two young sons captive.

The soldier marched up to the chest-high pillar and reached for the sphere. At the instant his fingers touched the luminous orb, his back arched and his face contorted in agony. A guttural rasp escaped his lips when he crumbled to the floor. His body convulsed several times, then lay still.

Shocked, Jessica stared at the motionless body. As if the persite was alive, she had felt its reaction to the foreign touch. It was insulted. She heard the soldier's heart slow and finally stop.

For a moment the Lord also stared at the fallen soldier. He turned back to the darkness behind him and pointed again. "You there, bring me the globe." His voice rang cold. The command was uncompromising.

Daenon. Jessica finally recognized his voice.

Another soldier appeared from the dark. He hesitated at the edge of the light, then slowly approached the stone pedestal, his eyes fixed on the ball. He circled it twice. When he reached for it, his hand shook. Within an inch of the prize he stopped and dropped the hand to his side.

Daenon drew a dagger from his belt. "Take that thing now or I'll kill you where you stand."

The man took a deep breath. Jessica concentrated on the globe. *Stop,* she moaned. *There's been enough death, don't kill him. Please, don't kill him.* Just before his fingers closed around the crystal, it ceased to glow. He grabbed the persite. Turning toward his master, a triumphant smile on his face, he held forth the crystal on his open palm.

Plucking the ball with his free hand, Daenon slashed downward with the dagger, plunging it through the soldier's palm. Jessica flinched. "Next time, don't falter in carrying out my orders." He placed the ball back on its stand then addressed the two old men. "Continue working on it. Let me know if it re-activates."

When the persite ceased to pulse, the shadowy edges of the room closed in. With the word 'activates' echoing in her mind, Jessica surrendered to the dark.

* * *

Ohhh, the pounding in my head. Consciousness came creeping back to Jessica. She lay on her side, the soft, mossy ground against her face. The cool vegetation, its aroma and rough texture, helped to revive her. What a ride. Were any bones broken? She rolled onto her back and focused on the sky above. Where was she? A bright, full moon and a few stars lit the semi-clouded heavens. Of course it would be nighttime, things like this don't happen during the day. Wait a minute, the whirling in her head slowed down a bit, one bright full moon and one three-quarter?

For several minutes she contemplated the alien sky, then pulled herself to a sitting position. Two moons…maybe she was dreaming again. The line between reality and insanity was not so distinct anymore. Though, she raised a hand to her throbbing head, she never had a splitting headache in a dream before. The evening air felt balmy, with a hint of a chill beginning to creep in, like late spring or, perhaps, early fall. Pulling her jean jacket closed, she fastened the buttons. Her hands shook.

A sensation of being watched pricked at her senses. It forced its way through the fog of pain. Alarm spiked in her throat. Choking back the panic, she twisted around to face the foreign presence and found herself nose to nose with the same pair of bright, golden-yellow eyes she had encountered after her expulsion from the hole. Blinking, she leaned back, trying to focus on the entire creature before her. It blinked back and in one quick move, licked her entire face with its massive, wet tongue.

"Oh, yuck!" She wrinkled up her nose in disgust and wiped the slobber with her sleeve. Jessica stared up at the huge beast, trying to place him into a familiar category. It took several seconds, but its appearance registered at last. "Why, you're a dog!" she blurted out. Not just any dog, but the biggest one she had ever seen, and…he was laughing at her. Little snorts came from his nose while his body gently shook. A sense of wonder replaced her apprehension.

Reaching up, she tentatively stroked the thick, dark yellow fur. He closed his eyes then leaned into her touch. "Do you like this?" He bowed his head at her question so she scratched behind his floppy ears. He leaned his great head further in and nuzzled her cheek. As he did, an image formed in her mind. An image of a word, or a name, swirled like a specter

35

upon her intellect. An odd tingling sensation forced its way into her consciousness. She closed her eyes in meditation, trying to 'see' the representation. At last the impression became clear; Varnack.

"Varnack?" she muttered, looking at the animal. He nodded and licked her once again. She wiped her face with her other sleeve, then scrambled to her feet to get a better look at him. In the brightness of the two moons, she could see his coat bore the same golden-yellow color as his eyes, but with wispy, white stripes scattered throughout. A black rim, giving the impression he wore thick eyeliner, defined his eyes. An enormous animal, his shoulders came to her waist and his head to her chest. He was about the size of a pony. Well-worked muscles swelled under the soft, short fur. His tail wagged in wide circles. Trust replaced her wonder.

"What's going on?" she muttered aloud. "I've got to be either dead, dreaming, or…"

A second impression sprang into her mind, forcing her to concentrate yet again. The word 'name'came into auditory focus as she heard it inside her head. Not an actual voice, but speech none-the-less.

"You're talking to me!" She cried in astonishment.

"Your name?" The animal asked again.

"Jessica." She narrowed her eyes. "Okay, this is just way too weird. How can I understand you? How are you doing this?"

He cocked his head. The impression came clearly, he did nothing…she did. "Me! I don't think so!"

"Certain?"

"Yes." She grew a little less confident.

"Gift."

"What gift?" She didn't remember anyone giving her a present.

"Talent."

"Ohhh." Jessica eyed Varnack. He sat in front of her on his hind legs. One back paw came up to scratch his ear.

She immediately thought of Sneakers and a comment her father had made. 'As usual Jess, I'm amazed. You and that cat have quite a relationship. It's uncanny how you two communicate.'

Her attention reverted to Varnack. "All people talk with their animals," she rationalized.

He stopped his scratching and gazed at her.

She frowned. "But I actually hear words when Sneakers meows."

She remembered the Siamese cat at Mark's party. The feline 'told' her about Jennifer's situation.

Her mind raced. Another impression from her new companion floated onto her consciousness. She could not give an exact translation, but it had the general meaning of 'I told you so'.

"This is impossible," she protested.

He shrugged his mighty shoulders.

Before she could ask any of the questions circling her mind or begin to have the nervous breakdown that was threatening to fracture her tenuous hold on civility, he commanded, "Rain. Go."

"Go where?" For the first time, she took notice of her surroundings. Tall, pipe-like trees encircled the tiny meadow she landed in. An undergrowth of dense, berry-laden bushes grew around the lofty trees. Thick, spongy moss covered the few patches of open ground.

As if someone were turning down a dimmer switch, the light from above gradually faded. Clouds covered one of the moons. Stars vanished, one by one, behind the moving, billowy curtain. She realized it would not be long before the second moon became obscured as well. The wind picked up and the clear scent of rain floated in the air.

Varnack moved past her and she ran to keep up with him. They traveled at a quick pace, taking advantage of the remaining moonlight. Varnack wove his way through the compact trees. The forest floor was smooth, oddly devoid of large pieces of debris, only small sticks and decaying leaves. Within minutes the precious light slipped away and gloomy night closed in. If she did not do something quick, she would probably lose him in the dark, so she grabbed onto his tail. She felt mild surprise come from him when she took hold of the soft appendage, but he made no complaints.

With the light gone and the wind gusting, they slowed their speed. "It won't be long before this rain hits. The smell is so strong I can taste it. I'm not looking forward to getting soaked," Jessica yelled above the blustering weather. Just when the first wet drops fell, the large hound shot through a wall of long willow vines and stopped.

Jessica released Varnack's tail and brought her hand within centimeters of her face. The dark of these new surroundings was so complete she could not see her fingers.

"Varnack, where are we?" Her voice sounded flat in her ears, muffled, with no echo. She could hear the wind rising in pitch, the rain splattering against the ground outside. "Is this a cave?" As if in answer, a flash of lightning gave brief illumination to the dirt enclosure. Before it went dark again, she caught a glimpse of Varnack coming toward her with a large bag in his teeth. He deposited it with a clunk at her feet.

"A sack??" Feeling the package, she fumbled for the opening. "Where did this come from?"

"Friends."

A cord bound it at the top and Jessica worked to free the knot. "So why aren't these friends with us?"

"Not safe."

"Not safe? What...Ah, there! I got the rope undone. So what's in here?" Feeling inside, she found a glass container about the size of a pint jar, something large and squishy made of soft leather, and several small packages wrapped up in what she thought was fabric, tied with string.

"Open glass."

"You're not a real conversationalist, are you Varnack?"

Holding the jar firmly, she removed it from the sack. With her fingers, she probed the top and found nothing but a string tightly binding a waxen lid, which crumpled into pieces when she pulled the twine. As soon as air came into contact with the powders of the jar, it glowed. Startled, she tossed the container down and jumped back. Within moments a bright light shone from the peculiar lantern.

"What a great lamp. I could have used one of these in that whirling tunnel. And speaking of tunnels..." she surveyed her new shelter.

This was indeed a small cave. Vines covered with long, thin, lime-green leaves covered the entrance. The cavern, however, was not gouged from stone, but was a man-made earthen dugout, reinforced with rib-like timbers. Hardened, jet-black dirt formed the floor, walls and ceiling of the enclosure. Undisturbed spider webs hung from the wooden supports and tufts of aqua-green moss grew around the entrance.

Rummaging through the contents of the cloth sack, Jessica removed the leather flask and several of the small packages. She unraveled two of them. Chunks of salted, dried meat were in the first and what looked like dried green fruit, and bread wafers in the second. "Are you hungry or thirsty?" She offered some meat and fruit to Varnack, but he shook his head.

"Me neither, just tired," she yawned involuntarily. "Ya know, I'm trying to decide if I should freak out...or not."

Varnack padded to her side and without warning pushed her with his mighty head. She fell over with a thud, barely able to keep her grasp on the food in her hands.

"What was that for!" she yelled at him in shocked surprise.

"Sleep."

She stared at him, her annoyance bubbling to the surface. "Fine." She muttered and jammed the food back into the cloth sack. "I had perfectly good hysterics all ready to go and you pushed them right out of me." Jessica took off her jacket. Using it as a barrier between her hair and the dirty floor, she laid down to rest.

In the quiet of the cave, with the soft, rhythmic splatter of the rain outside, Jessica's mind wandered over her predicament. "My dad's going to be worried sick when he finds I'm gone. He'll never know where I am. I don't even know where I am!"

Varnack did not respond, but trotted to the cave entrance. He inclined his head toward the bushes and closed his eyes.

"What are you listening for?" A low sense of danger dabbed at the edges of her imagination. Watching the great hound, she realized if someone were to surprise them, they would be in for quite a thrashing. She would not want to tangle with Varnack.

After several minutes, he opened his eyes.

"Well? What did you hear?"

He shook his head. "Safe."

"Your name, Varnack, that's a pretty cool name." Before she really thought, she blurted out. "Hey, could I call you V-dawg?" She put a lot of attitude into the appellation, complete with rapper-like hand gestures.

The mighty animal was trotting from the cave entrance to another small pile of supplies when she made her comment. He stopped in his tracks, his front paw in mid-air. He slowly turned his head and stared, unblinking at her.

"Oh...um...well," she sputtered, "Never mind."

He gave a curt nod before continuing to the pile. He seized a blanket in his teeth and brought it over to her.

"Where am I?"

"Planet Edia. Country Esparia."

"Can I *ever* go home?"

He curled up next to her, his warmth, along with the blanket, helping her relax. "Don't know."

The answer came as a surprise, but if he didn't know, then there was still hope. The jar's light gave simple comfort from the surrounding darkness. She was exhausted, completely exhausted. Panic...fear...She knew she should be feeling both emotions, but she simply did not have the energy. Maybe tomorrow she could freak out. Within moments, she fell asleep.

For the third time in two days, Jessica found herself surrounded by dream mist. *Not again.* Passing her hand through the phantom fog she felt disheartened. Yes, it was the same stuff. Knowing motion would prove no danger, she closed her eyes and pressed forward. With sight of little use in this murky, impenetrable cloud, its elimination allowed her to better concentrate on her sense of hearing. After traveling for what seemed an hour through the endless vapor, she finally caught the low drone of men's voices and turned toward them.

To her surprise, the closer she approached the voices, the colder the dense fog became. This was new. She folded her arms across her chest. When she drew near enough to hear the men, she knelt down into a tight ball, trying to conserve her body heat.

"Victory is mine," an icy voice proclaimed. "Haesom is gone, and Larone cannot hold Esparia together. Your information gave my force the edge it needed. The Dorsett fell with little effort." He gave a small laugh.

"My Elitet are thirsty for more victories. You've done well."

Jessica was grateful she was curled up, because her legs went weak at the sound of this familiar voice.

"Thank you, My Lord. As you know, I'm privy to many confidences at Ramadine and I've come with startling news."

"I already know Larone has summoned his brother." Daenon sounded confident.

"Yes, Anton's at Ramadine, but this is not what I've learned."

"Well? What's this news that's so urgent you rushed here, against my orders, to tell me?"

"I've learned the Protectors are not all dead."

"What?" Daenon snapped. "Explain yourself!"

"An heir of Graesion's still lives. Larone and Anton have conspired to bring him here."

"That's impossible! Haesom's sons are dead."

"Yes, my Lord, but his younger sister lived."

"What?" The question was barely a whisper.

"Haesom wanted everyone to believe she died, but his sister lived."

Someone paced on a carpeted floor. The rhythmic thumping of his feet betrayed uneasiness.

"Only one heir?" Deanon asked.

"That's my understanding."

"You said, 'him'. How do you know this protector is male?"

"Well...I just assumed..." The voice trailed off.

"Idiot! Never assume anything! Haesom's sister...Shallenon was her name...would be fifty by now." The pacing suddenly stopped. "In what manner does she come? By land? By sea? By magic?"

"That, I...I also do not know." The man's voice held real fear.

"You come with no details? Where has she been hiding all this time?"

"My Lord, I...I..." The informer barely whispered.

"You fool!" A loud smack caused Jessica to flinch. She tried in vain to see through the thick cloud swirling around her. The pacing began again. "How certain are you that this information is accurate? Could this be one of Larone's ploys? Are you suspected?"

"No. I believe my authority is still without question. I'm always your faithful eyes and ears, my Lord." Under the persuasive tones of this smooth voice Jessica could sense alarm. *Oh this guy's good...oily and reeking of insincerity. I wonder if Daenon will even notice.*

"Remember, once in my service, always in my service. Never give me cause to regret our arrangement." The cold edge in the voice sent a shiver up Jessica's back. "Go back to Ramadine and learn details. I'll begin an immediate search. The teams I've sent to kill Larone must now be diverted to find Shallenon. She must be found before we attack. I want no

Protector leading or even inspiring these people."

"Yes, Lord Daenon. I'll learn all I can, I swear."

"Don't get caught. Now go."

The retreating footsteps of the informer faded away, but the dull, rhythmic pacing continued. She counted each stride. One, two, three, swish…One, two, three swish.

"I will not be denied my victory by some brat of Graesion's." Daenon spoke aloud. The pacing stopped. "The green persite. I wonder if her coming caused it to glow." His heavy footsteps echoed off into the distance.

Jessica shivered in the cold fog. It was time to find a way out, but… where was 'out'? The chill set deeper into her bones and her fingers were numb. Warmth, she needed to find warm. She started to run. Faster and faster, her speed increased. She tried to escape from the mist and the terrifying cold.

In the first mist-vision, Sneakers incessant purring opened a channel to reality and with the sauna experience, Sophia's call pulled her back home. Now, however, she did not know where to find 'home'. Fighting the rising tide of panic, she tried to remember where she had last been. A cave…the remarkable dog. The dog! She seized upon the thought. *Varnack! Help! I'm trapped!*

Within seconds, Jessica felt herself rolling over and over. Something warm and moist touched her cheek. An inner voice called, bringing her out from the icy prison. Her eyes flew open. Varnack's face filled her field of vision, his nose nearly touching hers. Throwing her arms around his neck, she clung to him. He crouched next to her, not pulling away until she herself broke the embrace.

"You heard me. Thank you," she managed to whisper. He licked her cheek.

CHAPTER 5

Gaylee Goes Home

John was in deep sleep when a scream jolted him awake. He sat straight up, his heart pounding. His pulse raced. "What the..." It took him a few seconds to recognize his room, and when he finally did, he flopped back onto his pillow.

"I *never* dream," he muttered half-awake. "Never." The clock showed twelve forty-three. Stumbling out of bed, he shuffled over to the window which overlooked the driveway. Jess's car was there, so she was home. He listened, but the house was quiet. He crawled back into bed. Like a dull barb, unease prodded at the edges of his consciousness, but he could not identify the nagging discomfort. While he lay there, trying to fall back to sleep, he thought of Jessica. His little girl was growing up, graduated today. Soon she would move away to school. He turned onto his side. He should have been there more. He would make it up, travel this summer. That's it. Show he cared...give his time.

$$* * *$$

The kitchen lay in early morning shadow. John crossed to the bay window next to the door and pulled the wooden blinds. "Huh, Jess always pulls these." The usual 'gone running' note was not on the refrigerator door.

She must be sleeping in. She would be bouncing down any minute and then he would hit her up about the summer. They could ask Grandma Gaylee to come with them. There would be Disneyland... no...no, maybe eight years ago. Perhaps New York, see some plays, shop, whatever Jess wanted to do.

A half an hour later he still sat alone at the round kitchen table, a half glass of tomato juice accompanied by a piece of cold, partially nibbled toast were in front of him. The morning paper lay open on his lap, but he found it difficult to concentrate. Where was she? He wanted to hear about the party and tell her about the planned trip before he left. The clock on the microwave showed 7:50. He would check on her. He had barely passed through the kitchen threshold into the hallway when the side door dead bolt turned and Sophia strolled in.

Humming the last few bars of 'Amazing Grace', she spotted John. The tune died in her throat. "Dr. John, you're still here." She hurried over to him. "Are you ill?"

"Sophia, could you go check on Jess?" He held his voice calm. "She's not down yet, and that's not like her. I was about to go up myself, but since you're here...in case she's in the shower or dressing."

"No problem, I'll be right back." She slipped past him and hurried up the stairs. John went to the granite counter. He absently brushed a few toast crumbs onto the tiled floor. Sophia was back in less than a minute, her brows knit together in concern. "Her bed hasn't been slept in."

"Are you sure? Maybe she made it already."

Sophia shook her head. "I know it hasn't been slept in because as a surprise, I placed a rose on her pillow yesterday. The rose is still there, right where I put it."

Sophia's normally ruddy face lost its' color, fear filled her eyes. John's pulse increased. His mouth went dry. Without a word he walked out the kitchen door and straight to Jessica's car. The doors were locked. Her wallet and party bag were on the backseat, nothing seemed out of place. He circled the automobile twice, checking everywhere, but found nothing suspicious.

"What are you doing?" Sophia watched from the kitchen doorway, wringing her hands. "Should I call the police?"

John did not immediately respond. How could he tell her he was looking for scuffmarks or dents or even blood? "I'm looking for some sign, some clue of what could have happened." Slowly, he walked up the brick path leading from the driveway to the kitchen entrance. Not an inch of ground escaped his scrutiny. There was nothing unusual, until he reached the door. On a rosebush under the bay window, dangling from a small branch, were Jessica's car keys.

"At least she made it to the door." He pointed to the keys, but did not touch them, they were evidence. What an idiot! He hadn't dreamed the scream, he'd actually heard it. Why did he assume things were all right last night? Why didn't he look in her room! Shame, disgust, but most of all guilt welled up inside of him. Shaking his head, he rushed past Sophia and went to the phone. "I'm calling the police." When he reached for the receiver, the sound of screeching tires on the driveway filtered into the kitchen.

John hesitated, his hand in mid-air. "Who?" He glanced toward the door. Sophia still stood in the opening.

"Gaylee!" Agitation filled Sophia's voice. "Jessica, she's missing!"

"I know!"

John turned to face his mother-in-law when she ran into the house.

"You know?" His heart nearly stopped. "Where is she?"

An athletic woman with a pleasant, but no nonsense manner, Gayleena Saylon never ceased to intrigue John. Always carrying herself with poise and confidence, she personified elegance. By her own admission, she had seen nearly eighty-three years of life, but she did not look a day over fifty. Her short, bright red hair was barely showing signs of gray. Her attractive face carried but a few forehead wrinkles while several small crow's feet creased the edges of her sapphire blue eyes. Tall, though not quite as tall as Jessica, she emitted a noble air. She never interfered in John's life, but always managed to call or show up just when he needed a friend the most.

"John." She hugged him.

"So where's Jess?"

"On Edia, my home world." She said it matter-of-factly, as if he should know what she meant.

"Your what?" he stammered.

"Sophia, here." Gaylee handed her friend a thick manila envelope. "Those are legal papers, giving you and Jacob power of attorney over my estate. Pull out the top paper, that's the one John needs to sign."

"Gaylee!" John was thoroughly confused. "Where's Jess? Explain yourself."

She appeared to not have heard him, for she crossed the kitchen and began rummaging through a small broom closet next to the bay window.

"What are you doing?" he demanded.

"Looking for your gun. Sophia," she ordered, "get me a fresh shirt or two for Jessica, and a pair of her jeans. You know she's our fashion princess, so get her favorites. We'll take those with us." Without a word Sophia left the kitchen. "And grab a fresh shirt for John while you're at it," she yelled after her.

John, feeling thoroughly irritated, grabbed her arm. "Have you lost your mind? Where is Jessica?"

Gaylee pulled her arm free and faced him. "John, I've never lied to you before. I don't plan on doing it now, but there's a lot about me you don't know. I can explain later, when we have more time, but I don't know how much longer the portal will be active, so we need to hurry. I came here…here as in Earth…fifty years ago with Shallenon, when she was just a new born baby." Gaylee turned back to the closet and pulled a box off the top shelf. "My home was under attack. My husband died in the battle, but my two uncles were able to save me and Shallenon by sending us here." She pulled the gun, a 9mm Beretta semi-automatic pistol, from the box. "Where's the ammunition?"

He glared at her. "What?"

"Ammunition…where is it?"

He reached around her and grabbed a box of bullets.

She snatched a small duffle bag hanging from a closet hook. "I left my country behind," she talked while packing the gun and bullets in the bag, "my uncles, and my son."

"Your son?" Sophia had just entered the room. In her arms were an assortment of shirts and pants, both Jessica's and John's. "You left a son in Esparia?" She deposited the clothes on the table.

"I never told you, Sophia. It was too painful to talk about. Haesom. My little boy." Gaylee plucked two shirts and a pair of jeans from the pile and stuffed them in the duffle bag.

John was at a loss. "Haesom? But Jessica…"

"…thought he was made up." Gaylee finished the thought. "She assumed her dreams were in response to her mom's death, but they were very real. Haesom was her uncle, Shallenon's older brother." Gaylee stopped packing. "And two nights ago she saw them murdered." Her shoulders drooped and she took a long, deep breath. "Which of these shirts do you want?" She held up a button up and a pull-over.

John ignored her and turned on Sophia. "What's Esparia?"

"Her country…Gaylee was a Protector."

"Since Shallenon's dead, and now Haesom and his family are gone, the birthright falls to Jessica. She's the last of the Saylon blood line." Gaylee managed to cram both shirts into the bag. She zipped it and thrust it at John's chest. He instinctively caught it. "Will you sign that paper already? We need to go **now**."

John had never seen his mother-in-law so agitated. He slung the bag's strap over his shoulder, grabbed a pen lying on the counter top and scribbled his name on the legal document.

"Okay, I've signed." John put his hand on Gaylee's shoulder. "Where do you think we're going?" His voice was calm, quiet. He knew she had snapped.

"To Edia…To Esparia…To where ever my uncles took Jessica. We're going to follow her. I'm going home." She looked around the kitchen. "Where's your first aid kit?"

John pointed to a kitchen cupboard. He looked to Sophia, hoping for some help, but she was weeping into a dish towel.

"I'm going to miss you Gaylee," the smaller woman sobbed.

Gaylee paused after retrieving the small pack of medical supplies and put her arms around her friend. She kissed her forehead. She too had tears in her eyes. "Tell Jacob good-bye." Sophia silently nodded.

Gaylee walked out the open kitchen door, down the path to where the cars were parked in the driveway. John watched from the bay window as she retrieved a hooded cape from her auto.

Sophia stood beside him. "She's telling you the truth. I know her whole story."

"Hey, you two," Gaylee called. "Come out here, and Sophia, be sure to close the door behind you."

John shook his head, feeling completely bewildered, but decided to humor the woman. He would go along with her delusions, only to prove them false, before calling a psychiatrist. Sophia closed the door behind them and scurried to safety behind John's car. There was fear on her face as she crouched behind the vehicle.

John poked the first aid pack into the duffle, then he and Gaylee walked from the cars, up the brick path to the kitchen entrance. At the door, Gaylee felt around the trim, the deadbolt and the door itself. Nothing happened.

The brass handle remained the only hardware untouched. "How appropriate," she murmured, "a doorknob is the link to another world." She stared at the latch, her body rigid. She gripped her cape so hard her knuckles turned white.

"So, what now?" John was losing patience. He really wanted to make that 911 call.

"Jessica didn't tell you about all of her dreams from the other night, did she?"

"More dreams than Haesom's death?"

Gaylee nodded. "My uncle said that he set the mechanism with his own life force, so only family could activate it. If he hasn't shut it down yet, then this should work." Reaching out, Gaylee touched the metal knob. The moment her fingers connected, a small arc of electricity jumped from the metal to her hand and from her hand to John's leg. His muscle involuntarily contracted when the shock connected with his body.

A low rumble came from the other side of the door, like the soft purr of a contented kitten, but within seconds it increased in volume and intensity. The door trembled. John thought an earthquake had hit, but then the door dissolved away. Each molecule was drawn backward with such rapidity that it took only a few moments for the entire wooden structure to disappear.

John stared, open mouthed, in disbelief. He heard Sophia call from behind the car. "Good-bye. I'll take care of everything here."

A black oval materialized where the kitchen should have been. The shrill sound of rushing air exploded around them, immediately followed by a faraway whistle. Gaylee grabbed John's arm, her nails dug into his flesh. "I nearly died the last time I was in this thing," she yelled into his ear.

"What? You never said anything about dying!"

As the distant whistle grew in volume, an iridescent funnel of wildly spinning air appeared deep inside the hollow. The rotating cone hurtled forward until it reached the mouth of the opening. John glanced over at Gaylee. Her eyes were closed, her mouth was pinched tight.

He stared back at the hole to see the inside of a wild twister. Together, they were sucked into the funnel. Side-by-side, the two shot through the long dark tube. A loud, high-pitched swishing sound filled the conduit. Nothing in his previous life experience could be remotely compared to the reality of the spiral. He closed his eyes. Now he understood why Jessica screamed. She must have been terrified! He gulped at the air, trying to push enough oxygen into his lungs to avoid passing out. It took every ounce of concentration to control the buzzing in his head. His muscles cramped, his ears rang, and he wanted to throw up. With each passing second, he felt the powerful, forward pull on his body, as if he were attached to the end of a tightly stretched elastic string, snapping back at lightning speed to its point of origin.

The brief trip abruptly ended with a crash-landing on damp, mossy, ground. Over and over John rolled until a tree stopped his forward momentum. The spiral continued to spew air for a few seconds, then it collapsed inward and evaporated.

John fought the dizziness that threatened to plunge him into unconsciousness. He focused on breathing and keeping his stomach contents where they belonged. He managed to gasp in adequate quantities of air, but lost the battle with his churning gut. He was suddenly grateful that he had only sipped part of the tomato juice and taken just two bites of toast, but once they were up and out, he felt considerably better.

Unconscious, Gaylee lay on her side several feet away. Giving her a quick exam, he was relieved that none of her bones were broken, and her vital signs appeared strong. She would be coming around soon.

He pressed his hand down nearly an entire foot into the spongy, aqua-green moss. It immediately sprang back when he withdrew the pressure, gently showering him with a watery mist. It was this thick, soft cushion that saved them from being hurt on impact. He surmised it had recently rained. If Jessica had been here, all traces of her were long gone.

His head ached. He combed his fingers through his hair. The sun rested high in the sky, yet its warm rays did little to relax him. Jessica…Jess…where could she be? He tried to keep his frustration and fear in check. Hopefully, when his headache faded, he would think more clearly.

A gentle breeze rustled through the high forest canopy at the edge of the meadow. The trees were tall, thin yellow poles with thick foliage mushrooming out at the tops. From their underside the leaves were deep green, with a thin, white cotton-like puff at each tip. A few of the white puffs had ruptured, and blue bell-shaped blooms hung from them. The leaves were translucent, like stained glass, allowing the sun to radiate through to the forest floor. Each tree trunk was waxy smooth to the very top where the umbrella-like greenery intertwined with neighboring trees.

The circular meadow, just a few yards in diameter was the only place where unfiltered light touched the ground. It was only here that the moss grew. It stopped at the very edge of the woodland shade. Scattered clumps of dwarf purple bushes ringed many of the trees. They were loaded with plump, lavender berries that emitted a sweet, inviting fragrance. When his empty stomach rumbled, John wondered if they were edible. Squinting up at the sky, he thought the sun seemed normal enough, but seeing a second, enormous celestial orb at mid-day gave him quite a shock. A huge, gaseous ball shimmered green and purple in the blue sky.

Gaylee groaned. Her eyes fluttered open. She brought up a trembling hand to rub her head.

"How are you feeling?" John helped her to a sitting position.

"I hate this form of travel," she moaned and massaged her shoulder. "Any sign of Jessica?"

"No sign of anyone. This moss doesn't hold a shape. So where do we start?" He wanted to go.

"Oh...I'm dizzy." She lay back down and closed her eyes. "Let me rest, just a little longer." She made a slight smile. "So I'm not as crazy as you thought, am I?"

John grunted and idly pulled at the moss. "Did Shallenon know?"

"That she wasn't from Earth? Yes. She eventually figured it out. I tried to raise her as a normal earthling, but her link to this place, especially to her brother, was too great to be dismissed. She dreamed about him a lot more regularly than Jessica does...did. Their dreams began at about the same age, ten." Gaylee opened her eyes and turned her head toward John. "You need to understand," she said emphatically, "that it wasn't my decision to keep this from you, it was Shallenon's. From the moment she met you, she wanted you to think her a normal woman, and she desperately wanted Jessica to have a normal life. Think about it John, I'm an extra-terrestrial, so was Shallenon. Do I need to say more? She wanted it left alone."

John shook his head. "I knew there was more to your history than you ever divulged, but I'd always thought it had happened in Soviet-occupied Poland."

"When we came to earth through the spiral—it's called a spiral transhifter— we landed right in Jacob and Sophia's living room. I'd broken several bones on landing. Luckily, Shallenon was unhurt. Anyone else would have turned us into the authorities, but Sophia had lost her brothers, sisters, and everyone she had loved. She needed someone to care for...someone to love, and she took us in. Jacob went along with it."

John stood up and stretched. His headache was finally at a low throb and he was anxious to begin his search for Jessica.

"John, I know you're worried about Jess, so am I, but really, I need

48

just a little more time to rest, or you'll be carrying me the whole way. Besides, I need to tell you about the two other dreams that Jessica had." Gaylee briefly related the first mist experience confirming Haesom's death to Larone and the second one detailing the spiral plans. "You're not going to like this, but I don't believe my uncle Larone induced either one of these visions. I think Jessica brought them on by herself."

John listened to his mother-in-law in bewildered silence, not knowing what to make of her stories, but this last statement brought his irritation to the surface. "What do you mean?" He stared down at her.

"When Haesom died, it triggered something in Jessica...turned something on. Maybe a dormant gene, or a latent power. I don't know. Like it or not John, Jessica's heritage is half Esparian, and as she grows older, the Esparian part, and all that goes with it, grows stronger."

Anger flooded through him. He jumped to his feet. "This is crazy Gaylee...all of this." He gestured to the foreign sky and the alien forest. "I'm worried sick. How *dare* your uncles steal her away! She's been dragged, completely unawares, into, from what little I know, an extremely deadly situation. Her life's in danger, and she's all alone." John's voice rose to a yelling pitch.

Gaylee's face flushed red. She sat up. "Do you think I like this? Do you think I wanted this?" she yelled back. "I'm just as worried as you are, just as appalled. You're not the only one who loves her! She's all I have left too, besides you." She took some deep breaths. "She's not alone. Larone sent someone named Varnack to protect her. This Varnack must be a great warrior for him to be sent instead of Anton. I don't know what's happened, but I do know my uncles and they would never have done this without thinking it through and weighing all of the dangers."

Gaylee raised her hands toward John. "Help me up." He grabbed her hands and pulled. She drew herself erect and stared him in the eye. "My name is Gayleena Liedia of the House of Saylon. I am the High Protector of Esparia, the largest country on planet Edia. When Shallenon died, the birthright of the Protectors went to Jessica. I was born to the house of Liedia, and married Graesion Saylon. My status as High Protector came by virtue of that marriage, however Jessica is a true Saylon, a Protector by blood. I wanted to explain all of this to Jess this morning. She knew I was coming; we talked yesterday." Gaylee shook her head. "I thought I had more time, but when I woke up, I knew she was gone. I *felt* it and came straight over."

"And now we're here." He scooped up the duffle bag.

"Yes, we're here. She looked up at the gaseous planet above. "I'm home."

CHAPTER 6

The Salupathic Gift

The sun shone through the vines at the mouth of the cave when Jessica finally awoke for the day. She had just begun to tell Varnack about the mist-dream when a loud stomach rumble interrupted her explanation. "I'm hungry. You want something?"

He nodded. She reached for the knapsack and dumped the foodstuffs onto her lap. After handing Varnack three strips of the dried meat, she sniffed a piece of dried green produce. She nibbled a corner. "Oooo, sweet."

Varnack never blinked while she finished relating her dream between bites of fruit leather, jerky and dark bread wafers. She ended her narration by asking, "Varnack, are we in danger?" A jab of apprehension made her shiver.

"Not yet."

"Is that because they're looking for my mom?"

"Yes."

She picked up the still glowing lantern-jar, the extra food, and the now half-full water flask, then placed them back in the sack. After shaking the dust from her jacket and tying it around her waist, she was ready to go. To her surprise, they did not exit through the front, but followed a small tunnel at the back of the dugout, deeper into the hillside. It was a man-made passageway and reminded Jessica of pictures she had seen of nineteenth century coal mine tunnels. Reinforced on three sides with thick wooden beams, the dark conduit smelled musty and stale. Jessica retrieved the lantern from the sack and holding it high, gratefully noted it still contained an inch or so of combustible powder.

"Who built this place?"

"First Ones."

"Why?"

"Don't talk. Move."

She almost commented on his brusque manner, then thought better of it. Maybe this is how his species is. Maybe all of them hate talking. She considered the possibility for a while. How could she judge a whole species by one member? This must be who Varnack is...Probably a loner, definitely not a socializer. She must be driving him crazy. The thought made her smile.

Much to her relief, the path was free from cobwebs and little crawling creatures. There were no branching pathways. They followed the straight, dank, chilly passage for half an hour to its end. Here Varnack rose up on his back legs and using his powerful front paws, dug at a crack in the earth where several slender beams of light peeked through. Jessica coughed when the dust swirled around her. "Can I help?" she offered.

"No."

He created a small opening, barely large enough for them to squeeze through. A vast forest of tall, spindly trees and thigh-high lavender berried, red leafed bushes grew all around them. Each pale yellow tree rose nearly twenty feet. No outgrowth of branches interrupted the waxen, smooth trunks. From every tree's crown sprouted dozens of spoke-like arms, extending in all directions. They intertwined with neighboring limbs, forming an intricate lattice. Broad, translucent green leaves shot skyward from every point along the towering grid, while bell shaped blooms ranging from deep azure to delicate baby blue hung several inches below. Sun light filtered through the glassy leaves, bathing the forest floor in a muted green glow. Here and there, unfiltered beams of white light punched through the canopy above. Where it kissed the ground, thick velvety moss grew. After the musty tunnel, the forest smelled clean and sweet, with a hint of flowering perfume in the air.

"Come." Wagging his tail, Varnack led the way.

They traveled at a brisk pace, skirting around the thicker bushes and squeezing between clumps of the pole-thin timbers. It did not take long for Jessica to become accustomed to the rhythm of Varnack's gait and she easily kept stride with him. Still moist from the previous night's rain, the moss squished down when they stepped on the infrequent patches, spraying their legs with fine mist.

At length they reached a clearing. After the muted light in the forest, the brightness of the sun caused Jessica to squint, and she turned her face upward to catch a bit of the warmth. To her surprise, a large planet loomed high above, hovering in the cloudless, blue expanse. It reminded her of the many times she saw earth's moon after sunrise, just before it disappeared beyond the horizon, hanging like a softly focused picture with the sun's rays illuminating it's white beauty. Only this was no small moon, but a massive planet, at least a thousand times larger in the sky, and streaked with soft green and purple pastel colors.

"Varnack, what's that!" she exclaimed too loudly.

The immense hound dug his front paws into the ground and wheeled around, his fur on edge, his muscles tense. Seeing his attack position, Jessica winced and felt very foolish. "I...I'm sorry," she apologized, "I

51

didn't mean to startle you. I just wondered about that." She pointed skyward.

Without looking up, he grunted, "Ragus." He resumed their journey. She was keenly aware of his irritation.

The dark, aqua-green moss was finally drying out so it no longer gurgled when stepped on. Only the thudding of Jessica's feet on the soft soil disturbed the serenity around them. Varnack's paws made no sound. Several times they happened upon some pint-sized woodland rodents who chattered at them in alarm, and once Jessica glimpsed a single-horned, hairy beast behind a heavily laden berry bush.

The grape sized lavender fruit that dotted the red shrubbery emitted a strong, sugary fragrance, distinctively different from the flowery scent of the trees. Jessica yearned to try the botanical delicacy. However, having disturbed Varnack once already, she kept her desire to her herself and trailed behind him in silence. He seemed on edge, constantly turning his head to look from side to side and every fifty yards or so he would sniff the air.

When the sun drew straight overhead her guide came to a halt. Before them lay a vast planting of the twisted, fruit laden bushes. They grew so thick together, no tree could spring up in their midst, and no moss could grow under them. The strong sun flooded in, its heat making the heady fruit scent even more powerful.

"Food," Varnack indicated the shiny lavender berries with a nod of his head. "Dandle."

"Dandle berries, huh? I hope they're good." Picking a handful of the darker ones, she popped several into her mouth. When the sweet juice from the crushed dandle swirled around her taste buds, a moan of pleasure tumbled out. "Mmmm, these are great!"

She offered her companion the remainder in her palm. He shook his mighty head, then sniffed at the air. She ate them herself. "They taste like over-ripened raspberries from home." She maneuvered her way through the thornless, triangular leafed plants, plucking the succulent berries as she walked. Varnack contented himself with the fruit at the edge of the patch. Snapping all of the berries within easy reach, they soon ate their fill.

Happy for the brief rest, Jessica watched a tiny pink bug crawl across a broad red leaf. On reaching the lavender fruit, a small needle-like tongue shot out. Juice traveled through the translucent tongue, and as it filled the bug's belly, the insect turned from pale pink to dark pink and finally the same vibrant lavender as the fruit.

"So where are we going?"

"Ramadine."

More questions burned on her lips, but before she could give voice to any of them, the hair on Varnack's back bristled. Jessica stared in awe at her massive bodyguard. At once he transformed from a tranquil, yet grumpy escort to an alert warrior tensed for battle. She bolted to his side and crouched down beside him, her heart pounding in her chest.

"Too exposed." The silent message came into her mind, making her instantly grateful for the rare communications gift she possessed. On all fours she scurried after him back into the protection of the dense forest. Belly down, she waited.

Peering through the low growing foliage, Jessica caught sight of dark figures moving through the forest opposite the Dandleberry patch. She counted five altogether. They avoided the open berry patch and were soon out of sight. It took nearly half an hour before the hair on Varnack's back relaxed. She realized she could finally speak in safety, but held her voice to a whisper none-the-less.

"Where am I, Varnack, and who are you?" She felt sick to her stomach. "This is no game; even I could sense the danger coming from those guys." She stared across the top of the berry patch, trying to bring her pulse down to normal. "Who are they? Who's after us?"

He turned his golden eyes to meet hers. Her answers lay hidden there, but he responded with only one word. "Daenon."

Leading the way again, Varnack proceeded at a right angle from their original direction. The large planet, Ragus, lay at their back and the afternoon sun to their right.

Jessica broke a short stick from a dandleberry bush. She twisted her long, red hair on top of her head and used the wood to anchor it in place. To her dismay, her hands still trembled.

"Sorry Varnack, but I need to talk. You don't have to listen. I just need to calm my nerves, and talking helps." She began with her life back home. She reminisced about her parents, her friends, and a lot of her feelings. At several intervals in her monologue, Varnack grunted his assurance that he was actually paying attention. When she began telling him about her recent dreams, his ears twitched.

"Repeat," he requested. Surprised, she told him again, adding all of the details she could remember about Haesom's death and the several conversations she overheard in the mists.

"Varnack, I've heard Graesion mentioned several times now. I've got my suspicions, but can you tell me who he was?"

"Grandfather".

"*My* grandfather?"

Varnack nodded and picked up the pace. Further questions remained locked away, for now she jogged to keep up with him.

The forest floor turned from cushioning moss to a muddy, marshy consistency. The trees grew wider and their branches hung lower. Hardened insect mounds seemed to grow up from the mud. This new terrain did not slow Varnack. He bounded over buggy habitats with graceful ease, but Jessica found the going more difficult. She was a runner, not a hurdler, and she clumsily sidestepped the hardened mud hives. With her greater height, she needed to push aside some low hanging branches to avoid being slapped in the face. Eventually Jessica mastered the new challenges of the run. Just when she felt confident at spotting and avoiding the woodland hazards, Varnack stopped.

Just ahead lay a small hamlet, built on several acres of cleared forestland. A couple of dozen brick and wood buildings made up this out-of-the-way village. "Is this Ramadine?"

"No. Vorgen Hoffle."

Varnack led the way around the clearing to a small dirt road that transected the forest and led into the town. The cobblestone main street was deserted; pools of blood punctuated the roadway.

"Something's very wrong, Varnack." Jessica placed her hand on his back and felt his muscles tighten. "Hello," she called into the eerie silence.

Varnack's ears twitched. "There." He motioned to the largest of the brick buildings. Cautiously, they walked toward it. When they were within several yards of the structure, a male voice yelled from within, "Come no further."

"We're travelers and need shelter for the night." Jessica called back.

"You are not welcome, leave," a woman answered.

Jessica turned to Varnack. "This is your country, are the people always like this?"

He sniffed the air. "Death. Fear."

She stared back at the two-story building. This time an old man's face appeared in an upper level window. "We've been walking all day." she called. "Please, don't turn us away."

After many minutes the upper story window opened and the old man poked his head out. His cheek sported a nasty cut and a bloody patch covered one eye. "Who are you?"

Varnack's thoughts flooded Jessica's mind. "My companion is Varnack." She translated the thoughts. "He's a Trigal hound and comes to you from Ramadine." The old man's head jerked up and he turned to speak to someone behind him. Jessica continued, "Esparia is at war, the High Protector is dead."

The double-wide front door opened and three men stepped out onto a green brick porch. Each bore fresh wounds, the blood on their bandages still bright red. One held a bloodstained rag over a stump at the end of his right arm where his hand should have been. "What do you desire?" he asked, his voice tired, but wary.

"Oh, Varnack, what happened here?" Jessica swallowed hard. She shoved her horror back into the recesses of her mind. She was the daughter of a Colonel, she could handle this. "First of all," she strode toward the men, "I desire to help."

She shouldered past the three and marched into the spacious gathering hall. At least two hundred women and children filled the space. There were no tables or chairs, only wall to wall humanity. The silence was eerie, for a room filled with so many children should have been buzzing with their tiny voices, but here, not even a baby cried. Most sat dejectedly on the wood flooring. A few women were distributing drinks of water. Children huddled close to their mothers; the silent fear in their eyes spoke volumes. The three men on the porch trudged inside. The one with the missing hand sat heavily on a wooden chair while the other two kept an eye on Jessica, hands on their swords. Varnack padded to her side and sat on his hind quarters.

"Will someone please tell us what went on here?" she pleaded.

"Five men came," one of the female water bearers responded. "They were looking for a woman, a foreigner."

"I told them there was no stranger here," another woman offered. She sat in a corner, her knees drawn up to her chin with her arms clasped tightly around them. Three children pressed closed to her.

"It was obvious they were frustrated," the one eyed old man said from halfway down the stairs at the side of the room. "We told them they were in the wrong place, but they attacked, went from house to house."

Looking at the three younger men with weapons, Jessica asked, "Where are the other men?"

"Those still alive are upstairs." A woman, her tunic and pants smeared with drying blood, gestured with her eyes to the floor above. She held a basin of water, and a few dozen cloth bandages hung from her arm. "These three are the only men who can still stand. Those five assassins attacked so swiftly, we were unprepared for the fight."

"They fought for pleasure," the one-handed man added, his voice devoid of emotion.

"I am Tarin, High Older of Vorgen Hoffle." The old man with one eye made his way to Jessica and Varnack. "We gathered everyone here in case the black clothed riders return, as they threatened."

Varnack said to Jessica. "Our trail leads here."

Jessica felt ill. "Varnack, what are…" Before she could finish, he left the building.

"You're the one they were looking for, aren't you?" A fair-haired girl, several years younger than Jessica, stated. She was staring at the jean jacket tied around Jessica's waist. "Foreigner. They don't realize they should be looking for a girl."

"I'm so sorry." Jessica searched for words of comfort. "If these men return, my companion will handle them."

"A dog!" the woman in the corner spat. She rose to her feet, her face red with fury. "How can a simple dog defeat five butchers?" Her voice went higher in pitch and volume. "Who are you, to bring this on us?"

"Chana, enough!" the one-handed man commanded. "The girl said this Varnack is a Trigal Hound."

"Myth and superstition," Chana sneered.

"No," High Older Tarin cut in, "not myth, and certainly not superstition. Trigal Hounds exist." He turned to Jessica. "We have no strength left in us for another fight. Our men were taken by surprise and many now hover between life and death. Had we been prepared, weapons in hand, we would have beaten those five."

"Is there no doctor here?" The people stared at her blankly. "A physician?" Still no response. "A healer?"

"No healer. Our hoffle is too small," the woman with the bandages and water basin said.

"Why are those killers looking for you?" the fair-haired girl asked.

Jessica felt bewildered. She shook her head. "I truly don't know. I'm nobody."

Tears welled up in the young girl's eyes. "My father is upstairs dying. Are you saying he'll die for no good reason?"

Jessica groped for something meaningful to say. "My Grandfather was a man named Graesion. I think he was someone important."

High Older Tarin looked as if Jessica had just slapped him. "Graesion, of the house of Saylon?" he barely whispered.

"Yes." It was Jessica's turn to be surprised. "You've heard of him?"

Several others in the room gasped, but no one spoke. Chana's young son, a boy about ten years of age finally broke the silence. "Who's Graesion of the House of Saylon?"

Jessica needed an answer to that question herself. She looked expectantly at the old man. However, before he could answer, an elderly woman stepped up to the lad. With a disgusted expression on her face, the aged lady shook his shoulder. "What do you do in school all day, boy? Don't you know your history? Graesion was the great High Protector. He and Lady Gayleena were Lord Haesom's parents."

Jessica's heart skipped a beat. "Lady Gayleena?" Before she could connect any more dots, Varnack appeared in the doorway.

"They return," he alerted.

"Already?" Jessica barely breathed. "Varnack, I can fight, I've been trained," she offered. "Tell me..."

He cut her off. "Stay."

"But…"

"Everyone." His command left no room for argument. He spun around and sat on his haunches on the front deck.

"The riders return," Jessica warned. "Varnack wants us to stay here."

The man with one hand rose, "I'd rather die fighting."

Jessica hurried to block his path. "If Varnack says to stay, then we stay."

"I didn't hear him speak. How do you know what the hound wants?" he challenged.

"I just know, okay? We communicate. If Varnack fails, then you can still die fighting, but right now you'd be more a liability than a help."

"Sit down, Bareth," the high older urged. "No one doubts your courage."

With his remaining hand, Bareth pulled a dagger from his belt and sat back on the chair.

Jessica took up position in the open doorway. Some of the women cracked the shutters to better see the road outside. Tarin, the high older, shuffled to Jessica's side while the last two men fell in behind him. Within moments the dull patter of horse's hooves on hardened earth reached her ears. Five black clothed men, their heads shaved, rode on shiny black horses down the stony street. Even though-or perhaps because-the situation was so intense, Jessica needed to stifle a laugh. Black! Why was it that bad guys always seemed to wear black?

The five halted a few yards from Varnack, then dismounted in unison. One pointed to Jessica standing in the doorway and whispered to his comrade, a man distinguished from the other four by a red sash around his middle.

"Girl," the leader called, "come with us and we'll leave this hoffle. No one gets hurt."

Once spoken, the untruth issued from the man's lips as a thin black rope coiling and twisting into a knot just in front of his mouth. Jessica saw it so clearly that, for an instant, it actually obscured his lips. Outraged, she shot back, "You lie!"

Varnack's thoughts came to her. "Leave now," she translated. "Or Varnack", she nodded her head toward him, "will kill you."

The men laughed, they seemed truly amused by her warning, but before their smiles faded, Varnack lunged from the porch. Startled by his swiftness, Jessica jumped back, thumping into the one handed man who was standing close behind her. He swore under his breath.

Varnack moved with astounding speed. Razor sharp claws protruded from each mighty forepaw. With the left he slit a man's throat while simultaneously using the right to rip open another's chest. Varnack nimbly touched the ground on all fours. He spun around and kicked with his hind legs, connecting with such force on a third killer, that the human was dead before hitting the ground. The fourth man pulled his sword and lunged at the mighty animal. Varnack pulled back, barely dodging the weapon.

Before the assassin could swing again, he sprang. His teeth sank deep into the man's side, tearing the flesh away. The killer cried out in agony. A dagger flew from just behind where Jessica stood. It landed with a muted thud in the wounded man's heart.

"Justice, though I think my hand is worth twenty of that doogeroot's lives," Bareth declared in cold satisfaction.

The red-sashed leader, his face alive with shock and anger, leapt at Varnack. In each hand he held a long, jagged edged blade. Varnack twisted to the side as one of the knives slashed downward toward his head. He rolled away, but the second dagger caught his shoulder. Red blood oozed onto his golden coat. The hound jumped, snapping at the man's left hand. He tore the tiny finger off. The enemy grimaced but made no noise. He held onto his weapon in a blood soaked grip. He hacked again at Varnack, twisting the blades over and around with blinding speed.

Their dance had a deadly grace to it. Weaving and bobbing, Varnack would lung and nip, then prance back so swiftly that his feet did not seem to touch the earth. Scattered pools of red liquid dotted his sleek body. The two had maneuvered further down the street. Jessica and many of the townspeople now crowded onto the veranda to witness the fight. With surprising agility, the Trigal hound skirted behind his opponent. He connected with the man's left hand again and this time caused the blade to sail through the air. Spinning around after the elusive animal, the man was caught off balance by a hit to the side. Again, Varnack dodged a deadly jab. He sprang back, circled once more, and charged the man, biting into his raised right sword arm. The two tumbled to the ground. Varnack quickly released the arm and sank his sharp fangs deep into the neck of the red sashed leader. The man struggled to twist away, pounding at Varnack's head, but the jaws held firm. Within moments, he ceased to struggle. The warrior dog did not let go of the throat until his opponent's body completely ceased to quiver.

"I'll bet they thought Trigal hounds were myth and superstition too," High Older Tarin mused. "It's over," he announced to his people, "we are safe once again."

Jessica, gasping from having held her breath so many times, ran to Varnack. He licked at the clotting blood on his shoulder. "I've never seen anything like that before, and I hope to never have to see it again." She stroked his head. "Thanks, Varnack."

Chana's inquisitive ten-year-old boy appeared at her elbow. "Can I touch him?" The child reached out to Varnack.

"I think he'd like that, but be soft. Varnack, how badly are you hurt?"

"Nothing deep," came the reply.

The child gently stroked the powerful animal. Varnack seemed to enjoy it.

Jessica smiled with relief. "He especially likes scratching behind his ears," she suggested to the boy.

Before long, the other village children came to see their mighty savior. The sound of their laughter seemed to bring life back into the stricken village. Varnack romped away from the fallen enemy and played with the little ones at the side of the green brick building while several women hauled the dead away.

Jessica re-entered the meeting hall. The woman who had earlier held the basin of water and bandages was ascending the stairway. "I'd like to help. What can I do?" Jessica called to her.

She turned and stared in surprise. "You can help my friends prepare an evening meal."

Jessica grimaced. "You don't want me near the cooking. Trust me on that one, I'm a lousy cook."

The woman smirked, but remained silent.

"Let me help with the wounded. My father is a healer and I've helped with wounded before." She was not really lying. Though never having worked in a hospital, she had learned a great deal at the vet clinic during the past year. How different could human medicine be?

"All right, come with me. But I warn you, it's a terrible sight upstairs."

Even with the warning, Jessica was unprepared for what she found on the second level. The stench of sweat mingled with coagulating blood and vomit reached her before she traversed half the stairs. Forty-three men lay on large woven rugs, their wounds ranging from severed limbs to deep body lacerations.

"Hot water and more dressings will be here soon. I am Karree."

Jessica swallowed hard. She felt her cheeks pale and her breathing shallow. *Get a grip, girl. Think of this as the veterinary clinic.* She'd helped with surgery before. "I'm Jessica. Wh…where do you want me?"

The next several hours were spent disinfecting, stitching, and bandaging sliced flesh. As soon as Jessica began her service to the wounded, she ceased looking at the humanity and focused solely on the injuries. An inner authority took over. She worked automatically, almost instinctively. She understood at a glance how to best treat the mutilations. The intuitive knowledge surprised her, but the urgency of the moment forced her to not dwell on this ability. "We're missing something," she muttered. "Karree, where are your healing herbs?"

"We have none. No hoffler understands this type of healing, and no one here has the Salupathic Gift."

Jessica frowned. "What's the Salupathic Gift."

Karree raised her eyebrows in surprise. "It's the ability to harness the powers in the Expanse of Gonta to restore health."

"And what's the Expanse of Gonta?"

Karree stared at Jessica, her eyes wide. "You don't know what the Expanse of Gonta is?"

"If I knew what it was, I wouldn't be asking." Jessica snapped and Karree bristled.

"Where do you come from? Who are you?" The woman's eyes narrowed.

Jessica shook her head. She felt empathy for Varnack. Unwanted questions irritated her, too.

The next man Jessica came to had lost so much blood his skin was ash white. Unconscious, his breath came in shallow, short pants. His heart raced in his chest. He was among the last to be tended as the other three nurses skirted around him to aid the less severely wounded, though Karree had gone to him several times to pat down his brow and whisper words of comfort. "This guy's lost a lot of blood," Jessica observed.

"He's lost too much and his injury is too severe," Karree agreed. "I'm surprised he still lives."

Jessica lifted the temporary bandage covering his middle and winced. His inner organs spilled through the wide opening. "Oh dear!" She tried hard to control her stomach.

Karree glared at her. "Leave him alone," she hissed. "Let him die in peace."

"No." Jessica shook her head. "As long as he's breathing, there's a chance."

Two nurses stopped their work to watch Karree and Jessica. "He is my husband," Karree's voice became stern, "and you are a child. A gifted child, I'll grant you, but unlearned never-the-less. Leave him."

Jessica drew herself to her full height. "If you're so certain he can't make it, then let my try *anyway*." She felt her blood pressure rise. Anger spilled into her voice. "If he dies, then…he dies, but maybe, just maybe I can save him. Don't let him die without a fight. Never will I leave another human being to pass on without at least trying to help!"

Grim faced, Karree remained silent. Taking the silence for disgruntled acquiescence, Jessica washed her hands in the hottest water she could stand, then dipped them in a basin filled with hard liquor. She thought of her father and fervently wished he were there.

She repaired the mutilated organs as best as she could with the finest needle the women had, then carefully poked everything back in and pulled the skin tight. She worked quickly, trying to remember the reality surgical shows she had seen on television. With the last stitch knotted off, Jessica checked the man's pulse. She could not find it. His breathing came shallower and slower until it ceased altogether.

Karree knelt beside Jessica, tears in her eyes. "You tried. Your courage is greater than mine."

In despair Jessica shook her head. "No. No!" Her voice was hard and she hissed the words through clenched teeth.

She placed both her hands over the man's sternum, closed her eyes, and concentrated. Pumping down and up with a CPR rhythm she counted one, two, three... up to thirty, then gave two breaths and pumped again, one, two, three... Over and over she did the chest compressions and breaths. After what seemed an eternity there was still no response. Her arms burned with the effort. She was losing the fight.

Instinctively, she shifted her hands from his sternum and placed them over his heart. She pushed once, with all of her force. "Live", she commanded. Then she let up and commanded again, "Heal." Another push. "Live." Another release of pressure. "Heal." Rhythmically, though not as quickly as with the CPR compressions, she pushed on his heart. She threw all of her weight behind each downward shove, and breathed out the command, "Live". With each recoil, she uttered, "Heal." Slowly, rhythmically, down and up, directly over his heart, she pumped, pulling strength from every tissue in her body. Live. Heal. Live. Heal. Over and over she commanded, at first out loud and then in her mind, focusing her concentration on those two words as her hands pushed on the heart. Her will was intense. Live...live.

After dozens of pushes, a tingling, deep within her consciousness, began. It multiplied exponentially in power with each subsequent thrust. Within seconds an electrical current traveled from the crown of her head, down the nape of her neck and split at her shoulders. The intense heat generated by the energy descended through her arms, then flowed into her hands. It radiated from her palms and fingertips into the lifeless body of Karree's husband. She felt her hands meld with the flesh above his heart. Much of her consciousness poured into his body through the connection. In her mind's eye Jessica could 'see' every damaged organ. She willed them to regenerate. Her mind traveled along the major arterial lines, repairing and reconnecting. The energy was intense. She destroyed infecting microbes with zaps of electricity. She united severed nerves as if welding together two pieces of delicate wire and forced ripped muscle to knit into shape. Bone fragments realigned, then cemented into place. She activated the delicate aioli of his lungs. Like millions of tiny balloons, they slowly inflated with oxygen. The non-pulsing heart was her final destination. Here, she forced her own life-spirit to spark the atrial, then ventricular chambers. Blood pumped. Again, a spark. Again, the cardiac muscle contracted, sending blood throughout the body. A third spark, and the heart beat on its' own.

Jessica collapsed into oblivion.

CHAPTER7

Ider Hoffle

"Any idea where we are?" John felt completely lost. He was the stranger now, the extra-terrestrial.

If Gaylee had been homesick for her world, she never let on. He wondered if she would miss Earth now. As for himself, he had the oddest feeling he would never see it again. He pushed the thought away.

"As I remember, moss of this color and texture only grows in the Southern Greenwood, so we've landed in the southwestern part of Esparia. To give you a frame of reference, think non-arid, northeastern New Mexico." Gaylee looked at the forest surrounding the small, moss covered meadow. "Jessica could be anywhere."

The statement irritated John. He glared at her, but before he could make an obnoxious comment, she cut him off.

"Remember, John, she has Varnack with her. They're already hours ahead of us and probably on their way to Ramadine, so I suggest we go there too. It lies north, about five hundred miles, or in Esparian units of measure, filons from here."

"Filons?"

"A filon is a little further than a mile. Now that you're here, you'll need to get used to a few different words and their meanings. If Jess isn't at Ramadine, then my Uncle Larone will be the only one who can help us."

"If not to your uncle, then where else would Varnack take her?"

"Ramadine's the only logical place. Just remember, if something happens to Jessica, I will know it, the same as I knew when my son died. I will feel it, but right now I have no such foreboding. I know she's safe, I promise you. Now that I'm back on Edia, my intuitive powers are going to increase. I draw strength from my planet in a way I could never do on Earth." She gave a short laugh. "Poor Jessica. She's going to have a dramatic increase in her gifts too, but she probably won't understand what's happening or why. It's imperative we find her, not only for safety reasons, but to help her come to terms with her unique abilities."

"Come on Gaylee...gifts, powers, abilities? You make her sound like a witch. I know we've come through a portal of some sort, but there must be a scientific explanation for it. I don't believe in this other stuff, and you know that. Granted, you have remarkable intuition, but I don't want to hear any more about sorcery."

Her face remained placid, but her eyes shone brightly.

"All right," he nodded, "I believe when you say Jess is okay. So, what's Ramadine?"

She led their way out of the mossy meadow. "Compare it to the larger universities on Earth, with every type of specialty school imaginable: medical, dental, pharmaceutical, veterinary, and law, as well as an agricultural center and performing arts academy. Ramadine is a self-sustaining, independent city. There are many universities throughout Esparia, just as on Earth, but Ramadine is the oldest, largest, and most prestigious. Its origins date back more than ten thousand years. Larone is the Grand Advisor, something like a university president. The word Ramadine is taken from an ancient tongue. The literal meaning is City of Knowledge. 'Rama' means knowledge and 'dine' means city. In fact, the word dine is used on Edia instead of city."

"Larone's the head guy, huh? We have a few things to discuss when I arrive." At the concerned look on her face, he added, "Don't worry. I'll hear him out before I shoot him. I want to know why he chose Jessica. Why he didn't search you out instead?"

"I told you, Jess is a protector by blood. Anyway, I think Larone knew I would follow her. He also knew you would come with me."

"Me?" He was shocked. "Why would Larone hope I would come?"

She shrugged her shoulders. "You and Jessica have always made a good team. It's something to think about anyway."

"How are you so certain we're going north?"

"Ragus." She indicated the large, green and blue pastel globe in the sky. "It's always to the north."

"Ahhh, it's called Ragus. Took my breath away."

Gaylee smiled. "I'd forgotten how beautiful it looks, just floating up there."

"Are these berries any good?" John waved his hand toward a clump of red bushes in front of them.

"Dandleberries, yes. You'll find they taste a great deal like raspberries." She plucked a few as she passed a loaded bush and popped them into her mouth. He followed her example and was pleasantly surprised at the delicate, sweet flavor. He stopped to pick several more handfuls, then ran to catch up with her.

Leading the way through the slender trees, Gaylee reminisced. "I remember as a child, I traveled to every part of Esparia with my parents. My country is roughly the size of the continental United States, minus Texas. It also stretches between two vast oceans. Three smaller countries border us. Marone is on the north, while Hent and Galland are on the

63

south. When I left, our population was about thirty-five million, perhaps forty million now."

She talked about the giants who lived in the southern Colossus Mountains and the dwarf tribes that lived on a large island off Esparia's southwestern coast. She described the Central Mountains where her home had been, as well as the rich, fertile Northern Plains. To the west were the Deserts of Demar, covering a full one fifth of Esparia.

John kept quiet while she spoke, trying to picture in his mind the places she so vividly described. It was when she mentioned the Deserts of Demar that her voice grew sad and her verbal sightseeing tour abruptly stopped. "It's not hard to tell you've hit on a sensitive subject." John kept his voice soft. "What happened, Gaylee? Why did you go to earth and never come back?"

She stopped and put her hand out to a young pole tree for support. She leaned heavily against the sturdy trunk. Her voice was barely a whisper, but John caught every word. "I had three uncles. Larone, I've told you a little about. He's the oldest. Anton is the youngest. And then there was Segal, the middle son. He hated not being the oldest and he hated not being distinguished as the youngest. My mother was their sister, Segal's twin. My parents died shortly after I wed. Graesion was the son of the High Protectors. Our families were close, had been for generations, so my marrying him was almost a pre-arranged given. But he was the love of my life." She sighed, a deep, slow exhale through her parted lips.

"Segal killed Graesion's parents in an attempt to gain control of the government. Graesion, though young at the time, defeated him and exiled him to the Deserts of Demar. The inhabitants of the deserts are a blood thirsty, savage people," she explained. "They cannibalize anyone unfortunate enough to wander into their traps, as well as each other. Segal somehow mesmerized them--convinced them to follow him. I'm not sure how he succeeded, but he did. Only hours after Shallenon was born, I received a letter of warning from Segal's young wife, Naydeen, that Segal would attack. But it came too late. I was too weak to run, and Graesion barely mounted a defense. Larone and Anton were with us. My uncle Anton had been working on an astounding piece of fifth dimensional science, magical science...power found in the Expanse of Gonta. He had in his possession ancient manuscripts containing long lost, for lack of a better word, incantations that govern hyper-travel."

John bristled. "Magical science? Isn't that an oxymoron?" His voice dripped with sarcasm.

"I know you don't believe in this type of thing, but the people of your world once did. Haven't you heard the phrase, 'faith can move mountains'? That's a reminder of the power I'm talking about. It once had a literal meaning."

64

"Finish your story," he said quietly.

"Graesion died trying to buy my uncles enough precious time. Haesom was going to flee with us, but when he heard his father was dead, he stayed. Time ran out, so I kissed my son good-bye, took the baby and jumped. To earth Shallenon and I came." She pushed off from the thin tree and resumed walking. "There was no way to return, until now. And even if a way had presented itself," she smiled and looked at him, "I would never have left. Once Shallenon married you, my ties with your world became unbreakable. She would never have left you, and I would never have left her, just as I would never leave Jessica or you." She laughed. "Who would have guessed we would *all* end up back here."

John did not return her smile. He felt irritation at the ironic turn of events. "So, why? Why are we all 'back here'? What brought all this on?"

She shook her head. "I really don't know, but from the little information in Jessica's mist dreams, it seems I have a younger cousin, Segal's son, Daenon. I can only assume Daenon has become the new Demarian leader, and like his father before him, wants to rule the world."

As they picked their way through the forest, Gaylee talked all about her life in Esparia. She told of her courtship with Graesion and their wedding. She told of their years together and then finally being blessed with their son. And of many more years before she was finally able to have Shallenon. John listened in silence, too bewildered to make comments. She seemed happy to just talk, to let out memories that had long been kept quiet. Soon the shadows lengthened, and the filtered light dimmed. John checked his watch and to his dismay found it had stopped working.

"We'd better find a place to camp for the night," he suggested. "Looks like it'll be dark soon." He chose shelter within a circlet of cream-barked trees where a small patch of moss grew. They satisfied their hunger on some MRE's Gaylee had smashed into the pack, then settled into the now dry, comfortably soft moss.

For a woman her age, Gaylee was in excellent shape, but her exhaustion was visible. "Those military meals are pretty good." She yawned.

"Yeah, MRE's are a soldier's food in the field. Lucky for us I keep several boxes in that storage closet for hunting trips."

Gaylee smiled. "I feel like a foot soldier, tired and dirty. All I need is a rifle to complete the scenario."

"I could load my gun and you could pretend it's a rifle."

"No thanks."

"So you really are eighty-three years old?" John's medical mind was fascinated with that fact.

"You didn't believe me?"

"Yeah, I did, but only because I could do the math. Fifty years on earth, plus your age when you met Sophia, but you sure don't look it."

"Well, John," she yawned again, "I'll live to be at least two hundred, probably even longer. Play your cards right, and you too will live well beyond your normal life span." She soon fell asleep.

John tried to clear his mind, but the day's events refused to file neatly away. He reviewed the few facts he knew. He was sitting on Edia, and Ragus circled overhead. Gaylee, with her husband Graesion, once ruled Esparia. Hmm, she called herself a Protector. He reviewed the history Gaylee related during their walk.

"My people have lived in peace for centuries," her words echoed in his memory. "We were blindsided by Segal. We thought that banishment would be the end of him. In the past, our laws were sufficient to control any would-be dictators. Edian people are, by nature, more peaceful than those of Earth, with the exception of the desert tribes of Demar, but they never bothered us. They kept to themselves until Segal's banishment. My uncle wasn't just power hungry, he was truly evil. He destroyed anyone he even thought could oppose him. He enslaved thousands, butchered men, women and children in his quest for power. Graesion should never have banished him, he should have condemned him to death."

At last, sleep crept up on John. He lay down and mulled the last statement over. "I agree," he decided.

* * *

They had walked ever northward for nearly four hours when John asked, "Gaylee, you do know where you're going, don't you?"

"Yes," she laughed. "There's a hoffle...well, was a hoffle, but is now a large town or tiern actually, there's two new words for you, several more filons north of here. It's called Ider Hoffle. The people who live there are all soldiers, warriors. They train constantly; it's a source of pride with them. The elite of the elite. It was with their help that Graesion defeated and banished Segal the first time. Ten years later, when Segal attacked again, a garrison of three hundred Ider warriors was stationed at Saylon Dorsett, my home. Those brave men and women, along with regular soldiers, were the reason Graesion held Segal as long as he did, allowing Shallenon and me to escape."

"Maybe we can bargain for some transportation there. This walking is too slow; we need to get to Ramadine."

"Um...John, there's one more thing I need to tell you about my world." He raised an eyebrow. "Technologically speaking, unless there have been dramatic changes since I left, Esparia is much like Earth if you combine the Roman and Renaissance eras. We do have steam power and solar power, we use natural pressure for indoor plumbing and running water, and we have moveable type printing presses. However, we do not have oil-based power or electrical power. It's been like this for thousands of years."

"No cars? No computers?"

She shook her head.

"Then how could Anton harness a black spiral if your science is so primitive?"

"I didn't say it was primitive," she defended. "I said we don't use those types of power. This may sound odd, but my people are almost defiant in their resistance to change, even if that change would be for their betterment. The Protectors have had no good reason to advance things. Life on Edia is simple. To be honest, I found that modern Earth living gave me a headache, though I did enjoy air-conditioning. Many of Earth's advances have come as a direct result of war and famine. We haven't had war for millennia, that is, until Segal and Daenon came along. Also, the soil here is rich, yielding an abundance of fruits, vegetables and grains. No one goes hungry.

"Anyway, for some reason, my family genes produce people who can harness the power of Edia. My uncle Anton has a natural gift when it comes to understanding the laws of physics, much like your Leonardo de Vinci. But unlike de Vinci, who only dreamed of fantastic twentieth century inventions, Anton has the magical," John groaned at the word, "ability to make his visions a reality. This is the science of the fifth dimension, or Expanse of Gonta. Your scientists understand four dimensions, but they have yet to understand the fifth one. Don't take anything for granted here, our science is much more advanced than you think, and our magic is powerful. The two are closely intertwined. There are powers that some individuals hold which defy all logic. Larone is another case in point." Her tone was firm, almost commanding.

"All right, I'll reserve final judgment until I've been here a while. So, if there's no train or bus, maybe we could buy a horse."

"And what are we going to barter with?"

"I am a physician, dear lady. Do not forget. Maybe someone could use a good doctor."

"You're right. There aren't many healers in Esparia, since disease is almost unheard of. However, broken bones and such are not uncommon. You have a valuable skill, and I'm sure it can be used."

John took the lead when the dandleberry bushes thickened and their path became more laborious. They walked in comfortable silence, the soft ground muffling their footsteps. He marveled at the strange world around him and wondered once again if he would ever miss Earth. He was grateful Gaylee was with him. She seemed confident in her knowledge of the land and the people. If Esparians were as slow to embrace change as she indicated, then things would not have changed since her leaving fifty years earlier. He also enjoyed his mother-in-law's company. Gaylee was one of the few people who John could speak frankly with and not offend. Their relationship consisted of mutual respect and admiration.

By habit, he glanced at his watch for the third time that day. Still on his wrist, the watch remained a gentle reminder of Earth. If the science here was as good as Gaylee claimed, then maybe there was someone at Ramadine who could fix it.

With Gaylee in mind, John chose the easiest path possible. The dandleberry bushes grew fuller and taller in this section of the forest, with fewer ripening berries. When he parted a particularly full-leafed set of branches, a horse neighed. Uncertain of their security, he turned to Gaylee with a finger to his lips and motioned for her to crouch down beside him. "Heard something," he whispered. "Tell me if they're friend or foe."

Gingerly, he moved two branches so they both could peer through. Crossing their line of vision were several black uniformed men. John counted five in all, heavily armed and dressed head to foot in black save a red belt on one who rode slightly ahead.

Silently the men passed by, all five inspecting the ground, diligently looking for something. John and Gaylee hardly breathed. They waited a full half hour before moving from their place of hiding. "Who were they?" John whispered, concerned the men might still be able to hear him.

"I have no idea, but they felt dangerous." She shivered. "I can still sense their malevolence. All I can tell you is they weren't Esparian." She wrinkled her brow. "They must be Demarian. Daenon's men."

"Well, whoever they were, they were searching for something or someone."

"I'll feel much safer when we reach Ider Hoffle." Gaylee sounded worried.

John nodded. He retrieved the pistol from the bag, loaded it, then slipped it through his belt.

When the sun began its descent in the sky, John thought about finding shelter for the evening. He was about to suggest stopping when the forest abruptly ended. Directly in front of them lay a beautiful tiern. A four-foot high wall made of polished, burnt-orange and creamy white stones ran the outer perimeter. The land between the forest edges and stonewall was cleared of all natural foliage and planted with soft green grass. John estimated it to be three football fields wide.

"I assume this is Ider Hoffle."

"Yes." Gaylee put her cape on and pulled the hood up over her head. After tying it snuggly under her chin, she tucked the few, still visible hairs in around the edges.

"What are you doing?"

"Red hair is uncommon among my people. Brownish-red and strawberry blond are not rare, but flaming red, my color, Jessica's color, oddly enough, only runs in my family, the Liedian line. Unlike your world, where color can be acquired in any shade from a bottle, my family color is natural and very unique. I'm not ready to announce my arrival just yet, so I'm taking precautions."

She glanced at the gun at his waist. "You'll want to put the pistol away. We'll be safe here, so you won't need it."

"I feel better with it close by."

"I understand, but that's a weapon unheard of on Edia. Remember, I told you gun powder hasn't been invented here, so unless you want the responsibility of introducing new technology to my world, you'd better hide it in the bag."

"New technology, huh? All right, you win." He quickly zipped the loaded gun in the bag. "What about a zipper? Is that new technology too?"

"As a matter of fact it is, but it's definitely the lesser of two evils."

The bright colors and cleanliness of the large town made a deep impression on John. Not a speck of trash littered the street. All of the buildings were in excellent repair, and the air smelled clean and fresh. From the decorative wall surrounding the tiern to the pink cobblestone streets, Ider Hoffle was a living rainbow. Gaylee showed the way through broad avenues lined with light yellow, soft orange and gentle lavender stone buildings. Wide, delicately etched marble arches punctuated the major street intersections, and small, green parks flourished on every block. She pointed out several impressive theatres, her favorite one being made of deep aqua polished stone, its front columns reaching a full three stories high. Most of the buildings had pitched, light blue metal roofs, reminding John of huge mirrors as they reflected the sun's rays.

"I've never seen metal roofs that color before," he commented.

"It's Palium."

"Palium?"

"Yes. It's very pliable in its natural state, so its usage is quite extensive. Depending on how it's refined, Palium has multiple uses. Physicians use it to stitch torn flesh, rope makers weave it into thin cable strong enough to heft several oxen at once, yet light enough a child could carry one hundred feet of it with ease, even weavers make it into cloth. Long thin strands are like sharp wire, but woven together, at right angles, they bond in such a way as to become feathery soft."

Partway into the tiern, they turned onto a major boulevard where shops, both petite and major, offered all manner of goods and services. Several open-air markets, some still conducting business in the twilight, had elaborate displays of fresh produce. Curious, John stopped for a moment to examine a hairy, green, diamond-shaped food. "Palanto," Gaylee offered from beside him. "Quite sweet, and wonderful as a jam."

She pointed out numerous public restrooms and drinking fountains at different intersections along the thoroughfare. Down side streets John glimpsed brightly colored homes with neatly trimmed yards and flourishing gardens. Children played inside white lattice fences, their laughter adding harmony to the city rhythm. The smell of baking filled the air, making John's stomach grumble several times.

People were dressed as colorfully as the ornamental buildings they lived in. Bright colored cloth draped and twisted into men's robes and women's gowns; however, loose fitting pantaloons, flowing shirts, and tighter fitting tunics attired the majority of both sexes. On their feet they wore laced-up sandals, slip-on clogs, soft-soled moccasins, or shined boots, ranging in height from the ankle to the knee. The colors of the foot-wear ranged throughout the rainbow spectrum as well. Upon horse or in wooden buggy, on foot or crude scooter, the bare headed people of Ider Hoffle laughed and talked, shopped and sold. The feeling of camaraderie made John envious. "Does everyone know each other? Pretty big city for that."

Gaylee smiled. "Remember, John, you're in Esparia. You'll find the people are naturally friendly. There's little reason to be afraid of one's neighbor here. There are criminals, but very few. As I said, Edians are by nature a far less warlike people than those of Earth." As if to confirm her words, two men on horseback smiled and nodded when they passed the newcomers. Periodically, other villagers gave them friendly acknowledgement. It took a full hour from the time they entered the tiern for the two pilgrims to reach the central square.

Though not uncommonly tall by earth standards, at six foot two inches John stood at least a half head taller than every man he saw in Ider Hoffle, making him feel uncomfortable. "Are all Esparians short?"

"No," Gaylee laughed, a sedate, yet mirth-filled sound. "Ider Hoffle is uncommon. The people here are quite closed about marrying out of the hoffle, so the gene pool is not diverse. If you'll notice, no one is staring at you because of your height. The citizens are used to seeing tall men and women who come for the Military Academy. It's just that none live here in the hoffle."

They made their way to a pink stone bench next to a small, bubbling fountain and sat down, weary from the day's journey. Four fountains adorned the spacious square, each with two elongated benches flanking it.

"Are you hungry?" John asked.

"Yes, but be as nonchalant as you can when you unzip that thing. We don't want to draw attention."

John grinned mischievously. "This zipper could make me a rich man, Gaylee." He opened the bag only as far as necessary to extract some dried food. "MRE's might attract notice. Here, have a granola bar."

After a few minutes of people watching, John said, "I've noticed a lot of weapons. Do the people always carry swords and daggers? Makes me wish I had my big game knife I just bought."

"I told you, this is a warrior center. Carrying weapons is a source of pride with them. And trust me, every person you see knows how to use them."

"I can use a knife, too. So, what now?"

Before Gaylee could answer, a commotion, coming from what seemed to be another main thoroughfare at the far end of the square, interrupted their conversation. As if on queue, people poured into the large plaza from every direction. John rose up in surprise, Gaylee followed. Those in the gathering crowd appeared agitated and worried. Able to gaze over the sea of heads, John was unexpectedly grateful for his uncommon height. Two young men on horses rode onto the square at the opposite end. Both were bruised, bloodied and poorly bandaged. Even from a distance, John could see they were in bad shape.

The young men stopped at the fountain furthest from John and Gaylee. It was obvious by their uniforms and weapons, they were soldiers. Helped from their horses to one of the stone benches flanking the fountain, the two stood tottering side by side.

John's attention momentarily diverted to a petite blond woman standing next to the taller of the two boys. Tears rolled down her face. She held his hand in both of hers. A hush fell over the crowd when this taller boy spoke. His voice sounded weak and the listeners quieted even further. No one moved. John's physician eyes did not miss the fact the young man put a great deal of effort into keeping himself from collapsing. The smaller boy also fought to stay on his feet. Several hands went up to support him.

"I have come to give my report," the boy began ceremoniously. John thought of a young Marine.

"I've come from Saylon Dorsett." John felt Gaylee go rigid next to him. He glanced her way. Her jaw muscles were tight, her eyes fixed on the reporting youth.

"That's your home, right?" he whispered. She nodded.

"I bring grievous news," the youth continued. "The High Protector, Lord Haesom, is dead." A collective gasp came from the crowd. "Every member of the Protector's family is dead. So are the Assistant Protector and every Grand Council member who arrived early, ninety in all. Our legion of a thousand men, a third from this hoffle, is dead, save four, Rembert the archer and my Uncle Cordon who are, at this time, reporting to Healer Larone, and Jeema here beside me, and myself."

A moan rippled through the people. Many men and women openly wept. Others stood silent, their stunned faces reflecting the pain of their emotions. "We were attacked by Daenon and his army of Elitet. An unknown hand betrayed us. We held for five days…they took no prisoners."

A young woman next to John sobbed. A grim-faced man tried to comfort her. "No. No, this can't be," a deep voice from behind whispered. Gaylee let her own silent tears fall. "The four of us who survived did so because we were trapped under the bodies of our fallen comrades," the soldier explained. "That is my report."

He no sooner finished when both young men collapsed. The blond woman caught the boy who reported. Automatically, John rushed forward. "I'm needed," he shouted to Gaylee. He tried to fight his way through the crowd to the wounded soldiers, but he did not get far. The people were too thickly grouped.

"My companion is a healer, let him through," Gaylee commanded in a loud voice that quieted the distressed hofflers around her. A stunned hush spread through the crowd and her authoritative voice rang out again. "I said, let the tall one through! He is a skilled healer." This time a corridor opened. The crowd drew back. John sprinted through.

The blond woman looked up, her startled expression quickly changing to suspicion. She handed the fallen boy in her arms to a man at her side then placed herself between John and the young soldiers. Distrust played on her face, a hardened, unwelcoming look glowed in her eyes. She reminded John of a tigress protecting her injured cubs.

His first reaction was to push past her to the dying youth, but a subtle warning sounded in his head. This woman emanated danger. She was not someone to easily dismiss.

"Is there another doctor, or healer to tend these boys?" John demanded.

An older woman cradling the smaller boy, Jeema, answered, "No, our two healers were with the warriors at Saylon Dorsett." Tears streamed down her face.

"Well, I'm a doctor…a healer. My name is John Ernshaw and I've tended wounds like these before. If you do not want them to die, then move out of my way and **let me heal!**" he yelled at the blond. John's own military training rippled under the surface and he felt his patience evaporating.

"Please, Lyrista" the older woman begged.

For a moment the confrontation continued. Their eyes locked in combat and those nearest John stepped back. Lyrista's hand flew to the dagger in her belt, but she did not pull it. A collective sigh of relief came from the crowd when she moved aside, but she kept her eyes riveted on the tall stranger while he assessed the condition of both young men. Multiple stab wounds in soft tissue, lacerations cutting to the bone, patches of raw muscle, and massive blood loss were immediately discernable. Jeema had lost so much blood his skin was translucent white. He was by far in the more critical condition. "How he made it here and through that ridiculous report was an absolute miracle." John muttered to himself. This boy should be dead...would be if he didn't hurry. "I need a clean place to work. Did your healer have an office or place of labor?"

"Not in the hoffle," Lyrista said. "The closest healer's house is at the Academy."

"You can use my shop," a brawny man, about John's own age stepped from the crowd. With his mass of dark wavy hair and matching mustache, John thought he held an uncanny resemblance to Sophia's husband, Jacob Bartlowski. Not a tall man, but a commanding presence none-the-less, this man's jet black eyes held warmth and compassion. "It's over there," the man indicated a dark blue and purple granite-like building bordering the square. "I keep it dirtless and have some supplies you may be able to use. I'm an animal preptor."

"That'll be fine." An animal preptor? Puzzled, John followed several men who had gathered the boys up. The solemn group transported them to the offered building. John hoped the supplies referred to were sufficient for the surgeries that lay ahead. It was going to be a long night, and he was not optimistic about the outcome.

"I'm not sensitive and can assist you, if you desire. My name is Alberod," the animal preptor offered.

"That would be appreciated, Alberod." They entered the shop.

"To the back workroom," Alberod ordered, leading the way. One look inside the store and John knew what an animal preptor was. Alberod was a taxidermist. The boys were placed on two spotless worktables, then John and Alberod were left alone to do their work.

CHAPTER 8

Anton

Sunrays streamed through a small, four-pane window above Jessica's head. Blinking against the bright light, she heaved herself to a sitting position. A small, overstuffed mattress stretched beneath her. Nothing else furnished the tiny room. "Varnack," she called.

"She's awake," someone yelled from beyond the closed door. It flew open and Varnack bounced in, followed by High Older Tarin and an assortment of men, women, and children.

Varnack licked her face. "Worried."

"What happened? The last thing I remember was Karree's husband. He was dead and I was….trying…"

"Do I look dead to you?" A man's voice demanded from the hallway. The crowd parted and Karree's mate came through to stand before his benefactress, a broad smile on his face.

Shocked, Jessica sputtered, "How?"

"The Salupathic Gift." Karree stepped next to her man. "You have it, My Lady."

"No way! That's impossible. I…I couldn't have…"

Varnack nudged her hand, gaining her attention. He shook his head. "Later."

She swallowed hard, staring back at the healed man in disbelief. "I didn't catch your name."

"Brayon, My Lady. I hope to one day repay this gift of life you have given me."

"I'm still not sure what I did, but you're welcome. How long have I been unconscious?"

"Two full days," Tarin said.

"No wonder I'm so hungry." There was a ripple of laughter.

"Everyone out," Tarin ordered. "She has awakened, so there's a feast to prepare."

When the room emptied, Varnack lowered his head to Jessica's hand. "Scratch."

* * *

Varnack and Jessica were on their way the next morning. A hundred questions bounced around Jessica's head. Karree had answered one before they left Vorgen Hoffle. "The Expanse of Gonta, you asked what it was." She reminded Jessica. "It's a source of profound sorcery. It is seldom, if ever tapped, and few have found the keys to unlocking its power and mysteries." This single answer spawned more curiosity. Would Varnack expound? She doubted it.

The morning journey proceeded in silence. Jessica took the quiet time to reflect on the past few days. She felt certain Varnack would be grateful for the absence of her many queries. The innocent faces of the Vorgen Hoffle people were burned into her mind. Bareth's valor, Tarin's leadership, Karree's courage and Chana's parting kindness of food for the journey all served to kindle a love for the people of Esparia and loathing for the man responsible for their pain.

During the previous night's feast Jessica witnessed firsthand the fruits of the nursing labors that she, Karree and the two other women had performed, for all but three of the once injured men were in attendance. She was astounded at how fast the wounded had healed. It seemed supernatural. Most smaller cuts had vanished with not even a scar remaining. Again, more unanswered questions.

After a few hours of traveling, Jessica's thoughts turned to home and family. She wondered how her father was handling her absence. Was Thomas liking Italy? How did Rachel Bartlowski, her dearest friend, feel about her disappearance? She heaved a great sigh. She would go crazy if she worried about all this now. She would worry about it later.

"All right Varnack, your down time is over. I've got some more questions for you and don't put me off. Oh, by the way, if there's water anywhere close by, I'd love to clean up. There's still grease under my fingernails and my hair smells like smoke. I didn't take any personal time at Vorgen Hoffle this morning."

Varnack abruptly changed direction.

"Graesion is, or was, my grandfather. Right?"

"Yes."

"The old woman back at Vorgen Hoffle mentioned a Lady Gayleena was his wife."

"Yes." Varnack picked up the pace, forcing Jessica to run.

"You always do this when you don't want to answer any more questions."

Jessica mulled over the few facts she possessed. Grandfather...**her** grandfather. He must be Grandma Gaylee's husband. Grandma never talked about him, only that he died.

Grandma Gaylee was from Edia? The thought was incredible. That meant Grandma was an extra-terrestrial…and that meant mom was too! So that made her… "OH, MY GOSH!" She almost tripped over a twig when the impact of her heritage hit her. Did Dad know?

From what pieces of information she remembered, she tried to piece together her genealogy. "Varnack, who are Larone and Anton?"

"Old uncles."

Old uncles? Then they were Grandma's uncles. Graesion was her husband and Haesom her son. For some reason Grandma and Mom were sent away. Larone called Daenon his nephew and that could only mean Segal, Larone and Anton were brothers. Poor grandma. Her husband was dead, her daughter was dead, and her son was dead. Only two uncles and she remained. Segal and Daenon, father and son, caused all of this pain. At that moment, the full realization of who and what she was, fell on her. She was a Saylon, heir to the throne, so to speak. *She* was the remaining Protector.

She now understood what the dreams had meant. Remembering Haesom's final moments shattered the hold she held over her emotions. Grief welled up, spilling out through unchecked tears. She cried for herself. She cried for her mother. Water flowed for her father, her grandmother, and a boy, Thomas Banks, all light years away on a planet she would probably never see again. She wept for her mother's brother whom she would never meet and his wife whom she would never touch, and finally for her cousins, Big Red and Little Red, murdered in their youth. She could hardly see Varnack or the ground directly in front of her through the watershed of tears. When her companion came to an abrupt halt, she barely avoided colliding with him.

Wiping the salty moisture from her eyes, she tried to blink away the melancholy that demoralized her. A small, clear blue lake filled her field of vision. For much of the shoreline, the forest grew down to kiss the water's edge, but Varnack and Jessica stood on a small, pebbled beach outside of the leafy woodland canopy. The sun beat down, its heat piercing through Jessica's despair. "Varnack, what a wonderful surprise!" She dropped the sacks tied around her middle and plunged into the cool water.

Her apprehension washed away with all of the dirt. Varnack sat on the shore, his head resting on his front paws, while she happily washed herself clean. She scrubbed her hair with her nails and tried rubbing her clothes with the fine sand.

After several minutes of floating on her back, Jessica beckoned to Varnack with a wave of her arm. "Come in. You've got to be hot and tired. The water's wonderful."

It did not take more prodding. The large animal stood, stretched, then splashed in after her. A small tidal wave shot out in response to his massive body pushing through the surf, its force lifting Jessica off her feet. She dove under it and came up laughing. They romped and played for several minutes. Just when her uncertainties had melted away, a sudden surge of nausea hit. The feeling came with such intensity she barely stopped herself from throwing up. Where did that come from? As if in answer to her question, an arrow whizzed by her ear.

Instantly Varnack tensed. Three more arrows zipped into the water around them. "Swim," he commanded, then seized her shirt in his teeth and pulled her further out into the lake. The air and water were filled with the lethal projectiles. They swam for their lives.

Crossing the lake, after jogging through the forest for most of the morning, strained Jessica's muscles to the breaking point. She urged herself forward, concentrating on pulling her body through the placid water. She put her mind in a race situation. She could...she would swim this lake. Though not a champion swimmer, she matched Varnack's speed and in time passed him. With great relief, she finally touched bottom on the opposite shore. She stood in shoulder-deep water, taking in huge gasps of air, her chest heaving up and down with the effort.

"Varnack?" She spun around. With a hundred yards still to go, his eyes and nose barely showed above the waterline.

"Varnack!" She dove back in. Summoning everything she had left, she reached him just when his head slipped under the water. Throwing an arm around his neck, she heaved him up and towed him to a treeless section of the shoreline. In the shallow water, she crumbled beside him.

She fought to catch her breath. When enough strength returned, she sat up and ran her hand down his head and back. There were no outstanding wounds. His side too appeared all right, but from underneath him, blood oozed onto the pebbles.

"Oh, no!" She rolled him over and hissed an "Oh-my-gosh!" between clenched teeth. The flesh of his back right thigh lay ripped open, exposing many inches of crème colored bone. No blood gushed from the laceration, but steadily dripped into it from all sides, then trickled down his wet fur. "How did you ever swim that lake with this? You've lost so much blood, you're hardly bleeding anymore."

She looked to the forest for anything that could help. A small, purple fern growing under a scrawny tree about ten feet away caught her attention. Somehow, instinctively, she knew it held healing properties. Forcing her muscles into action, she stumbled over to the plant. Pulling it up, root and all, she carefully carried it back to where Varnack lay. The short stem felt mushy. With a thumb nail, she punctured it. Thin white sap trickled out. By gently squeezing the tender stalk she was able to control the liquid's flow and drizzle it throughout the dreadful gash. The plant's feathery fronds were then placed over the ripped flesh. Using the sleeves ripped from her shirt as bandages, she bound the leg together.

"We really need to find cover, Varnack. We're too open here. Whoever shot at us will be coming around for a second chance. Can you walk?"

Varnack rose on three of his feet. He managed to hobble several yards, to the first line of trees, then collapsed. "Run."

"That's not an option, Varnack. I won't leave you."

He closed his eyes. He passed out.

Deep within the forest, a twig snapped, then several branches cracked. Something or someone was fast approaching and within seconds footsteps pounded toward them. Jessica placed herself between Varnack and the unseen threat. Crouching, she braced herself for an attack.

From out of the dense woods, a massive, bearded man thundered toward the tiny beach. He pushed past Jessica with little effort and before she could cry out or stop him, scooped Varnack into his arms. "Come!" he ordered as he ran back into the forest. Jessica did not hesitate, but ran after him, not because he commanded it, but because she worried about Varnack.

The massive man carrying Varnack moved with surprising speed and agility. Keeping pace with him required focus and stamina, which Jessica pulled from her years of cross-country training. The swim across the lake had extracted much of her strength, and with little respite to replenish it, she now called upon the raw instincts deep within to keep her legs advancing. Run, run. The thought forced her to throw one foot in front of another. The relentless pursuit by those who wished to destroy them drove her beyond usual thresholds. Her lungs burned with every stride and soon she fell behind the burly rescuer.

Uphill they ran, through the compact trees and twisting shrubbery. At length, they reached a stream where this seemingly tireless man splashed upstream at the water's edge. She stumbled after him, and within minutes, heard the faint thunder of rushing waters. The bubbling roar increased with every step until the pounding liquid matched the pulsing blood in her ears. After rounding a sizeable protrusion of jagged rocks, she beheld a waterfall cascading a hundred feet into a clear blue pool.

Holding Varnack's limp body above the water, the man waded into the pool up to his chest. He walked directly toward the waterfall, then disappeared into it. Jessica, panting for all she was worth, hesitated for only a moment. She followed the same course, but with the water much deeper for her, she fought to gain footing and the force of the falls pushed her under. She came up in the middle of the pond, sputtering and gasping for air. Struggling to where she could touch bottom, she realized her stamina was all but gone. The famous 'wall' that many athletes hit, loomed only inches away. She steeled herself for a second attempt at plowing her way past the dense sheets of falling water. In she plunged. Just when she felt her feet slip once again and the shadows of the misty deep yawn wide to embrace her, someone seized her arm and pulled her to safety.

Jessica found herself standing next to the hulking man she fleetingly thought could have been a center for any pro-basketball team. Well over seven feet tall and powerfully built, his sharp, sapphire blue eyes glowed in a weathered face half-obscured by a bushy, salt and paprika beard. His shoulder-length, unruly hair was auburn in color, with slight graying at the temples. His costume reminded her of a cross between an old Tennessee frontiersman and a knight of the round-table, complete with moccasins and chain mail vest.

"Can ya stand?" he asked, his loud voice echoing in the small cave.

She locked her knees, then nodded.

Letting go of her arm, he stepped toward the backside of the waterfall. "Wait for me," he ordered, then disappeared through the cascading wall.

She knew that voice.

Her energy gone, she sank to the stone floor. It was a long time before Jessica could move. Varnack? He lay several feet further in, his back to her. She crawled beside him and inspected the makeshift bandage on his thigh. No blood stained it. Well, that was either good, or bad. She was unsure which. Not knowing what to do, she left the leg alone, hoping for the best. Gently she stroked Varnack's head. His eyes were closed, his breathing shallow.

"Please don't die, Varnack," she whispered.

Light filtered into the cave through the watery curtain. Jessica was surprised at the soothing effect of the falling droplets. Scanning her surroundings as far as the light would allow she found the high-ceilinged cave completely empty. Carved from solid stone, it scooped back into the cliff. Fifteen feet at the widest point and about twenty feet wide, the expanse felt damp and cool, but it was free of dirt, bugs and spider webbing. There was a triangular opening off to one side near the back.

"Incredible." She slid closer to Varnack, placed her arm around his neck and held him close. Both of them were soaking wet, but she hoped their combined body heat would help him warm up. The exhausting day finally crept to a close.

A crackling fire and the smell of cooking meat awakened Jessica. A warm, woolen-like blanket covered both her and Varnack. Sliding her arm off the animal's neck, she rolled out from under the grayish blanket, then tenderly tucked it in around his back.

"Was wonderin' when you'd wake up," a deep, pleasant voice came from behind. She let out a yelp and spun around. A smokeless fire with a spit of roasting fowl positioned over it was being tended by the large man. The flames gave out the only light in the cave, as the waterfall was now a curtain of black, shielding them from the outside world.

"Anton?"

The man's bushy eyebrows shot up.

"I don't think you'd believe me." She held up her hand to stop the questions from being asked. She walked closer to the fire, then sat with her legs crossed under her.

"Ya look a lot like yer Grandma." Anton pulled the roasting bird off the skewer. He ripped a piece of meat and handed it to her. She did not realize how hungry she was until she took the first bite. The smoky flavor elicited little sighs of satisfaction and she thought the bird tasted remarkably like turkey.

"My Dad says I look like my mom. You came just in the nick of time." She glanced over at Varnack. His breathing was now deep and regular.

"We knew ya were in danger, so I came fast as I could." His voice seemed too big for the size of the cave, yet it harmonized well with the rumble of the free-falling water.

"We?" she asked.

"Me 'n my brother."

"Larone?"

This time his eyebrows really shot up.

"So who shot at us?" Jessica asked. "I thought my coming was supposed to be a secret?"

"It was! Some doogeroot betrayed us. We don't know who yet, but we're workin' on it."

"Why shoot at me though. They're looking for a woman, right? Like my mom."

He shrugged his shoulders. "Varnack's a dead giveaway that yer someone important. Maybe they've smartened up and figure yer a girl. Elitet are after ya."

Jessica shivered. "Who are they?"

"Daenon's Elite Shield, glorified name for a killer squad."

"Do they dress all in black, except one with a red belt?"

"Yeah." Now Anton sounded as shocked as he looked. "Ya know an awful lot for just gettin' here."

"Actually, I've been here a couple of days." Jessica related all that happened after being spit out by the black spiral, her walk with Varnack and the battle at Vorgen Hoffle, everything except the healing episode. That still mystified her, scared her, and without knowing her new found uncle better, she did not feel comfortable in sharing this spiritual experience with him.

"So the Elitet are trying to kill me."

"No, if they wanted ya dead, ya would be. They don't miss. Most likely, they were tryin' to kill Varnack. They want ya alive, capture ya. Yer swimmin' behind him stopped 'em from finishin' him off. I saw the whole thing up the mountain. Couldn't get down fast enough to warn ya though. Now how's about ya tell me just how ya know who I am."

Jessica reached for the cup of water Anton offered her, then told him about her mist dreams, all of them.

While he listened he never took his eyes from her face and when she finished he said so softly, so angrily, it made the hairs stand up on the back of her neck, "So there is a traitor at Ramadine".

"I don't know who he is, but there's definitely a spy. Varnack told me Graesion was my grandfather." Anton shot a quick look at Varnack. "It doesn't take a mastermind to figure out the genealogy after that. You're my blood relative. I have none on Earth, besides Dad and Grandma."

Jessica finished eating. She searched for something to wipe her greasy hands on and finally settled for the front of her pants. "Varnack also told me this is Esparia, but he doesn't elaborate much, so my information is still pretty sketchy. Could you tell me about this place, this world, Uncle Anton?"

At the word 'uncle', Anton flinched. He stared at Jessica, his face placid, but his eyes filled with wonder. His muscles tensed, his mouth opened as if to speak, then closed again, the words unuttered. He averted his eyes and for many minutes stared into the fire. She sensed an inner struggle raging inside him.

What did she say to cause this reaction?

At last he looked up from the fire, cleared his throat, and spoke about Edia. He explained its location compared to Earth, using Edian astrophysical terms she had never heard before. It soon became apparent to her his everyday speech belied his true genius. He told her of Esparia, its history, the different peoples and the lay of the land. He explained about the Protectors, how they ruled in peace for centuries. Finally, he told her about her family, about Graesion and his son Haesom, then Segal and his son, Daenon.

"Last of all are me, 'n my brother, Larone. He's a great healer while I like playin' with magical sciences. I don't like people much though," he shrugged. "Lived most my life wanderin' all over Esparia. I don't think there's one place I haven't seen, except the Deserts of Demar. No one in his right mind goes there," here he paused, then gave a little snort, "maybe that's why Segal managed so well there. He was always a little touched. Ya probably noticed I don't talk too good. I haven't had much use for speakin', pretty much a loner, so I'm not real used to it 'n I don't much care. Fact is, this is more talkin' I've done tonight than in the last five years pulled together."

Varnack moaned, then gave a little cough. Jessica and Anton both went to him.

"How ya doin' there Varnack?" Anton gently picked him up and moved him closer to the fire.

Jessica translated his words. "He says he's hungry, sore and tired."

"Ya really can understand him then?" Anton held Varnack's head while Jessica gave the thirsty animal a drink of water from the cup.

"Yeah, I can." She stroked his head and scratched behind his ears. Pulling meat off of the bird bones, she fed him small pieces. He ate everything she gave him, took another long drink of water, and then closed his eyes.

Anton sat back, watching Jessica care for Varnack. "We'll need to leave here before full mornin' light. It won't take the Elitet long to find this place. Ya'd better catch some more sleep."

"First, tell me why I'm here."

Anton hesitated. Jessica could see him choosing his words carefully. "Well, it's like this. Yer cousin Daenon killed yer uncle 'n his family."

"Right...saw it happen."

"Yer the last o' the blood-line Protectors. It's a long story, but to make it little, yer the one decreed to bring Daenon down."

Jessica stared at her uncle. "That's a little bold, isn't it?"

He shrugged. "Look deep inside. Ya'll see I'm telling the truth."

After the Salupathic healing experience, Jessica did not want to feel 'deep inside'. Unsure of what she would find there, she chose to ask another question. "Can I ever go home?"

Anton nodded. "Yep, ya can." Jessica brightened as hope took hold. "Not right now though, it takes blue persite to break into the Expanse of Gonta 'n I don't have any with me. What little's left is at Ramadine, just enough for one more journey." A look of compassion crossed his face. "Jessi, if, after ya've heard all the facts, 'n met Larone, 'n thought about everythin', 'n ya don't want to stay, I promise, no matter what, I'll send ya home."

Tears stung her eyes as the possibility sunk in. "Varnack mentioned Ramadine. So that's where we're going?"

"Eventually, but I'm pretty sure the Elitet know that, so we'll have to go in a real round about way. Ya'll get to see lots o' country. Now, go to sleep."

"You need rest too. I've been asleep for hours and I'm not tired anymore. You sleep while I keep watch."

He opened his mouth in protest, but she raised her hand to stop him. "I'll wake you if I hear anything odd. I'll also wake you if I get tired." He tried to protest once more, but this time she cut him off. "I mean it, I am not tired." She retrieved the blanket once used for covering Varnack, whose fur now felt dry. After shaking it out, she laid it over Anton. "You sleep."

He lay down with a scowl on his face, but within minutes the scowl faded and his snoring competed with the waterfall for sound supremacy. Jessica smiled. The snoring was actually quieter than his speaking.

She amused herself the rest of the night by playing in the fire with a long stick. She kept one ear open for approaching footsteps and one eye on the waterfall to catch the first glimpse of dawn.

CHAPTER 9

Lady Saylon

Gaylee remained dignified and silent throughout the commotion in Ider Hoffle central square. A few people stared at her, curiosity on their faces, but once the wounded soldiers were carried to Alberod's building, the crowd dispersed. A heavy mood hung in the air. Most of the hofflers left in tears. The sun had set during the young soldier's report, so the two silver moons now dominated the heavens above.

Alone, both physically and emotionally, Gaylee turned her face to the sky. A profound sadness filled her soul. The young soldier's report brought her deepest thoughts to the surface. Dearest Haesom...my Haesom. Rather she would have died than he. Oh, how she wished to see his face one more time, but he was gone from her. *Rest in peace, my son, your sacrifice will not be in vain.* She wandered over to the building she had seen John, the wounded, and several others, probably family members, enter and sat on a wooden bench in front of its dimly lit show window. If anyone could save the two boys, John could.

A lamplighter stepped onto the square, a single bright torch in his hand. He moved from post to post, bringing soft illumination to the friendless plaza. The click of a boot heel on stone cut through the hushed night. A lone figure, bare headed, but clad in a long, dark cape crossed the deserted square. A slight limp in his gait caused an uneven clip-clop in his footsteps. He did not hurry, but came steadily forward, his course set for Gaylee. When the man drew closer, she noticed a long, thin scar above his left eye. His face stirred an old, vague memory.

Directly in front of her, he fell to one knee. Smartly snapping his left fist to his forehead and then left breast, he saluted her. "My Lady, you have come home," he spoke softly and bowed his head.

Gaylee caught her breath. He recognized her. Taking good appraisal of the man, she suddenly knew him. "Ophir, my friend, it has been too long." Leaning forward, she touched his shoulder.

Before they could speak further, the shop door opened and Lyrista, wide eyed, astonishment clearly showing on her face, stood in the open frame. She stared at Gaylee. "Ophir?" she questioned, not taking her eyes from the stately woman's face. "Why does the Commander of the Esparian

Security Academy give the Salute of Loyalty?"

Without a word, Gaylee stood, then walked past the suspicious woman and into the tidy shop. Ophir followed behind. The store abounded with animals, large and small, mounted on walls, logs, and in naturalistic settings. The displays were as lifelike as anything found in nature. This taxidermist does beautiful work, Gaylee thought.

Besides Ophir, Lyrista, and herself, eight other people crammed into the store. The room fell into silence. Untying her hood, she slipped it from her head revealing her short, bright red hair. A gasp of recognition came from the older hofflers.

"My friends, may I introduce Lady Gayleena Liedia of the House of Saylon, Protectoress of Esparia," Ophir announced. One by one, as the magnitude of this introduction sunk in, the persons in the room fell to one knee, saluting her. Two older men were first, with the two older women next.

"Ophir, introduce me to these kind people." With her former general at her side, Gaylee went to the nearest man. She motioned for him to rise. "This is Jannir, the father of the young soldier, Jeema."

"Your brave son is in the hands of the finest healer I know."

The woman who cradled Jeema in her arms knelt beside Jannir. Reaching down, Gaylee took her by the hand and helped her stand. Ophir introduced her as Kayta, Jeema's mother. In a flash, a picture of an aged Jeema, surrounded by children and grandchildren came into Gaylee's mind.

Gaylee barely whispered. "I don't have visions very often." Looking deep into the smaller woman's eyes, she continued. "Your son is going to live and he will be a great leader in your hoffle. I've seen him, an old man, highly respected, with many loved ones around him."

Kayta gasped at the prophecy and fell again to one knee. "Thank you, My Lady...Thank you."

The next kneeling man was the High Older of the hoffle and beside him his wife, Geilin. Gaylee smiled at them both. "I commend you for your leadership and for showing compassion by being here with the families of these wounded soldiers."

Two young men in uniforms of navy blue trimmed with silver braid at the neck, shoulder, cuffs and waist were next. They knelt with heads bowed, their shoulders slumped. Neither would look at Gaylee when she stepped before them. She looked to Ophir for explanations.

"Garrett and Mica, My Lady. They were originally part of our three hundred soldiers stationed at Saylon Dorsett. They were both excused from duty a week ago to be with their wives, who each have since given birth to sons. They feel shame, for they missed the great battle."

"We should have been with our men." Garrett's voice choked with regret.

"Do you honestly think two more warriors would have changed the final outcome?" Gaylee queried, but before the soldier could answer she counseled, "Do not be so quick to wish for death, my young friends. Your courage and skills will yet be needed. There will be battles enough for you to fight, battles without treachery, battles which can be won."

Two young women knelt beyond the soldiers. "Jeema is our childhood friend," the first explained. Both girls wore the tan britches and white tunics of Ider Warriors in training. Each female trainee had her hair tightly braided and knotted on top of her head. The girls looked remarkably similar, even down to a black handled blade sheathed at the waist.

"Your friend is receiving the best possible care," Gaylee addressed them.

Last of all, Gaylee came to Lyrista. For the first time during his introductions, Ophir addressed Gaylee formally. "My Lady Gayleena, I have the distinct pleasure of introducing you to Lyrista, daughter of General Gammet, your friend from long ago and fallen commander of Protector Haesom's forces at Saylon Dorsett."

Gaylee took Lyrista by both her arms and lifted her up. She gazed into the hazel brown eyes of General Gammet's youngest daughter and liked what she saw. "I knew your father," Gaylee spoke kindly. "He was a fine man, an admirable soldier. I considered him a friend and am deeply saddened by his loss. I will miss him. Please accept my sincere sympathy."

Lyrista squared her shoulders. "Thank you, madam." She choked back tears. "I'm also the aunt of the boy who gave the report. His name is Reese."

The shop door opening interrupted the interview. Several women carrying clear glass trays piled with food walked in. "The evening nourishment has arrived," Geilin, the High Older's wife, announced. The two female trainees cleared a main display table, then the three serving women squeezed goblets, two-pronged forks, and small platters, all made of blue Palium, on top of the wooden slab. Trays of black roasted meat, steamed vegetable pods, sliced red and yellow fruits, and unleavened white bread were placed in the center of the table. The serving women kept staring at Gaylee. Geilin gave them a few hurried words of explanation and gratitude, then ushered them out of the building.

Gaylee sat at the table's head, with Ophir to her right. The meal had scarcely begun when the door to the back of the shop creaked and young Reese shuffled out. Lyrista darted to his side. Clean and sporting fresh bandages, the young man leaned heavily on his aunt.

"Jeema has lost too much blood. The healer says he'll die unless it's replenished. He requires Jeema's mother or father to come and give some. This is not without danger. There's a chance the blood could kill him, but without it, he is dead for sure." Without hesitation, Jannir hurried through the door to the place of surgery.

Lyrista guided Reese to Jannir's freshly vacated chair. Geilin piled one of the thin blue platters with food. The meal proceeded with no one speaking, but all intently watching the pale soldier. He ate a large amount of the food placed before him. With warm food to give him nourishment, the young man's color had dramatically improved.

Gaylee also watched the young man from across the table. When he had finished his meal she spoke. "I know you're tired and you need rest, but tell me young soldier, how are you so certain you were betrayed?" From his first accusation, she felt disturbed. She did not disbelieve him, the opposite was true; treason was the single possible explanation for Haesom's total defeat. She desired more information about who this traitor could be.

Reese looked at Gaylee with obvious confusion in his tired eyes. "I'm sorry, my lady," he said. "But…"

"Reese," Lyrista said gently, "this is Lady Gayleena Saylon, High Protector Haesom's mother."

"His mother?" he said softly. Some of the new found color faded from his cheeks. He swallowed hard.

"My Grandfather, General Gammet, was warned of the attack. However, the informer reported that the Elitet were yet three days away. We began organizing our defenses, but had we known they would attack that night, we would have immediately evacuated the Protector and his family." His voice broke and he fought for control of his emotions. "Lady Saylon, Lord Haesom's wife, asked for a few hours to pack some things. General Gammet thought there was sufficient time and agreed."

He gazed at Gaylee, his eyes filled with pain at the memory. "We had no idea we were out of time. When the attack came, I led fifty others from our hoffle with the assignment to protect the High family. Our defenses were not all in place, but that should have made no difference. We should have been able to hold the attackers until reinforcements came. Gammet dispatched three men through a secret tunnel to go for help." Gaylee nodded. She remembered the tunnel he spoke of. "Somehow, the Elitet knew about the tunnel. Our runners were cut down before they were even out. The enemy flooded into the Dorsett through it. They targeted our weakest defenses first and before long we were overrun. Only a traitor in our midst could have given so much detail to the enemy about our defenses." He hung his head and continued, "I'm sorry, My Lady. I failed. I did not protect your family."

Lyrista, tears floating in her eyes, wrapped an arm around her nephew's shoulders.

"You would have been proud of your son and two grandsons," Reese whispered hoarsely. "They fought like true Ider Warriors. My last service to the family was to find their bodies and bury them beside Lord Graesion, then Jeema and I came directly here." His voice broke, his head hung low.

Gaylee stood, took his face into her hands, and raised it so she could see into his tear-filled eyes. "Reese, I know you would have died for them. You nearly did. I do **not** hold you responsible for what happened there." Lowering her hands, she asked, "Who falsely warned General Gammet of the coming attack?"

Her words seemed to bring calm to Reese. "I don't know, My Lady. He came in secret, meeting only with my grandfather and his close advisers. I was not one of that circle. Since everyone who would have known is now dead, we may never find out."

"Thank you, Reese."

"We'll leave now." Lyrista took the young man's arm. "Reese needs to rest. When you're ready, please come to my home, I have room for you there. Ophir will show you the way." Her request was more of an order, and Gaylee noticed not even Geilin raised objection, though she bit her lip and fidgeted with a large ring on her finger. Supporting Reese, Lyrista left the shop. Gaylee could see this was a very capable woman, used to being in command.

"Reese is more Lyrista's son than nephew," Ophir explained. He had left the table and wandered among the handsomely displayed animals during Reese's interview. But Gaylee knew her former general missed nothing of the conversation. "Her only sister died giving birth to him, and since the father is a soldier, not often here, Lyrista raised him. She's also one of our best trainers at the academy. You'll find few more skilled at close combat than Lyrista. I for one would not wish to fight her."

Gaylee took a chair, placed it by the large display window and sat down. "Ophir, I have been gone fifty years and for fifty years I've wondered what took place that terrible day so long ago, when you burst into that room and informed me of Graesion's death. Tell me what happened after I left."

Everyone in the room focused on Ophir. Gaylee knew only she could have asked such a question of him and she fully expected an answer. He walked to the table, took a chair of his own, and placed it beside Gaylee's. "When young Haesom decided to stay, and not travel with you through that...whatever it was, I pledged my loyalty to Healer Larone. Once you disappeared, I headed to the front hall to check on the battle, but Gammet met me in the main passageway with ten others. They were all that remained of our force. We raced back to your uncles and managed to escape through the tunnel Reese just spoke of. Once out of the Dorsett, we sheltered Haesom as best we could."

Ophir made a slight smile. "Graesion trained him well. That little boy could truly handle a sword. We cut our way through Segal's troops to freedom. I've never seen anyone fight like your Uncle Anton. Only eight survived, Gammet, your uncles, Haesom, three soldiers, who now lie dead at Saylon Dorsett, and myself. Through the years, Larone gave your son all the love any father could give a boy. Rest assured of that."

Gaylee wiped a tear from the corner of her eye. She had spent many worried nights wondering if her thirteen-year-old was thrown into a man's world without any parental love or support. Now she realized how unfounded those concerns were. Of course Larone would treat him as his own child. This was the kind of man Larone was.

The opening of the surgery door interrupted Ophir's tale. John walked out, followed by Alberod, the animal preptor. John was silent, his face showing no sign of emotion, but Alberod was all smiles. He addressed Jeema's mother. "Kayta, you can go in now. Jeema will be all right. Your husband's blood gave him back his life." The woman wasted no time in rushing through the open door.

The High Older offered the two healers chairs at the table and Geilin busied herself with serving them. From now on, Alberod would always be referred to as a healer.

"Please, continue," Gaylee urged Ophir.

"Segal was foolhardy. He marched into the heart of the country in his efforts to kill you and your family. It didn't take long for us to rally the people. We surrounded Segal. Victory came swiftly, but still he managed to slip away. For five years we gathered and trained anyone willing to fight for freedom. Hundreds of thousands rallied to Haesom. I personally finished his training and served as his bodyguard while Gammet organized our defenses. Like a man possessed, Gammet worked day and night, knowing Segal would return.

"When Haesom turned nineteen, Segal attacked again, with a force of five hundred thousand. He built his army through flattery, bribery, coercion, and alliances. Many of our people deserted over to his side, lured by hollow promises of power and wealth." He gave a mirthless laugh. "As if Segal would share any of it. The war lasted eighteen long, brutal months. The end came at Blue Mountain. With the enemy defeated, we stormed the fortress. We found Segal's body in the courtyard; he'd been stabbed to the heart. To this day, no one has any idea who did it. Maybe Daenon killed him. Who knows?" Ophir shrugged. "At least he was dead. Daenon and the seventh bars fled with most of the Demar desert warriors when they saw they were about to be captured."

"What of Naydeen, Segal's wife?" Gaylee asked.

Ophir shook his head. "We never found her, nor has she been seen since that time. I'm sorry."

Ophir's emotionless telling of the story finished and a sober mood fell over the occupants of the room. Gaylee went to John. She placed her hand on his shoulder. "This man is John Ernshaw." Unmistakable pride filled her voice. "He is a great healer and my son-in-law."

"Son-in…is your daughter here also?" Geilin asked.

Gaylee shook her head. "No, Shallenon died ten years ago. However, my granddaughter is here, somewhere in the Southern Greenwood. That is one of the reasons for my return. She precedes us by a day and we don't know where she is. We're on our way to Ramadine to find out what Healer Larone may know concerning her whereabouts."

Ophir jumped to his feet. "Your granddaughter! You should have said something. I'll waste no more time, My Lady." He headed for the door. "I'll search for her immediately."

"No Ophir, wait. I'm very concerned for her, but she's not alone. Larone sent a great warrior to protect her."

Ophir raised his eyebrows at this news.

"A warrior named Varnack." She said.

Ophir's mouth dropped open. Nearly everyone in the room gasped. "Varnack, you said?" Ophir asked.

"Yes," Gaylee looked from Ophir to the High Older, who had the same open-mouthed look on his face, and back again.

"We searched for signs of them." John spoke for the first time. "But it rained between our two arrivals, so all traces vanished. We came here hoping to arrange transportation to Ramadine, where Larone is. Gaylee thinks her uncle is our best hope for locating my daughter."

Eagerly, every person in the room offered some sort of aid. "I shall have my own carriage prepared to take you there," the High Older insisted. The two soldiers, Garrett and Mica, volunteered to accompany the carriage to ensure its safety. The young women offered to prepare food and drink and Ophir promised he would still search for Jessica.

"However," he added, "if Varnack is with her, then she is better protected than with ten of our warriors. Since it's night, Varnack will be well hidden and I would never find them. I must search by the light of day."

"Ophir, who is Varnack?" Gaylee asked.

"He's a Trigal Hound."

This time Gaylee gasped. "Healer Larone has a Trigal Hound for a companion?"

"Yes, a golden one."

"What's a Trigal Hound?" John asked.

Gaylee thought hard before answering his question. She chose her words carefully. "Visualize a dog the size of a small horse, but with different colored coats and eyes to match their coats of red, green, blue, orange, white, gold, et cetera. Now picture this animal, not as an animal, but with the intelligence of a human, minus our capacity for speech."

"I would very much like to meet this Varnack," John commented. "He must be quite a guard dog."

"No John, not a dog, but a warrior. A Trigal hound," Gaylee reiterated. She knew John well enough to realize he was just barely containing his sarcasm. To her relief he simply nodded.

"It's been a long day," John exhaled, then turned to the High Older. "Thank you for the offer of your carriage, we gratefully accept it. We'd like to leave in the morning, after I've checked on my patients."

"Come," Ophir opened the door to the shop. "I'll take you to Lyrista's house, it's not far."

Gaylee reached for her cloak. Once in the open square, John rubbed his face with both hands and asked, "Who's Lyrista?"

"Reese's aunt," Ophir answered.

"You know, the attractive blond woman who threatened you earlier," Gaylee prompted.

"Ooooh, yeah. Her."

Poor John, Gaylee chuckled to herself. It really has been a long day.

Lyrista's home was one of many two level, stone dwellings on the street. A small, neatly clipped yard edged with lush miniature ferns and robust coral flower bushes attested to the woman's gardening abilities. A three-foot high stonewall marked the property boundaries. Lyrista answered Ophir's knock and told him to take John upstairs to her father, Gammet's room.

"I've prepared this room for you, My Lady." Lyrista led Gaylee to a comfortably decorated chamber on the main floor.

"It's more than adequate," Gaylee said.

"Good night, Lady Gayleena."

After the day's long march and the emotional histories, Gaylee fell into a deep sleep moments after her head hit the feather pillow.

* * *

John woke to the smell of hot bread. He found shaving equipment on a table next to a small sink in the bedroom. When he turned a metal tap, he smiled at the running water. He remembered Gaylee's pride when she spoke of the pressurized plumbing. He cleaned up, then went looking for the source of the wonderful smells filling the house.

He found Lyrista in a tidy kitchen. Close to the doorway stood a square, wooden table, covered with a yellow cloth whose edges were embroidered in bright pink and green flowers. Four sturdy wooden chairs surrounded it. Four settings of glass plates and cups, Palium metal knives and two-pronged forks were neatly arranged on the cloth. A large metal pitcher of lavender juice he assumed to be dandleberry, along with a wooden bowl of hairy, green diamond-shaped fruit Gaylee had called palanto was placed in the center.

John lingered in the doorway for a moment, contemplating the slim, well-toned woman. Her straight, white blond hair was cut short and he remembered from the night before that there had been flecks of green in her hazel brown eyes. She moved with grace around the room. Dressed in gray pants and a light brown shirt, she would have looked like any ordinary woman pulling a pan of brown, round biscuits from a fire driven oven if it weren't for the deadly dagger attached to her leather belt. He cleared his throat to attract her attention.

"You're awake. Good morning," she said pleasantly.

"Good morning. It certainly smells good in here. Is there anything I can do to help?" He entered the cooking center.

"No. Just have a seat, everything's ready. Reese should be up soon and I think I heard Lady Saylon earlier."

"Reese? Is he here?"

"He's over there," she pointed with a wooden spatula to a long, cushioned bench, easily seen from the kitchen doorway. "He never made it to his bed, just collapsed in the front room and fell right to sleep. I thought it best not to move him."

The couch was in the center of the room, facing a large stone fireplace. John was so exhausted the night before he never noticed the boy resting there. Entering the living space, he noted how cozy and inviting Lyrista's house felt. The front area had a thin, light yellow and chocolate brown rug on the wooden floor, nearly covering it from wall to wall. Richly carved, red wooden tables flanked the couch while two large, wooden chairs, accented with deep green cushions, were placed, one beside each table. Three tall, wrought iron candleholders were positioned close to the furniture. Robust looking green and yellow grass plants completed the decor. Bright morning light streamed in through a large, yellow curtained picture window, located next to the front door.

Being careful not to wake him, John examined the boy. His color had dramatically improved from the night before and his temperature felt normal. No infection showed around the stitches and all but one wound had completely ceased to ooze. This was remarkable, if not impossible. John was thoroughly amazed. He had never seen anyone heal so rapidly.

Reese's dark, curly hair had dirt and dried blood matted into it. His uniform looked more like a pile of rags than soldier's attire. John shook his head. He hoped the wounds were just physical. He could only imagine the horrors this kid had seen.

Going back to the kitchen, he slumped into a chair at the table. If war was truly imminent, he pitied the poor guy who would have to run it. All war was terrible. He wouldn't want to be the one sending some young kid to his death. Afghanistan was all the battle he ever wanted to see. When he reached for the Palium pitcher, Gaylee, looking thoroughly refreshed, walked into the room. Her home world certainly agreed with her. "Sleep well?" he asked.

"Very," she answered. "It smells wonderful, Lyrista. Thank you for your hospitality."

Lyrista. John pondered the name. She dropped some fried eggs onto his plate. Yes, he liked that name very much. He ate quickly, anxious to go to Alberod's shop and check on Jeema. Of the two patients, Jeema was, by far, in the worse shape and John had left orders he not be moved. When finished eating, he excused himself from the ladies and walked out the front door into the crisp, morning air.

Ophir sat on the short stonewall surrounding Lyrista's building. His back was to the house. John wondered if the man had been there all night. "Ophir." The warrior turned at his name and smiled at John. It was a warm smile that lit up his eyes. "Could you direct me to Alberod's? I want to check on Jeema."

"His parents transferred him to their home this morning. It's not far from here; I'll show you the way."

"What? This morning?" John frowned. "They felt he was strong enough to be moved?"

"His mother was anxious to have him home."

Annoyed at the blatant disregard this mother held for his orders, John set off at a brisk pace. The two men did not go far before John became keenly aware that nearly every person they passed, man or woman, bowed to them.

"You must be quite an important man to receive such respect," he commented.

Ophir stared at John in genuine surprise. "It's not me to whom they bow, but to you! Word has spread. The entire Hoffle knows what you did for Jeema and Reese. The High Older has been busy throughout the night making certain everything is ready for your journey to Ramadine. He has turned away hundreds of offers to help. Here we are," he motioned to a moderately sized, wood and brick house, "this is Jeema's home."

After a quick exam, John commended Jeema into his mother's care. As with Reese, the young man was making a remarkable recovery. Leaving the house, he wondered that if he were wounded, would he heal as fast in this environment?

When John entered Jeema's home, he left Ophir on the street, empty handed. The aging warrior now held the bridles of two beautiful, white horses in his hand.

"Where did you find those?"

"I told you, hundreds offered to help. The Second Older's servant insisted I take these and present them to you. He's not a man one says no to."

"The Second Older?"

Ophir shook his head. "The servant."

John took one of the leather reins. He stroked the animal's neck. A knot formed in his stomach when he realized the creature was for him. Facing enemy fire or jumping from an airplane in full combat gear never fazed John, but the thought of riding on a horse filled him with dread. John did not like horses, or rather, he felt horses did not like him. Though he had ridden only twice before, disaster struck in the form of blood and bruises during both of those equestrian experiences. Riding in a carriage to Ramadine was a form of travel John could live with, but the prospect of riding a horse the entire way was not a pleasant one.

"What's his name?"

"Fireguard. Come, I'll show you Ider Hoffle" Ophir swung easily up on to the second animal. Swallowing hard, John mounted his large stallion. He tried to relax while Ophir took him on the brief tour.

"Ophir, while Gaylee and I traveled here, we nearly collided with a group of black clothed riders, five in all. They seemed pretty dangerous, so we stayed clear of them. Are there bandits around here?"

Ophir scrunched his eyebrows together. "Five black riders? Did one have a red sash around his middle?"

"Yes. He seemed to be the leader. Who were they?"

"Daenon's private soldiers, the Elite Shield, or Elitet. They usually team in groups of five, and are led by a Shield, the one distinguished by the red sash. Shields are the highest ranking Elitet. How far from Ider Hoffle were you?"

"Due south, about four hours walking distance."

Ophir called to a soldier on the street. "Go to the Academy and inform Second Commander Garn there may be Elitet in Southern Greenwood. I'm imposing full alert status and want an immediate sweep of the province. Red currier Larone at Ramadine and send messages to all other posts."

Turning to John he explained, "Elitet are deadly, suicide units. Their presence here would be as spies or assassins or both. The sooner you are at Ramadine, the safer you'll be."

Back at Lyrista's, John hurried into the house. He felt like a complete idiot. It was an emotion he hadn't felt in years. He had tried to conceal his lack of horsemanship from Ophir, but was fairly certain he failed miserably. He really was no horseman, but vowed to master this riding business, even if it was the last thing he ever did.

To his pleasant surprise, Reese was awake, dressed in a fresh uniform and eating breakfast in the kitchen. Gaylee sat beside him at the table, a large map spread out in front of her.

"How are you feeling, Reese?" John asked from the living room.

"Much better, thank you." Reese swallowed down a half-chewed piece of bread. "I owe you my life."

"Well, don't lose it now by choking on your breakfast," John laughed. He glanced into the kitchen. "Where's Lyrista?"

"Changing," Gaylee answered.

"I'm going to grab the duffle bag. It's about time to go." John ran upstairs and retrieved his bag from the bedroom. Back in the living room, he checked the contents and repacked. Ophir entered the home.

"John, can you give me some idea of where your daughter arrived?" Ophir asked. "That's where I would like to begin my search. I apologize for not having left yet, but I have my reasons for postponing my departure."

John nodded. "Thanks for going after her. I'd come with you, but I'd only slow you down, and the sooner Jess is found, the better. I trust you Ophir, I trust you with my only child."

Ophir's features softened, just a little.

"I don't know the location, but it's the same place where we arrived, so Gaylee could probably tell you." John stuffed the last few things into the bag. "You mention our 'arrival' as if you understand how we came here. Do you know about the portal?"

"I was present when Lady Gayleena and her daughter disappeared into the black tornado fifty years ago. I assume you came back here using the same mode of transportation."

"'Mode of transportation', that's a good way of describing it," John smiled.

Gaylee walked in from the kitchen. Ophir half-bowed to her.

"Lyrista gave me a map and I've been going over it. I've marked the place where you should begin searching for Jessica." Reese brought the map into the main room and placed it on one of the small side tables. "The location is due south from here, about thirty-three filons." Gaylee pointed to a location on the parchment.

Ophir nodded his head. "I know the meadow." He placed his hand on John's shoulder. "Don't worry, my friend. I promise I'll find your Jessica."

"Take the horse," John offered.

"Thank you, but no. My steed is not as young, but he is well trained and I prefer what I can trust."

"Of course."

"May I go with you, Master Ophir?" Gaylee, John and Ophir stared at a weak, but determined Reese. "Please, I must go," he insisted. "I'm still honor bound to protect the family Saylon, and this girl, Lady Jessica, is a

Saylon. I'm a good tracker and am getting stronger by the hour. Please, Master Ophir, accept my service." His face was set.

Ophir eyed the young soldier. "Do you think you can ride?"

"Yes sir."

Turning to John, Ophir said, "I'll take the second horse after all, for Reese."

Nodding in agreement, John now understood the reason Ophir postponed his leaving. Reese would want to come. Would need to come. Ophir could help him work through his experiences at Saylon Dorsett.

John's admiration of the older soldier was increasing with each new circumstance. "The animal is yours. I don't think Lady Gaylee will be too upset if she isn't able to ride a horse to Ramadine." Briefly explaining about the horses being gifts, John insisted on Reese taking one of the strong, beautiful animals.

Ophir left to fetch his preferred mount and his already packed supplies. He promised he would inform the First Older that Lady Gayleena and Healer John were ready to leave. When he returned ten minutes later, Reese stood ready, and to everyone's surprise, so did Lyrista.

Dressed in a snappy, deep blue and silver uniform, fully armed with sword, knife and bow, she announced, "I'm going to Ramadine with you. Reese mentioned last night that my brother is there. Together, we'll find the one who betrayed our father and our friends." No one argued with her.

The excited buzzing of voices filtered into Lyrista's house. Gaylee went to the front window. "What's all this?" she asked. John joined her. Hundreds of people were gathered outside the home.

"The news of your return has spread," Ophir explained, "and many want to see for themselves your son, the great healer."

"Son?" John was caught off-guard.

"In our law, once you married Shallenon, you became my son." Gaylee explained.

"It's an honor, Gaylee, but I don't need a law to tell me that."

Lyrista opened her front door. She nodded to Gaylee, "After you."

"All right." There was an acquiescent tone in Gaylee's voice. She straightened her back and raised her head high. Turning to John she counseled, "Just take a deep breath and you'll be fine." She walked out the door with Lyrista following.

John motioned for Ophir and Reese to go before him. He stopped in the doorway and stared at the respectful onlookers. A hush fell over those assembled when the High Older approached Gaylee. Six men, each dressed in turquoise robes of office, accompanied him.

"Protector Gayleena and," the High Older was forced to peer around Lyrista, Ophir, and Reese to address John, still standing at the front door, "Great Healer. The people of Ider Hoffle are here to pledge our loyalty and our swords to you. We have been forever bound to the Esparian Protectors, but this day we life-honor ourselves to the House of Saylon." Every hoffler, including Ophir, Reese and Lyrista, fell to one knee and gave the Salute of Loyalty. What the Olders pledged, each man, woman, and child were now obligated to honor.

Gaylee stepped forward. "I thank you. We, in return, life-honor our commitment to free this land from the specter of tyranny and oppression. As long as a Saylon heir holds the office of Protector, the Rights of Liberty will be upheld."

The crowd rose and gave a great cheer. Gaylee held her hand for silence. "You must now prepare for war. I need Ider warriors to travel from hoffle to hoffle and dine to dine, up and down the border. Warn the people to be on their guard."

The High Older bowed in acknowledgment.

Sensing the brief ceremony over, John left the protective doorway and marched to the waiting carriage. He opened the door for Gaylee and helped her in. After stowing his bag at her feet, he mounted his new horse, Fireguard. Garrett and Mica, the two young soldiers from the night before, were in full dress uniform and armed to the teeth. The soldier driving the carriage was also heavily armed. Lyrista, astride a magnificent roan mare, took point, leading the carriage with its escort north, through hoffle streets filled with cheering people.

No one but John took notice of the two lone riders who headed south in search of a young woman and her legendary companion. "God speed, Ophir," he whispered. "God speed."

CHAPTER 10

Elitet

Anton doused what was left of the fire with water from the pool that lapped at the edge of the cave. The back of the waterfall was a scant three feet further away. He leaned his head into it. Pulling back, he scrubbed his face and beard with a wet hand and smoothed the mass of long reddish hair out of his eyes. "I got horses in the back," he said to Jessica.

Varnack sighed, "Thirsty."

"Varnack, you're awake." Jessica grabbed the cup and gave her friend a drink of water. "How are you going to travel?" He was still very weak.

"Got that one covered," Anton said. He folded the blanket into long thirds, then gently placed Varnack into the center. After tying both ends together, he pulled the makeshift sling over his head and one shoulder, then hoisted the large animal up, onto his back.

Varnack's weight did not seem to bother the huge man as he led the way through the triangular door at the back of the cave. Two horses stood fully loaded and ready for travel. Anton mounted his animal with ease. Varnack's extra weight did not seem to faze the animal, for he never readjusted his footing after accepting the additional load. Jessica stared at the massive creature. The short-haired coat shimmered blue-black with patches of light brown accenting feet and forehead. Anton stroked the long neck and playfully flipped the animal's ears.

"This here's Jin. Yer horse's name is Web."

Jessica mounted the smaller, cola brown animal. She admired the wisps of white running through his coat, which gave the impression of a spider's web spun all over him.

Anton opened a small jar of combustible powder and light flooded the area. They rode single file through a long corridor, Jin barely able to fit and Anton ducking half the time to avoid the tunnel ceiling. Jessica checked around her soft-padded saddle and found a bulging knapsack along with two water flasks tied to it. Shaking the containers, she found them to be full. "Hey," she called. "I see food and water here, but no weapons. Don't I get something? I mean, a cool gladiator sword, or a Xena flying ring, or maybe even some of those ninja stick things..."

Anton turned nearly all the way around in his saddle, not an easy feat for a man carrying such a huge cargo as Varnack on his back. "What?" His eyebrows were raised nearly to the hairline.

"Well…a weapon? You know, something to fight with."

"Do ya know how to use anythin'?"

She thought for a moment. "I've been trained in hand-to-hand fighting."

"Then ya got yer weapons with ya." His tone left no room for argument.

After what seemed an hour of riding through underground twists and turns, a small stream of sunlight grew visible up ahead. Anton snuffed the combustible powder. Long vines hung over an exit doorway. They grew so thick, they allowed only a few light rays to penetrate into the tunnel.

Once outside, Jessica squinted against the shock of bright sunlight. Shading her eyes, she turned her face away from the sun. The hill behind them was wrapped in layers of burgundy vines. They in turn were covered by large yellow blossoms. The foliage camouflaged the cave entrance so effectively she was unable to ascertain its exact whereabouts.

Single file, they traveled in silence, trotting in what Jessica deemed an eastward direction through the wooded lands. She was not a horsewoman, though she did not have the morbid fear of horses that her father did. Vacationing as a child on a dude ranch constituted the extent of her equestrian training, so she spent the first two hours getting the feel of the animal's gait, then the next two trying to relax. After a while, she unwound enough to let her mind wander. Questions, questions. However, one look at her uncle's rigid posture and the questions remained unasked.

Every few feet Anton turned his head, scanning the terrain from side to side. Each muscle in his neck stood out. The tension emanating from him made even the horses skittish. Jessica could sense Web's fear and confusion. "It's okay, boy," she soothed and gently stroked his neck. She felt completely useless, almost a burden. She had no training as a tracker and was not sure she could even distinguish a deer, if there were deer on Edia, from a tree.

The going was slow. They skirted around tree clumps, plowed through dense underbrush, and plodded over thick, spongy moss. The only sounds in the forest were the occasional bird chirps and their own muted strides.

They never stopped moving, not even for lunch, so Jessica rummaged in a few of the packs and found more of the same dried fruits, breads, and meats as she'd found on her first night in Esparia. By midafternoon the forest began to grow thinner, the moss less dense and the dandle shrubbery replaced by tall, willowy grasses.

Anton slowed his horse and motioned for Jessica to pull up next to him. "We'll take a short break before we pass out 'o the forest. There's a solid group 'o trees over there, if ya need some privacy." He dismounted and allowed Jin to chomp on the new growths of tender grass.

Grateful for the pit stop, Jessica swung down off of Web. When her feet touched the ground, her legs nearly buckled. Rubbing her cramping muscles, she hobbled to the shelter of the dense thicket.

Ten minutes later, they were back on their horses. "We're goin' for another couple hours," Anton warned. "Ya up to it?"

She nodded.

"Once out 'o this forest, we'll be exposed. Elitet travel in teams of five. I don't know how many teams are after ya, but if we run into trouble I want ya to head in a straight course followin' the big planet in the sky, that's Ragus. This time of year it has a northern orbit to Edia 'n if ya follow it, y'all be led to dines where people can take ya to Ramadine."

"I understand." His seriousness frightened her. And worse, she had more questions. Dines? Better not to ask. She guessed they were probably cities or villages of some sort.

Within minutes, they left the forest behind. The tall grasses of the open plain ahead grew nearly five feet high. Jessica ran her hand over the tops as they trotted through the vast sea. The pointy tips gave way to her touch, like a feather's edge bends when stroked. Towering rock formations and huge, single boulders punctuated the terrain, scattered in random patterns as if sprinkled down from high above by a gigantic shaker bottle.

Their vulnerability now increased substantially and Jessica felt Anton tense even more. He scanned the ground ahead, as well as from side to side, always searching, constantly watching their surroundings. Without the cover of the trees they could be easily seen, and the tall grasses could hide an ambush. Jessica was on her guard too, straining her senses, squinting to see as far ahead as possible. They finally stopped when both moons were high overhead.

Anton chose the shelter of an immense rock for their first campsite. "I'm not goin' to light a fire. There's dried food in yer sack."

"I already found it."

Opening her pack, Jessica shared her meat and water with Varnack.

"How ya holdin'up, Jessi?" Genuine concern filled Anton's voice.

Not wanting to complain or be more of a burden she simply smiled. "Fine. A little tired, but fine." Ohhh! She inwardly moaned. She was not fine. She was sore and her inner thighs burned with fire. They felt red and raw from rubbing against the saddle all day; she was not used to any of this.

Anton grinned at her. "Sure ya are," he said sarcastically and he rummaged inside his sack. Producing a bottle with lotion in it, he tossed it to Jessica. "Larone figured ya wouldn't be used to all this ridin', so he sent this stuff. Go over there," he pointed to a sheltered place by the edge of the rock formation. "Rub that everywhere yer sore. Ya'll be a lot better by mornin'."

Without protest, she took the bottle, and shuffled over behind the large rock. She poured a generous amount of the lotion onto her palm. It smelled like honeysuckle. When the soothing balm touched her sore flesh, the burning pain immediately subsided. "Oh!" She let out a squeal of delight. This stuff was great!

When she finished, she returned to the campsite and placed the lotion in her own knapsack. "Much better. Thank you, Uncle Anton."

"Yer welcome. We'll want to leave before sun up, so ya'd better catch some sleep."

She didn't complain. Tonight she felt exhausted. As she laid out a blanket found in her knapsack, Varnack spoke to her. "How did Larone know we would be in danger?" he asked.

"So you can speak in full sentences." Jessica laughed at her friend.

Anton looked expectantly at the two of them.

"Varnack wants to know how you and Larone knew we'd be in danger and need help?"

"Two Ider warriors, half dead from the Saylon massacre rode into Ramadine, a couple o' days ago. Said they'd been betrayed. We'd known about the massacre for a day, but the news of a traitor, well, that took us by surprise. We figured it likely Daenon knew about ya comin', 'n if he did, he'd send Elitet after ya. I left right away. When ya hadn't made it to any of the checkpoints, I knew ya were in trouble. If I was Varnack, I'da headed for Clear Blue Lake, away from the usual trail, so that's where I went. Good thing too, I saw those black robes through the trees 'n rode hard to get ahead of 'em."

Anton's explanation brought up more questions for Jessica, but before she could ask them, Varnack spoke to her again. It took some focus to understand everything he conveyed. Usually he spoke little, but this time he had a great deal to say and she wanted to translate it correctly.

"He wants to thank you. He also wants me to tell you he's not tired. Your back is comfortable and he slept quite a bit. He says he'll stand guard and awaken you if there's trouble. He wants you to rest."

"Ya sure you're up to this?"

Varnack nodded, his ears swaying with the action. Anton scrutinized the animal. "Fine," he sighed. "Ya know the danger here. I guess I won't argue, if yer really feelin' strong enough."

Jessica knew her own questions could wait. Lying on her back, looking up at the foreign sky, her thoughts turned to family and friends and the last four days. She wondered what Dad and Grandma were doing right now. She wondered where Thomas was, if he'd seen the leaning tower or the Vatican. She desperately wanted to talk with Rachel. Would her friend even believe her? Jessica wasn't sure if she believed what was happening!

Everything was so unreal.

Anton's snoring brought the reality sweeping back. "Varnack", she whispered, "can you read my thoughts?"

"No, and you can't read mine unless I let you."

She sighed deeply, rolled onto her side, and soon fell asleep.

About an hour before sunrise Anton woke Jessica. She rubbed more lotion on her legs, then ate a cold breakfast. Varnack was placed back in the sling and once he settled, they took off at a brisk pace.

The terrain remained the same as the afternoon before, tall grasses interspersed with boulders and rock formations of various sizes. Still wary, but less strained than yesterday, Jessica noticed wild flowers as tall as the grasses. The bright pinks, oranges, and lavenders lifted her spirits. Had they not been in a hurry she would have enjoyed picking some and experiencing their various fragrances.

Anton and Jessica traveled side by side in silence, each on their guard while Varnack slept most of the day. Several times the riders scared up some fat, gray and white spotted fowl nesting in the grass, and once Jessica spotted a grouping of antlerless, deer-like creatures. She counted seven large birds of prey circling overhead, but never set eyes on another human soul.

When the sun hung low at the horizon, the unmistakable sound of distant thunder drifted in on the quickening breeze. Before long, the air became heavy with the smell of rain. "Looks like we're in for it," Anton looked at the glowering sky. "I'll try 'n find some shelter, but get prepared for a good soakin.'"

He managed to find a small outcropping of rocks low to the ground, barely large enough for the three of them to fit under if they crawled. Jessica went in first with Varnack next and Anton last, his back to the opening to shield his charges from the wind and rain.

"It's a good thing I'm not claustrophobic," Jessica muttered. She touched the stone ceiling only inches from her face. The wind howled for hours while the rain came in intermittent bursts through the night. By morning the storm passed, leaving the air cool and the ground soaked through for several inches.

"This isn't good." Anton surveyed the soil. "This mud'll show every print for days." Jessica nodded, the worry in his voice echoed her own grim thoughts.

The days melted into each other. The warm spring sun beat down on the wayfarers. In the evenings, Jessica described Earth, then Anton would talk of his travels around Esparia and her northern neighbor, Marone. It had been up in the furthermost reaches of the continent where he had first found blue persite, just a rock, glowing in the snow.

Once he tried to explain the dimensional specifics of Transmirian spirals, but when he started into particle physics and blue persite sorcery and the Channels of Gonta, she gave up trying to understand. He seemed to derive great pleasure in expounding his insights, so she politely listened, ooing and ahing where she thought appropriate. Jessica grew fond of the great man protecting her. She found him to be without guile, a straight forward individual.

After the evening meals, Jessica peeked at the edges of Varnack's wound. No purulent oozing or signs of infection contaminated the area. He never complained, so she basically left well enough alone. Each night the mighty canine stood watch. He grew stronger with the passing of every uneventful day.

When they traveled, Jessica entertained herself by keeping track of the wildlife and noting any new flora. One day, they passed close to a small herd of elephant sized bovine animals. She had seen several herds from a distance, and up close she thought they resembled gigantic, hornless cattle. Several of the gentle creatures looked up from their grazing, but seemed unperturbed by the strange riders passing by. She wondered if they tasted anything like beef.

After five days of unvaried terrain coming and going, Jessica wondered if the grasslands would never end. Toward mid-afternoon of the sixth day, a few long-needled trees appeared on the horizon. Brushing up against one of the branches, she was surprised to find the needles were feathery soft. Once she spotted the first trees, they quickly multiplied, and by early evening a lush forest lay ahead. Unlike the arbors of the Southern Greenland, tall and pole-like, this woodland boasted fat, Christmas-tree-shaped firs ranging from mere saplings to gigantic seventy foot behemoths. Anton did not stop until they were well into it.

After finding shelter at the base of one huge granddaddy which was surrounded by a dense growth of eight-foot-high saplings, Anton deposited Varnack next to Jessica, then went to tend the horses. With a bit of sunlight remaining to the day, Jessica decided to give Varnack's wound a thorough inspection.

"Varnack, I think it's time to replace the bandages on your leg. You haven't mentioned anything about it for two days now, so let's have a good look at it." She untied the sleeves to the arm bandages and took a deep breath to strengthen her stomach against what she might find. She removed the fern placed there a week earlier. It had shriveled into several mustard-pink fragments. To her astonishment, the wound showed dramatic improvement, more than she could ever have imagined. The flesh mended together over the previously exposed bone. Only an inch more to go and the gash would be completely filled in, but without scar tissue. New muscle was generating. Already, wisps of fur were growing at the healed edges of the once shredded flesh. Using a gentle hand, she probed the area, checking Varnack's face for any sign of pain. When he did not wince, she knew all would be well.

"You'll have some great stories to tell your kids." Varnack licked her hand, and then his injury.

Anton knelt beside her. He poked at the crumbling fern, then gazed at her with interest. "How did ya know to use this plant on the wound?"

She shrugged her shoulders. "I have no idea. Pure instinct. I somehow knew it was the right thing to use. I broke it open to let the white sap drip into the hole, then placed the rest of the fern on top. As you can see, I used my shirt sleeves as the bandage."

Anton nodded his approval. "Ya did good. Ya saved his life." He patted her on the shoulder.

For the first time since leaving the cave, Anton built a small fire. "Our food is runnin' low," he announced. "But, tomorrow we should find quite a bit in the forest. We'll travel more in a true north direction. Ya've probably noticed I've been avoidin' hoffles. Yer red hair is a sure sign yer a Protector. This color isn't common here. In fact, no one but our family, I mean the Liedias, not Saylons, has red hair. Cause of Haesom 'n his boys bein' bright redheads, this color was known as the Protector's color. I don't know who's friend or who's foe right now, so I don't want to take any chances."

"I understand. Where are we?"

"This is Feather Forest, named for the trees. We just passed through the Rocky Plains."

As they unrolled their respective blankets for the night's rest, Jessica took measure of her kin. "Uncle Anton, I didn't tell you everything that happened at Vorgen Hoffle."

He squirmed into a comfortable position on his blanket. "I'm listenin', Jessi."

She told him about rescuing Karree's husband back from the brink of death and healing his fatal wounds. "Karree called it the Salupathic Gift. I don't understand how it happened. I only know I wanted this man to live, then power, like life itself, traveled through me to him. It put me into a coma for two days. Scared me, Uncle."

Anton remained silent for a long time. Jessica thought he had fallen asleep, so when he finally spoke, she jumped. "Larone has the Salupathic gift. It's what makes him such a great healer. He'll be the one to explain it all to ya. I don't understand it myself, but the power comes from Edia 'n from the Expanse of Gonta. It's not scary, but ya need to respect it."

As with the previous nights, Varnack sat guard while the other two benefited from some much needed sleep. Having a keen sense of hearing and smell, Varnack made a better night watchman than Anton. He would know if someone approached long before Anton could hear.

The first rays of light breaking through the firs awoke Jessica. She hopped up and stretched. Growing accustomed to sleeping on the hard ground, she felt well rested this morning. The first few days she awoke stiff and sore, but today, her muscles were relaxed and pain free. Anton had also just risen, so Varnack, relieved of duty, laid his great head on huge front paws and closed his eyes.

"Let me help with the horses this morning, I'd like to learn how to care for them."

"All right." Anton handed her Web's lead rope. He showed her the pads, the bridles, and the saddles. He explained the function of each, then showed her how they fit on the animals. She copied his every move and followed his directions precisely. Soon her horse stood ready for travel.

"One more thing," he added. "Everythin' comes off in the opposite order we put it on, 'n when that's done, we wipe the animals down with this," he reached into a second pack attached to his saddle and pulled out a brush, "like this." He pretended to brush down the horse with a few strokes.

Jessica had never observed Anton care for the horses in the evenings. Her task was to help Varnack, so this was the first time she had seen the brush, and gaped hungrily at it. "A brush!" she cried out. "You have a brush?"

Anton stared at her, staring at the brush in his hand. "Yes," he said slowly. Her sudden and unusual behavior obviously startled him.

"Uncle Anton…give me that brush."

His mouth opened, then closed. "Is there a spell on it?" He actually managed to whisper. He did not move a muscle.

With his hand frozen in mid-air, she walked over to him and plucked the instrument from it. "It's a girl thing," was all the explanation he received, and turning on her heel, she began picking out the horsehairs. When she finished, she used it to start detangling her own long mane.

For the first time since Jessica met her uncle, he burst out in full, hearty laughter, his voice echoing through the forest. Shaking his shaggy head, he gave her a huge bear hug, then placed Web's reins into her free hand. "Well, Varnack," he turned, still laughing, to the large golden hound, "how ya doin' this mornin'?

Still putting the horse brush to good use, Jessica listened to the response and translated. "He's much better today and wants to walk for a while."

"All right," Anton agreed. "Just let me know when yer tired. I'll go slow cause ya've been up all night."

Within five minutes they were ready to go. True to his word, Anton went at a much slower pace so Varnack, following behind on all four feet, could easily pick his way through the light underbrush. Jessica gave her mount a free rein while continuing to work at her long, matted hair. She realized Anton still chuckled, but it didn't bother her. So, maybe she was a little vain, she conceded to herself, but she couldn't stand the tangles any longer. Anyway, it was good to hear her uncle laugh. He'd been so serious and so tense, he deserved a little respite. If that was at her expense, then she didn't mind. Besides, she held the brush up and admired it as if it were the most precious thing in the entire world, she had a brush. It took her two full hours to completely comb through her red tresses.

The sun blazed directly overhead in the clear, azure sky when Jessica's inner clock let her know it was time for lunch. She was about to suggest a short break to Anton, but an incapacitating, unexpected sense of foreboding forced her silence. Confused by the unexpected onslaught she tried pushing it away, but the foreboding quickly deteriorated to a sick feeling in the pit of her stomach, abruptly giving her the urge to vomit.

"Anton!" she screamed. "Danger!" Reacting instantly, he yanked back on his horse and dove to the ground, his sword in hand. Jessica followed his example just as five arrows went zipping through the air. She remembered him telling her, whoever was after them did not want her dead, so she slammed herself into Varnack, forcing him onto his side and shielded him with her body. From the corner of her eye she realized Anton was hit.

"Varnack, stop squirming," she hissed. "Play dead! You can't fight arrows."

A mock show of grief was needed to set a trap. "Oh, Varnack!" she wailed loudly. "They've killed you!" She flopped over to Anton, crying louder than ever while making a quick assessment of the wound in his back. Blood flowed from an arrow lodged deep in his left shoulder. It hit at an angle, penetrating the flesh exposed at the edge of the chain mail vest. He stared, unblinking straight ahead. His chest did not rise and fall.

"Anton?" she sobbed in real fear. Sensing rather than hearing the attackers approach she tensed. For all her years of self-defense training, Jessica had never actually put her knowledge to use. She had been in a few competitions, but did not enjoy fighting for the sake of the sport. With nerves on edge, she frantically tried to remember the moves she had been taught.

Her back to the assassins, she continued to make a fuss over Anton, while searching for something to use as a weapon. Spotting a small log beside Anton, she focused. At the instant someone touched her, she lunged for the log. Grabbing it, she turned and sprang at her attacker.

The Elitet wore a mask, only his dark eyes showed through stitched, round holes. He did not jump fast enough to dodge the log in her hand. She threw her whole body into the force behind the blow aimed at his head. One down.

106

The four others rushed in. Relief flooded through Jessica when both Varnack and Anton jump to their feet. Anton's wound went deep and his back was saturated with blood. Two of the Elitet were on him, their blows aiming to kill. Jessica's worry turned to the Trigal hound. She knew the long walk in the woods, coupled with little sleep the night before, had drained a good deal of his strength, leaving him much weaker than normal.

She twisted away from her own attacker and flew at the one thrusting his sword at her friend's chest. She sunk her teeth into his raised sword arm with all the power her jaws held. He yelped in surprise and pain.

From behind, an Elitet seized her hair, jerking her around. She twisted in his grasp and kicking with her leg, connecting with his groin. Adrenaline pumped through her as never before. He fell backward into a spike-leafed bush, but managed to keep his hold on her hair, pulling her down with him. Using her elbow, she jammed the bony point into his ribcage. This time, the man's grip slackened and she wrenched free, leaving a thick clump of red strands intertwined through his fingers.

Varnack fought beside her. Fresh blood oozed from his paw, but the Elitet received slash wounds of his own. He jabbed at Varnack, the tip of his sword disappearing into the animal's side. With her right shoulder lowered, Jessica ran at the attacker and smashed into his back. The blow knocked him off center.

Before she could catch her breath, her adversary bolted back. He grabbed her by the neck in a crushing grip, then brought his fist down into her face. The blow made her head reel and her legs buckled under her. Darkness tried to close in, but she fought it, wanting to stay conscious. Her arms were wrenched behind her body so forcefully she thought the bones were going to break. The Elitet threw her to the ground and smashed her face into the dirt. His knee ground into her back, forcing the breath out of her lungs. She gasped for oxygen.

All at once, the weight on her back was gone and her arms were free. Two men dressed in blue and silver had joined the fight, quickly evening out the odds. An older man fought at Anton's side while a younger one battled the Elitet who had held Jessica. She immediately recognized him as one of the two Saylon Dorset survivors she had seen in her video game incident at Mark's house many nights earlier. A black shrouded body lay in a heap beside Varnack, a bloody mass where his throat should have been.

"Varnack!" She crawled to where he had collapsed. His left shoulder was slashed to the bone, as was his right paw, and a hole at his side dripped red where a sword point had penetrated the flesh. Searching for something to stem the crimson tide, she tore the shirt from the fallen attacker.

A man lay at Anton's feet. Anton's sword dripped with blood. Beside Anton, the older man leaned on a red-stained sword, his lifeless opponent sprawled beside him. They watched the younger warrior disarm the last attacker, the one who nearly broke Jessica's arms. Momentarily, her attention shifted to a deep-red sash about the Elitet's waist, then back to the young man. He raised his sword to finish the enemy off.

"No," Jessica cried. "Don't kill him. We may need him." The young man hesitated. His mouth was drawn down at each corner, his jaw clenched. The muscles in his neck were taught, causing the veins to bulge and pulsate with each heartbeat. His gaze was fixed on the black robed assassin. Quick as lightning, the Elitet pulled a concealed knife and lunged, but faster yet, the older rescuer threw his own dagger with pinpoint accuracy. The Elitet fell dead, his hand still gripping his blade.

The only sound in the forest was the heavy breathing of the three standing men. Jessica turned her attention back to Varnack. She ripped the shirt in her hands into several long strips and bound up his wounds. Anton sank to the ground. He neither uttered a sound nor winced when the elder rescuer dug the arrow from the back of his shoulder. The younger man went from enemy to enemy, checking life signs on each. When he came to the one Jessica had hit with the log he announced, "This one's still alive."

"Bind him tightly," the older man ordered. "Elitet take a suicide vow."

Having never killed anyone before, Jessica felt relief that the man lived. The thought of taking another life caused a shiver of horror to run the length of her body. She knew how sacred life was. 'Thou shalt not kill' was a premier command in all cultures since the dawn of time. However, she now knew, if forced, she could take a life, but not to save herself. No, never for something as selfish as that. She thought of Varnack, Uncle Anton, and the innocent villagers of Vergan Hoffle, the children. For them she could do the unthinkable. To save them, she could kill in the heat of battle. She shuddered and put the thought to the back of her mind.

Turning her doctoring attentions to Anton, she held her hand to his wounded back. The hole left from the arrow was the size of a quarter, and blood continued to drain from it, but no air whizzed out. "Man, you must live right. Your lung's not punctured." She rinsed the wound with water from her flask, then folded a large piece of black cloth and placed it firmly over the opening. She secured it with a second bandage wound around his shoulder and back.

The two men in blue moved the bodies of the four dead Elitet through the trees beyond Jessica's sight. When they returned, she addressed the older man, "Are you wounded?" She scanned him for signs of blood.

"No, I am unhurt, Protectoress."

Too concerned with his wellbeing, Jessica barely noticed his use of the title. She crossed to the younger man. Blood stained his upper arm. "Sit down," she commanded, ripping his sleeve away. She cleansed the slash mark with water, and using the last of her black cloth, bound his arm. "Any place else?"

"No, My Lady." He stared at her. Under his gaze, she became mindful of her own appearance. Touching her hand to her face, she felt it moist and sticky. Bringing the hand down, she was shocked at the sight of her own bright red blood. It took a moment to realize her lip was bleeding.

"I'm surprised my nose isn't broken as well," she mumbled and searched the ground for something to wipe her face. The elder warrior tore a piece of shirt from the bound Elitet, then brought the cloth to Jessica. He fell to one knee before her and when the younger man joined him they simultaneously touched their left fists to their foreheads and then left breasts.

Taken aback by the soldiers' actions and the realization of who Reese was, Jessica was uncertain how to react. She looked to Anton, hoping for some guidance. He formally addressed her. "Protector Jessica, may I introduce General Ophir, commander of the Esparian Security Academy at Ider Hoffle 'n his companion, Lieutenant Reese, grandson of General Gammet, commander of the forces at Saylon Dorsett."

Realizing something needed to be said, she stammered, unsure of what words to say, "Thank-you," was the best she could come up with. But then quickly added, "I think we would have been lost without you."

"Oh, I don't know 'bout that," joked Anton lightheartedly. "I thought we had things pretty well in hand."

Jessica gaped at him in disbelief. "Yeah, right," she laughed, as did the two kneeling men. "Please stand up," she begged. "I'm not used to this."

Ophir rose first, he looked admiringly at Jessica. "You look a great deal like your grandmother."

"You knew my Grandma?"

"Knew! I know your grandmother. She's here, My Lady, and your father accompanies her."

Jessica felt the blood rush from her face and Reese sprang to her side. He helped her sit down. The shock of this news was more than she could have hoped. She held up quite well after the rush of adrenaline from the fight, but now her emotional defenses were drained and tears stung her eyes.

"Gayleena is here?"

"Yes, Anton." Ophir briefly explained the events at Ider Hoffle.

Captivated by the story, Jessica reined in her crumbling emotions. She used the rag to wipe her face once again. This time she winced at a pain in her chin and found it too was split. However, emotionally, she felt much better for having shed the tears. They were on Edia. Her Dad and Grandma were here. Her heart felt lighter than it had in days. She would see them soon at Ramadine and she could hardly wait.

Ophir started a fire, then retrieved the five Elitet horses while Reese hunted for food. Soon they were all fed, except the captured Elitet. He refused to eat.

It was determined Ophir would stand the first watch, sword in hand, while the others slept. None of them were naïve enough to think this was the only team of Elitet on their trail.

CHAPTER 11

Lyrista

The journey to Ramadine began with a flourish. Since news of Protector Gayleena's return preceded them, crowds lined the streets to watch her small coach speed by. Everyone sought a glimpse of the great lady, and curiosity concerning the tall, handsome healer who accompanied her ran high. It was no secret he was her daughter's husband, and rumor had it he came to help the people. John felt extremely uncomfortable being the object of so much interest.

The richly forested land surrounding Ider Hoffle was surprisingly flat. The pole trees were no longer thin, but grew fat, some nearly three feet in diameter. Their waxy branches grew lower on the trunk and the leaves were more opaque. The thick dandleberry bushes stretched upward, with few berries on the pointy red boughs. Slender, eight-pronged spider plants crisscrossed the forest floor, sending out ribbons of twisting bright green and brown vine in all directions. Many of the vines twisted up around the pole trees. Small bunches of grass-type bouquets, ranging in height from a fraction of an inch to nearly a foot, dotted the ground.

The road out of Ider Hoffle cut a straight path through the dense foliage. Every crossroad was well marked with distance signs and directional arrows to the nearest dine. It was a broad, well-kept highway that provided ample room for the carriage, oncoming traffic, and spectators who stood three to four people deep at both sides. Many of the brightly dressed inhabitants smiled and waved, others pointed or nodded their heads in acknowledgement. A non-stop buzz of excitement filled the air from the moment the party left Lyrista's home. Not one section of the roadway was without onlookers for several filons. The crowds gradually thinned away as the last of the farm steads dwindled behind them.

Lyrista took command of the journey. She positioned Mica and Garrett, the two young soldiers who had offered their services, at the rear of the coach. They had strict instructions to stay alert and have their weapons at the ready. The driver acknowledged his instructions--keep up and have weapons beside him. John was simply told to stay close. She took point and set a quick pace, never looking back, but constantly scanning the crowd and the forest beyond the highway edge.

John was out of his league. To carry any sort of weapon on a horse he could not ride would have been a disaster waiting to happen, and he knew it. He spent the first hour trying not to fall off of Fireguard. With the horse alternating between a fast cantor and slow gallop, the rhythm never settled in. He finally decided to relax, and once he did, he was surprised at how much easier it was to keep his balance. By the end of the day, after much trial and error with posture, leg placement, knee squeezes, and leaning in different directions, he felt he had established some basic stop and go parameters. He was not sure if the horse was training him, or if he was actually in control, but at least Fireguard was following commands.

The distinguished group traveled as swiftly as the two coach stallions could manage. At Gaylee's request, they paused briefly in some of the larger tierns and dines for her to tell of the massacre at Saylon Dorsett and warn the local Olders to be on their guard for possible attack. Each settlement, whether big or small, was enclosed by a short, decorative stone wall. The buildings within these boundaries were similar to those of Ider Hoffle, complete with the blue Palium roofing. They were clean communities, with no signs of poverty.

Lyrista organized their lodgings on the first evening and took up guard duty at Gaylee's chamber door. John, Mica, Garrett and the coach driver slept in an adjoining room. At least Mica, Garrett and the coach driver slept. John tossed and turned, only managing to catch snatches of sleep. Unaccustomed to horseback riding, his body ached all over from the full day atop Fireguard. Finally, somewhere between the second and third watch of the night, he rolled out of bed, pulled his shirt back on, and left the snore filled room.

Lyrista was still where he had last seen her, standing watch over Gaylee's room. "I'm here to relieve you," John said matter of factly. "If you don't get some rest you won't be any good in the morning."

"I've gone much longer periods before without sleep," she replied curtly. "I'll be fine."

"I have no doubts as to your abilities to be on your guard," John said more gently. "I just can't sleep any more. I'm wide awake. I'm grateful for all you're doing for Gaylee - for us. Trust me when I say I'm very capable of handling protection duty. If I get into any trouble I promise I'll scream." Lyrista smiled, but didn't move.

"Seriously," John continued, "take my offer and get some sleep. Now go." She still hesitated, but her face had relaxed and weariness showed in her eyes. "Go." John repeated, and with one finger he pushed at her shoulder. She slowly stepped toward Gaylee's room. "Sleep." John said firmly. She opened the door and walked through. In the morning, they were off before the sun was up.

As they took their journey along the road, John was acutely aware of

Lyrista. She handled her horse as if the mare were an extension of her own body. There was grace in every movement she made. She had her bow within easy reach at her side and a full quiver of arrows was strapped to her saddle. Two daggers attached at the front of her belt, a third and fourth were strapped to each thigh. A short sword hung at her right. Garrett, Mica, and the coach driver seemed comfortable with her leadership and that meant quite a bit. These men treated her with the utmost respect.

John couldn't help but compare himself with what he felt her abilities might be. He was good with a bow. His childhood fascination with the hunting prowess of Native Americans had fueled a passion for bow hunting. It was one of his few hobbies and he was good at it. He also had skill with a knife, thanks to his comprehensive military training. It was the sword that made him feel inadequate, a feeling he intensely disliked. He wondered how hard it would be to learn the art of sword fighting. Would he even be here long enough to need that skill? His plan was to retrieve Jessica and return to Earth. Staying had never crossed his mind.

John possessed great self-confidence, almost to the point of arrogance. He knew his skills as a surgeon, a teacher, and a politician, but when it came to women, he found himself at a loss. In a normal work environment, he thought of his female colleagues as 'one of the guys', never as potential companions. Since his wife's death, he never dated. So now, his attraction to Lyrista threw him off balance. With a desire to know her better, however, he pushed his uncertainties aside and on the morning of their second day on the road he struck up a conversation.

"Lyrista, how far is it to Ramadine?"

"About five hundred filons."

"And how long should it take?"

"Normally, a good horse can reach the Ramastar in five or six days, but that's really pushing hard. Because of the coach, we can't go nearly that fast, so we should arrive there in eight or so."

John hid his disappointment. He hoped it would take less time. Each passing day brought more worry about Jessica.

As if reading his thoughts, Lyrista sympathized, "This must be awful for you, not knowing from day to day if your daughter is safe. Ophir will find her. I've known him all my life and I don't trust anyone more. I'm sure this Varnack is very good, but rest assured, no one, not even the great Anton is a better tracker and warrior than Ophir."

"Do you know of Trigal hounds? Is Varnack adequate protection?" John hoped her answer would give him some measure of assurance.

Lyrista pursed her lips in thought. "Trigal hounds are part myth, part legend and part reality. In my mind, the three blend together. This much I do know as fact: their clan lives in the farthest northern regions. They don't interact with humans, so for Healer Larone to have one as a friend is quite amazing. My father told me, when he was young and exploring the northern mountains beyond Marone, that he had met one. It was a great red creature, with bright red eyes. It would not let my father go any further and forced him to turn around - leave the area. It never spoke, but made its wishes known through unmistakable body language. My father had the distinct impression this was an animal capable of killing him quite easily if it had wanted to."

"So you're saying Varnack is a worthy guard."

She nodded. "From my father's description, yes. I, for one, would not wish to challenge him."

They rode together in silence. John thought about a large hound watching over his daughter and shook his head. Finally, with nothing more to say, he slowed his horse until he was even with the driver of Gaylee's coach. He judged the man to be several years older than himself, though exactly how many was difficult to tell, with the Edians aging so differently from Earthmen.

"How goes it?" John yelled over the din of the galloping horses and rolling carriage wheels.

"The road is smooth and the horses respond well," the driver called back.

"Maybe later you could teach me how to handle this thing," John gestured at the vehicle with his thumb.

"I'd be honored."

Realizing that conversing over the noise of the carriage, compounded by the chatter of the crowds, was nearly impossible, John gave up his efforts with the driver and let Fireguard fall behind the coach. He joined the two soldiers who served as rear guard. He soon discovered them to be amiable fellows and spent the rest of the day in their company.

The older of the two, Garrett, stood a full four inches taller than Mica. A garrulous speaker, Garrett found great pleasure in the sound of his own voice. Once John asked a question, any question, it took nearly half an hour before Garrett finished lecturing on every aspect of the query. Mica, on the other hand, when Garrett paused for breath, would offer his short, to the point opinions.

John found, once he sifted through the life histories of these two childhood friends, Esparian life was no different for them than it was for Gaylee. One topic they were able to provide a measure of illumination on was Lyrista herself. John began his probing by asking about Cordon, her older brother. "Reese mentioned he has an Uncle, a soldier named Cordon."

Garrett, eager to show his knowledge, no matter how slight it might be, took John's nudge and ran with it. "Cordon is Lyrista's only brother. They had another sister, Reese's mom, but she died when he was born.

Since Reese's father is a career soldier, Lyrista raised him. Cordon's father is, er...was, Gammet. He and Ophir were best friends, like Mica and me, and life-long defenders of the Saylons. Lyrista's whole family, for generations back, has produced famous Ider Warriors. Cordon followed Gammet as a member of the Saylon bodyguard while Lyrista decided to teach at the Defense Academy. She trains in hand-to-hand combat. Her specialty's dagger dexterity."

When Garrett stopped his oration to flick at a fly, Mica spoke up. "I've never worked under Cordon, but his reputation and skill are well known. The Saylon bodyguards were always the most elite warriors in the country. Everyone knows Lyrista. She's taught at the academy for nearly ten years and remembers the name of every student she's ever had. I don't know any man who wouldn't be honored to serve under her in battle."

Garrett picked up the conversation. "Lyrista speaks her mind. Once I had…"

John quickly cut off the side story. "So is Cordon married?"

"No," Mica spoke quickly, "but he's kept company with a lot of women, even courted my mom for a while, before she married my dad."

"Truly?" Garrett's eyebrows rose in surprise. "He was with my oldest sister for a time."

John laughed, "Sounds like Cordon just hasn't found the right girl yet."

"Lyrista hasn't found the right man either," Garrett offered. "My sister said Lyrista's always had a warrior's way. Most men are afraid of her."

"I wouldn't annoy her," Mica added. "She's a fourth bar officer."

"Fourth bar?" John said. "Out of how many bars?"

"Seven."

John did some quick calculating. That would make her a captain, or possibly a major.

"Mica, I can't see you annoying anybody," Garrett said. "You're the easiest going guy I know."

"That's why I'm still your friend," Mica chuckled.

After the second day on the road, John's legs were on fire, for the leather saddle chafed his inner thighs raw. When he helped Gaylee from the carriage that night, he looked longingly at the empty seat opposite her. "Your ride looks comfortable."

She smiled. "Yes, it is. Are you ready to swallow your manly pride and ride with me tomorrow? I'm impressed you've lasted this long on the horse."

"I was hoping you'd offer," he laughed. "To be honest, I'm not sure I could ride another day." His voice took on a serious tone. "Any premonitions about Jessica?"

"No, none. I promise, I'll tell you if I feel anything, even the slightest tremor."

As much as John hated to admit it, he quietly confided, "I may not believe in your fifth dimensional disciplines, but I know from experience you have a unique sense of family. You're the only link I have right now."

* * *

John found the luxurious coach to be a pleasant form of transportation. Its motion was made smooth by large metal springs on each wheel. The shock absorbers worked remarkably well considering the speed with which they were traveling. The beige leather of the interior was velvety smooth with ample padding in the seats and side rests. And even though the open windows were excessively large, John felt much less exposed to the curiosity filled eyes of the Esparian people.

As their caravan pulled away from another small hoffle whose major roadway had been lined with cheering, waving Esparians until the last large farmstead, John sat back and watched Gaylee as she watched happily out the window as the farms fell away. "Gaylee, I've got a question I've been thinking about the last few days. That ceremony in Ider Hoffle just before we left, what's a life-honor?"

"It's a solemn oath. A promise here is not given lightly, but the most sacred of oaths is the life-honor. For an oath to be truly binding, it must be bound by the life force of something. Some people swear by their children or their parents, but the greatest pledge is the pledge of self. It means if the oath is broken, the life of the oath breaker is forfeit."

The fourth day on the road dawned overcast and drizzling, with a biting chill in the air. Even though the coach was warm and comfortable, John decided to try riding again. As they made their way back onto the highway via the main street of the charming hoffle where they had spent the night, he pulled his mount close to the carriage window to speak with Gaylee. "You seem to have the royal wave down. Doesn't your arm get tired?"

"Well, a little, but I can't get out to shake every hand, not when we're trying to reach Ramadine as fast as possible. So I wave and try to make eye contact with as many countrymen as I can."

"About that, I can't believe all the people. Every day it seems the entire population of any given hoffle or tiern we pass through is out along the roadside. How does word get out so fast? How do your people communicate such large distances if you don't have telephones?"

With a twinkle in her eye, she suggested, "Why don't you go ask Lyrista that question. I've been gone fifty years, things may have changed."

"Ask Lyrista?"

Gaylee nodded.

"Lyrista, huh? Well, why not?"

As usual, Lyrista rode point ahead of the carriage. Her back was straight, rigid with tension. She continually scanned the crowd. John felt a twinge of guilt as he kicked his horse to catch up with her. He was a well-trained soldier himself, capable in any combat situation. But riding a horse, instead of in a Jeep had taken some getting used to. Now that he was finally getting his rhythm with Fireguard, he could be more help in keeping an eye on the surrounding forests.

"I want to thank you for taking charge of this trip. You've done an amazing job of organizing things and caring for Gaylee."

Lyrista seemed to relax ever so slightly. "Thank you. Having Lady Gayleena in my care is a privilege. My family has a life-honor to protect the Saylons. Having taught at the Academy all my life, I never thought this duty would fall on my shoulders."

"It seems the entire country knows Gaylee's back. How is it done? How does news travel so fast?" he asked with a true desire to understand Esparian way of life.

Taking her attention from the road ahead, she glanced sideways at him, a hint of questioning in her eyes. "I think it's pretty much the same everywhere, Esparia, Marone, Galland, even in the Deserts. How does news travel where you're from?"

"Assume that it's quite different where I come from, not at all like here."

Her eyebrows shot up. "All right. We have the Red Feathers. It's a system of carrier birds. Transfer coops, called Red Feather Centers, are in every major tiern as well as some strategic hoffles. You'll find no other bright red buildings in the entire country. No matter where they fly, the birds know a red roof means home and they go straight to it. We also have a letter delivery system, running daily by coach, to dines and larger tierns and by horse to smaller tierns and hoffles. Coach takes about two weeks to travel from one end of the country to another. The same distance is traveled in about three days by carrier bird, but coach is much less expensive."

John nodded. This was something he could easily understand given the current technology, or lack of it.

"Of course, there's also the Sighted," she continued, "but the newspapers employ most of them, when they're not using the birds."

"Sighted?"

"Yes, you know, those who see what's happened."

"Those who see…ohhh," he groaned. "Expanse of Gonta stuff, right? Fifth dimension?" He vainly tried to keep a scoffing tone out of his voice.

"Of course." She gave him her full attention. "You don't understand the expanse, do you?"

"It's not a matter of understanding. I simply don't believe it. Hocus pocus...mumbo jumbo...no, I think it's all a bunch of, well...I don't believe in it."

She pursed her lips and went back to scanning the crowd. After several minutes she said, "You'll like Ramadine, it's very beautiful."

She surprised him by the change of topic. "Ramadine? What has that got to do with the expanse..."

"Nothing." She cut him off. "I don't want to argue about something you obviously know little of; it'll do neither of us any good."

"Fair enough. You mentioned your brother's at Ramadine."

"Yes. Cordon." Lyrista nodded. "He's one of the Saylon Dorsett survivors. I'm anxious to see him, perhaps as anxious about seeing him as you are about seeing your daughter. I can understand your feelings of concern. Really, we're traveling as fast as we safely can."

"I know that. Lyrista, I'm sorry about your father. I too lost my dad in a terrible war. I understand Gammet was a great man."

"Thank you. He was." Lyrista signaled the driver to slow the coach's speed as a large city lay just ahead and the road was quickly becoming more congested than usual.

"It's like bumper to bumper rush hour traffic," John muttered.

"What was that?" Lyrista shot him a queer look.

"Lord Healer," the carriage driver called, "Lady Saylon wishes to speak with you."

John leaned back on his horse, slowing his pace and allowing the carriage to catch up with him. "You wanted me?" He spoke through the large open window.

Lowering her waving arm, Gaylee studied John, a serious expression on her face. "I promised I'd tell you if I felt anything about Jess. It's hard to describe, but I felt apprehension for a while, a feeling of dread. She's safe now, but something..."

"You're sure she's safe,"

"Yes, of course. The feeling lifted moments ago."

John shook his head. He stared past Gaylee, out the large open window at the opposite side of the carriage. The never ending line of Esparians waving from the roadside passed by in a blur of color. He focused beyond them, to the tree line, where the forest began at the highway's edge. Several black forms stood out from among the cream and green branches of the thickly grown trees. In an instant, John realized each aimed an armed bow directly at them. Lyrista shouted a warning at the same moment he launched himself from Fireguard's back into the coach through the large window. Flying through the sizable opening, he grabbed Gaylee as he shot past her. They both tumbled to the carriage floor a split second before three arrows thudded into the cushioned bench where she had just been sitting.

John grabbed his duffle bag and nearly destroyed the zipper in his haste to retrieve the gun. In the few seconds it took him to get it, an arrow slammed into the carriage door and another whizzed through the window, landing on the seat only inches from his head.

"Stay here," he commanded, then bolted out the carriage door, ready for a fight, but the would-be assassins had already vanished into the woodland. Garrett was at the head of the now stationary carriage, one hand on the bridle of the lead stallion, the other holding a sword. His face was grim, his mouth went taught when he caught John's eye. Mica circled the coach on his horse, his bow at the ready. Both men motioned to the agitated crowd to stay back.

One deadly projectile had found its mark in the carriage driver's left breast. He lay slumped back in his seat, the horse's reins still in his hand. John shoved the gun into his belt, then scrambled up beside the man, however there was nothing he could do but gently press the lifeless eyes closed.

Lyrista sat on her horse, her left arm hanging at her side, an arrow shot through her shoulder, its point protruding from her back. In her dangling hand she clutched her bow. Her right hand was pressed tightly to a wound in her side and blood oozed between her fingers. Without a word, John jumped from the driver's seat and ran to her. Reaching up, he pulled her off her mare and into his arms.

Gaylee appeared beside him, the first-aid kit from the duffle bag in her hand. "Tell me what to do."

"Lady Gayleena," Lyrista gasped, "you're too open to danger here. Get back in the coach."

"Lyrista, there are more armed men here right now protecting us than in two full Ider Hoffle regiments," Gaylee soothed. She was right. Many in the crowd had pulled their weapons and others had plowed into the forest after the would-be assassins.

John deposited Lyrista on the doorstep of the carriage, then snapped off the feather end of the arrow. "I need to pull this through. I've got some lidocaine in the kit," he said to Gaylee. "Fill a syringe."

Waiting for the anesthesia, John inspected the gash in Lyrista's side. "You lost a piece of muscle."

"I'm pretty sure I shot one," Lyrista breathed through clenched teeth. "We really need to be moving."

"Mica's got things under control," John assured her. He numbed both her wounds with the anesthesia. "Okay, grit your teeth."

Lyrista closed her eyes when John grasped the sharp arrow point and pulled. He threw the broken shaft to the ground and finished treating her shoulder and side. With the task completed, he gently lifted her into the carriage.

"I can ride," she protested.

"I don't think so, not today anyway. You've lost a lot of blood, and I don't need you passing out on me while galloping on a horse."

Lyrista's eyes flashed. "I won't pass out, and who do you think you are, telling me what I can and cannot do?"

John met her anger with cool resolution. Lyrista took on patient status is his mind and he now dealt with her on that basis. "You will follow my orders, or I'll tie you to this seat."

Before Lyrista could respond, Gaylee intervened. "Lyrista, I think having a guard inside the carriage would be a wise move. I would like no one better than you to be with me right now."

Lyrista continued to glare at John, but nodded in agreement. "Very well, Lady Gayleena. For the rest of this day, I'll ride with you, but only because *you* have wished it so."

Turning his attentions to the commotion around him, John barked orders to Garrett and Mica. "Garrett, you're our driver now. Mica, you're in charge at the rear."

Mica shot a look of surprise to Garrett that John did not miss.

"I'm not just a healer, but where I come from I'm a sixth bar, now move," John snapped in a tone that demanded compliance.

"Yes, sir," Garrett and Mica simultaneously chimed.

Two runners appeared at the forest edge and came to the carriage. "Well?" John asked them authoritatively. He stood at his full height. His entire demeanor was one of command.

One runner snapped to attention. "We found a thick trail of blood, but no body. Others are still searching, but whoever they were, they seem to have disappeared."

John nodded. He knew they were vulnerable while on the main highway. "Are there any who are willing to accompany us to Ramadine?" he called out to the crowd. About fifty men, swords still in their hands stepped forward. "I'm grateful to all of you," John acknowledged, "but we have no time to waste. So those with horses at the ready will come with us now." There was a bustle of activity as swords were sheathed and a dozen men ran for their tethered mounts at the forest's edge. John turned to a bystander who looked particularly disappointed at not being chosen. "This man," John pointed to the body of the dead coach driver now lying on the ground, "is from Ider Hoffle. He needs to go home."

The bystander squared his shoulders, gave the Salute of Loyalty, and promised, "It will be done."

Astride Fireguard, John positioned himself at the head of the group. In his hand he held the loaded Beretta. The twenty new escorts took up positions around the coach. Tense and alert for the rest of that day, as well as the following two, he led their way northward. Luckily the road to Ramadine was well marked. He rode harder than ever, forcing all to keep pace with him. They traveled late into each night. John knew they would never be truly safe until they reached Ramadine, so he pushed the horses to exhaustion to cut a full day from the journey.

On the seventh morning Lyrista insisted on riding again. She rejoined the procession to lead their way at John's side into the legendary city, Ramadine.

CHAPTER 12

Ramadine

As they approached the ancient city, hills rose to meet them and the highway started to climb. Uniformed soldiers replaced the crowds of civilians as the carriage, with its small escort, made its way along the last few miles of the journey. This final portion of smooth cobblestone highway cut uphill, through a dense, lush forest. The pale yellow pole trees had vanished the previous day with thick trunked broad-leafs replacing them as giants of the woodland. Short branches sprouted from base to top of each mighty tree and were completely covered with silvery-white bloated leaves. They were huge, pointed puff balls, thrown together in random bunches. Dandleberries still grew in abundance where the sun streamed through to the open patches of ground. These bushes lined each side of the road, spiraling upwards to ten feet.

At the first sign of soldiers along the road, John's tension level lessened. For the first time since taking lead for the journey he let himself feel greater curiosity and anticipation as they neared the ancient university he had heard so much about.

"Not much farther now," Lyrista said from beside him. They rode side by side, with the carriage following and Mica guarding their rear. "In fact, you should be able to see Ramadine after we round the next corner."

Built of pastel colored stones, the sprawling complex loomed atop the highest plateau. From their distance, it looked like a mighty, shimmering fortress floating on the forest canopy of silvery white puff leaves. Many of the buildings were domed while others were topped by tall, thin spires of shiny metal, glistening in the setting sun. The many hues melted into a rainbow of soft colors, gently blending into each other. A great wall surrounded the entire campus, with large turrets built into it every eighty feet. The glossy white barricade was between forty and fifty feet high. John guessed it was also made of stone. At the entrance, two enormous, deep blue Palium gates stood open. This was the only visible opening built into the formidable wall and the road led straight through it.

Thousands of soldiers, clothed in navy blue and silver, stood at attention on the deforested land surrounding the Ramadine wall. This was a large area, spreading six hundred feet from the edge of the forest to the massive stone barricade. Every battle tower had at least eight men staffing it and the top of the wall was filled with uniformed humanity. As the coach passed the impressive honor guard and entered the city through the ornate metal gates, each warrior gave the Salute of Loyalty.

The buildings of Ramadine were constructed of massive stone blocks ranging in color from light pink to deep green and soft gray to creamy yellow. Each building was uniquely decorated with delicate botanical carvings and ornamental statues depicting humans, wildlife, nature, and the abstract. Stained glass windows added more color and dimension. Each structure had a smooth, polished finish, giving it the look of elegant marble.

The grounds of Ramadine were just as striking as the buildings upon them, with neatly trimmed lawn and countless well-groomed flowerbeds. Smooth, pale green walkways serpentined between buildings, efficiently connecting them while not detracting from the overall landscaping. Tall, ancient trees gave plenty of shade and several large fountains flanked by stone benches accented the surrounding areas.

A bell, deep and rich in tone, tolled repeatedly. It heralded their coming and scores of people poured from the campus buildings. Men and women of all ages, handsomely dressed in bright clothing, jostled for a glimpse of the travelers. John and Lyrista, side by side, led the small procession up the main road to the largest of the visible structures. Constructed of lime-green stone with four-story-high columns and a sharply peaked silver roof, it stood out as the most ornate and notable. Lyrista held her hand up as a signal to stop.

Gathered around the newcomers were uniformed soldiers, civilians dressed in all manner of tunics, skirts, pants, shirts, robes and dresses, as well as older professor-types in red and brown robes of distinction. However, it was a tall, thin man wearing a simple gray robe who caught John's attention. He stood erect before two large wood paneled doors leading into the green stone building. Neatly trimmed, snow-white hair crowned his head. A smile brightened his clean-shaven, aging face and kindness showed in his sapphire eyes. His gray robe bunched at the waist, a white cord keeping the thick fabric in place. Opened slightly at the chest with loosely fitted sleeves, the plain garment hung to his ankles. The smile on his face reminded John of Shallenon's smile, the strong genetic resemblances in this family were remarkable. No one needed to tell him this was Larone, the Great Healer.

John and Lyrista dismounted. A teenage boy stepped from the crowd offering to take the animals. Walking to the carriage, John opened the door and helped Gaylee descend. Larone came forward at a brisk walk, a smile on his face that lit up his eyes, and as soon as Gaylee's feet hit the ground she ran to him. He embraced her tenderly, as any loving father would embrace a long lost daughter. The onlookers were hushed in respectful silence. Larone whispered something to Gaylee and tears streamed down his face. At last, they withdrew a pace from each other. The crowd, unable to contain themselves, burst forth in a mighty cheer.

Gaylee wiped her cheeks and beckoned John to join them. He first went to Lyrista, who stood by the carriage horses, and offered her his arm. Tentatively, she took it. Together they joined Larone and Gaylee. John motioned for the two young soldiers, Garrett and Mica, to follow and the small group entered the green building.

Once through the massive doors, Larone turned to John. "There is no news of your daughter, but that is good. If something had happened to her, I am certain we would have heard. In this case, no news is good news. Varnack, a very trusted and capable friend, is with her. As soon as we knew about the traitor in our midst, Anton left to find them. That was nearly a week ago. I know there is much you have to say to me, questions, much deserved recriminations and smoldering frustrations. However, you must be hungry. Refresh yourselves first, then we can talk more."

Through a jumble of emotions, John reluctantly agreed. This was not what he expected. Larone seemed like a decent guy. John was expecting…well, he was expecting a know-it-all, someone self-absorbed, and proud. But Larone seemed the opposite of those. John's gut reaction was trust.

"You know about Jessica's arrival on Edia?" Gaylee asked.

"Oh, yes. That's why I chose Varnack to protect her. Other than Anton, I trust no one better."

"Weren't you expecting Shallenon?" Gaylee looked perplexed.

Larone smiled. "No. I knew when Shallenon's life force darkened ten years ago and passed on. It greatly saddened me. Haesom took it especially hard. But I have also known about my great-grandniece, Jessica, for some time. Her connection with Edia has grown stronger this past year. Only Anton, Haesom and I knew of her existence. We kept Shallenon's passing a secret. This betrayer would assume that Shallenon, a grown woman, not a girl of Jessica's age will return to claim the Protectorship. If Daenon suspects anything, it will be a woman of fifty, not a girl of eighteen that he will search for."

One of the many knots in John's stomach slowly unwound at this bit of unexpected news. "That's good to know." He looked at Larone. "Gaylee and I saw a band of Elitet by Ider Hoffle. They were definitely searching for someone."

Larone frowned. "I'm glad they did not find the two of you. Though," he openly appraised John from head to foot, "I think they would have had a difficult time capturing you. You may be a healer, but you have the bearing of a warrior."

John nodded. His thoughts flickered to the Beretta, safely wedged

124

into his belt and hidden by his untucked shirt. He knew swords were no match for bullets.

Larone led them down a wide, tiled corridor. They passed several open classrooms and finally came to large double doors. Larone pulled on a thick metal handle. The door easily swung open to reveal a spacious hall filled with rows of long wooden tables and benches. Wide windows lining the outer wall allowed the fading sunlight to filter in.

The large room was deserted save for two young women who were busy transferring platters of food from a wooden cart onto a table in the far corner. Larone conducted his guests to the simple slab. Ten large chairs surrounded it.

"Please sit down. You must be tired and hungry." Larone gestured to the banquet.

John found himself sandwiched between Gaylee and Lyrista, with Mica, Garrett, and Larone opposite them. The two serving girls brought warm, moist towels so each diner could wash, then Larone began passing the food.

"Your accommodations are prepared," the dignified healer explained while they ate. "I thought the soldiers would be more comfortable staying in the barracks with their comrades." The two men nodded in agreement. "The Ladies Gayleena and Lyrista will be in the private section next to my chambers and Healer John in the guest room within my chambers."

Good. John approved. That would give the two of them a chance to speak in private.

The dining room doors opened. A lone soldier entered the hall. Using a cane for support, the man limped partway in, then scanned the room, and upon spotting the small group, hastened to join them.

Lyrista gasped when she saw the newcomer, nearly upsetting her chair as she flew from the table to meet him. "Cordon!" she cried.

"Lyrista!" His face split into a wide grin. They embraced each other fondly, then with her arm around him for support, came to the table.

"Lady Gayleena, I'd like to present my brother, Cordon," she said proudly. He tried to bow, but Gaylee quickly stopped him.

Rising, she extended her hand. "I'm honored to meet you, and wish to express my deep appreciation for everything you tried to do for my family."

Cordon took her hand, kissed it, then shook his head in protest. Before he could give voice to his thoughts, John interceded, "Please, won't you join us. We've heard great things about you. I'm John Ernshaw." He held his hand out and Cordon shook it firmly. John immediately liked the man.

After sitting, Lyrista explained to Cordon how John had helped Reese and saved Jeema. John noticed how intently Larone listened, as if hearing the story for the first time, but he knew better. He was certain that not many events happened in Esparia that Larone did not know about.

When Lyrista finished, Cordon openly appraised John. "I owe you a great deal of thanks."

"I did what I'm trained to do, but I'm glad I could help your nephew after all you've done and sacrificed for Lady Gayleena's family," John said.

"Speaking of family," Gaylee said to Larone, "what of Daenon? It's been over a week since the attack on Saylon Dorsett. What precautions are being taken to keep the western borders safe?"

"I knew of the massacre the day after it happened. Within an hour of my information, I sent two hundred volunteers to spy out Demar and eight thousand troops to reinforce the border. I have contacted the High Older at Ider Hoffle asking him to send what men he could to each of the larger border tierns of Verdure and Ramana to organize militias. Our people are constantly on guard. Several of the spies have returned. They tell me Daenon is gathering his troops well within the Deserts. He has not begun to amass them along the borders. He must surely know we are watching for him, and an invasion force would not go unnoticed, as it unfortunately did eight days ago."

Suddenly, Larone looked old. His shoulders drooped and his face filled with sorrow. "Gaylee," his voice faltered, "I am so sorry. We had no idea so many of the Elitet crossed over our borders. I would be dead myself, if not for an emergency here at Ramadine delaying my departure. It was the yearly summit meeting at the Dorsett, with the entire governing council. Now they are all dead. We did have a few hours warning, and I sent a trusted messenger to warn Haesom, but he arrived too late. The battle had already begun. The cursed night hindered my sending a carrier bird. Everything worked against us."

"I don't hold you responsible, Larone," she said gently. "No one could have foreseen that day, or that someone would betray you."

A somber mood fell on the group. "If your protectors and governing council are gone, then who's running your government?" John asked Larone.

"I am. But I cannot do it much longer. It will not take long for shock to wear off and the grieving period to end. My authority will be challenged, as it should be. I am not a legal Protector."

Little more was said. Each person had their own thoughts to contend with.

When the meal came to an end, Larone turned to Cordon. "You and Lyrista have much to talk about. Would you please show the soldiers to the barracks? I am sure Lyrista would like to accompany you." To Lyrista he explained, "Many of your former pupils have expressed concern for your safety. We heard about the attack on your party. Your wound is healing, I assume?"

126

"Yes, I've had good care." She blushed slightly.

Addressing Cordon once again, he finished, "When Lyrista is ready to retire she will be staying with Lady Gayleena in the guest rooms adjacent to my own."

With a nod of understanding, Cordon led the soldiers from the hall. Garrett asked about the regiment's meal schedule just before they exited through the main double doors.

Gaylee and John followed Larone through a small side door. "This route is closer and more private." The three of them walked in silence down a short hall that was lit by several tall, thick candles and up a flight of stairs. Turning to the right at the second level, Larone stopped in front of adjacent doors. "Gaylee, your rooms are here on the right and mine are on the left. Please come into my chambers after you freshen up." She nodded, leaving the two men in the hall.

Larone opened his door and walked in, with John right behind him. They entered a small sitting room that looked a great deal like a library. Two of the four walls were covered, floor to ceiling, with books of every size and color. Two stuffed chairs, a small square table and several candle stands, already lit, finished the simple furnishings and décor.

Visibly tensing up, Larone turned to face John. "You have every right to be angry with me," he began. "I stole the one person who meant everything to you, without warning or permission. I will make no excuses. You have seen the aftermath of what my nephew is capable of in Reese, Jeema and Cordon. I am a desperate man, desperate for my country and desperate for my people. Your daughter is the one person who can defeat Daenon." The man's entire face pleaded with John to understand.

The sincerity in Larone's voice vanquished the last of John's anger, but the frustration he felt for nearly a week came tumbling out. "Anger is not the emotion I'm feeling right now, so rest assured I'm not going to hit you, but why? Why Jessica? You say she can defeat this Daenon, but what gives you the right to make that determination? Why not Gaylee? I've come from a six day journey with Gaylee and have seen how the people respond to her. They don't even know Jessica. Why would they rally to her, she's a child?"

"She is a young woman," Larone corrected. Shaking his head, he sighed. "I cannot explain what I *feel*, but I know without her we can never win." John rolled his eyes. "John." Larone's voice took on a stern tone. "I knew Gaylee would follow Jessica. I also knew *you* would come with her."

"Me? Look Larone, don't change the subject. Jess is a kid. I've come here to bring her home."

Before Larone could respond, a sharp knock at the door begged their attention. Gaylee strode in, a concerned look on her face which melted

127

away upon seeing the two men standing together. "I'm glad there's no blood. Larone, I thought for a while John might do you bodily harm."

"And I would have deserved it." Larone pulled both of the chairs back from the wooden table in the center of the room. "Please, sit." Gaylee took the one closest to her. John shook his head, preferring to stand. With a deep sigh, Larone took the second. "John, Varnack is with your daughter. I would, and have, trusted my life to him. You have never met Anton, but trust me when I say he will find her, if he has not already done so. He is a mountain of a man, a formidable fighter with excellent instincts. When you meet him, do not let his appearance fool you, he is much more than what he seems."

"Larone, what happened to Anton?" Gaylee asked. "Lyrista told me about his wild man looks and his reclusive lifestyle. He never used to be like that."

"I do not know." Sadness filled his voice. "The change came fifty years ago, after the battle of Blue Mountain, when Segal was found dead and his forces defeated. I have asked many times what pain he carries, I feel it in him, but he refuses to answer. His work is his only true passion."

John was irritated. His few moments alone with the old gentleman were unsatisfying. The only real information Larone gave him was that he knew John and Gaylee would follow Jessica through the spiral. And that only fueled John's frustration. How could he have *known* such a thing? How could he claim to *feel* another person's thoughts from light years away? It was all a bunch of garbage. Still annoyed, John excused himself.

Lying on a comfortable bed in the guest chamber with the muffled voices of niece and uncle drifting through the closed door, John mulled over Larone's words. So he knew John would come, did he? Gaylee's homecoming was understandable, but him? What did that crafty old man have in mind? John extinguished the candles lighting his room. Yeah, Larone was crafty all right, but heaven help them all…John's gut still said to trust the old guy. He tried to clear his mind, but thoughts of Jessica, a golden Trigal hound, and transmirian spirals continued to barge their way in. After staring at the ceiling for an eternity, he finally fell asleep.

Each day that went by began with John asking Larone about Jessica. The answer never varied. "No news, but that is good." To keep sane, John kept himself busy at Ramadine. In the mornings he worked out with the soldiers, beginning his first lessons in swordsmanship alongside a batch of new recruits. There were some private lessons with Lyrista in hand-to-hand combat and dagger training. He was a little rusty, but after two sessions she could no longer beat him in hand-to-hand. However, combat use of a dagger was not his specialty and she cut him several times.

He surprised everyone, especially Cordon, by placing second in the daily archery contest. "I'm used to bows and arrows," he explained.

"Where I come from, I'm a hunter and I use a bow, not a gun."

Cordon looked at John with interest. "What is a...gun?"

John was taken aback; the word 'gun' came out of his mouth before he realized what he had said.

"It's an instrument of death." The explanation seemed to satisfy Cordon. Maybe Gaylee was right. He shouldn't introduce something new where the basic discovery had not yet been made by local scientists. He would guard his speech in the future.

The afternoons were filled with classes on Edian herbs and medicinal plants. He toured Larone's impressive laboratory where he learned how they made some of their antibiotics and medications. In turn, John taught Larone about some of those found on Earth.

One day John showed Larone his watch. "Shallenon gave me this timepiece just before she died. It stopped working in the Transmirian spiral. Gaylee thought someone here might be able to fix it?"

Turning the watch over in his hand, Larone examined it closely. "There are several fine craftsmen here who can repair this. The band is very functional, I myself, carry a daykeeper in my robe." He extracted a small, silver circlet from a pocket at his side.

"You have a watch?"

"If a daykeeper is a watch, then yes. Most men and women carry them in their pockets. Yours may be a little different from ours, but I am certain it can be made functional again."

"Great."

"I want to speak with you about Cordon," Larone said. "His wounds are healing nicely, but he still limps. Twice I have mentioned he needs to strengthen the leg, but I do not know if he completely understands the importance. He is too young."

John was surprised. He never would have categorized Cordon as being young. By earth standards, the man looked to be in his late thirty's. The shock must have shown on his face for Larone laughed, a full, deep resonating sound. "By our standards of aging, Cordon *is* young and I have found the young do not always take care of themselves as they should."

John pursed his lips. "Cordon's not much younger than me. Do you think I'm a child?"

Larone laughed again, his eyes twinkled with mirth. "Do any of us ever really grow up? I look in the mirror and an old man stares back at me. But inside, I am in my youth."

"You avoid my question; actually you have a knack for it."

"In a word...no. You are no child." He smiled, a gleam in his eye. "However, you still have far to go, but you are on the right path."

"Right path? I don't know Larone. Few minutes go by without my wondering what I'm doing here."

The older man nodded. His smile relaxed. His face reflected wisdom and patience that can only come with age. He looked at John, his eyes slightly squinting. John knew that look; he had seen it several times now. He was learning that it meant 'Wait a while longer, and you will come to understand what I already know'. The look annoyed him.

"Okay," John sighed, "I'll look at Cordon. There may be some therapy I can help him with."

"Thank you. I think he will listen to you."

Summoning Cordon to Ramadine's hospital, John examined his leg and other wounds. As Larone indicated, the various stabs and slashes were nearly healed, causing John to once again marvel at the recuperative abilities Edians had, but the leg needed work. Having been thoroughly shredded, the muscles had reknit, but the massive amounts of scar tissue lacked flexibility and needed stretching.

"You need to bring elasticity back to the muscle with some exercises I have in mind," John said.

"You sound like Larone."

"I'll tell you what, teach me some moves so I can hold my own against Lyrista's dagger, and I'll help you with your leg. I'm sure we can use some of the same actions for both purposes."

CHAPTER 13

Protectoress

The morning after the Elitets attacked, Jessica woke to bright sunlight streaming down on her through random gaps in the forest canopy. The three men in her party were already up, packed, and ready to go. She realized they had allowed her to sleep as long as she needed. "You should have wakened me, but thanks, I think I needed the extra rest." Anton and Ophir smiled, while Reese gave a single nod.

When she rose to her feet, a painful throbbing in her right side shocked her. She ignored it. She took hold of her blanket to shake out the dirt and feather needles before packing it away, but the moment she raised her arms, the throbbing spiked to a stab, tearing through her chest. Stifling a screech, she caught her breath, then gingerly felt her ribs. Unsure of the full extent of the damage, she surmised at least one, probably several, of her rib bones were cracked. *Oh no...no, no, no!*

Yesterday, all her pains blurred into one, but now, with the adrenaline rush worn off and no one needing her attention, Jessica felt every tender point in her body. She was not about to tell anyone though. Nothing could be done for cracked ribs anyway, other than wrap them...and she was out of bandages. After stuffing the dusty blanket in her knapsack, she headed for her already saddled horse.

Two of the Elitet horses were harnessed together with a blanket secured between them. Ophir and Reese lifted the wounded Varnack onto it. With Anton also injured, Varnack could no longer ride on his back. Jessica went to her furry friend.

"How ya doin?" she asked. He opened his eyes, they were full of pain. A sympathetic tear slid down her cheek. "I'm sorry I don't have any purple fern for you. At least I stopped the bleeding in fair time, you should be better soon." She reach up to stroke his fur, but shockwaves of pain rolled through her own chest.

"You're hurt!" his thoughts came to her. He tried to rise in the blanket. "You rest, I walk."

"No." This time she brought her hand up and held him down, biting her lip so as not to cry out at the sharp pangs near her right lung. "Look at your paw, you're lucky it wasn't cut completely off. You won't be able to travel on that for several days, at least. Don't make me get Uncle Anton after you."

He snickered at her weak attempt at humor. "Anton? Too weak, hurt bad."

She scratched behind his ears then turned toward Web. The captured Elitet happened to be positioned between her and Web. He sat tightly bound to his horse, a gag in his mouth. He stared straight ahead, his face calm, with every muscle relaxed. When she started toward him, he looked directly at her. His dark eyes narrowed when he focused on her face and she was suddenly grateful he was gagged.

From behind her Anton said, "The doogeroot wasn't talkin' nice, so we silenced him. If ya can't say anythin' nice, then ya shouldn't say anythin' at all."

"This guy's dangerous." She turned toward her uncle.

"Yeah," he nodded. "But, so am I."

She thought of her uncle as warm and kind, but realized he was also lean, strong, and very well trained. Yes, he could be exceptionally dangerous. The Elitet became insignificant. Yet Jessica circled wide around the prisoner. She found when she drew near him, a sick, cold feeling welled up in the pit of her stomach. When she reached her horse, she moaned. "Oh Web, how am I ever going to get up on you," she whispered. "I can hardly walk." She leaned her forehead against his large neck and rested, trying to summon up the courage to heave herself onto the animal.

"Help, J'ca." The horse whinnied, but Jessica heard the words in her mind.

"Oh, please." she whispered in astonishment. "I could use any help you could give." In response, he shifted around to nuzzle her chin with his nose.

The men, mounted on their horses, waited patiently for Jessica. Reese's lips parted in surprise when Web knelt down on his front legs and lowered his body as close to the ground as he could. Ophir's eyes grew wide at the strange sight, but Anton looked on with keen interest while Jessica carefully maneuvered into her saddle. Only after she settled onto his back did Web rise and join the others.

Jessica tried to appear cool, as if nothing out of the ordinary had just happened, but the throb in her side forced her to breathe in short, shallow gulps and she clutched at Web's mane to steady herself. When they left the small meadow, Anton followed unusually close behind her.

They rode in silence, one strictly behind another. Ophir led, picking the way northward to Ramadine. Varnack was next, followed by Jessica, Anton, the Elitet and Reese. Jessica was exceedingly grateful for the two soldiers who accompanied them. Her ability to be alert and watch for possible traps was lost in the fog of pain that she drifted into. It was all she could do to hang onto her horse. Mercifully, while the long hours passed, the pain let up. It never fully went away, but decreased to a tolerable level.

Late in the afternoon, Ophir ordered a brief rest to drink, eat, and allow the horses to nibble at the grasses growing on the forest floor. Jessica found that as long as she did not move too much, nor breathe too deeply, the pain in her side would not escalate, so she remained in her saddle.

Giving Web free rein to wander in search of food, she gazed up through the thin, feathery canopy at the sky, to the planet Ragus, forever hovering in the north. Web stopped moving and little snorts of contentment came from him as he gnawed at the plants around them.

"Find something good, boy?" Jessica patted his neck. To her delight, just to the left of where Web was tearing at a tender green shoot, she spotted a large, purple fern, just like the one she had used to heal Varnack's leg.

"Uncle Anton," she called. "Look what I found."

He pulled his horse over. A smile spread across his face when he dismounted. Using the point of his dagger, he carefully sliced the plant at its base and handed it to Jessica.

"This will help your shoulder, won't it?"

"Yeah. This aids in the healin' of any open wound. It works so fast, some think it's magic."

"Then turn around and I'll redress you shoulder." She untied the bandage and carefully inspected the hole. "It's a good thing I'm not squeamish." She broke a piece of the fern and let the white liquid sap drip into the wound. She placed the rest of the piece over the hole and retied the bandage.

"Feels better already," Anton said flexing his shoulder. "The liquid has a way of stoppin' pain."

Taking some of the fern from Jessica, Anton went to Varnack and attended to the great hound while Jessica rode over to Reese to redress his arm. She noted they were about the same height, but he seemed a few years older.

"There," she said with satisfaction, "your arm should be as good as new in a few days."

"Thank you," he responded. "I wish I had some of that plant a few weeks ago."

"Here," she held out the rest of it to him. "The past cannot be changed, but maybe this will help in the future."

"Thanks." He took the precious fern and carefully placed it in his saddlebag.

When they stopped for the night, Anton dismounted next to Jessica. Before she could move, he tenderly lifted her off of her horse. "Too bad that fern can't be used on broken bones," he tried to say quietly in her ear.

However, he made her ear ring for several minutes.

"You know!" She was shocked. "I was trying so hard not to let on. But they're not broken, only cracked, I think. Right now, everything's gone numb, so I'm doing okay." She walked over to a fallen log and gingerly sat down. Varnack limped over to sit at her side. She affectionately stroked his big head and back.

That evening the decision was made to forge a straight march to Ramadine. "It's time we let the world know Jessi's in Esparia," Anton said. "Daenon knows she's here, 'n if there are more teams of Elitet out there, our best defense will be crowd safety. We'll announce Jessi's arrival and let the people see her. They'll help protect her. The news'll go ahead of us to Ramadine that we're safe. I'm sure her dad's especially worried. I know I would be."

"If we're going to go somewhere public, then I need a bath," Jessica announced. The two soldiers stared at her in surprise.

"That may not be wise" Ophir cautioned.

"I understand," Jessica countered, "but, just the same, I can't be seen like this." She gestured to her entire body with both hands. "I can't...I just can't." She looked for help to her uncle. "Uncle Anton, please."

He heaved a deep sigh and nodded. "I guess it's a girl thing."

$$* * *$$

Morning came too soon for Jessica. She was sore and dirty. She had never considered herself a girly girl, but she would have given anything for a toothbrush.

"Just for you Jessi, we're headed to a small stream this mornin'," Anton said. "Not much water there, but hopefully enough for ya to wash up some."

"Really?" Jessica was elated.

Ophir chuckled. "I have little understanding of women, Lady Jessica, but I can appreciate the need for cleanliness. The stream is not far from here."

"Thank you. Thank you. And by the way, my name's Jessica. The 'lady' thing is too strange for me. Please, just call me Jessica and I'll call you Mister Ophir. That goes for you too, Reese," she called to him, "call me Jessica."

Reese gave her a nod and mounted his horse.

Ophir finished adjusting a strap that held Varnack's sling in place between two of the extra horses. "All right, Jessica it is, but only in private. In public, you will always be referred to as Lady Jessica. That is the title of a Protector." He swung up onto his horse. "And my name is simply Ophir."

Anton went to Varnack and stroked the animal's head. "Doin' okay?" Varnack licked his friend's hand.

"Well, ya look a lot better this mornin'." He gave Varnack one more pat, then went to Jin, the beautiful stallion who carried the big man with ease.

They rode in single file again through the soft needled forest. Jessica scanned the ground for more purple ferns, but was disappointed to reach the small stream without finding one.

Anton helped her dismount, then took Web's reins. "We'll be right over there if ya need us," he said gesturing to a spot beyond her line of vision. Ophir had already disappeared behind the row of trees and Reese was right after him.

"Thanks. I won't be long," she said. She felt foolish to make the men go out of their way for her, but the dried blood in her hair mixed with the dirt of camping out for over a week, and her filthy clothes were almost more than she could bear.

Jessica waded into the shallow brook where the deepest point came to just above her knees. Sitting down, she washed as best as she could in the refreshingly cool liquid. Her face felt sore and tender from the blow she had received and her ribs hurt with the effort of sitting, but she was clean. Closing her eyes, she lay down in the water, letting the gentle current sweep the grime and blood away.

The peaceful moment did not last long. Nausea flooded into her stomach while adrenaline pumped into her bloodstream. Jessica scrambled to her feet. The tall firs and dense underbrush were undisturbed; nothing seemed out of sorts, but her intuition was unmistakable.

Her friends were to her right, just beyond the first row of trees, yet something cautioned her to keep silent. If arrows were pointed her way, her call could mean their instant deaths. Sensing, rather than seeing her attackers, Jessica paused for one brief electric moment, then dove into the two and half-foot deep water and swam for her life, the meager current helping push her downstream. Twigs snapped behind her.

Jessica did not travel very far in the water, when the stream became shallower. She would have to make a run for it. Grabbing a fist sized rock from the stream bed she scurried out and dashed into the forest, adrenaline overcoming any pain from her ribs. She let out a piercing scream, hoping Varnack would hear it.

She could hear her pursuers closing in while she dodged trees and plowed through bushes. Her efforts to avoid capture were short lived, for two Elitet on horseback easily caught up with her. She dropped to the ground, just when they reached out to grab her, eluding them for the moment.

Pivoting around, she headed back upstream to where she hoped her uncle and the others would be. Again, she did not run very far, for one of the horsemen quickly turned his mount. He launched himself from his saddle, striking like a missile into her side, and throwing her to the ground with a crushing force. She heard the sickening crackle when three of her ribs broke.

With adrenaline's magical strength running through her veins, she slammed the rock, still in her hand, into the man's face. The force pushed him backward and Jessica kicked him off, but the second horseman rode up and the three other members of the deadly team crashed through the bushes toward her. Still on the ground, she found herself completely surrounded.

For a moment no one moved. The men stared at her, their eyes flashing daggers of hate. She knew if their orders were not so strict to bring her in alive, they would have torn her apart. Jessica's chest throbbed; she could not fight anymore. Suddenly, the distinct impression to lie down and duck flowed into her mind. *Varnack!* She curled up in a ball, with both arms protecting her head. She closed her eyes tightly. There was a menacing growl, the zing of flying arrows, the thud of falling bodies, and the clash of a single sword fight.

Jessica did not move and she did not want to look. She had seen and smelled enough of death these last two days. Someone gently picked her up.

"Uncle Anton, the ribs are definitely broken now," she whispered. "I heard them snap."

With Varnack limping along beside them, Anton carried Jessica back to their horses, leaving the grizzly clean up to Ophir and Reese. Setting her down on a fallen log, he walked over to the bound Elitet and ripped off what was left of his black shirt. With the garment completely stripped off, the tattoo of a snake's head was revealed on the Elitet's right forearm. The man's eyes were full of the same hate Jessica saw only a short time before from his compatriots. Once again, she felt grateful he was gagged.

Anton used the torn shirt to tightly wrap his niece's torso. Rummaging through her knapsack, he took the horse brush from it and gently brushed out her damp hair. By the time Ophir and Reese returned to the makeshift camp with the Elitet's horses, supplies and weapons, Jessica's hair was detangled, shining and tied into a pony tail with a piece of black cloth.

"I wanna get out of this forest," Anton said. "As soon as possible."

"I heartily agree," Ophir nodded. "Two Elitet units in barely two days are too much."

Though pale and weak, Jessica insisted on riding her own horse. The men protested, but she held her ground. "In Vorgen Hoffle, the people asked me who I was. I told them I didn't know. Well, I didn't then, but I do now."

Anton raised his eyebrows, Ophir smiled slightly, and Reese looked at her expectantly. "I am Jessica Ernshaw, Graesion and Gayleena's granddaughter, the last living blood-heir to the House of Saylon. In my veins runs the blood of Esparian heritage. Daenon thinks me a person of such import he sent at least three teams of Elitet to find me. I am a Protector of Esparia."

Ophir's smile grew, his eyes shone. Anton nodded, pride on his face. Reese bowed at the waist. "I will ride my horse, my head held high. How can I be any sort of Protector to these people if I crumble at the first injury I get? Esparians need to see their Protector, not some wimpy girl."

Anton remained close to Jessica's side while they rode. After an hour of slow, silent travel he said in the quietest voice Jessica had heard him use yet, "Impressive display back there. Do you really know who you are?"

"Yes, I do. While you brushed my hair, I went over everything that's happened since I arrived here. The people of Vorgen Hoffle, Older Tarin, Karree, Chana, the children...I came to respect them, admire them, even feel affection for them in those few days I spent there." She shook her head. "I just thought about everything, Anton, and something deep inside says I belong here. I don't understand the strange powers I feel, they scare me, but they are real. I had them on Earth, though not nearly this strong."

"Larone can help ya understand the expanse of Gonta. The sooner we get to Ramadine, the better."

It took another day before they reached a heavily traveled highway cutting through the northern tip of Feather Forest. Buggies, carriages, wagons, horses and people on foot journeyed in both directions. When the rag-tag party of two heavily armed soldiers, one huge man, a tightly bound and gagged Elitet, a limping, golden Trigal hound, and a white faced, brightly red-haired girl emerged from the forest, traffic came to a standstill. People stared in wonder. They made quite a sight, but it was to Jessica most of the stares were directed.

She met the onlookers with calm assurance. Yes, she finally knew who she was, though she had no thoughts of greatness. She would never rule, she didn't want to. However, she was a symbol for authority. In her, the protector line continued and this could inspire the people. But would they accept her? That remained to be seen.

An elderly woman, using a walking stick for support, threaded her way to the forefront of the gathering crowd. She used her cane to bully those in her pathway aside.

"Uncle Anton, look." Jessica gestured toward the old woman.

"Ophir, do ya know this lady?" Anton asked.

Silence fell on the crowd when the woman advanced to Jessica's side. She looked Jessica up and down then pursed her lips. "Finally," she said,

"You're too young to be Shallenon, but you definitely belong to Lady Gayleena."

"I'm her granddaughter, Jessica. My mother was Shallenon."

Ophir peered closely at the old woman. "Radlia," he said. She turned at her name, her eyes brightening in recognition of him.

"Ophir, my boy!" she exclaimed warmly. "How good you look."

"Lady Gayleena has come home," he told her, a blush in his cheeks.

"Yes, I've heard, but this child is unexpected!"

Jessica sat taller in her saddle and took a deep breath. "I am Jessica Ernshaw, Granddaughter of Lord Graesion Saylon, High Protector of Esparia."

"Granddaughter? Graesion? A protector? Her hair!" A buzz of excitement swept through the crowd.

Turning to Radlia Jessica asked, "How do you know my family?"

"I attended to Lady Gayleena at the Dorsett and I loved your grandmother. I've missed her these many years. I'm traveling to Ramadine to see her." Tears welled up in the woman's old eyes. "When I heard about Protector Haesom's death, I cried. Such tragedy. Then the news of Lady Gayleena's return reached my tiern and my mourning turned to joy. But seeing you…a grandchild of Lord Graesion's, my joy turns to *hope*." Her joyous voice rang out loud and clear. "A Saylon lives!" Many bystanders echoed her words.

A lump rose in Jessica's throat. Maybe, just maybe, her coming here would be useful after all.

Anton urged the horses forward and the crowd parted. Many bowed when they rode past while others still gaped at the young Protectoress. Traffic on the congested highway inched along. By the time the group reached the first hoffle, people lined the streets by the hundreds to look at the beaten and battered group.

When Gaylee traveled to Ramadine, the throngs of people cheered her. Where ever Jessica traveled, the throngs of people saluted her in respectful silence. At the first tiern they came to, Anton made one short, eloquent speech in the city square. "I am Anton, son of Paulus, of House Liedia. My companions are Varnack, the Trigal hound, Ophir, Commander of the Esparian Defense Academy at Ider Hoffle, Reese, grandson of General Gammet, and Protectoress Jessica Ernshaw, granddaughter of Protector Graesion of House Saylon, blood niece to Protector Haesom of House Saylon. She has come from far away to lead our people to victory against he who would destroy us all, Daenon of the Demarian Deserts."

Jessica did not realize at the time what impact this speech had on the people. Just the fact these famous warriors traveled in the same party was news to send hundreds of birds flying. By the time Jessica reached Ramadine, everyone in the country knew about her.

* * *

A little over a week after first coming to Ramadine, John was working out on the military training ground when he spotted Larone running full speed toward him. Out of breath, his silver hair in need of combing, he came panting up to John and Cordon. Every activity ceased on the field. All eyes turned to the stately gentleman, who at that moment looked exceedingly unstately.

"I knew…you would want to hear…the news…and I have looked everywhere…for you. Jessica is going to be all right. She is on her way here…with Anton, Varnack, Ophir and Reese…they have a prisoner, an Elitet Shield."

"A Shield!" Cordon exclaimed before John could say anything. "How did they capture a Shield?"

"I do not know. My news is limited, but they are on their way."

"Finally," John said with relief, but then, "wait a minute, what do you mean, 'Jessica is *going* to be all right'? What's wrong with her?"

"As I said, my information is not complete. Jessica is noticeably weak and hurt, but rides without assistance. Varnack limps at her side."

"I need to go to her."

"No, my friend." Larone placed his hand on John's arm. "Everywhere she goes the people salute her because of her courage and her bearing. Do not take that away from her. If anything were life threatening Anton would waste no time in seeking medical attention. They have not done so, and stop only to eat a little and sleep before continuing their journey here. Wait, and receive her with the others when they come. They are hailed as heroes. Let it be so."

Reluctantly, John agreed. "How long will it take them to reach Ramadine?"

"I estimate four, perhaps five days."

To fill those days, John threw himself into studies and training, however, that dedication was interrupted after three days when the great bell in Ramadine's Central Hall rang out. It only rang on special occasions. Out on the training field with Lyrista, they heard the clear tones. Soldiers and students left what they were doing and ran to the main square. John and Lyrista joined Larone and Gaylee in front of the lime-green Administration Building. A troop of soldiers, dressed in Esparian deep blue and silver, rode through the gateway. The silent onlookers bowed their heads when the group passed. Halting in front of the Great Healer, the leader dismounted, took a long, thin wrapped package from his horse and walked toward Larone. The soldier bowed, then turned to Gaylee and saluted her. Falling to one knee, he took the package in both hands and offered it up.

Gaylee accepted the bundle. Turning it over in her hands, she unwrapped it. When the fabric fell away, a beautiful sword was revealed. "Oh my," she gasped, and tears stung her eyes. "This is wonderful, thank you, very much. Where did you find it?"

The soldier looked at Larone, and after receiving a single nod explained, "My Lady, Healer Larone chose my comrades and I from a group of volunteers to bury all the dead from the Dorsett massacre. It took us many days, but we've finished our sad duty. We found your son, Protector Haesom, and his family already buried next to Protector Graesion. We discovered the sword hidden under many bodies in the basement of the charred remains of the Dorsett. I cleaned the blade, wrapped it, and brought it back for you."

John could see it was a magnificent weapon. Made of fine steel, the blade glittered in the sun. Three large diamond shaped crystals, perfectly clear like glass and surrounded by ornate carvings, were set into the golden hilt. Smaller rubies and emeralds accented the crystals. He guessed it was perfectly balanced, and by the way Gaylee held it, unusually lightweight.

"This is the Sword of Judgment. It was a gift to Graesion on our wedding day from Uncle Larone and Uncle Anton," Gaylee explained to John. "It belonged to their father, and was one of two sister swords handed down in our family. After Graesion died, Ophir rescued the Sword of Judgment and gave it to Haesom." Gaylee turned back to the soldier, who now stood before her. "Thank you again," and looking at the other nineteen still astride their mounts, called out, "I thank each of you."

Without hesitation, in front of the people at Ramadine, she held the sword out to John. Astounded, he hesitated. "John," she announced loud and clear, "this sword belonged to my husband and then to my son. It belongs to a member of my family and you are my son as Shallenon was my daughter. From this day forward you are officially known upon the records of this land as my legal heir. Please, accept this with my love and appreciation, John Ernshaw of the House of Liedia-Saylon."

The chirping of a bird in one of the tall trees sliced through the silence. John looked from the sword to Gaylee. He realized this to be a defining moment and that his present actions would affect the rest of his life. For an instant, time stood still. As clear as if she were standing next to him, John heard Shallenon's voice.

"Help my people, John. Help *our* people."

The sword, glistening in the bright sunlight, came back into focus. John took a deep breath and accepted the weapon.

"Thank you," he said huskily. "I'll honor the Sword of Judgment and be true to what it stands for." When his hands closed around the blade and hilt, the three crystals came to life. For many seconds they glowed brightly, encompassing John in an aura of white light.

"The sword has accepted you as its master," Larone whispered in his ear.

The crowd seemed to have sensed the enormity of the occasion also, for after John accepted the weapon, several more seconds of silence passed, then the reverence was shattered by thunderous cheers and applause.

* * *

Once more, the great bell of Ramadine rang loud and clear. It heralded the approach of some extraordinary, weary travelers. Larone, John, and Gaylee assembled in front of the door at the Administration Building. The visibly worn-out group entered the great city through the massive front gates. Jessica rode slightly ahead with Anton on her right and a limping Varnack on her left. Ophir and Reese trailed a little behind them with the captured Elitet coming last of all, the nine extra Elitet horses, gathered from the two battles, tethered to his. They moved slowly up the bricked roadway.

Every soldier they passed gave the salute of Loyalty. John stood solemn and proud. Jessica's white pants were permanently gray and torn in several places. A dark bruise on her cheek stood out against the pallor of her face. Her silk blouse was tattered and smudged with bloodstains. Anton signaled a stop when they came to the large, green colored hall. He dismounted first, then lifted Jessica from her horse and set her feet on the ground. She smiled at her father and grandmother, her head held high, a look of triumph in her eyes. She had made it.

CHAPTER 14

Family

It was late in the evening when Jessica, dressed in a white cottony nightgown borrowed from Lyrista, crawled into a soft bed with clean sheets. She had taken a hot bath with lots of soap and felt, at last, completely clean. Having refused to leave her side for the night, Varnack lay comfortably on a soft rug beside the bed. Jessica's chamber was one of three small bedrooms in the guest quarters at Ramadine. Gaylee and Lyrista occupied the other two. All three rooms opened to a small communal sitting parlor, similar to Larone's next door, only without so many books.

Jessica was exhausted, both emotionally and physically. She had been strong for her father; he would worry if she had broken down in front of him. However, when finally alone with her grandmother in the sitting room, she had crumbled into her arms and sobbed while Gaylee held her and softly stroked her head. Jessica never kept her emotions inside for very long. Allowing them to escape was her way of coping with life.

The tears had brought a cleansing effect, so now Jessica felt at peace, ready to sleep forever. Just when she snuggled into a comfortable position, a quiet tap at the door called for her attention. With Varnack close at her side, she answered the summons.

"I come bearing gifts," her father said, a wide grin on his face. He held out a neatly folded pile of clothing. "I didn't have the chance to give this to you before--too much going on, but I thought you could use these."

Folding his arms across his chest, he leaned against the door frame and watched her face while she inspected the gifts. "Oh, Dad! My jeans, my favorite polo, my green t-shirt and track sweats!" She threw one arm around him, then kissed him on the cheek. He gingerly hugged her back.

"As much as I'd like to, I can't take the credit for these. It was your grandma's idea to bring the extra clothes and Sophia picked them out. At the time, I thought both women were crazy, but I've been the designated pack mule for these, and so I get to give them to you. Now it's time you sleep, Jess. I love you." He kissed her forehead and left.

Jessica admired each garment before she laid it at the foot of the bed. She wondered what impact the new style clothing would make on Edian fashion. She could hardly wait until morning.

Sunlight poured through veiled windows when Jessica awoke to Varnack licking her hand. Opening her eyes, she moaned, "Okay. Okay. I'm awake." She longed to stay in the comfortable bed, but slid out and opened the door so Varnack could leave. She waved to Lyrista who looked comfortable in an overstuffed chair in the sitting room. The new clothes were still on the bed, exactly where she had left them. Cautious not to disturb the bandages around her ribcage that Larone had so carefully wrapped the previous night, she dressed. Choosing the jeans and designer sweatshirt, she relished every moment of putting the fresh clothes on.

"Good morning, Lyrista," Jessica said when she walked into the small common area.

"Good morning." Lyrista smiled back. "Your grandmother left early this morning. An elderly woman has come. I guess she used to be Lady Gayleena's personal maid."

"Radlia. I've met her."

"You look terrific! What are those?" Lyrista nodded at the denims.

"They're jeans." Jessica spun around. "Like 'em?"

"Very much. Now that you and Anton are here, Larone's called a meeting, but it's not until this afternoon, so we have a few hours before it starts. If it's all right, I'd like to show you around Ramadine."

"That'd be great, but first I'm starving!" As if to confirm her declaration, Jessica's stomach rumbled loudly.

Lyrista gave a light, gentle laugh. "Dining hall is this way."

* * *

Ramadine bustled with activity. Several gardeners paused from their work to nod when the young Protectoress and fourth bar officer passed by on horseback. Lyrista smiled back in response. People hustled from class to class or talked in small groups on the grass. Jessica had been to several universities before, but Ramadine was a full city and seemed magical, with its green brick pathways and shimmering pastel buildings. The morning sun reflected off the polished stone facades, making it all sparkle.

Lyrista pointed out the various science and art buildings, the business and mathematical centers, and some of the theatres and performing arts pavilions. At the bell tower they dismounted. The seven story monolith reminded Jessica of a grain silo, tall and cylindrical in shape. Stained glass windows punctuated the entire exterior clear to the bell opening at the top. A high open archway was built into the wall and Lyrista led their way through it. Sunlight beamed through the colored glass windows, bouncing rainbows of color off polished white marble walls. They entered a closet sized platform lift located in the center of the tower. Lyrista easily pulled, hand over hand, on a rope inside the compartment and the elevator ascended. "I thought this might be easier than walking our way to the top." Lyrista explained with a smile. She stopped just below the gigantic bell. They stepped onto a staircase that ran around the inside of the tower from the bottom floor to the bell level. They took the final few stairs up to an open air loft which had been built around the bell, and from this height they could see beyond the fortified walls, in all directions. To the north grew the vegetable gardens, orchards and livestock pastures, most of the houses and apartments lay to the west, and in the east were the soldiers' quarters, military stables and training fields.

It took a little over four hours to take an abbreviated tour through the City of Knowledge. The final stop was the military school.

Rounding the last of the soldier barracks, they came to a large expanse of open land. The exercise field accommodated hundreds of men. To the far right stood the military stables, three large buildings built of wood and stone. Between the stables and the field lay a complicated equestrian course, where would-be cavalrymen practiced their horsemanship. One young recruit fell from his mount when he tried to jump several bales of hay. Directly in front of them spread a large, grassy lawn filled with exercise apparatus geared to training a soldier. Men in blue pants and white tunics practiced their swordsmanship, others ran an obstacle course. Off to the left was the archery field. Jessica recognized Ophir, bow in hand, demonstrating how to accurately hit a moving target.

Lyrista spotted John beyond the swordsmen and pointed him out to Jessica. He kicked and lunged, twisted and jabbed, working on defensive moves with Cordon, so the ladies maneuvered closer to watch. Jessica assessed the changes in her father. He always tried to maintain good physical form, but three years at a desk job had taken its toll and softened him up.

Now, however, he looked well-tanned and toned. She assumed much of this was due to Cordon. When meeting Lyrista's brother the night before, she observed the easy friendship between him and her father, so she particularly took notice of him. She was impressed with Cordon's agility. His movement reminded her of her former teachers, martial arts instructors long forgotten. It was entertaining to watch her dad practice skills he had not used in many years, but after one particularly nasty blow from Cordon that he failed to deflect, Jessica decided it was time for a rescue.

"Hey, Dad," she yelled and dismounted Web. "Pretty impressive! If my ribs weren't broken I could show you a thing or two."

His eyes lit up at the sight of her and he motioned for Cordon to follow as he ran over to talk. "Saved by your yell," he said, rubbing his bruised shoulder. "You're on, Jess. When you're completely healed, I expect a firsthand demonstration. I'd like to see the results of all the money I spent on lessons for you. Lyrista, your brother's killing me."

Jessica did not miss the way her father looked at Lyrista, who had also dismounted and joined them, when he spoke with her. She had noticed the previous evening how often he glanced her way. At first she was surprised, but now she found it sweet. She truly hoped things might work out for him. She understood his loneliness, and she liked Lyrista. The woman was candid and straightforward.

"Hi, Cordon." Jessica smiled. "I see you're whipping my Dad back into shape."

"He has remarkable reflexes." Cordon slapped John on the back. "Another session or two and it'll be me rubbing a bruised shoulder."

"Well, I'll leave you to your bruises, Dad," Jessica laughed. "Lyrista has shown me some of the campus, and now I'd like to explore a little on my own."

She said good-bye to everyone and walked back to Web. Lyrista accompanied John and Cordon back onto the field. Just before mounting her horse, Jessica spotted Reese, with two soldiers, walking toward the training field. She tried to hide behind Web before he saw her, but was not swift enough. He called, "Lady Jessica, how are you doing this morning?"

She blushed, but walked over to him and his buddies. "Please don't call me *Lady* Jessica, just Jessica." She smiled at his two friends. "I'm doing a lot better, thanks."

"These are my friends, Garrett and Mica. They rode here from Ider Hoffle with your father and Lady Gayleena."

"It's nice to meet you." She shook their hands. An awkward silence followed. Finally, Jessica excused herself. "Well, I'm off to explore. I'll see you around." She nearly ran back to Web in her desire to be freed from the uncomfortable situation. *That didn't go very well. I absolutely froze.* For an instant, her thoughts turned to a boy light-years away, someone who made her feel at ease and whose presence brought a light to her eyes. *Will I ever see you again?* The thought was too unpleasant. She ruthlessly pushed it aside.

She forced the encounter with Reese out of her mind as well, and astride Web, wandered aimlessly around the campus. She checked out several of the older buildings, marveling at the architecture and ornate detail. Many looked almost ancient, yet they were beautifully preserved and still in usable condition. They stood out from the more modern structures by their darker, muted coloring and smaller sizes. Most of these roofs were not metal, but constructed of cement tiles in colors ranging from deep green to burnt amber. The flat, smooth walls were well worn with not as much floral design etched into them, but more geometrical shapes. When she explored several, she found they were used primarily as classrooms and for storage.

When she passed close to one of the six massive stables interspersed throughout Ramadine, she heard a horse yell. "No! No go." The words formed in her mind with a force that shocked her. Alarmed, for the animal was truly distressed, she stormed into the enormous barn to find the source of the protest.

"Come on Jin," someone tried to whisper. "We need to leave now."

"Uncle Anton?" Jessica half asked, half stated. "What are you doing?" He stood next to his saddled horse. Jin was loaded down with supplies.

"Are you leaving? Without saying good-bye?" She felt both confused and hurt.

"I'm sorry Jessi, but I can't stay here. I need to be on my way." Bewildered, she stared at him. "I've done my job, now it's time I get goin'."

"Uncle Anton," ignoring the dull pain in her side, she ran to him. "You can't go." Her mind raced, thinking of all the arguments she could give for him to stay. She opened her mouth to let loose the flood of words welling up inside her, but he softly placed his hand over her mouth and shook his head.

"I need to go."

Panic swelled in every cell of her body. How could he leave? She had just found him...Her uncle, someone she trusted, a blood relative when she thought there were none left. Family meant everything to her and here was another one slipping away. There were no Ernshaws left. Her dad was an only child, orphaned at fifteen. Her mother was gone, Haesom and his family were gone, and now he was leaving her too?

"No!" she squeaked, pushing his hand away. Her voice had gone hoarse. "Why? Just tell me why?"

He refused to meet her gaze.

"Did I do something wrong?" She felt sick, trying to remember the journey to Ramadine. "I'll try not to be a burden, I'll try..."

"Jessi, no!" He looked horrified. "It's not you, not at all. It's me...I don't deserve...I can't get close...It's too hard." His shoulders slumped. His voice dropped in defeat. "It hurts too much."

The pain in his eyes jolted her out of her own self-pity. She felt his intense sadness, and then she felt his fear. That surprised her. Yes, she could feel his fear and she understood it. She knew it as she had lived it herself after her mother's death... the black hole in the center of the soul. Maybe understood it better than he understood it himself, but she had faced her fear, her loneliness, her intense sadness, and conquered it. He was still struggling, drowning in his own mental anguish.

Placing her hand on his arm, she spoke softly. "I know what you're doing." His eyebrows arched in question. "You're running away...not from actual responsibility or tasks, but from us, from people." When he turned away, she knew she was right. "You've been hurt, right down to the center of your being. I don't know how, when, or by whom, but it went deep. I know your ache, I've been there and it comes because you cared so much. Someone once told me deep anguish is directly proportional to profound love, and it's true. You're avoiding being injured again…by avoiding those you care about or *might* care about…your family, your friends, people in general and as a whole. All of these years, you've been alone, pushing everyone away, building your walls. You think if you don't feel, then you can't have those feelings hurt."

Staring at the ground, he shuffled his feet, but remained silent. "After my mom died I wanted to shut the entire world out. I hurt so badly that for a while I wanted to die myself, just to stop the pain. But, I didn't die, I had to live and cope with my loss. There was nowhere for me to run, so I decided to build thick walls around my heart. I thought if I didn't let anyone close to me, I couldn't ever be hurt again, but I was wrong. I would never be completely alive until I faced my feelings and dealt with them. On a conscious level I could maintain my wall, but when I slept, my pain came crashing through."

At this, he gave her a hard look. "Uncle Anton," her hold on his arm tightened, "the only way you can deal with your pain is to face it and allow the love of other people to heal you. When you let someone in, when you let many people in, you build a strong support group. If, for some reason, one of them fails you, the others will still be there. Uncle, I always wanted to be part of a large family, but that wasn't possible. For so many years it has been just my Dad and my Grandma and me. But now there are more of us, there's you and Uncle Larone. Since I've found you both, I won't lose either of you. I will hang on to you with everything I have."

She gripped both of his arms. "It's time to come home, Uncle Anton. Grandma has come home, I've come, even my Dad is here, now you must come too. There's such a thing as being too alone. Come home and allow the love of your family to bring you peace."

He sighed long and deep. "You don't know what yer askin'."

"Yes, I do." Her voice remained firm. "I'm asking you to rejoin the human race and that takes a lot more courage than it does to run away. Come home, Uncle. We need you. *I* need you."

His arms hung limply by his sides, his shoulders still slouched. After many quiet minutes, he finally straightened. "I will stay." The promise was barely audible.

Coming forward from the shadows of the stable door, Larone rushed to his younger brother, tears streaming down his cheeks. When the two men embraced, Jessica realized she now intruded on a very private moment. She left the brothers alone and went to find her grandmother.

* * *

The sun was long set when the family, accompanied by Ophir, Lyrista, Cordon and Reese, gathered in Larone's office, a small room with a cluttered desk and two scrawny potted plants flanking each side. A large map of Esparia hung from one wall. The others were bare. More chairs had been brought in for the meeting, making the room especially cramped. Varnack managed to squeeze in and sat at Jessica's feet.

Larone appraised those gathered. "I apologize for the lateness of the hour. I scheduled this meeting for the afternoon, but I have been waiting for the return of two important ambassadors and they have yet to arrive. However, we can postpone no longer. My friends, in this room sit the new leaders of Esparia." John frowned. "Our military leadership now rests with Ophir and Cordon. Our governmental leadership returns to the Protector line of Saylon." Larone paused. "John?"

John raised his chin.

"You're a military man. Have you given any thought as to what you would do if you led our people into battle?"

"What are you getting at, Larone?" John asked, suspicion in his voice.

"Just a 'what if' question, John. I would like to know your opinions on the subject." Larone waved his hand as if to dismiss the matter altogether. "We need to begin…" A knock at the door interrupted the meeting.

"Come in," Larone called.

A short, middle-aged man of medium weight and build walked in. He sported a thin, light brown mustache and his scant amount of long, blond hair was pulled back in a thin ponytail. Surprise showed on his face when he looked upon the group, then shock when his eyes fell on Gaylee, but he bowed to Larone and crossed the room to him.

"Ah, Quirt. You have returned at last. I almost sent a search party after you," Larone smiled kindly at the man.

So this is Quirt. He looked nothing like Jessica had pictured and she took an instant dislike to him. *I don't trust him. I'm surprised Uncle Larone does.*

"I was delayed in Marone," the gravel-voiced man explained. A wisp of smoke twirled from his mouth. It coiled above his head and slowly disappeared. Jessica knew she was the only one to see the smoke, for she was the only one who knew he had just lied.

Larone explained to those in the room, "I sent Quirt as an ambassador to our northern neighbor, Marone. I asked for their aid in our fight against Daenon. If he succeeds in taking over Esparia, it will only be a matter of time before he turns on Marone. So Quirt, what was their answer?"

Quirt looked miserable. He shook his head. "They've refused to involve themselves with our internal matters. Thus my delay, I spent a great deal of time trying to convince them to help us, but they're still upset about Naydeen and refuse to believe her child would attack them."

Jessica's insides churned. She could almost smell the foul vapors as they spilled from his lips. She glared at him. "Liar," she breathed. Varnack looked up at her. Jessica briefly met his eyes and instantly communicated her feelings.

Larone frowned. Jessica wondered if he too realized the man did not speak the truth. Unwilling to take any chances, she opened her mouth to speak, but another knock at the door interrupted them. A second courier had just arrived from his ambassadorial mission to the south.

"Good to see you, Keran. Please wait for me in the conference room across the hall," Larone ordered. Turning to the others he announced, "I know we have barely begun, but let us adjourn our meeting until tomorrow after breakfast. I need time to obtain details from Quirt and Keran before I can give you a complete picture of our situation. Good night." With that, he abruptly left the room. Quirt followed him, then Varnack followed Quirt.

With the meeting dismissed, the group members went their separate ways. In the hall Jessica managed to speak to her father alone. "Dad, that Quirt guy lied."

"What?"

"He was lying. He never went to Marone."

"You're absolutely certain? That's a pretty strong accusation with serious ramifications."

"Come on, Dad. You know me. Have I ever, even once, been wrong about liars?"

They walked together in silence, until they reached their rooms. "It makes sense Jess, that's why Larone looked so astonished."

"And why Varnack followed Quirt," Jessica agreed. "I told Varnack about the lies. He's protecting Larone now."

John nodded. "I'll wait up for Larone and tell him about your insight. We'll get to the bottom of this, I promise." He kissed her cheek. "Good night, sweetheart."

Jessica went into the guest chambers where Gaylee and Lyrista were already preparing for the night. "Grandma," she called. Gaylee appeared at a bedroom door.

"Yes, Jess?"

"Quirt wasn't telling the truth."

Lyrista's poked her head out from her open doorway. "What was that?"

"Quirt lied about Marone refusing to help us. He never stayed there. I don't think he ever even went there," Jessica shook her head. "I told my Dad, so he's going to wait up for Uncle Larone and talk to him about it. Lyrista, I always know when someone is lying. It's just something I've always been able to do."

Lyrista gazed steadily at Jessica, then nodded her head. "That's quite a gift. I'm bringing you along next time I interview one of my soldiers."

Gaylee gave Jessica a goodnight hug. "Don't worry dear. Your father and Larone will know what to do. Now let's get some rest."

Slumber did not come quickly for Jessica. A nagging feeling something was wrong kept her tossing and turning. She tried to pinpoint the suspicion, and finally decided Quirt had upset her more than she originally thought. At last, she drifted off into a fitful sleep.

Jessica jolted awake when someone yanked her out of bed. A crushing arm went around her waist and a smothering hand pressed down on her mouth. She tried to twist out of the hold, but was squeezed even harder. Pain stabbed through her chest, causing her to nearly pass out. Being dragged from the guest chamber, she noticed a cobra head tattoo on the bare arm of her attacker. The Elitet? But he should be in a prison! *Dad,* she screamed in her mind. She could hardly breathe, the hand clamped so tightly over her nose and mouth. *Dad, help!* Was her last conscious thought.

* * *

John awoke in a cold sweat, his heart raced, his pulse pounded in his ears. He had fallen asleep in a sitting room chair while waiting for Larone, and tried to clear his foggy brain. The glass candle lamp on the table still burned and cast an eerie glow around the room. He remembered the night Jessica was pulled through the Transmirian spiral. No! Not again!

Bounding in four strides to his room, he grabbed the first weapon he saw, the sword Gaylee had presented to him. It stood against the wall next to his bed. Gaylee had insisted he unload his gun and hide it away. She had taken the bullets for it, removing all temptation to use the firearm. Her resolve to keep new technology hidden before it was logically discovered had been annoying, but now it was stupid. He cursed her under his breath, then cursed himself for having listened to her. John was not a good swordsman, but the weapon was well balanced and felt good, almost natural in his hand.

Dashing into the hall, he noticed the door to the women's guest chamber wide open. He ran in, straight to Jessica's open door. In the pale light he could see she was gone. *NO!* Racing from the room, he fought the panic in his stomach. Flying down a staircase, three steps at a time, he bolted through the building and out the front doors. He stopped at the main road, his eyes searching the deserted street. The two moons shone down on the campus, their light adequately illuminating the area. Spotting shadowy movement in front of the nearest Mathematics Center, he chased after it; unsure if what he saw was even real. When he rounded the building, nothing suspicious lay in sight. *Come on, Jess. Come on.* He stood motionless. Closing his eyes, he strained his other senses. He had never believed in the ability to *feel* things. Gaylee and Larone were constantly alluding to their psychic power and it was all he could do to keep his skeptical comments to himself. But now, with each second pounding at him with the weight of a mountain, he wished that he had the same gift. He bowed his head. He listened. The sword in his hand grew warm, so warm he opened his eyes to stare at it. The crystals in the hilt pulsed with life, blazing bright white in the handle. Stables! The word flew into his mind with such force it nearly knocked him over. Running full out, he flew through the deserted streets of Ramadine. The huge barn was just ahead. Roaring Jessica's name, he burst through the wide double doors.

CHAPTER 15

Traitors and Spies

An Elitet held the unconscious Jessica over his bare shoulder. He was poised to mount a saddled horse. Seeing John, the kidnapper dropped his prisoner and pulled a sword from his saddle sheath. Jessica moaned. For an instant, the two men stared in hatred at each other, then the Elitet flew into action.

John's knowledge of sword fighting consisted primarily of the lessons he had taken during his short time at Ramadine. Swordsmanship was a daily training class, and he had progressed well beyond intermediate level, but Cordon had not yet shown him the finer points of using the blade. The only time John ever used a similar weapon was at West Point, where he took a fencing class. There he won first place in a novice tournament, but fencing uses a delicate foil, not a bulky glaive. Fortunately, the Sword of Judgment felt lightweight and perfectly balanced. This was the first time John had actually handled it and now his life depended on making no mistakes.

Jess. Must win for Jess. He parried the furious blows as best he could, grateful the Elitet was weak from his self-imposed fast. John realized that if his opponent had been in good condition, he would have finished him off in minutes.

John battled the trained warrior, receiving many nicks and slices, but managing to avoid the deadlier thrusts. His adrenaline pumped strength into his arms and helped him focus on the flashing steel. Several times the crystals in his sword of Judgment glowed and each time they did, his hand moved as if with a mind of its own, each move blocking a potentially life taking strike. John was constantly on the defensive. He was able to hold his ground for a blow or two, but then needed to back away from the deadly blade thrusts.

He twisted around a vertical support beam, his opponent's sword gouging out a chunk of the wood after a quick downward slash. Three more lunges were parried, then John nearly fell over dodging a blow to his neck. He began to tire, the adrenaline receding from his system. The Elitet gave him no openings.

Suddenly the move that won him the fencing tournament so many years before came flashing into his memory. Gripping the sword with both hands he awkwardly performed the maneuvers meant for a fencing match: parry right, feint left, riposte and lunge. The bizarre tactic seemed to take the Elitet by surprise for he briefly let his own blade dip. It was the edge John needed and he plunged the tip of the razor sharp Judgment deep into the Elitet's left breast; the terrible fight was instantly over. The man gaped at him in astonishment before crumbling lifeless to the ground.

Air came in huge gasps as John stared at the motionless form on the floor. For all of his military training, he had never deliberately killed anyone in hand to hand combat and now, with the adrenalin all but gone, he understood the responsibility of what he had just done. He did not regret taking the Elitet's life, but he would never forget what had just transpired.

The stable doors crashed open behind him and at the sound he whirled around, raising his weapon to a defensive angle. Two soldiers ran through the doors, but halted when they saw John. They stared at the fallen Elitet. John lowered his weapon.

"Mica," he panted. We need to find out what happened at the jail. How'd the prisoner escape!" Mica nodded and left at a run. "Garrett, take this thing out of here," John gestured at the fallen body. The soldier dragged the fallen Elitet out through the stable doors.

Dropping his sword, John rushed to Jessica. The pain in her eyes infuriated him. "How did that killer get free?"

As if the question were directed to her, Jessica shook her head. "I don't know," she whimpered. She described to her father, in halting breaths and between the throbs of pain, how she was hauled out of bed and passed out.

Moments later, heavy footsteps outside the barn door announced Anton's arrival. He barreled through the stable doors, sword in hand and ready for a fight. After a moment's hesitation, while he took in the scene before him, he sheathed his weapon, then grabbed a horse blanket and two brooms. He made a crude stretcher out of them and helped John lift Jessica onto it.

Larone reached the stable doors just when they were exiting. "I've made the healing station ready," he told John while they walked. "Lyrista found the prison guards. One is alive. Barely, but alive. He needs your immediate attention; Lyrista is transporting him as we speak. The other was not so fortunate. They were both stabbed in the back."

John was grim. "I sent Mica to investigate what happened there."

"You're wounded," Larone observed.

John checked his arms and chest. Blood oozed from the many cuts he had received, others were already staunched by coagulation. He briefly wondered how many would require stitches. In the heat of battle he had never felt any of them. "I'll be fine. You can take care of me later."

Once at the infirmary, he left Jessica in Larone's capable hands. Lyrista was waiting at the surgery door, pacing the floor, her face flushed with worry. "You're okay. What about Jessica?"

"She'll be fine, Larone has her."

Visibly relieved, she offered, "Let me help you. The soldier in there was a student of mine and I've never been good at sitting around. It nearly killed me to wait while you worked on Reese."

"You're okay with blood?"

"I've drawn it enough times on an opponent, you included. I think I can handle it."

"All right, grab some soap."

* * *

"Uncle Larone." Jessica grimaced. She sat on a table in a small examining room, while her uncle treated the battered ribs. "What's the Salupathic Gift?"

"It is the ability of one being to pour their life force into another. It cannot bring back the dead, but it can bring healing to one on the brink. Why do you ask?"

Jessica recounted the experience at Vorgen Hoffle. She told him every detail, every feeling as she healed Brayon's many wounds and brought the spark of life back into his heart."

He listened intently, with no facial expressions betraying his thoughts. "So you were only incapacitated for two days afterward?"

She nodded.

"You were very fortunate."

"If it's my life force I'm giving, then could this gift shorten my life?" The thought frightened her.

"No, my dear. However," his voice suddenly became stern, "I must caution you that you can give your entire life force to save someone, which *would* result in your death."

"Karree seemed to know quite a bit about this ability. Do many people have it?"

"It is not as rare as many think. Most people do not realize they have the gift, mainly because they have never needed to use it. Others may have experienced brief moments when they have felt the power, but it frightened them, and so it goes undeveloped. Most of our healers have the gift, to some extent at least, but few can do what you did."

"You can."

Larone smiled. "Yes."

"There's one other thing I need to tell you. Quirt lied when he claimed the people of Marone refused to help. He also lied when he said he stayed there and tried to convince them to change their minds."

Larone finished wrapping her ribcage in silence. When he finished he sighed, "I thought as much. Certain of their support, I was stunned at their refusal. I realized he could not be telling the entire truth."

Walking to the door, he called out, "Anton, please come in."

Anton and Varnack came into the examining room, with Gaylee close behind. Varnack licked Jessica's hand.

"Jessica, tell Anton what you just told me about Quirt." Stroking Varnack's head she told about her first impressions of Quirt and the lies he had told.

Anton rumbled, "I knew there was a spy...a traitor here, but who'da guessed the doogeroot was Quirt?"

"Who exactly is Quirt?" Gaylee asked.

"He has been with me since the Battle of Blue Mountain," Larone explained. "He saved my life. He asked me to train him; he desired to be a healer. To his great disappointment, he did not have the gift, but he has been a tremendous help these many years and a trusted friend. The thought of his treachery is unbelievable."

"Maybe he has a good reason for lying about Marone," Jessica suggested half-heartedly.

"We'll find out," Anton assured her. He reached over and picked her up.

"Uncle Anton, I have three broken ribs, not two broken legs."

"Yeah, well...that's fine, Jessi."

She shot an appeal to her grandmother, but Gaylee only smiled. Leaving the examining room, they made their way to the surgery area to wait for John. They found Ophir, Cordon, and a third officer, someone Jessica had never seen before, already there. This waiting area was the section of wide hallway next to the surgery door, where a few wooden benches lined the bare walls.

"No information yet," Cordon said. He introduced the officer as Ballian, the Commander of Ramadine's Defense Academy. The older man was smartly dressed in a pressed blue and silver uniform, polished boots and shining sword. She could not help but notice how brilliantly his sword glittered in the lamplight. It had a single enormous ruby set in the hilt. The stone was blood red.

Larone went into the operating room. While he was gone, Anton requested Jessica tell her story once more for Ophir and Cordon. When she finished, Ophir left without a word.

Commander Ballian was a quiet man, who kept to himself in the corner. Jessica continuously glanced his way. He made her feel uneasy, though she had no explanation as to why. *Cordon seems to like him, but I'm sure glad Uncle Anton's here.*

155

"Uncle Anton, what's a doogeroot? I've heard you use that expression several times now."

Anton blushed. "Well...um," he stammered and looked to Gaylee for help.

"You're on your own for this one, Anton," she laughed.

"Jessi, it's a...uh. It's a plant that grows in animal...uh...stuff." Again, he appealed to Gaylee.

"It's a plant that thrives on animal excrement," Gaylee offered. "Anton uses the word as a profanity."

"Ohhh," Jessica nodded.

The door to the surgery opened and Larone stepped through. "John is nearly finished. The guard has an excellent chance of pulling through." Ballian seemed pleased and excused himself to relate the good news to the rest of his men. Relief flooded through Jessica when he turned a corner and was gone from sight.

"It was interesting to watch your father work as I worked on him. He did not flinch once as I stitched his wounds while he operated on the young guard," Larone commented to Jessica. "He has certainly proved himself. I don't think there is one man here who would not follow him now. He has shown himself to be an expert archer, a natural swordsman and a master healer." Jessica felt a surge of pride. Coming from Larone, this was no small compliment.

John and Lyrista walked out of the surgery a half hour later. John looked haggard, but was hopeful with how things had gone. He had nothing but high words of praise for Lyrista as a surgical assistant. "She anticipated my every need during the operation. I could not have asked for a better nurse."

Cordon grinned at his little sister, blatant admiration on his face. She too had a glow about her.

"You okay, Jess?" The crow's feet around John's eyes deepened with concern.

"I'm okay, Dad, honestly. Uncle Larone gave me some great painkiller. I'm just sleepy."

"I think each of us had better take some much needed rest," Larone suggested. "Let us meet in the morning, right after the breakfast bell. The conference center across the hall from my office would be a better room. I think we were too cramped in mine." No one objected.

Lyrista reached for Cordon's arm. "I don't know this commander Ballian very well. He left Ider Hoffle Academy shortly after I arrived there, so come with me. I want to visit the barracks, and personally reassure the men that their friend will be all right." He nodded and together they left through the main corridor.

"I have a few things I wish to finish here." Larone stated. "I will be along presently." He walked back into the surgery.

Anton handed the Sword of Judgment to John. "I went back to the stables while Larone was fixin' Jessi and got it. Didn't trust no one else."

"Thanks. I didn't mean to leave it."

"Dad," Jessica admired the sword, "tell me about this weapon. It's beautiful." She ran her hand over the blade and fingered the crystals in the hilt. "Are these diamonds?"

Varnack accompanied Gaylee, Anton, John, and Jessica back to the main building where their quarters were located. While they walked John told his daughter about the brief ceremony when the soldiers returned from burying their comrades at the Dorsett and of his public adoption into the House of Saylon. "This is called the Sword of Judgment. Your grandma mentioned it was one of two sister swords passed down for generations in her grandfather's family," he finished.

"Yeah." Anton rubbed his beard. "This one's a warrior's weapon, meant to go from father to son, but Larone and I aren't true warriors and neither of us has sons, so it was only right we gave it to Graesion, then to Haesom, and now to you, John. Ya proved tonight yer worthy of it." He clapped John firmly on the back. "Those aren't diamonds, Jessi, they're white persite."

"So this is the sword that Daenon so desperately wanted. Haesom's last act was to deny him access to it," Jessica remembered.

"What happened to the other sword?" Gaylee asked.

"Dunno," Anton shrugged. "It wasn't meant for warfare…Was called the 'Sword of Mercy'. As I remember the story, it was forged at the same time as this one," he indicated the weapon in John's hand, "but it's a lot more delicate and as the steel cooled, it was sprinkled with diamond dust, so it glitters from every angle when the light hits it."

They reached the lime-green building and stopped before the doors. "I only saw it once, when I was a little boy. It truly was beautiful and the light danced off it, but my Dad wouldn't let me touch it. He told me it held some sort of power, but it's all pretty hazy in my memory. Larone doesn't even know what happened to it. Well, goodnight."

Morning came swiftly. Varnack had spent the night as guard at Jessica's door. When she slid off the bed to let him out of the room, she was pleasantly surprised to find she still felt no pain. *Uncle Larone's medicine is great stuff.* She dressed swiftly, then joined Gaylee and Lyrista for breakfast in the sitting room. Larone had ordered white bread, butter, honey, milk and several pieces of a pink, round fruit to be sent to their chambers.

Smelling the soft fruit, Jessica asked, "What's this?"

"Taya." Gaylee put emphasis on the second syllable. "It's tart, but not so much like a lemon that it'll make you pucker. Try it, I bet you'll like it."

Jessica bit into the juicy ball. "Hmmm. It's almost like a tangy banana flavor." Juice dripped down her chin.

Lyrista handed her a cloth. "Don't eat too much; it can really make you want to go to the bathroom…a lot." Her light laughter filled the room.

The morning bell rang, its high tone a dramatic difference from the rich baritone quality of Ramadine's great assembly bell.

The conference room was much larger than Larone's humble office, but just as bereft of decoration. A window on the far wall, framed with dark green drapes, allowed the sun to flow in unchecked. The bare, wooden floor was well worn and in need of a good refinishing. Two small round tables with five chairs surrounding each were the only furnishings.

Ophir was already there with Quirt, bound hand and foot, next to him. Larone, Varnack and Anton entered after the women, with John, Cordon and Reese not far behind. When Reese walked in he hurried over to Jessica. "Your father has been telling me about last night. Are you all right?"

"Yes, thank you." His concern surprised her and she felt her cheeks flush.

Once everyone was seated, Ophir took charge. "Last night, after Jessica told us about Quirt, I went to find him. If he was innocent, then he would understand. If he was guilty, he needed to be stopped from doing more harm. I found him in a stable, saddling his horse, but he came quietly."

"Untie him," Larone requested. Quirt looked uneasy, barely able to remain calm.

"Quirt, my friend," Larone's voice was soft, "you have some explaining to do. Jessica will notify us of any untruths you may tell. Let us begin with your mission to Saylon Dorsett. Did you reach General Gammet?"

Quirt rubbed his wrists with shaking hands. "Yes, I did."

"What did you tell him?"

"That a force of a thousand Elitet rode to destroy him and all who lived at the Dorsett, but I arrived too late. The attack came before he could adequately organize his forces. I told you, everyone died."

"Not everyone," Cordon snapped. "You are looking at a survivor of that battle."

"Two survivors," Reese intoned just as icily as his uncle.

All color drained from Quirt's face.

"How much time did you tell General Gammet…my *father*, that he had before the attack was to start," Cordon demanded.

Quirt remained silent.

"Answer him," Lyrista sternly commanded.

"Three days."

158

Cordon's chair fell over when he bolted to his feet. "Three days!" he bellowed. "We only had hours! You deliberately lied to him. You betrayed us all. How did you know our defenses so well? How…" He quieted down when John placed a hand on his arm.

"You knew they only had a short time," Larone shook his head in disbelief. "*Why* did you tell Gammet he had three days?"

"They captured me before I arrived at the Dorsett," Quirt choked. "They promised if I cooperated, I would be spared when the attack came. They were very convincing, Larone." His eyes darted from Cordon to Reese, then back to Larone. "They gave me money and told me never to return to Ramadine, but I did anyway, to tell you about Haesom's death. When we met and you gave me a new assignment, I was terrified. I went to the east coast instead of Marone. I don't know what happened to me," he bowed his head and shook it. "Those Elitet and Addex." Jessica flinched at the name. "These last two weeks, I've done some deep, inward searching and I decided to come back."

Larone looked to Jessica. She nodded, "He's telling the truth."

Quirt stammered at Cordon, "Believe me. I knew n…nothing about your defenses. I'm not a military man. I don't even know w…what you're talking about. I told Gammet he had three days instead of three hours, but I betrayed nothing else. I s…swear. How can I betray something I know nothing about?"

"You were trying to leave when I found you," Ophir cross-examined. "Why?"

"Why? You ask me why?" his voice was becoming hoarser by the minute. "I heard the Elitet was loose. I wasn't about to stay around and let him kill me!"

"Kill you?" John shot back. "He wasn't after you, he wanted Jessica."

For the first time Quirt looked directly at the girl. "Wanted you, but why? You're nothing but a child. Granted, you have red hair, but the Lady Gayleena is the real power here. You're nothing. Why would an Elitet be interested in you?"

Jessica felt thoroughly offended, but before she could say anything John stated matter-of-factly, "You didn't free the Elitet."

Quirt gaped at John, "I may be a coward and a deserter, but I'm no fool. I'd never free an Elitet! Those guys are crazy."

There was stunned silence and it was Gaylee who finally voiced each of their thoughts, "There is someone else. A second traitor is in our midst."

"But who?" Lyrista asked.

"Maybe I can help answer that question," a male voice from behind offered. This unexpected interruption startled every one and together they turned to see a rugged, travel worn man standing in the doorway. Heavily armed and in need of a shave and bath, his torn clothes were caked with dried blood from several deep cuts on his chest and arms, but he stood tall with his hands clasped behind his back.

"Lepsis!" Larone sprang to the man's side and placed an arm around his shoulder. "Come, sit down. You are wounded."

"Nothing too serious." Lepsis closed the door behind him. He shot Quirt a menacing glance.

Ophir jumped to his feet and drew his sword. Anton also stood, staring at the newcomer, but his weapon remained where it was.

"Sheath your sword Ophir, Lepsis is a friend." Larone soothed. "We have been in communication for many years now. How do you think I obtained the information to warn Gammet at Saylon Dorsett of the Elitet's attack?"

"I risked everything to send that information in time to save those people," Lepsis fumed. "Because of this worm," he motioned to Quirt, "it was all for nothing." His green eyes were cold, full of anger.

Cordon, still on his feet from threatening Quirt, offered the man his chair. "I served at the Dorsett. I'm Cordon, Gammet was my father."

"Not was...is. He's still alive." Lepsis sat heavily in the offered chair. He removed his bow and quiver and let them fall beside him. Cordon's face went ash gray and Lyrista gasped. "That's one reason I've come. The other is to warn you there is another traitor here, worse than this maggot," he gestured again at Quirt, "but I see you've figured that out on your own. I also can't stomach being around Daenon any more, fifty years is long enough."

Anton walked over to the man and pulled him upward into a huge bear hug. "Lepsis m' boy, yer the exact image of yer sister. How are ya son?"

Lepsis was visibly shaken. His hard exterior fell for a moment and a vulnerable, sensitive man stood there, but he certainly was not a boy, he was older than John.

"It's been an interesting life, Anton."

"Tell those in this room, who do not know you, a little about yourself," Larone prompted.

Lepsis looked at those seated around him. "I'm a prince of Marone. When my mother died I came to live with my sister Naydeen, wife to Segal. I hoped Daenon would be the brother I never had." He shook his head and sat back down in the chair. "I was fifteen when Segal and Naydeen died. I made the decision to stay with Daenon, hoping to continue my sister's efforts at making amends for what Segal had done, but it was too late. By the time Daenon reached fourteen he was already like his father. The most I could do was try to control the damage he did. I think...I hope anyway, I did some good while I lived at Rendaira. About ten years ago I contacted Larone. I knew Daenon was gearing up for an attack and I've been keeping Larone informed on each new development. I'd still be there, but when Quirt was caught trying to warn Gammet, Daenon knew he was betrayed. I barely escaped. There've been a couple Shields on my trail the entire way here. It's a good thing your sentries knew my name and let me in."

Jessica felt both compassion and respect for this man. She recognized her own thoughts reflected in her father's face and knew he would be Lepsis' friend.

"You said my father is alive," Lyrista barely whispered, her pale face a mask of calm.

"Yes. He's being held at a high security prison in the Snow Peak Mountains. That was the last information I acquired before escaping."

"You also claimed you could help us find the spy," Ophir reminded him.

Lepsis leaned forward on his chair. "He's a military man, someone who knew every detail of the Dorsett's defenses. I never saw the man's face, only caught a glimpse of him when they sneaked him into Rendaira after the battle to receive his reward. He wore a blue and silver uniform and carried a sword. I remember the sword quite well, very unique. The biggest, blood red ruby I've ever seen was imbedded in the hilt."

For one electric moment Cordon locked eyes with Ophir then they dashed from the room at the same instant. Lyrista was only a step behind and the others quickly followed. They ran to the main entrance.

"Garrett," Cordon yelled towards one of the lofty guard towers that flanked the front gates. "Have you seen Commander Ballian?"

"Yes," he hollered back. "He left Ramadine a short time ago, just after that man came." Mica pointed to Lepsis who brought up the rear of the posse.

"Aaauuugggghhhh!" Cordon threw his hands up in the air. "So close, and he slips through our fingers!"

"Larone," Ophir spoke up. "Word must be sent to every outpost that Ballian is a traitor. He needs to be taken, dead or alive."

"I'll do it," Reese offered and ran toward the Red Feathers Center.

One by one the exasperated leaders turned back to the Administration Building with Jessica and Lepsis being the last to move. She continued to stare down the road from the open front gates. "How maddening," she mumbled to herself. "It would have been one less headache to have that guy in prison." When she turned to follow an already retreating Lepsis, a nearly overwhelming wave of nausea hit her. Not again! In a split second she ran at full speed, straight for Lepsis. Catching him completely off guard, she tackled the large man, throwing him to the ground with a loud thud. A well-aimed arrow whizzed past Lepsis as he fell, narrowly missing his head.

"Commander Ballian?" a surprised soldier just outside the main gate queried in complete astonishment. The sound of a retreating horse, galloping away at full speed was barely heard.

Cordon yelled at group of nearby soldiers. "Go after him! Commander Ballian's a traitor!" The soldiers grabbed their tethered horses and galloped out the gates.

"Perhaps we better start exposing Ballian's treachery here, with our own troops," Larone, who came running up with Ophir suggested. The old warrior nodded.

Anton reached Jessica first and gently picked her up. "I told you I needed you, Uncle Anton," Jessica smiled through the pain in her chest, "it just wouldn't feel right for someone else to scoop me off the ground."

John helped Lepsis to stand. "I'm John Ernshaw. And this little powerhouse is my daughter, Jessica." To her he asked, "Are you all right? How are the ribs?"

"Well, Uncle Larone's pain killer has definitely worn off, but I had a soft landing. I think I'm okay."

"Lepsis, I'm a healer. Let me take care of those cuts, you're bleeding."

"The fall must have opened some of them." Lepsis inspected his arm. "My death would have been quite a trophy for Ballian. Thanks to you, Lady Jessica. You saved my life." He squinted down the road, out the open main gate. "You have excellent eye sight, to spot someone with a bow aimed in here."

"Oh, I didn't *see* anything, I *felt* it." The explanation tumbled out before she thought about what she was saying and she instantly regretted it.

"You *felt* that Ballian was aiming at me?" Lepsis cocked his head.

Jessica moaned. "No...I, ugh...I didn't know exactly where the danger came from, just that it existed. It's hard to describe, it's not a very pleasant experience." She did not want to talk about it. She herself barely understood the physical aspects of the warnings, and she had no idea as to why they happened. However, she saw her friends and family were waiting for her to continue the explanation. Larone seemed particularly interested.

"From nowhere, a horrible feeling comes over me. A foreboding or type of terrible premonition, then there's this almost overpowering urge to throw up. This is only the fourth time it's happened, so I don't know all the fine points yet. How did I know you were the specific person in danger?" she shrugged her shoulders, "I just knew. I *felt* it. It doesn't sound very scientific, but that's how it works."

She looked at her dad, waiting for a sarcastic remark to her pitiful explanation. To her surprise he nodded. "I believe you, Jess."

CHAPTER 16

Acceptance

After John and Larone tended to Lepsis's wounds, the council meeting resumed in the modest conference room. Jessica noted Quirt's absence, but Lepsis joined them. He had exchanged his tattered clothing for the same simple-styled gray robe Larone wore. His thinning blond hair was smoothed back and he had washed up. He looked much less threatening, but Jessica knew how deceiving looks could be.

Larone began. "Daenon controls the Deserts of Demar, and two of our western provinces, Snow Peak, which voluntarily seceded to him forty-five years ago, and Palium, which he acquired four years ago. He has made an alliance with our southwestern neighbor, Hent. We do not know the exact numbers of the Demarian army, however Lepsis has informed me that since Segal's defeat, the Demarian women have become obsessed with having children. The harsh environment of the desert, and lack of food and water, proved a hindrance to large families, but Daenon, through his southern alliance, has overcome that obstacle. The population has exploded and the children of the last four decades have been raised on a constant diet of hate. These are Daenon's Elitet.

"After hearing from Lepsis ten years ago, Haesom contacted the Olders of Ider Hoffle and set their training program into full operation. We converted some of Ramadine's buildings and land into a training center. Twenty-five other ramastars around the country added training centers. Since that time, every center has been filled to capacity. Haesom did well to prepare our people for what is coming, and Ider Hoffle soldiers have done an outstanding job organizing our western defenses these past two weeks."

Larone paused and looked at John, who sat staring at the ground. He seemed grim and Jessica sensed he battled some inner turmoil.

"The second courier last night came with good news," Larone continued. "Our other southern neighbor, Galland, has signed a treaty with us. The Gallish are not as foolish as the people of Hent. They know Daenon's promises are full of wind. We still need to send an emissary to Marone, but I am confident they will help."

"I'll go," Lepsis volunteered. "I haven't been home in half a century, and it's time I went. You'll have your alliance."

Larone nodded. He cleared his throat. "Haesom was the High Protector of Esparia. With his death, his children's death and the deaths of most Council members, we are virtually without a central government. I was only president of the Grand Council, not the federal head. It is true I have given orders these past few weeks, but I do not wish to continue. I have many responsibilities here at Ramadine and here is where my heart is. I will help in any way I can, even to giving my life if necessary, to see that Esparia remains free, but I do not want to lead. I do not have the vigor or youth necessary to fulfill the position of Protector."

He turned to Gaylee. "Gayleena, my dear, you are the rightful leader. It is up to you to decide what should be done."

"I knew if I ever came back, the reins of government would probably be thrust into my hands,"

Gaylee responded. "I've been gone too long and grown too weary to take on this task." She stood and walked to the large window at the end of the room. "I'll remain a figurehead; however, a true leader is someone who's used to giving orders, used to making the hard decisions and following through. Someone who understands war, for this has become a matter of war. We need someone with military experience, yet a cool head and able to lead. Someone who took a sloppy Afghanistan MASH unit and turned it into the finest field hospital the Army had. Someone with West Point training. I'm appointing my son, John Ernshaw of the House of Saylon, as commander of the armies of Esparia and Protector of the Rights of Freedom."

John's head snapped up. He looked trapped. "Stop right there Gaylee. I came to find Jessica and bring her home, not *lead* a country."

"John, do you truly think I needed that formal sword ceremony to make you my son? I love you as I loved Haesom." Gaylee smiled at him. "I only made the adoption official and legal for the sake of others." John opened his mouth, but she held her hand to stop him. "Because of the adoption, you are considered as much an Esparian as I am. In the eyes of the law, you are a legal Saylon, and as Jessica's father, with both her support and mine, no one can question your authority. No one will dare."

John took a deep breath. "I understand what's happening here; I've definitely become more than a casual observer. I don't mind giving you my support and expertise, but being an official Protector…"

"That's why you'd be perfect for the position," Cordon cut him off. "You don't want it, so you wouldn't abuse it. We know you're a soldier, an officer, used to giving orders. From what I understand, you've had wartime experience. No one here has, except Ophir and Anton. You and Jessica are the next rightful Protectors. The law allows you to take undisputed control. We can be united under you. If not, we run the risk of being fragmented under several would-be leaders."

"Three provincial regulators are already campaigning for the office of High Protector," Larone added. "Gayleena's arrival has dampened these movements, but they still smolder. Jessica is the rightful heir, but she is young and inexperienced. Under our law, your adoption makes you a Saylon, as if you were *born* a Saylon. You now have a blood right to the Protectorship."

John still did not respond. Seconds ticked by in profound silence. "Dad," Jessica said firmly. "I've decided to stay."

"What?" John turned to her in disbelief.

She knelt beside him. "I told you about Vorgen Hoffle, my journey to Ramadine through the cities and villages along the way. I'm Edian, Esparian, and I have to stay to explore this part of me that for eighteen years was hidden. If I go back now, I'd be half a person, forever wondering 'what if'. Your entire life has led you to this point in time. Like it or not, you *are* a bit of a politician and you are definitely a soldier, not just any soldier, but a high-ranking, West Point graduate with a penchant for dangerous assignments. Granted, you opted for medicine instead of a military command, but you have the background. You had to compete against the entire graduating class at West Point in order to earn your place in the Department of Defense uniformed Services University of Health Sciences. Not many people can get their medical education while beginning an officer career. To top it all off, your father, a career military man himself, taught you more about strategy than any book could. You told me that. John, call all it fate or whatever you will, but you are here and you are destined to lead."

"Destiny." John gave a short laugh. "This is why you wanted me to follow Jessica." John looked at Larone.

The older man met his gaze. "Yes," he answered softly, "I knew you would follow, just as I know you will lead."

"John?" Gaylee breathed.

"Yesterday Larone asked '*if*' I were to lead in this war, what would I do? Yes, I have given this some thought. What *would* I do? How would I begin to gather an army, to train it? Who would I ask to lead with me and how would I counter Daenon's Elitet?"

With a deep sigh, John rose to his feet. "I decided, when I accepted the Sword of Judgment, that my honor would be bound to this world, though I didn't anticipate this kind of commitment." He looked at Larone. "You're not so subtle hints haven't gone unnoticed." He let out a long breath between pursed lips. "Yes, I will take command," he said very, very softly.

Ophir let out his own breath, a wan smile on his face. "I don't envy your position, but I promise you my sword for as long as you need it."

Anton grinned from ear to ear and Lyrista reached up to squeeze

John's arm.

"Thanks, Ophir." He walked to the front of the room, then he squared his shoulders and took charge. "Larone and Gaylee will run the government from Ramadine. I want Anton, Reese and Jessica to travel throughout the country gathering all who are willing to fight. From what I've seen, you don't have much of a standing army. With Lepsis's information I did some math and figure Daenon has at least three million well trained, disciplined men at his disposal, probably more."

"Are you serious?" Cordon asked, his face going ashen. "Three million?"

"Unfortunately, yes," he nodded. "Lepsis, you need to leave at once for Marone. Take what men you feel necessary, I don't think those Elitet Shields will give up on killing you. As soon as you've secured Marone's aid, begin mustering an army. Keep in touch via the Red Feathers and await your orders. You'll be the Seventh bar in charge there. You have a lot to do, without the luxury of much time."

"Don't worry; you'll be amazed at how quickly my people will respond."

Nodding his head, John walked to where Gaylee previously had stood by the window. He gazed absently up at Ragus. "Cordon, we'll need to find Lepsis a new uniform."

"Good as done."

John's voice softened when he directed his remarks to Lyrista. "I want you to head a Special Operations Task Force. We need advance scouts, people who can track and keep well hidden. We need expert bowmen, archers who can hit a target at five hundred and fifty feet... er, five hundred and fifty sheks I mean. I want units capable of quick search and destroy missions, and your best men are needed to form five man squads capable of countering the Elitet. We need hundreds."

Lyrista nodded, her eyes filled with excitement. "I'll contact Ider Academy. I know just what to do."

Ophir was next to receive orders. "We need to send someone to Galland, to spearhead our forces there. Will you take that responsibility?"

Ophir gave one nod. "Honored to do so."

"We'll need maps," John spoke to Larone, "of Demar and Esparia."

John next addressed Anton. "Road trip, Anton. It's time to mobilize the entire nation, not just the west. Take Reese, Jessica, and if he's willing, Varnack with you. Cordon'll pick ten of his best men to travel with you as security escort. Travel the country, gather troops and send them west. Time is short. We don't know when Daenon will invade. I'm sending Jessica to inspire the people as a rightful Protector. Reese goes because he has proven himself in battle and Lyrista has mentioned he has a good eye for leadership. I trust Lyrista's judgment, therefore I trust Reese to appoint and approve officers.

"Reese, to give you the appropriate authority for your assignment, you're promoted to the rank of fifth bar. Anton's presence will give your promotion legitimacy among the provincial Regulators. No one will question you."

Reese looked startled by this high praise and stared inquiringly at his aunt.

"You judge well. You're the right man here," Lyrista confirmed.

The young man blushed slightly. "Okay."

Anton seemed especially pleased. "It'll be good to be out again," he boomed.

Lastly, John knelt in front of Varnack. "Will you protect my daughter?" Varnack licked John's hand in response. He smiled. "Thank you."

"Gaylee, will you travel through this section of the country?" He turned to face her. "I'll send two fourth bars and another security detail of eight soldiers with you to finish coordinating the units the Ider Hoffle soldiers organized."

"Of course."

John took a deep breath. "Cordon, I'll need any advice you can offer as we look at the maps and plan tactics. Finally, I noticed from the day I arrived here, Ramadine flies no flag. Is there a national symbol?"

"No." Larone shook his head. "Some dines have adopted certain colors but there is no emblem of countrywide importance."

"Then we must adopt one. A national flag people can rally around and carry into battle is all-important. It inspires everyone who sees it and reminds them of who they are and where they come from."

"That's a wonderful idea," Jessica bubbled. "We'll carry it where ever we go and it'll be our standard, our Banner of Freedom."

"But what should it look like?" Lyrista asked.

"I know," Gaylee's eyes sparkled, her voice deepened with emotion. "John's right, we need something, and Jessica has given it a name. We need a Banner of Freedom. I've seen grown men cry when they watch their flag rise; people salute its meaning and treasure it. I've designed it time and again, wondering if I could ever unfold my vision. Our uniforms have been blue and silver for thousands of years, so the banner must reflect that. A blue, square banner; blue for loyalty and truth, with the square bringing to mind honesty. The banner will be fringed with silver. Silver standing for justice, for justice must always encompass truth and loyalty. Finally, a red ring positioned at the center, with red signifying courage and strength. It is at the center of truth and the ring represents eternal, never ending courage."

Ophir grinned at Gaylee in approval. "A large blue field, fringed in silver with a red ring positioned in the middle, yes, the banner is simple and the symbolism clever, justice encompassing truth and loyalty with courage at the center."

Larone actually looked excited. "This is good, very, very good. I will have our textiles department start on it immediately. By the time you are ready to set out, we should have enough for each of you to carry several. I will send word to every point of our great country--we have a leader and a Banner of Freedom."

In only a few hours, twenty flags stood ready for the travelers, just as Larone had promised. Reese's uniform displayed the extra bars on it as proof of his promotion; Lepsis wore a new uniform, and an armed troop of twenty men from the Maronian contingent followed him. Ophir was ready to march south with a thousand well trained men.

When Ramadine's great bell rang out at mid-afternoon, the staff and students crowded along the main road, while the soldiers assembled in strict formation outside the broad, open gates. A pole had been erected on the northern gate tower. Gaylee, John and Larone stood atop the battlement.

Gaylee held a newly made flag in her hands. Holding it high for all to see, she shouted. "This Banner of Freedom will fly over every school, Justice building and Tiern Center throughout Esparia. It is a perfect, honest square of loyal blue, fringed by the silver of justice and centered with an eternal ring of red courage. Let every man, woman and child who looks on it remember the day when a new Protector came to aid us in our struggle against tyranny."

Her speech finished, she gave the flag to John and Larone, who hoisted it up the new pole. Every onlooker gave the Salute of Loyalty, then a mighty cheer filled the air.

Once down from the tower, John and Gaylee went to Jessica.

"We'll see each other soon." John sounded confident. "I'm very proud of you." He gave his daughter a gentle hug, being mindful of her still tender ribs.

"I love you too, Dad. Everything will be all right, you'll see." Jessica tightly squeezed Gaylee. "Good-bye, Grandma. I'm proud to be a Saylon."

"I know you'll bring honor to our name." Gaylee smiled with pride.

Lastly, Jessica bade farewell to Lyrista. "We've only known each other for a few short days, but I feel I've known you a lot longer. I know you'll be busy organizing your Special Units, but could you do me a favor and keep an eye on my Dad?"

Lyrista's cheeks went a deeper shade of pink. "I'll do my best, but I don't know if I'll be seeing much of him. When he won't be with Larone, Cordon has him scheduled for the training field, but I'll see to it he eats and rests a little."

Larone and Anton nodded to each other while Reese waved good-bye to his Aunt Lyrista and Uncle Cordon. A lightweight buggy was prepared for Jessica with her horse, Web, harnessed to it. Jessica felt embarrassed by not being able to actually ride her animal, but if she was to make this journey, she needed to travel this way until her ribs healed more.

Amidst great fanfare and wild cheering, the ambassadors rode out of Ramadine. Anton led the grand procession, with Reese and Jessica directly behind him and the ten security soldiers directly behind them. Varnack trotted at Jessica's side, strong and alert, the worst of his wounds nearly healed. Lepsis and his men followed while Ophir with his thousand came last.

Anton's loud voice could be heard over the crowd as he passed through the soldiers assembled outside the main gates, "Hey Jessi, ya got yer brush? It's a girl thing, Reese, a girl thing."

* * *

The following week flew by for those left at Ramadine. Anton sent daily messages and John received communiqués from both Lepsis and Ophir. The Red Feathers Center had not been this busy in years. Lepsis was successful in securing Marone's aid and was busy organizing an army. Marone was not as large as Esparia, but the people were a hardy lot and quite fierce by nature. Living in the northlands made them strong.

Ophir had his hands full with the people of Galland. The Gallish were willing to help, but were far from ready for a battle of any sort. Had Daenon been aware, he could have crushed the small country in less than a week. Ophir was frantically fortifying the border between Hent and Galland, and John's first business was to send five divisions of ten thousand each to aid Ophir. He knew it was easier to maintain land than it was to retake it once lost.

John spent his days busy with maps, strategies, training and establishing supply lines. At the end of the first week, to his great surprise and delight, the animal preptor turned physician, Alberod from Ider Hoffle, rode into Ramadine. John wasted no time in training Alberod with crash courses on medical procedure. He wanted the taxidermist with him on the battlefront as a medical man. The kind of injuries they would encounter would require a skilled sewing hand and Alberod scored among the best John had seen.

Lyrista held to the promise she made to Jessica. Several times she nearly sat on John to make him take food and once she threatened him with bodily harm if he did not rest.

"I swear, John, I'll take you out myself if you don't go to bed. You'll be worthless without some sleep. You cannot make the best decisions or retain what you're learning without resting your mind for at least a few hours." Realizing she was right, he agreed to take better care of himself.

At the beginning of the second week John met in his new office, formerly known as the conference center, with Larone. Several maps of the southern border lay open on the desk. John pointed to the Colossus Mountains, a thousand filon long barrier between Galland and Esparia. "Tell me about these mountains."

"They are enormous. Even the plant life grows to mighty proportions. They are nearly three hundred filons wide and consist of over two hundred soaring peaks."

"Gaylee once mentioned giants live in these mountains, is this true?"

"Yes, they live there, but we have little contact with them. They do not welcome outsiders. They do not speak Esparian, and I am not aware of anyone who knows their tongue. Anton met a giant once. He had wandered in the Colossus Mountains for several weeks, trying to make contact. Then one evening, a man, at least five heads taller than himself came into his camp and through basic sign language told Anton to leave."

"Do you think they would talk to me?" The potential aroused John's interest.

Larone thought for a moment. "Anything is possible, but you do not have weeks to wander around, John"

"I know, but I want to try. I have a gift for languages, maybe that'll help. I'll take Cordon and we'll leave tomorrow. You and Lyrista can wrap up the details here. You know where to deploy the troops. We need to finish fortifying the western borders."

"Lyrista and I will handle the western front. The giants would be valuable allies. In fact, if I were a few years younger, I would go with you. The possibility of seeing a giant is tantalizing."

In the morning, John and Cordon began their expedition to the Colossus Mountains. John rode the magnificent Fireguard while Cordon used one of the best stallions Ramadine could offer. During the journey from Ider Hoffle, as well as the days spent at Ramadine, John had taken extra effort to care for his animal. As a result, a bond of affection had been forged between the two. John now felt confident as a rider, fully trusting the intelligent horse.

After nearly three long days of constant, high speed travel, the western rim of the Colossus Mountains came into sight. Each peak in the range rivaled Earth's Mount Everest in size and height, the summits being lost in white, cloudy mist. On a clear day it would have been difficult to see the actual tips from the range base, they reached so high.

It took another day and a half to reach the range base. While the two men made their way into it, John admired the majestic redwood-like trees towering above. "If I were a giant, I'd live here, this place is spectacular."

Everything in the forest grew to enormous proportions. Multicolored mushrooms, the size of dinner plates, spread across many of the tree

170

trunks. Tall, feathery ferns arched up to a height of nearly twelve feet. Clumps of green vegetation with stalks the width of John's arm and six foot long leaves dotted the forest floor.

"This is overwhelming," Cordon said. "It makes me feel insignificant. I don't like it. We could travel for weeks and never come across another soul. In fact, we've been traveling for hours now and I haven't seen one sign of human life."

"Larone did say they were masters of concealment," John mused and he reined in Fireguard. Cordon stopped beside him. "They're probably watching right now. I'll bet they've been keeping track of us since we entered the forest this morning."

"We passed a small clearing about half a filon back, why don't we return there and make camp," Cordon suggested.

"Works for me." Upon reaching the meadow, John's first course of action was to cut a sturdy sapling, then strip its branches with a dagger. Cordon held the new pole while John retrieved a Banner of Freedom from his saddlebag and attached it to the makeshift staff. After gathering a pile of rocks, they planted the flag.

"We'll stay three days and nights, that's all the time we can spare. Larone can handle things for a while, but I don't want to be gone too long," John decided. "Hopefully, curiosity will overcome their mistrust long enough for us to communicate. We only need a few minutes."

Cordon built a blazing fire, a constant signal of their presence. They passed the long hours by practicing swordsmanship and exchanging stories of their youth. On their second night of camping out, John decided to broach a sensitive subject.

"Cordon, why have you never married?"

"You're brave," Cordon grinned. "Not even Lyrista has the courage to ask me that question."

Fully expecting a reply, John waited, but when Cordon remained silent he felt a prod was needed. "Well?"

"I'm a career soldier," was all Cordon offered.

"So was I, but I married Shallenon."

"Were you ever home?" The question shocked John, but before he could answer Cordon continued. "My father is a career soldier, and he was never there. I remember how difficult it was for my mother to raise three kids alone. Late at night, when she thought everyone slept, I would hear her crying." He shook his head. "I couldn't do that to a woman I loved or my kids. A family deserves to have a real husband and father, not a phantom in their lives. If it weren't for Lyrista, Reese would have been an orphan. After our sister died, his father came around even less often than mine did. No. Career soldiering and family do not go together."

"I understand how you feel, but I disagree. My father was army. In fact I'm third generation military. We moved around a lot, but I have good memories of my dad. He went missing in action in a conflict my country was involved in many years ago. Until that time, however, he always tried to be there for us. Shallenon and I had a great relationship. I tried very hard to make her and Jessica my number one priority. I was home as much as I possibly could be. I never took on extra work, unless it was vital to someone's life, and I found creative ways to keep in touch. My hobby was my family. Being married was my lifeline, it kept me grounded." He threw another log on the roaring fire.

"I do understand how Reese's dad felt though," John continued. "Losing your greatest friend and lifelong companion is devastating. I know firsthand how effective hard work and new challenges are in filling the void. When Shallenon died, I was lost for a long time. Luckily, Jessica had Gaylee. It's ironic, just when I'd decided to change my workaholic ways, she gets transported here. I just hope my fatherly efforts aren't too late."

"It's never too late to be a dad. When I was newly graduated from the Esparian Defense Academy, Gammet and I came to terms. I was fortunate to work beside him these last fifteen years. I'd say I understood him better than anyone, even better than Ophir."

John nodded. "I'd never give up the twelve years I had with Shallenon, even though the last ten have been tough without her. But I know how fortunate I am, I have a great daughter in Jessica."

They sat in silence, both men staring into the fire. After a long time, Cordon spoke. "After the war, I'll give family life serious consideration."

John was beginning to feel like a boy scout again, sleeping under the stars and foraging for wood to keep the fire constantly blazing. Finally, on the evening of the third day, a loud thud shattered the quiet twilight. Mindful not to draw their weapons, John and Cordon stood and faced the sound.

After several tense moments a deep voice asked from behind, "Why have you come?" John jumped and Cordon whirled around, his hand instinctively on his knife. A towering man stood before them. At least thirteen feet tall, this giant would have made Anton feel small. He was clean-shaven with long, thick white hair pulled back in ponytail fashion. He appeared to be alone, but John sensed others were around. To his amazement, he basically understood what the giant said. He felt both relieved and stunned. He quickly gathered his thoughts.

"I am the Protector of Esparia," John said. "We need help to defeat a murderer. If he takes Esparia, he will soon invade your mountain home."

The giant regarded John suspiciously. "What is that?" he motioned to the Banner.

"Our Banner of Freedom, our flag. Blue is loyalty, silver is justice and red is courage," John explained. "Our honor. A gift for you."

The giant looked from the flag to John and then to Cordon. "Leave by morning," he commanded. "Do not return." He left as quietly as he had come. Within seconds he vanished into the darkening forest.

John and Cordon stood speechless. After sitting back down next to their fire, Cordon stared at John, mouth open and eyes wide. "How did you do that?" he asked breathlessly.

John was confused. "Do what?"

"You spoke Giant, John. I mean, YOU SPOKE GIANT!"

"No I was speaking like we are now, Edian."

Cordon laughed. "No, you spoke Giant. I don't know what language it was, but I was sure glad you could do it. I'm not a man who easily panics, but I was a little concerned when I saw that guy. And then there you go, just rattling off some weird language." Cordon gave a brave smile.

After translating the brief conversation John shook his head. "Well I don't know how I did it."

"You must be tied into the Expanse of Gonta more than you know," Cordon said firmly.

John opened his mouth to protest, but quickly thought better of it. He had no idea what had just happened and if it made Cordon feel better to think it was some sort of magic, then fine. He would ask Larone about it later. "Yeah, maybe. Let's get some rest."

The next morning John and Cordon awoke to find the Banner of Freedom gone.

"Well, what do you know?" Cordon gave a deep, heart-felt laugh.

"At least they took it. I hope it's a good sign," John said.

* * *

Troops and supplies poured in and Ramadine was never a busier place. It took John two full days before he could question Larone about the newfound ability to understand Giants. Larone seemed perplexed by the surprising ability also. "I have been pondering for some time now your ability to speak Esparian. I have questioned Gaylee and she has told me of her ability to speak both a language called Polish and your native tongue of English without even realizing she was speaking them."

John was stunned. "What do you mean? My speaking Esparian? I'm speaking English."

"No my friend, I assure you...you are speaking Esparian. It is impossible that our two languages would be this compatible. You are definitely speaking Esparian."

"But there are some words that are foreign to me and Gaylee has had to teach me their meanings." He protested.

"I can't explain the full impact of what happened to you when you went through the Expanse of Gonta in the spiral to come here, but you definitely absorbed some power to communicate. Perhaps," he mused, "not as much as Gaylee did when she traveled to earth or Jessica when she came through, but you absorbed something."

"Something, huh," John grunted. "What else happened to me in there?"

Larone shook his head. "I do not know. No one has traveled between our worlds in millennia. And the writings of those who may have made the journey have been lost. We may never know the full extent of how your travel has affected you."

"And what about Jess?" John was feeling anger begin to rise in him. "Does she realize she's speaking Esparian?"

Larone shook his head. "I doubt it. Has she spoken to you about it?"

"No," John sighed, checking his anger. "And she has so much to think about right now, I'm not going to mention it." He shook his head. "This is too weird."

During the next week, before Anton, Jessica, Reese and Varnack returned, John filled his time with heavy training and meetings with division and regimental commanders from the eastern provinces. John liked these men, Reese had done a good job approving and appointing them to their positions. They seemed competent and unafraid. Several officers wanted to attack the Deserts right away, but John convinced them it would be suicide.

"Our maps of the Deserts are incomplete at best. Without knowledgeable guides, we would be walking into ambush after ambush. We will wait for Daenon to make the first move," John commanded. "We can interrogate our prisoners and gain more knowledge of the terrain. I won't go anywhere half-blind."

Lepsis and Ophir kept daily communication with Ramadine. They hastened to complete their respective tasks. John sent another six regiments to Ophir. When men arrived, he deployed more troops to the western outposts and made sure the supply lines from the Northern Plains were well secured.

Having completed her tour of the western provinces, Gaylee returned one day before Jessica and company. Since the West lay in Daenon's direct path, the western peoples had already begun mobilization under the Ider Hoffle soldiers.

Gaylee met with John and Larone in John's new office to brief them on her tour when, halfway through her report, Lyrista burst through the door. Pale, her mouth set in a grim line, she handed John a small piece of paper. "I just received this." She walked over to gaze out the window.

John read the neatly printed message out loud.

Commander Lyrista,

Enemy troops amassing on the Palium border. Received word of similar troop movements on the Snow Peak border. Please advise.

Fourth Bar Ru
Acting Commander Advance Scouts

CHAPTER 17

Green Persite

Esparia consisted of fifteen large provinces. The country stretched from the Eastern Ocean to the desert borders of Demar, and from the country of Marone on the north to Hent and Galland on the south. With Gaylee bound for the three western provinces of Verdure, Ramana, and Kine, Anton and company needed to cover the remaining ten in three weeks. Snow Peak and Palium were not on the list, for they were under Daenon's control. Larone sent word through the Red Feathers to the provincial capitals and universities, or ramastars, informing them of the impending visits.

Anton mapped their course and put them on a strict timetable. Reese carried their standard, the Banner of Freedom, in a special holster made to attach to his saddle. Jessica kept the extra banners folded in a bag at her feet. The buggy she drove was small and handled well. Web didn't seem to mind the burden.

Varnack seemed quite content to run beside the buggy, every now and then darting in front of Web in a bizarre game of Trigal hound chicken. Feeling Web's growing irritation, Jessica scolded the hound more than once. She noticed he didn't bother the accompanying soldier's horses.

"Not as much fun," was his reason.

They headed northeast at a brisk clip toward Lyson Hoffle, nearly fifty filons from Ramadine, in the fertile province of Uberty. There was no time to keep things slow, so they pushed the well-conditioned mounts to their limits.

With the Banner flying before them, they made an impressive group. Reese looked handsome and stately in his crisp uniform, a direct contrast to Anton's rugged, wild appearance. Varnack always made an impression, and Jessica was striking with her long, bright red hair flying behind her in the wind. The security detail rounded out the company. Some of these men would ride beside her, trading positions every hour or so. Some rode by Reese, but none rode by Anton. Jessica felt quite safe, as she was certain these men were the best of the best.

The last golden rays of sunlight were fading into the horizon when Jessica noticed the glow of distant lights. Anton maneuvered his horse next to her carriage. "That's not Lyson up there. The dine's at least another half hour away just over that little rise, so be on yer guard," he warned. Within minutes a faint cheer drifted to Jessica's ears. Hundreds of people, all bearing torches, lit their way. The glowing lights grew in number with every filon until, when they reached their destination; the night was lit almost as if it were day.

At Lyson's gates, the High Olders met them with great fanfare. So many people came with greetings that barely enough room remained to maneuver the horses and buggy down the street. The four ambassadors were led to a spacious, brightly lit field where a platform had been erected. The field was packed with people from the city and the surrounding tierns.

Once on the stage, Anton stepped forward and a hush fell over the crowd. "My fellow Esparians, the time has come for each man to look deep inside and determine what he is made of. Your country calls you to arms. Not for over a thousand years has our liberty and freedom been so threatened. Rise up, and for your wives, your children, your parents, and everything you hold dear, don your armor and take up your weapons. Hoist this Banner of Freedom from every tower and take to heart what it stands for. We are Esparians and we will never bow to tyranny."

A cheer went up and a sea of drawn swords, held high, glittered in the firelight. Jessica was totally taken by surprise at her uncle's perfect speech. *So he can talk well if he wants to,* she thought. But now it was her moment to step forward and be heard, so she focused on her own words. She gave the same address that her Grandmother had given that afternoon at Ramadine, with a few minor changes. "A Protector has come from afar to lead this land. My father, John Ernshaw of the House of Saylon, officially adopted by Lady Gayleena of Saylon House, wields the Sword of Judgment. Let the Banner of Freedom fly over every school, Justice building and Tiern Center throughout Esparia. It is a perfect, honest square of loyal blue, fringed by the silver of justice and centered by the eternal, red ring of courage. May every man, woman and child who looks on it remember the day when a new Protector came to aid us in our struggle against tyranny, and freedom remained secure."

Reese raised the flag for everyone to see. Each person in the crowd fell to one knee and gave the Salute of Loyalty.

Anton addressed the High Older, "Have the troops assembled and ready by mornin'. I'll need to see yer musterin' records. Fifth Bar Reese'll approve yer officers and appoint new ones if necessary. Now we need food and rest."

* * *

"Get up." The message came through loud and clear. Jessica opened her eyes to see Varnack nose to nose with her. He licked her face.

"What time is it?"

"Late."

"What do you mean, late? How late?" She jumped out of bed and opened the door to let him out.

"Go."

Having been too tired to change, she had slept in her clothes. So she grabbed a chunk of warm, yellow bread and piece of yellow-brown fruit from a platter the inn keeper offered, and hurried out the inn door to the adjoining stable. Anton, Reese, and nine soldiers sat waiting for her. The horses were saddled and her buggy stood ready. Before she could protest being left out of the morning's activities, Anton bundled her into the carriage and they were off.

Anton's plan called for ten capitol cities and twenty of the country's twenty-five universities to be visited in twenty-one days. It was a grueling schedule, and Jessica knew he was determined they keep it.

"Uncle Anton," she said when they were in stride. "I appreciate the extra sleep, but tomorrow, I want to wake up when you and Reese wake up. Unless you're willing to give interviews, you'd better let me handle the public relations end of this journey. I can be the main spokesperson for our group. If there are any news people or questioning hoffle elders, you might want to let me handle them."

"Well Jessi," Anton took on a fatherly tone, "I don't want ya to overdo it. Ya need to keep up yer strength."

"I promise if I get tired, I'll let you know. Okay?"

He frowned. "Oh, all right."

"And what happened to security guard number eight?" she asked. She hadn't had time to learn their names, so in her mind she had given each a number.

"Left him behind to help gather men and train 'em before sending 'em off to the border," he replied.

The country they traveled through was flat and fertile. They passed numerous small farms with green fields of ripening grain, row after endless low of tubers, edible roots and above ground vines. Orchards of pink dwarf taya and gigantic, green hairy palanto trees grew in abundance.

"Hey, Reese," Jessica called out, "I know next to nothing about Esparia. Come and tell me about it."

Reese brought his horse next to her buggy. "Uberty. Farmlands and orchards. Most of the nation's food is grown here. I'm sure Anton will settle agreements with the farmers."

"Yer right there lad," Anton interjected. "I have lots of agreements to get signed from every province. Time to put those taxes Haesom collected to good use."

"There's not much else to tell. Uberty is, well," Reese shrugged his shoulders, "Uberty."

Jessica laughed. "Ask a stupid question...men."

By late afternoon they reached Cardine, the capitol of Uberty, where bright green and yellow flags lined the main road and throngs of excited people, pointing and waving, escorted them to a wooden platform in the center square. Anton and Jessica gave their same speeches while Reese stood at attention holding the Banner of Freedom. The three ambassadors knew their respective tasks, so with the ceremony completed, they wasted no time. Anton inspected the troops and made arrangements with the provincial authorities to have food sent to the front line.

Reese interviewed and approved the current officers, appointed a few more, then gave orders to secure the province from guerrilla attacks. As most of the supply lines would be coming through Uberty, they needed to be well guarded. Anton left another soldier from their security detail in charge there to ensure the safety of those supply lines.

Jessica met with the three news people and one tiern Elder, answering what questions she could. She tactfully declined to answer queries concerning her whereabouts the past eighteen years and firmly stuck to the matters at hand, namely, raising an army, supplying it, and winning a war.

Varnack's duty was given him directly from John. He was Jessica's bodyguard. Alert and attentive, he watched the news people interview Jessica with an intense interest. On several occasions she needed to put her hand on his head to stop him from growling and keep him in check. By the end of the news conference, his irritation was palpable.

"It's over, Varnack. Calm down. I could hardly answer those last few men, your exasperation kept bellowing in my head."

"Hate questions."

"Well, try to think of this as an exercise in patience," she sniggered and scratched him behind the ears. On impulse, she threw her arms around his head and kissed his forehead. "I know this is hard on you and I shouldn't laugh. I'm just glad you're here."

Sunrise saw them back on the road, cantering toward the first of twenty military Defense Academies. This one was located at Uberty's center of learning, Uberty Ramastar. The country they traveled through consisted of endless grain fields, green with freshly spouted plants.

"Not much to look at here," Reese remarked.

"Reminds me of a place called Nebraska."

"Is that where you're from?"

"No, but it's a province in my country, or rather, the country I grew up in."

"So is your country anything like Esparia?"

"Yeah, it is. In fact I'm surprised at the similarities. Plants are a little different and so's the wildlife, but the people…well, I guess people are the same wherever you go. All they want is to live their lives in peace. The dines are larger, but not nearly as colorful, and the air's not as clean."

"Not as clean? How can air be dirty?" He frowned.

"There're a lot more people where I come from, a whole lot more, so we burn a lot of fuel. The air in the large dines is filled with smoke all the time. It's called pollution."

He wrinkled up his nose.

"There're many ramastars, like here. In fact, I'm supposed to go to the ramastar in my state, or province, this fall."

"What do you wish to study? Will you be a healer like your father?"

"No. I want to be a scientist like Uncle Anton and study biology and chemistry. Many of my people suffer from terrible illnesses called cancers and I'd like to help find a cure."

"I think you'll do well in whatever you choose."

"Thank you, Reese." Jessica felt her cheeks grow warm. Their conversation would have continued, but at that moment both Reese and Jessica spotted a lone rider far down the straight road. As he galloped toward them, his blue and silver uniform revealed his military affiliation. After several more minutes passed, she could see he sported a full, black beard, but no mustache. Reese gasped beside her.

"Papa!" he called, then clicked his horse into a gallop.

"Papa?" Jessica questioned, looking at Anton for explanations, but none were offered.

The time at the Defense Academy went rapidly. Reese's father, Geldric, was the commander of the facility. For a brief moment, Jessica managed to corner Anton. "I had no idea Reese's dad was around. Why is he such a phantom in his son's life?"

"I dunno," he shrugged his shoulders. "Maybe the death of his wife was more than he could bear. Maybe puttin' distance between himself and the only other thing that could hurt him was how he coped with it."

Anton would say no more, but she saw the sadness in his eyes. How she wished she could reach inside his mind and find out what had happened. He held a tight lock on his pain.

Within a few hours Anton and Reese completed their work and the party left for Province Florio. Jessica had found the Defense Academy impressive, but she was amazed at how much it resembled the training center at Ramadine.

As soon as they were in stride, she asked Reese about it. "I was surprised by how much the layout of the Defense Academy resembled the one at Ramadine."

"Actually, the resemblance isn't to Ramadine directly. More correctly, it resembled the Academy at Ider Hoffle. All training grounds have been built as similarly to Ider Academy as possible."

"How are the commanders, like your father, chosen?"

"From the Academy staff at Ider Hoffle. Only the best are chosen to head the other schools. They have to lead as well as teach. Lyrista's been asked several times to command a ramastar Defense Academy, but she prefers to stay in Ider Hoffle. You don't have to be a native of Ider Hoffle to be a commander, there are many commanders from other dines, you just have to be an Ider Hoffle teacher. Someday, I want to command a Defense Academy."

"Just like your dad."

"Yeah, like my dad."

They said nothing more, but he continued riding beside the buggy. The silence felt comfortable and Jessica was pleased to have him by her for the remainder of the day's journey. More than a few times she stole a look at him. With classically handsome features and thick, dark, curly hair he cut a striking figure. Though not much taller than herself, his muscular physique more than compensated for the lack of stature. She found his boyish shyness quite charming; it reminded her of another young man, worlds away.

Toward the eventide, the walled fortress of Koradine appeared in the distance. The capitol of Florio rose like a spired coronet atop the rich, flat fields surrounding it.

"You're looking at one of the oldest settlements in Esparia," Reese explained. "It's called Koradine, or City of Plenty, and is tens of thousands of years old. It's been built in three distinct sections or layers. There's an ancient Inner Dine preserved as a museum, it's the original city. Then the Middle Dine was built about twenty thousand years ago and the Outer Dine is only three thousand years old. Most of the government buildings are located in the Middle Dine, so I think that's where we're going. It's really fantastic, to see how the people have kept the buildings in such good repair for so many years. They're very proud of their history and have gone to enormous lengths to keep everything from decay."

Traveling through the Outer Dine toward the Middle Dine, the buildings resembled more and more those at Ramadine. The outer buildings were built of colored brick, some red, some green, others blue, yellow, peach and violet. All were accented along blue Palium roofs and down each exterior corner by white stones. Each building was smoothed to a glassy finish. The structures of the Middle Dine were more ornate and of pastel hues, but shined to the same high gloss. Here the roofs were of copper and pastel tiles of all colors.

They stopped before a large building, heavily ornate with grand arches and sculpted flower garlands. Jessica was enthralled by the intricate detail of the edifice. When she exited her buggy, she did not notice her foot had become entwined in the reins of her carriage and she fell, head first, onto a smooth stone sidewalk. A weak, brief screech of surprise escaped her lips as she thrust her hands outward to break her fall.

Anton and Reese, as well as three passers-by ran to her aid. Reese unraveled her foot from the leather lines while Anton swept her into his arms. Filled with embarrassment, she tried to wiggle down, but Anton held her firm, his face wrinkled in concern.

"Uncle Anton, I'm all right," she tried to assure him. "I don't feel any pain."

"That's 'cause yer takin' Larone's painkiller."

As he carried her into the elegant building Jessica looked at her hands. To her dismay they were scraped, her right much worse than her left. She squeezed them tightly to try and slow the bleeding. "That pain killer really does work well", she mused. "I don't feel a thing." With Reese and Varnack close behind, Anton marched up to the first person he saw and demanded, "Where's the High Older's office?" Luckily for the individual, he knew just where to send the large, worried man and his delegation.

"We need a healer," Anton announced when he burst into the High Older's office. "Jessi here had an accident and I want her attended to right now."

Realizing that she may really need some medical attention, Jessica resigned herself to Anton's fatherly attentions

The High Older, a portly gentleman with short, gray hair stared in stunned silence at the intruders. He quickly recovered his composure. "We have one of the finest healers in the country here, Orin," he boasted. "I'll send for him immediately." He waddled out of the office, leaving the four alone.

"Orin, huh? I've heard of him," Anton commented. "I would say only Larone is better known."

Having been deposited in a comfortable, overstuffed chair, Jessica waited with her friends for the High Older's return. There was little to do and she felt extremely foolish. "I'm sorry for upsetting the schedule," she apologized. "I was too engrossed in the beauty of the buildings instead of being careful."

"It's all right, Jessi," her Uncle comforted. "We're ahead of time, so this shouldn't set us back any."

Varnack licked her hand. "Worried."

"Really, I'm okay."

Reese stood at a small window, gazing down at the street. "There's a crowd gathering in front of the building. Our presence here is known."

Anton joined him. "Yeah, well I guess we could get started. As soon as the High Older returns, I'll tell him to show you to…" Before he could finish the sentence, the door to the plush office opened and the Older stood there, his faced flushed.

"You are very fortunate!" he exclaimed with such excitement Jessica worried his eyes would pop right out of his head. "Healer Orin seldom comes to the dine, but today he was here and I found him walking down the street over there." The Older flicked his hand to indicate the general direction he was referring to. Standing in the doorway, the large man blocked any view of this famous healer. When he finally moved aside, allowing Orin to enter the room, Anton and Reese gasped in unison while Varnack jumped to his feet, wagging his tail in obvious delight. Jessica blinked in astonishment.

She shot a questioning glance at her two companions positioned by the window. Reese's mouth lay open in shock and the color had completely drained from Anton's face. She looked from the two, to the healer, and back again. This tall, slender man held an uncanny resemblance to Haesom, her murdered uncle. He was older, and his hair was auburn, not blazing red, but from his sapphire blue eyes and to the dimple in his chin, he was an older version of the dead Protector.

If he noticed any of their reactions, he did not show it, but focused his full attention on Jessica. "I heard you took quite a tumble."

Jessica swallowed hard and pulled herself together.

Orin knelt down and took her hands in his, examining the scrapes. Varnack nosed the man on his cheek and Orin chuckled quietly. "You have a very friendly Trigal Hound there."

Jessica stared at the man kneeling in front of her. He was definitely older than Haesom, in fact, she had the distinct impression he was older than her grandmother, but by how much was uncertain. His light, auburn-brown hair had just begun to gray and there were lines around his eyes and mouth. When he took her hand she felt great kindness emanate from him.

"My niece has some broken ribs," Anton boomed, his brusque voice sounding with a calm that belied his still stunned expression.

"Then I will need some privacy," Orin advised, and the others quickly filed out of the office.

"So you were in the tiern for a visit?" Jessica ventured.

"Yes, I was not going to come to the middle dine today, but I felt prompted to. I came in about an hour ago to visit a friend. I had just left his home when the High Older found me."

"Lucky for me you were around. I thought poor Uncle Anton was going to have a heart attack right on the spot where I fell."

"It is a privilege to meet you, Lady Jessica. I understand you have come from a great distance, both you and your father, to aid my people."

"Yes, it was a long trip." She felt comfortable around this kind stranger. "Now we're traveling throughout the entire country, well, almost the entire country. It's beautiful here, very diverse."

"Beautiful...yes, I agree, but do not let the beauty of the land lull you into thinking there are no dangers."

Jessica was surprised. "Daenon can reach this far into the country?"

"No," he shook his head. "Not Daenon. It is difficult to put my suspicions into words. Have you heard of the Winds of Malana?"

"No." Her interest was piqued.

"Malana and Bree were sisters," Orin began. He poured a yellow liquid from a small vial onto her palms and wiped them. "Their story is as old as Koradine itself, for it was their father, Korad, who founded Koradine and brought all of the nomadic tribes of Esparia to peace. He became the first Protector. Bree was the younger of the two sisters and she loved the land and all that was part of it. Our first records of white persite come from her writings." Orin pulled a fine needle from his bag and threaded it. "She learned to harness the power of persite and used it to bless all living things. She traveled this entire planet, crossing the oceans and visiting the isles of the sea. Everywhere she went plant life thrived. She lived to an ancient age. The persite extended her lifespan to many times that of normal people. Malana was the oldest child in the family." He stitched the shredded flesh of her right palm as he spoke. "She wanted to rule and was furious when her father chose one of her younger brothers to succeed him. Knowing that persite held great power, she went searching for a crystal of her own. With it she hoped to force a coup and reign in her brother's place. She found what she was looking for, but was unable to unlock its power. When Bree refused to help her, Malana fled to the western jungle. At that time Demar was not a desert, but a lush, tropical garden covering a third of our country. Malana spent many years trying to control the persite's power. Eventually, she succeeded; however before she could attack her brother, Bree intervened. The sisters battled day and night for weeks. In a desperate effort to increase her power, Malana pulled the life forces from the jungle plants surrounding her, turning her white persite to green. Bree was able to tap into the strength of Edia, anchoring herself to the planet. In that final, terrible battle, Malana consumed the Demarian gardens, rendering the land barren and desolate of all life for millennia. The effort of battle, using the persite as weapons, threatened the existence of both women. Malana absorbed so much of the green persite's energy that her body could not contain it. Her flesh transformed into the green crystal and exploded into thousands of pieces. A tremendous, violent wind was generated by the blast and the crystals were carried to all parts of this land. In the process, much of the country was devastated."

Orin secured the last bandage on Jessica's palms and turned his attention to her ribs. "It is said that Malana did not die in the blast, but became the wind and vented her fury. Even now, when a destructive wind manifests on land or sea, you can hear Malana's evil laugh. Hence, the

Winds of Malana…destructive, dangerous, evil. Bree, encircled within the safety of Edia, survived. The last we know of her is that she left to go visit the Colossus Mountains, and never returned. Those who were closest to her say that she merged with our planet. Her connection with Edia and the power of persite preserved her spiritual essence and she became guardian to all living things."

Orin finished re-wrapping the bandages around Jessica's middle. "Malana, the Winds of Malana, have always been associated with green persite, and green persite is associated with evil. As I said, I have suspicions. I have felt something quite evil, I cannot explain it, but believe me," he looked earnestly into Jessica's eyes, "green persite is real, and someone has unlocked a piece of it. I understand you're traveling the country. I don't believe this to be a coincidence."

Jessica remembered the green rock she had seen on the night she came to Esparia. She nodded. "I do believe you, Orin." She wondered if Daenon had finally succeeded in tapping the crystal's power. "I think I should say something to Uncle Anton."

Orin nodded in agreement. "Well, as near as I can judge, you are a very lucky girl. The fall did not do greater damage to your ribcage and your scrapes will heal in a couple of days."

"Thanks. Have you ever been to Ramadine?" she asked.

"No, I have not. I was born here in Florio and educated at our local ramastar. I prefer staying close to home, but I would like to go there someday. I am no longer a young man, but I am not too old either," his eyes twinkled, "so perhaps after the war I will travel a bit. Right now, the ramastar has placed me in charge of training other healers to aid in the coming battles. I have three hundred students."

Jessica stood up and offered her hand to the man, then remembered the bandages. Orin gently took her hand between both of his. "I hope to meet you again," she thanked him, "and I'll tell Uncle Anton of what you've felt. We'll be on our guard for anything out of the ordinary."

"Until next time." He smiled and bowed slightly. "Now I must be going." He opened the office door, but paused and looked back at her. "It has been strange meeting you, Lady Jessica, as if I already know you." He shrugged his shoulders and left.

Jessica felt the same about him. Not only did he look remarkably like Haesom, but his speech patterns completely mimicked Larone's. Jessica burned with questions for Reese, Anton and Varnack. Never before had she seen Varnack react to a perfect stranger with such affection. He still had not totally warmed up to her father. Never far from her, he trotted back into the makeshift examination room.

"Varnack, you liked Healer Orin a great deal, didn't you?"

"Yes"

"That surprised me. I've never seen you be that friendly before at just the first meeting."

"Yes, you have."

"I have? When?"

"The night I first met you."

She gently stroked his back. "You're my best friend, Varnack," she whispered.

On the road the following morning Jessica called out to Reese. "All right, I can't stand it! Who is this Orin guy? Why did he look so much like my Uncle Haesom?"

He pulled his horse next to her buggy. His brow wrinkled and he shook his head. "It's as much a mystery to me as it is to you. I tried asking Anton. He said he doesn't know, and I believe him. I think it really shook him up."

Jessica agreed. She knew Anton well enough to realize he dealt with personal feelings by burying himself in his work, so she braced herself for several days of hectic activity.

In the province of Arboret, a land covered in forests, Anton secured top quality bows, arrows and javelins for the army. Palinium, noted for its fine steel and Palium production, was the provider of varied swords, daggers, shields and armor, both chain mail and solid plate, for men and horses.

While traveling through Wasseria, a land filled with flowing rivers and large bodies of water, Jessica came to fully appreciate the Esparian way of naming landmarks. The first lake they spied was large, but quite shallow and appropriately dubbed Shallow Lake. During their journey they crossed three long, winding rivers, one called Serpentine River, another Longshore River and the third Rapid River. Anton explained the bodies of water were titled for their intense colors and unique shapes, mountains for their outstanding features, while forests and plains were called after the prominent plant life growing therein. Even most of the provinces took their monikers from their major economies.

Jessica realized a wealth of hydroelectric power lay untapped in Wasseria. There could be enough electricity from this one province alone to supply half of Esparia. *I'll remember to tell Dad, in case he wants to introduce the concept to the people.* She was certain the Esparian scientists could come up with the necessary technology once set on the right path of discovery.

With each stop they had lost a security soldier. Anton had assignments for every man and left them behind to finish what he had begun. They were down to four extra men by the time they reached Jewlett. The road they traveled was straight, with only small tufts for green shrubbery on the landscape for as far as any of them could see. The security soldiers were divided with a pair up front leading the way, and a pair trailing a behind to protect the rear. It was here that Jessica had a rare moment to talk with Anton. "I've been telling Reese about how my country compares to Esparia. He's been good about not prying, but I know he's curious. Do you think I should tell him the truth about where I come from? I'd like to be honest with him."

Anton thought for a moment, then nodded his head. "He's a good man and would keep whatever ya told him in confidence. It would be agreeable with me."

Jessica waited for the right opportunity to talk with Reese. It finally came when they stopped for the night. Anton chose a small glade where the shrubbery grew tall and thick, not too far from the main highway, for their campsite. Their evening routine had become well established. Anton built a fire, Reese and the soldiers took care of the horses, and Jessica unpacked their picnic meal. After eating, the soldiers drew lots as to the order of their sentry duty for the night. The bed rolls were laid out and everyone settled in. The soldiers were usually the first to fall asleep, as they took advantage of rest time between their turn at guard duty. Even though the hour had grown late, Jessica wanted to tell Reese about her home while they enjoyed a quiet moment.

When she heard the soft snoring of the three off duty soldiers and saw the fourth checking on the horses, she said quietly, "Reese, I have something I want to tell you."

Anton looked at her and nodded in agreement.

"I want to tell you where I come from, but you must promise to keep it to yourself. My Dad and I aren't ready to let the general populace in on our secret."

"Of course."

She hesitated. "This is more difficult than I thought it would be. Um…Uncle Anton, where is Earth?" She waved her hand toward the heavens.

"It's over there." He pointed to a section of northwestern sky. "It's in a cluster of faint stars beyond that bright one right there."

Reese looked at the sky where Anton pointed, then back at Jessica. She smiled weakly and explained, "I'm not from across the ocean; I'm not even from Edia. I come from a planet in a neighboring solar system. My planet is called Earth and it's located in the section of sky Uncle Anton just pointed to."

Reese looked back at the sky. He gave a short laugh and shook his head. "I believe you. That explains a lot. You've tried hard to fit in, but there are subtle differences. So Earth is your home world."

"Yes," she sighed. "And the United States of America is my country. Now you understand why I want it kept secret. I don't think many people here are ready to have an off-worlder as a Protector."

"I see what you mean." He thought for a minute. "How did you come here?"

"Uncle Anton brought me through something called a Transmirian spiral. It was a wild ride and when I came out, Varnack was waiting for me. My grandma and dad followed a day later."

"That also explains a great deal."

"All right," Anton interrupted. "Now ya know, Reese. Varnack's already asleep, let's go to sleep too." The conversation was terminated.

A low growl brought Jessica out from a deep sleep. Varnack crouched beside her, glaring into the shadowed bushes surrounding them, his muscles tense, ready to spring. The night was quiet. Both moons were still high in the star filled sky. She turned her head, ever so slightly, to glance over at Anton and Reese. They both lay motionless only a few feet from her. The soldier on guard duty had his back to them and stood looking out toward the main highway. Closing her eyes she tried to listen. Silence. She strained her senses trying to pick up whatever had set Varnack on edge. To her complete surprise she felt the presence of several life energies. They were nearly surrounded, but not by Elitet. These life energies were different, less evil, but just as deadly. Her skin prickled, goose bumps rising on her arms. There was a power here, something totally foreign to her understanding. Malignant...vicious. Electrical tendrils, invisible and subtle, snaked into her soul. Almost imperceptible, the tingling slithered around her free will. It squeezed, very gently, sending warmth that dulled her senses. With a start, she shook them off.

She tried to call out, but her voice only squeaked. It seemed to be enough though, for the sentry turned and the others stirred. Slowly, as if in a dream, she rose to her feet. Instantly she knew the armed assassins surrounding them could be dealt with. They were dangerous, but not enough to overwhelm her companions. The real danger centered in the person controlling the others. Hate emanated from this unseen enemy, a rage bent on destroying them. *Go back to where you came from,* the message hung in the air. *You are not welcome, you are not wanted.*

A score of armed men dressed in simple farmer's clothing rushed at them from every direction. Anton, Reese, and the soldiers sprang to their feet. The sentry leapt into action. Varnack jumped forward, his teeth bared. One man went down, his sword arm ripped in shreds from gnashing teeth. A second attacker's leg became Varnack's next target. Within seconds the man was writhing on the ground next to his friend. Three others were no match for the powerful hound. Reese threw daggers, aimed not to kill, but to maim, felling two men in mid-stride, then pulled his sword. Each soldier stood his ground and Anton fought hand to hand.

Jessica stood in the midst of her guardians, trying to quash the invisible power that threatened them. *I warn you, leave us in peace,* her mental admonition penetrated the surrounding vegetation.

A mirthless laugh reverberated in her mind. *Die!* A green ball of energy burst from the nearest thicket. It flew like an arrow of emerald fire, slicing through the flesh of Jessica's forearm and barely missing the bone. The heat from the bolt exploded through her body and mind. Her back arched in agony and every muscle quivered in seizure, freezing her where she stood. She wanted to scream, but her throat would not function. Her breathing ceased. Darkness quickly closed in.

Anton's voice drifted through the fog in her mind. "By the voice of T'Aalin, through the Expanse of Gonta, I call on the powers of Bree, to vanquish the foe, the Winds of Malana, flee away to the Torbuchhi sea."

Jessica fell to the ground while Anton repeated the chant. She shook herself. Anton stood between her and the threatening menace. He faced the dark hedge, his arms stretched forward at chest level, his palms outward, as if to hold back another power blast. A circle of white mist, a foot in diameter, yet only two hairs thick, swirled inches in front of his hands. Again and again he chanted the same spell. Varnack, Reese, and the soldiers continued the fight against the few remaining assailants.

Jessica pulled herself up to shakily stand by Anton, her every muscle straining with the effort. A green energy, swirling like fire enveloped the shrubbery directly ahead. The high resonance of a woman chanting contrasted sharply with Anton's deeper voice. The green fire expanded, spreading its greedy fingers to neighboring saplings and plant life. The vegetation withered as their life forces were instantly drained from them. Another bolt of jade lightning arched toward them.

It pierced the small vaporic shield, hitting Anton full in the chest. He fell to his knees, the chant dying in his throat. Jessica reached for him. His face was contorted in agony. When her fingers touched his back, the searing heat of the blast traveled through him and into her own hands. She moaned in pain, but clamped her hands firmly on Anton's shoulders, willing the deadly energy into her own body. She allowed her tears to flow, expelling the green poison with the salty drops.

Anton began the chant again. It was a whisper at first. "By the voice of T'Aalin, through the Expanse of Gonta, I call on the powers of Bree, to vanquish the foe, the Winds of Malana, flee away to the Torbuchhi Sea." Then it slowly grew in volume.

I've got to help...must help. Jessica centered on Anton. T'Aalin...Bree...T'Aalin...Bree...T'Aalin...Bree. She dug her bare toes into the brown earth beneath her. A warm, tingling sensation began in the soles of her feet. In a split second, heat traveled upward, through her legs, then flew to her shoulders, soothing her blistering nerves along the way. Down her arms it went, through her finger tips, directly into Anton. A second flash of warmth followed behind the first. When the pulses increased in frequency, the temperature also rose, yet it did not burn. Within moments, hot energy flowed from Edia, through Jessica, and into Anton.

He roared out the incantation. The white shield reappeared, a solid wall of protection. Anton leaned into Jessica, bending his arms at the elbows and pulling his out facing hands to his chest. Like a compressed spring exploding, he shot his arms forward to their full extension. The white shield hurtled toward the green inferno. An explosion rocked the glen, throwing Jessica several feet backwards, onto her backside. With the wind knocked out of her, she fought to remain conscious. Her breath, when it finally returned, flowed through her mouth in short, shallow gasps. Her heart pounded with the effort of expanding her lungs. At her side, Varnack licked her face, his eyes full of worry.

"I'm...okay," she panted. "Gotta...get...my breath. Anton."

"I'm all right." With Reese supporting the huge man, he limped over and collapsed beside her. "Thought I was a gonner."

Reese, his sword still in his hand scanned the surrounding area. Two soldiers were sprawled on the ground, the other two poked through the ashes and burned shrubbery.

"You can relax, guys," Jessica assured. "There's no one left out there." She saw them hesitate. "Trust me, I'd know." They went to aid their comrades and Reese sat beside Anton. "Your friends are okay," Jessica assured her guards. She could sense their heart beats, strong and clear. "I think they were knocked out by the blast." As if to confirm her words they both shifted and sat up.

"Uncle Anton, what just happened?"

"I'm not sure. Why don't ya tell me yer feelin's first, then maybe I can make some sense out of it?"

While Reese bandaged her wounded arm with the purple fern she had given him on their last journey, Jessica related how she had sensed their attackers and the one who held the source of power. She told of the odd message to go home as well as the death threat. She explained how she felt Edia's energy flow through her body and into Anton's. She ended her brief account with a question of her own. "That first green bolt nearly took off my arm. It hit you full in the chest. Why aren't you dead?"

"There's a lot to tell, Jessi." Anton looked old and tired.

"Well," she said with a drawn smile, "take your time, I'm not going anywhere."

"Thousands and thousands of years ago, magic with all its sorceries and potions and incantations and...well, ya know, magic was everywhere. Reese, ya won't know anythin' about this. Neither will you guys." He waved at the four soldiers who had come to join them on the ground. "It's not a part of our history we teach the young 'uns, 'cause it was a dark time.

Magic itself isn't evil, it's the people who use it, and there were a lot of corrupted people back then. Two great sorcerers arose…brothers, Alderic and Tiard. Family history has it we're descended from Alderic, Jessi. Anyway, the brothers bound the magic, locked it in the Expanse of Gonta and destroyed all the persite spheres they could find, not just the green, but even the blue and white.

"Persite amplifies magic. White is the most powerful, followed by blue, then green. In times long gone, green was the persite of choice fer people who exercised dark magic. In fact the darker the green, the more powerful the magic could be. It's interestin' that Orin could feel it. It's almost like the persite has a mind of its own. White could never be used for dark magic. Don't know all the particulars 'bout it, that stuff is lost, but persite is a part of Edia. It's grown inside her, so maybe it's a part of her spirit comin' through.

"Any written spells, potions and such were destroyed too. Most of the brother's writin's were burned, but a few survived deep in the catacombs of Ramadine. I have two sets of papers, that's how I first learned about Transmirian spirals, but the manuscripts weren't complete. Took me years to find some persite, and much more time to figure the right incantations for spirals. Along the way, I've learned a few magic tricks. That chant I was sayin' is very powerful. That's why I'm not dead, it protected me and finally, with yer help, destroyed the green persite."

"You say those words have power," Jessica commented. "I wasn't sure how to help, until I focused on the chant. Bree …I sort of understand. Orin mentioned her, that she became a sort of guardian. On my planet, I would call her Mother Nature. And Gonta is sort of like a fifth dimension. But T'Aalin, what is T'Aalin?"

"Not what," Reese interjected, "but who? Who is T'Aalin?"

"Okay, then *who* is T'Aalin?" Jessica felt a little irritated at the correction.

"T'Aalin," Anton quickly answered, "is the sacred name for Edia herself. Each planet, each star has a soul and T'Aalin is the soul of Edia."

"Soul? As in Edia might be alive?"

"Yes." Anton sounded firm. "Everything has a soul; the spirit gives life to the physical, even a planet. Ya felt her power, yer able to somehow draw on it. Bree had done the same thing in her life time."

Jessica suddenly knew how her dad felt. She was dumb struck, but could not argue that she had indeed tapped into something powerful.

Reese broke the silence. "You're not the only one who's uncovered some ancient spells, Anton. I heard a woman chanting her own magic charm."

"But Daenon's not behind this," Jessica pointed to the wounded, unconscious men all around them. "Those aren't Elitet."

191

Anton nodded. "Yer right, Deanon wants ya alive, Jessi. It'll be tough to find out who's after us right now. That explosion destroyed not only the green persite, but the woman controllin' it. If she was workin' alone, then we're safe, but my guess is she had a master."

"Why farmers?" a soldier asked.

"I had to kill one," another said sadly. "But I didn't kill any others."

"I tried to knock them out without hurting them too badly," said a third.

"Varnack did the same." Jessica translated his low grunt. "They were definitely being controlled," she commented.

"That's the power of the green persite. Nasty stuff," Anton added.

"It may be Daenon who's actually behind this." Jessica said.

Anton raised his eyebrows in question.

"When I first came here, I saw a vision where Daenon had a huge green crystal," Jessica explained. "He was desperate to unlock it. I didn't understand what he was trying to do, or what it all meant. So I never gave it much more thought, but now I'm educated. This could be really bad if he's learned how to use it."

"If it was Daenon, I think he'd have attacked by now," Anton said. "He'd be unstoppable."

"I wonder," Jessica thought out loud. "Reese said Koradine is thousands of years old, that the ancient section is a museum. If Ramadine has lots of tunnels and hidden places underground, I'll bet the Inner Dine does too. There may be information hidden there on the ancient sorceries that you're not aware of."

Anton nodded. "I'll send some fellas I know who love old stuff to do some explorin'. In fact, I'll even go myself as soon as we're done with this trip, that is, if the war don't get in the way." He shook his shaggy head. "I got a lot to talk to Larone about."

"Yes," Jessica agreed. "First topic is a guy named Orin."

Anton just smiled. He looked to the horizon. "Sun'll be up soon. Let's fix these guys up best we can," he motioned to the farmers on the ground all around them, "then be on our way. I'll send help back here from the next hoffle. Ya up to travelin'?"

"Yeah, I think so." Jessica gingerly fingered her bandaged arm. "That purple fern really works for killing pain."

"It'll help the wound heal without scarrin' bad, too. We've got Seadom on the coast, Rosidia, Tropica and Colossus left to visit. No more sleepin' in the open. Let's get to it."

CHAPTER 18

The Prophecy

After learning the Demarian forces were amassing on the border, John called an emergency meeting in his modest office at Ramadine. Jessica, Varnack, Lyrista, Cordon, Larone, Anton, Gaylee and Reese were all in attendance. They sat on simple wooden chairs arranged in a semicircle facing John's cluttered desk.

Anton gave a full account of the three-week journey to the provinces. All ears perked up when he related the attack in Jewlett.

"It seems we have more enemies than we realized," Larone declared. He looked at his younger brother with concern.

"Yeah, well, I just hope whoever was behind it all doesn't foul us up any." Anton turned to John who sat on the edge of the desk facing his seated friends. "Enemies within can be a lot harder to fight than those from without."

John nodded. "I was thinking the same thing. No idea who it was, huh?"

"Nope." Anton shook his head. "When Reese checked the woods out, all he found were a few scraps of clothing and pieces of fried flesh."

"I didn't mean to kill anyone," Jessica moaned.

"Ah, Jessi," Anton boomed. "It wasn't you. I'm the one who channeled yer power and destroyed the witch. Don't go feeling guilty now, it wasn't yer fault."

She nodded, but still felt the heavy responsibility of having participated in taking a life.

"Look, honey," John sympathized with an endearment he seldom used, "self-defense isn't murder. It was a simple case of kill, or be killed. This is war." He reached over and squeezed her hand. "It seems your power saved all of you."

"You said 'power'." Gaylee smiled. "Does that mean you are finally coming to believe?"

John gave a short grunt. "For lack of a better word, Gaylee. Just because I recognize Jess has certain unexplained abilities, does *not* mean I believe in magic or sorcery or whatever."

"It's okay, Gaylee," Anton winked, "we'll win 'im over yet. Now back to my report. Agreements, agreements, and more agreements." He detailed the papers he had signed for weapons and supplies as well as the number of troops they could still expect.

Cordon described the brief encounter with the giants. It surprised everyone when he mentioned that they acquired the Banner of Freedom.

"Well, at least they took it, that's a good sign," Jessica suggested.

"Your father said the same thing," Cordon laughed, an easy, deep laughter that softened his features and made him look years younger.

Next, Gaylee summarized her western tour. "The people are equipped and organized. Their memory of how quickly the provinces of Snow Peak and Palium fell is still vivid, even after ten years. Being on the western fringes…well…you can imagine their fears."

John updated everyone on the efforts of Lepsis and Ophir. "Lepsis has finished marshaling the armies of Marone. The leaders there have been well aware of the situation in Esparia. When Snow Peak fell to Daenon's influence ten years ago, they recognized the coming danger and began their preparations back then. In fact, they expressed amazement at the length of time it took Esparia to actually do something about him. Lepsis' cousin sits on the throne, and from what he said, welcomed him home with open arms.

"Ophir, on the other hand, is struggling. The leaders of Galland never anticipated conflict. Their level of readiness was basically non-existent, but what the people lack in preparation they make up for in heart. They're training, literally day and night. The men and extra supplies we sent have helped a great deal, so he's fairly confident they can hold the line against Hent. I plan on sending him another fifty thousand to bolster his armies."

Finally, Lyrista recapped her efforts in organizing the Special Operations groups. "I've sent three hundred spies out to the Deserts. They're well qualified and know the risks. There are fifteen companies of expert archers, twelve companies of the best swordsmen you could ever hope to find, and three companies of trackers. Each company consists of five hundred and can be further divided into smaller teams as needed. I have twenty thousand men, as good as any Elitet Daenon can come up with, arranged in groups of five. I've dubbed them the Guardians, and they're ready for assignment."

"Great," John approved. "Many of your scouts have reported back. Daenon's marching thousands of troops to the Demarian border, so I think we have only a few days before he attacks. I'm sending Cordon to take command of the Northern army. He'll be able to free his father from there, and any other prisoners who might be held at the Snow Peak Prison. Lepsis indicated he thought there were others."

Addressing Anton he asked, "Will you go with him? Those are your mountains and as I understand it no one knows them better. You'll be second in command, after Cordon."

"Yeah, I'll go. I've got a few ideas for ya Cordon."

"Fine," John continued, "Lepsis knows you're coming and is marching to meet you. He's in command of the Maronians. Now Anton," John's voice took on a stern tone, "if you're going to be a commander, it's time you wear a uniform."

At Anton's moan and look of disgust, everyone laughed.

"We've taken the liberty of having one made for you," Lyrista piped up. She walked to the corner of the room where a large bag sat and pulled a new uniform from it. "I hope it fits." She grinned when she handed it to him.

He accepted the gift and looked it over. "Thanks." A slight smile lit up his whiskered face.

"Reese and I will go to the Southern command post," John nodded at the young man. "Lyrista, you and half of your units will move to the center of the front. You'll be better able to direct them from there. We'll discuss the deployment of the other half right after this meeting." She nodded.

"More soldiers arrive here daily. Larone and Gaylee will dispatch them where necessary, keeping at least one division of ten thousand to protect Ramadine. I also need you to handle the money and goods flowing in from the provinces," John addressed Larone. "We'll try and send word daily as to what is happening so you can make prudent decisions."

John paused to look through his papers. "I guess that's about all. If there are no questions, then we leave within the half hour."

Jessica sat patiently listening to her father give orders to every person in the room. Now he wanted to bring the meeting to a close without so much as a nod in her direction and she was not happy. "Just a minute, Dad, you've given an assignment to everyone but me and Varnack."

"Varnack knows his job."

"Dad!" Jessica protested, but before she could say more he cut her off.

"Look, Jess," he leaned toward her, "I am your father. I'm also commander of this entire operation. I can't be both right now. You need to stay put, where I know you're safe. Then I can completely focus on the war."

She felt crestfallen. She wanted to be with him, to be an active participant of the fight to maintain Esparia's freedom, but his reasoning cut through her protests. "All right, Dad," she sounded dejected. "I'll stay. I'm sure Uncle Larone can use me."

"Yes, I can. You will not be disappointed for staying," Larone promised, then stood and faced John. "There is one more item we need to discuss, something I have not explained, but the time has now come."

"Are ya sure, Larone?" Anton's voice boomed through the room.

"Yes, Anton. Before this war commences, they must know the

warnings."

Anton nodded his agreement. "Go ahead."

"John, you better sit down. You are not going to like what I have to say, but I would not take extra time if this were trivial. It will not take long." After a moment's hesitation, John took Larone's vacated chair.

"I need to give you a little background first. Jessica, this has much to do about you."

A little startled by being singled out, she gave him her full attention.

"Anton and I are the two remaining children of Paulus and Shallenon, the fifteenth generation of great healers. Our parents were extraordinary people. From our mother comes the fire-red hair that you and your grandmother have. Your mother was named after mine. Mother had a remarkable gift with animals, she could communicate with them. Not actually talk—it was more a telepathic link, but she could understand them, and they her. She once told me her grandmother had the same gift. I can only assume it runs in the family, showing up every couple of generations. She also could sense deceit. She had an ability to know when someone lied or spoke the truth."

"Yeah," Anton chuckled. "Do ya have any idea what it's like to be a rowdy kid and not be able to tell yer mom it wasn't you who tied the cat to the horse's back?"

"What?" Lyrista laughed, her gentle sound a sharp contrast to Anton's booming snicker.

"To see how fast it could go, 'o course," he explained. "If the cat or the horse didn't tell her it was me, she still always knew when I wasn't tellin' the truth."

Larone smiled affectionately at his brother and continued. "Our father, from whom comes our blue eyes, was a renowned healer. He could draw on T'Aalin herself to heal. Each generation of his family, going back several thousand years, has produced at least one with this ability."

Larone walked over to the window. He absently gazed at the large, ghostly planet hovering in the sky above. "Mother was the first to die. Anton and I have suspected for many years our brother, Segal, poisoned her. Father died shortly thereafter. I think Segal also had a hand in his demise. Just before he died, he had a remarkable dream, so vivid in detail and physical sensibility as to call it a vision. From what he saw, he made a prophecy and asked me to write it down. They were the last words he ever spoke."

Larone turned from the window and faced the group. "I have it memorized."

> "A cry of war, from shore to shore
> The land of peace will be no more.

196

Like thunder from a distant storm
Approaches slowly, takes on form.
Dark of hate, of lust and greed
Steadily grows, a forceful weed.
Potions rare, hungers power

He will not stop till all do cower.
From afar a light grows steady
Safe from harm till she is ready
Within her hand she holds all gifts
Of truth and speech, healing of rifts.
Opposing cousins take a stand
Protector new will lead the land
Mercy and kindness from his lips
Upon this course the balance tips.
Dark succeeds to twice arise
With army fierce in strength and size
When light returns with allies strong
Keep justice true, do not go wrong.
Here is a warning, heed it well,
For patience strong will break war's hell
If anger rule and vengeance take
Countless years of darkness make."

Larone finished the verse in a near whisper. "There's a little bit more, but this much is important right now."

"Why in verse?" Lyrista asked.

"My father loved poetry and often spoke in verse," Larone explained. He walked over to stand next to Anton. He placed his hand on his brother's broad shoulder. "Anton and I have remained silent about this, not wanting to influence the natural course of events. So far, everything my father predicted has come to pass. Two cousins are standing against each other and a war is about to begin. Daenon, like his father before him, lusts for power. And like his father before him, he has a gift for potions. He was educated in chemistry, herbology, medicine and dark sorcery. Daenon is a master at using strange medications, from powerful hallucinogenic drugs to slow acting, undetectable poisons."

"That's how he took over Snow Peak and Palium provinces," Anton interjected. "'Bout twelve years ago he flooded 'em with a powerful, cheap drug and got the people so hooked they would do anythin' to have the stuff. After that, he just walked right in and took 'em over, without a single man resistin'."

"That was when Haesom set up the training academies and began taxing our people," Larone explained to John and Gaylee. "Ten years ago, there was no standing army in Esparia, it was disbanded after Segal's defeat at Blue Mountain. Only the warriors from Ider Hoffle stood between Daenon and the rest of the country. When we realized the power of his narcotic, we broke all relations with Palium and Snow Peak, then Ophir's men sealed the border. This, as well as great vigilance, has saved the rest of Esparia from being poisoned with the drug."

"I wondered why Haesom never came to Palium and Snow Peak's rescue," John commented.

Larone looked hurt. "My nephew did not abandon them. It was a peaceful takeover and no one asked for help. Daenon managed the deed quietly, quickly and very efficiently. The takeover was complete before Haesom realized what happened. He would have sent troops in immediately if he suspected treachery, but it was many months before the truth of the takeover came out, and by then Daenon's army had fortified the borders. We were not prepared at that time for an all-out war."

"Esparia is not held together as the United States is." Gaylee explained to John. "The central government has power, but the individual provinces are just as strong, perhaps more. If one province wanted to secede badly enough, it could. There would be no civil war, as your country had so long ago. Think of the European Economic Union, several independent countries held together by a common governing power. For Europe it's economic power, but for Esparia it's political. The Protectors, along with a Grand Council, made up of elected officials from the provinces, comprise our central government. We have political power, but not as absolute as the US federal government."

John nodded, seeming to understand this explanation, though Cordon and Lyrista had inquisitive looks on their faces.

"European Economic Union? United States?" Lyrista looked to John.

"Now you know how I felt when I first heard about Esparia, Hent and Marone." John smiled. "I'll explain later."

"Please Larone," Gaylee gently urged, "you were explaining Grandfather's prophecy."

"There is a passage about Jessica." Larone quoted again, "'From afar a light grows steady, Safe from harm till she is ready, Within her hand she holds all gifts, Of truth and speech, healing of rifts.' Earth is as far from Edia as one can get."

"Earth?" Lyrista's eyebrows shot up again.

"I promise, I'll explain later," John reassured.

Anton spoke up. "Jessi has the Healin' or Salupathic Gift and we've seen her Truth skills. She even understands Varnack."

Larone nodded. "The prophecy contains two strict warnings, *patience strong will break war's hell*' and *If anger rule and vengeance take Countless years of darkness make.*'" Looking at John he confessed, "I was immensely relieved when you resisted the temptation to attack Daenon first. I believe that would have proved disastrous."

Addressing the entire group again he finished, "The second warning is quite clear, this is not a war of vengeance. Mercy needs to be shown. This is the only way to peace."

For a long time, no one spoke. Finally, Cordon broke the silence. "You failed to mention another stanza of the prophecy, something like, *'Protector new will lead the land'*." Cordon looked directly at John with an expression of 'I told you so' on his face. John wrinkled his brow and took a breath, as if to say something, but then swallowed it and remained quiet.

"I have explained the lines which are important for now, the warnings. However, I believe as you do Cordon, the 'new Protector' is John; the problem is *he* does not believe it. He must come to that conclusion on his own."

When John still did not respond, Larone turned to Jessica. "I am pleased you are willing to stay here for a while longer. I can teach you how to control your gifts and more fully develop them. With patience, you will come to understand your heritage and achieve your full potential."

"It's no secret how I feel about magical powers," John finally spoke. "But if this prophecy brings any of you comfort and guidance, then who am I to discredit it. Now, if there are no other surprises," he paused, "then it's time to adjourn this meeting. Good luck everyone."

* * *

Mid-morning found Jessica in Medicinal Plants class. Her ability to concentrate waned while the seconds ticked by. Normally she enjoyed the fascinating class, but the instructor, a middle aged woman with a whiny voice, had chosen as today's topic 'the value of the Purple Fern' and Jessica already knew, from personal experience, how the plant functioned. Her arm was nearly healed, with only a small scar to prove she was ever wounded.

The only thing on Jessica's mind was the sad thought that Varnack would leave that afternoon for the home of the Trigal Hounds. She understood the importance of his mission, the hounds would make invaluable allies, but her heart felt heavy at losing her best friend.

She wouldn't have much time to dwell on the loss though. Larone had her on a demanding schedule. As soon as she said good-bye to her father and the other departing leaders, Larone and Grandma Gaylee began her Esparian education. That was a little over a week ago. Since then she had suffered through tutorials of every form, from early morning to late evening. Before noon, traditional classroom instruction of the medical profession filled her time. The lessons ranged from Birthing Babies to

Emergency Medical Care. These classes she actually enjoyed, for they were fast paced and full of practical information. The afternoon schedule consisted first of laboratory work...moderately interesting; second, Esparian history and culture...excruciatingly boring; third, weaponry...not as fun as she originally thought it would be, and finally horsemanship...best of the afternoon bunch.

Jessica felt the evenings, spent with Larone and Grandma Gaylee, to be the most worthwhile time in her day, for it was then she learned to hone her abilities. The first half of each evening found them at Ramadine's farm where Larone had Jessica practice her animal communication skills. She improved dramatically during the week and decided she liked talking with the pigs best, as their quirky sense of humor made her laugh.

The second half of each evening was devoted to exercises specific for development and control of her psychic powers. These proved to be the most difficult of all. There were relaxation exercises and precise drills for controlling her mental state, practicing her visualization as well as developing mental protection. It took a great deal of dedicated concentration and she found the mental exertion was, ironically, more taxing than any physical labor she had ever before performed. As a result, she fell into her bed each night completely exhausted.

At last, a bell ringer came through the hall signaling the end of the purple fern class. Scores of bell ringers were employed at Ramadine. Their job was to attend to the sundials and announce the time at each hour throughout the day. Silently, Jessica blessed the bell ringer who ended the Medicinal Plants lecture. She filed out with the rest of the students and headed for Dental Emergencies when Quirt singled her out. "My Lady...Jessica," he huffed, somewhat out of breath, "Lord Larone...wants you right away. He's...in his office."

"Thanks, Quirt," she said, then made her way across campus to the large, green building. Larone had allowed Quirt to stay at Ramadine, but the man was stripped of his previous authority and was now little more than an errand boy. Jessica felt pity for him because she understood how truly penitent he was for his betrayal, but no amount of remorse could bring back the thousand lives lost by his false information that fateful day at Saylon Dorsett.

Jessica found her uncle sitting at his desk, studying a small piece of paper in his hand. "Quirt said you wanted to see me," she knocked on the open door.

"Yes, come in and sit down, my dear. I have just received another communication from your father." He indicated the small paper. "Daenon still has not attacked. His troops are arrayed within Palium and Snow Peak, approximately five filons from our border, and yet he waits."

Jessica pursed her lips. "Maybe Daenon's waiting for something else.

He must have spies around. He might be trying to infiltrate further into our lines before he makes the first move, attack us from within as well as without, or cut off the supply routes."

"Perhaps." Larone set the paper aside. "I will send warnings to take extra precautions and double the guards where necessary, but that is not the reason why I called you in here." He pulled a piece of thinly hammered bark from his top desk drawer. "I received this last night by Red Feathers; I believe it to be from the giants."

He handed it to her. It was yellow in color and slightly thicker than regular paper. A short line of handwritten characters was scrawled across it. At first glance the characters seemed foreign to Jessica, sort of blurry on the paper. But as she stared at them they seemed to come into focus.

She read it out loud. "Meet again, John"

"Hmmm," Larone stared intently at Jessica. She became uncomfortable under his scrutiny. Finally he said, "So, they desire another meeting with your father." He took the yellowed paper out of her hand and studied it. "That is not possible, since he is not here." He looked at Jessica. "I do not wish to disappoint the giants. This meeting could prove extremely beneficial to us. Would you go in your father's place?"

Jessica's heart skipped several beats. "I would love to go, but are you sure this is from the giants?"

"It was delivered to a Red Feathers Center closest to the base of the Colossus Mountain range by a giant. The Redman in charge of the center was terrified. I will send an escort of men with you. Not a large troop, I do not wish to alarm the giants, but enough soldiers to protect you in an emergency. They are expecting only your father and possibly Cordon, not an entire regiment."

"How soon do I leave?"

"Can you be ready by this afternoon? It will take at least four days to reach the mountains, and I do not know how far into them you will have to ride before making contact. I will instruct your escort to take you to the Golden Meadow, since that is where your father had his first contact with them."

"This afternoon will be fine." She tried to keep her voice steady, but inside she jumped with excitement. She could not wait to see the majestic mountains her father had so vividly described, and she was already mentally reviewing her German, and wishing she'd paid more attention in class.

Two hours later, a group of soldiers, fresh from Ider Hoffle, stood ready at the gate. Their leader was a young man who had recently arrived at Ramadine. When Jessica and Web approached the troop, the leader dismounted and bowed to her. He introduced himself as Jeema, the soldier her father had saved in Ider Hoffle a few weeks earlier. He did not look much older than she, but knowing how deceiving looks could be, she gratefully accepted his leadership.

Jessica said good-bye to Gaylee and Larone. Varnack came to her and licked her hand. "Not happy. Go with you."

"I'm not happy about this either, Varnack, but Uncle Larone needs you. You're our only emissary to the Trigal Hounds."

"Don't trust soldiers."

"I'll be fine. In fact, I bet I'm back before you are." She scratched his head when he licked her once more, then Jeema gave the signal to head out.

Traveling south-eastward, the trip took the four and a half days Larone predicted it would. Jessica felt grateful she had taken equestrian lessons the week earlier, especially since none of the escort offered her any assistance in tending Web. He was, however, very helpful, and even told her he was impressed with the improvements she made in her care for him as well as her riding skills.

Jessica found these Idle Hoffle soldiers to be a well disciplined and close knit group. In the evenings, they quietly joked with each other, but limited their interaction with the young Protectoress. Jeema was polite, but never made an extra effort to involve Jessica in his plans or decisions. All of the men seemed to keep their distance from her, not physically, for they stayed in a tight group, but emotionally, isolating Jessica from their camaraderie.

This somewhat hostile behavior was puzzling until on the evening of the third day out, Jessica overheard the whisperings of a several soldiers. Feigning sleep, she strained to hear their conversation.

"I think I caught a glimpse of those mountains before the sun went down," one commented.

"I did, too," another responded. "We should be there soon."

"Not soon enough," a third quipped. "The faster this mission is over, the faster we go west, where the real action is."

"I agree," said the first. "This is torture. Knowing the Demarians are ready to attack, and we're here, having to escort this child to a meeting that may or may not take place. It's a waste of time. We're Idle Hoffle warriors, not some sub-standard soldier from Jewlett."

The others muttered their agreement.

"Enough," a rough whisper silenced the group. Jessica recognized Jeema's voice. "This is our assignment, and we will fulfill it. We'll prove ourselves, no matter how trivial the task, then the greater challenges will come. Now go to sleep."

Jessica felt the emotions of anger, astonishment, insult, and finally sadness course through her in seconds. She stifled the impulse to grab Web and ride on alone, knowing those actions would disappoint both Larone and her father.

When the travelers finally reached the base of the Colossus mountain range, the entire troop stood still, staring in awe at the peaks before them. Not one person had been there before, and the towering, cloud hidden spires left each man speechless. John tried to describe the enormity of the mountains, but no words could adequately express the reality. Each peak in the range seemed to touch beyond the sky, and the range stretched on for as far as the eye could see.

The massive trees and truck sized bushes made Jessica feel as small as one of her old Barbie dolls. She half expected to see giant insects, but only ordinary flies and bees whizzed around. Even though the plant life grew to extraordinary size, the enormous flowers they produced held ordinary pollination centers.

"We'd better proceed with caution," Jeema suggested. "Algor, which way from here?"

The troop navigator checked the sky, consulted his map, then pointed off to one side. Jessica pulled the giant's message Larone gave her from her pocket. She wanted it handy in case of a surprise meeting with any giants to prove she was sent in her father's place.

They traveled about an hour, winding through the majestic hardwoods on an ever-upward course when Jessica felt uneasy. "Jeema," she called. "Stop. Something's not right here."

Jeema brushed her off with a wave of his hand and continued moving forward. "Jeema, you arrogant..." she called again, more urgently, "Stop!" She reined her horse to a halt and soon found herself at the back of the advancing column, as the other soldiers continued to follow their leader. The last to pass her turned in his saddle, and with an exasperated look on his face, motioned for her to catch up with him.

Jessica had learned to control some of her abilities, but the urge to throw up was one side effect she was still working on, and right now that urge rose in her throat. She tried one last time to warn the soldiers. With all the force of spirit she could muster, she shouted vocally and mentally, "Jeema! Run!" To her horror the men still did not listen, but fortunately, their horses did. Thanks to her additional training during the past week, her message penetrated to all living creatures, and the animals bolted, scattering in different directions, with their riders, in stunned surprise, hanging on for their lives.

She had little time to run herself, for two teams of Elitet materialized from behind the mammoth trees to quickly surround her. In her brief, but desperate attempt for freedom, Jessica dropped the giant's note. She realized, far too late, it was fake.

While her hands were being lashed together in front of her, Jessica managed one blood curdling scream before someone jammed a gag into her mouth. A rope was tied to her left ankle, then threaded under Web and tied to her right, binding her securely to the animal. Once her scream died away, an eerie hush fell on the forest. The Elitet worked quickly in the profound silence, taking only moments to restrict Jessica's ability to move.

Enclosed on every side by men cloaked in black, she was swiftly escorted out of the area. While they galloped along, an appalling realization struck her. *This is why Daenon hasn't attacked Esparia yet. It's taken his men this long to set this trap. The guy wants a backup plan...me!* They rode directly toward the setting sun. West...due west. Straight to the Deserts of Demar.

CHAPTER 19

The Prisoners of Snow Peak

Cordon's encampment lay positioned in a lightly wooded area on the Verdure-Snow Peak border. Verdure was directly north of Ramana, the province where Ramadine and Saylon Dorsett were located. One of the major agricultural provinces, Verdure's security was vital, not only to the war effort, but to the nation as well.

The Maronian army, under the command of Lepsis, was already digging in and making fortifications all up and down the northern half of the Verdure border when Cordon's force of three hundred thousand men marched throughout the southern half. The two seventh bars were assigned to protect Verdure and keep Daenon out of Marone. The western perimeter of Verdure bordered all of Snow Peak and the northern third of Palium. Cordon split the Verdure boundary in half, giving Lepsis, with his army of nearly two hundred thousand Maronian men, stewardship over the northern section and himself the southern.

Wasting no time, Cordon deployed his men along the border of the southern territory. Cordon's command hub lay centered on the Verdure line. Lepsis was only ten filons north with his command headquarters, and the two met every few days to compare strategies and send combined reports to John.

No one could understand why Daenon did not attack. Cordon felt Daenon was playing mind games. John sent a communiqué saying he felt something more sinister was afoot, but he did not know what. No one did. After a week of speculation, they were no closer to solving the mystery, but Cordon had his men continuously training and gathering as much intelligence about Daenon's strength as possible.

On the eighth day after leaving Ramadine, a regiment of fifty well-trained Guardians rode into Cordon's command camp. Their leader, a small, muscular man with jet-black hair, shiny black eyes, and black lock beard walked into the command center tent. Clicking his heals and bowing, Fourth Bar Ru handed Cordon a sealed letter. Opening it, Cordon recognized Lyrista's hand.

Dearest Brother,

While Daenon frits away his time, I cannot wait one more day. I have sent you fifty of my best men. Put Lepsis in command. Ask Anton to go with you and free our father.

Lyrista

Cordon reread the short note several times, then stuffed it in his pocket, his eyes gleamed. "Wait outside with your men until I return," he ordered the fourth bar, barely able to control his excitement. "I'll have hot food sent to you."

Having barked the orders to a nearby second bar, Cordon ran to where Anton's private compound was set up. Only a short distance from the main body of soldiers lay a small clearing with a brook running beside it. The big man claimed sole camping privileges at this pristine location and Cordon allowed him his solitude.

"Anton," Cordon called before he entered the clearing. He wanted to give ample warning of his approach. Anton tended a small fire. Cordon felt a slight rush of relief when the loner exhibited a welcoming grin.

"Cordon, m' boy. Good to see ya. What can I do?"

"How long does it take to get from here to Snow Peak Prison?"

Anton exhibited no surprise to the question. "Depends on how fast ya travel. If ya make good speed, it's about four days goin' round the base of the mountains, two if ya cut through the Narrow Passes, but by usin' the passes, ya gotta leave yer horses behind. Why?" The gleam from Cordon's eye took hold in Anton's.

Cordon handed over Lyrista's note, then waited by the fire for Anton's response. A smile spread across the big man's face. He picked up a cooking pot and strode over to the stream. Filling it with water, he doused the little fire. Cordon jumped in the air, threw both hands and gave a fierce war cry, making Anton stare in amazement at the usually sedate man.

"Thank you, Anton! I'll inform Ru we leave in a few minutes," Cordon hollered before he left the camp at a run.

When Cordon returned to his tent, he found Lepsis there waiting to begin their scheduled meeting. "Lepsis, I'm glad to see you," Cordon nearly bounced with enthusiasm. "Lyrista has sent me fifty of the best men she has. Since Daenon is waiting to attack, I'm going to Snow Peak Prison to free my father. You're in full command." At his desk he quickly scribbled the necessary authorizations. Lepsis stood silently, watching his new friend. "We're taking the Narrow Passes. Anton is the only man in Esparia who knows about them, so we'll have the element of surprise. I should be gone six days, two and a half there, one to take the prison, and two and a half back. If I don't return within a week, inform John."

"He's going to be furious," Lepsis warned.

"Not if we're successful."

Lepsis shook his head. "And if Daenon attacks while you're gone?"

Cordon stood still, staring at Lepsis. He clenched his jaw while he thought about what to say. "Everything is in place, our defenses, our strategies, everything. We sit here," he spat, his frustration and anger rising to the surface. "While I do nothing, my father dies a little more each day. I am one man. Just one man. The officers know what to do. You're more than capable of commanding this region. I cannot...no, I *will not*, wait any longer, not when I'm so close to freeing him."

Lepsis sighed, "I've been expecting this. I think Anton was too. He asked me three days ago to show him a current map and exactly where the prison was located on it. I've never been there myself, but I've seen the location dozens of times at Rendaira. For some reason, Daenon's very proud of the prison and keeps a painting of it hung on one of the walls in his office. It's odd, even for him, but I believe there is someone of great importance imprisoned there, though I don't know who."

"We'll find out. We'll free every one of the prisoners."

The rescue party rode single file to hide their numbers from would-be trackers. They traveled swiftly, with Anton leading the way. They did not stop until the two moons were well up in the night sky, then grabbed a few hours of precious sleep before riding hard again.

When dawn broke on the morning of their third day out, the Snow Peak Mountains loomed in the distance. Cordon noticed how small they looked in comparison to the Colossus Mountains of the southeast, but they were still quite beautiful. The Snow Peak range, named for its tallest spire, was known for its sharp peaks and deadly, sheer cliffs. Geologically speaking, the range was young. Not a great deal of erosion had taken place to round out the edges and smooth it down. Each of the summits within sight shimmered with white ice caps.

Anton turned to the northwest and the band of rescuers entered the range from its eastern foothills. Once in the lightly wooded mountains, their trail rose steeply, and soon they climbed high up to oxygen thin elevations. It was nearly noon when the riders reached the Narrow Passes.

Cordon was impressed Anton remembered where the Passes' opening lay. They arrived at a small clearing where Anton slowed their pace and finally dismounted. He poked at a wall of foliage that blocked their path with his sword. After a second probing, he chose an area and hacked at the bushes, using his sword as a machete. Cutting a small opening, he disappeared into it.

"Cordon," his voiced boomed out, "we'll need some torches."

While the men prepared the fire brands, they could hear Anton chopping at more plants. After nearly twenty minutes of branches breaking, leaves rustling and Anton swearing, there was silence. Finally, the big man reappeared with a broad smile on his face.

"All right fellas, light yer torches. We're footin' it from here on out." With his drawn sword still in his right hand, Anton led the way through nearly ten feet of dense growth. Behind these tall bushes lay the opening to a small, man-made tunnel which cut through the side of the mountain.

Nearly three hundred feet long, the tunnel was filled with cobwebs. A thick layer of fine dirt covered the floor. It was clear to all that no human foot had disturbed the dust in decades. Cordon felt relieved. At least this end of the trail was free from ambush. At the end of the tunnel lay a natural pathway, about three feet wide, protruding from the mountain's side. Motioning for those behind him to stay close to the mountain wall, Anton stepped out onto the narrow trail.

The treacherous passes were, in fact, not true passes at all, but a series of narrow pathways, formed by thick rock ledges jutting out on three separate peaks and connected to each other by palium rope bridges. The trail was barely wide enough for a man the size of Anton. Cordon, who followed directly behind, was uncomfortable watching his large friend cautiously inch along. One edge of the path was the mountain itself and the other a sheer drop, at hundreds of feet down. These slender passageways were only accessible during the summer months, for they were snowbound fall, winter and spring.

As Cordon carefully rounded each blind corner, he hoped Daenon's people were not guarding the way. However, if resistance were encountered, he and Anton would be the first to know it. Being isolated from the other peaks, the rescue party was safe from archer's arrows, for with the steep rise of the mountain, no one from below or above could attack. Only an adversary directly on the path would pose a threat.

With the approach of evening, the band of Guardians came to the end of the third and last path. As with the trail's opening, thick bushes grew over the pathway exit and Anton cut their way through. With the opening cleared, the soldiers filed silently onto the steep face of the sparsely wooded mountain. Dense, short shrubbery grew throughout the mountainside, providing some cover from spying eyes down below.

"There." Anton pointed to the buildings on the valley floor.

From their vantage point behind a cluster of boulders, Cordon could see the prison was built up against the side of the steep mountain wall directly below them. "It's a smaller compound than what I imagined," he whispered. "I make out two high towers flanking the one main building as well as a barracks near the front gate."

Anton nodded. "Fortress wall...new," he tried hard to whisper. The complex was surrounded by a thick, fifteen foot high, stone wall.

Fourth Bar Ru silently slid in next to them. "I've made a quick inspection. This thick foliage gives adequate cover, but will make our descent to the prison more difficult. The sharp slope doesn't help either. The ground is soft, muddy in some spots, so could prove dangerously slick. I don't know how stable the trees are, but they're all we can anchor our ropes to. I don't trust the boulders; they could jar loose at any time. There seems to be little else to hinder our operation."

"At least the prison looks asleep," Cordon whispered. "What an isolated spot. I'd hate to have duty here. Look," he pointed to the ground under his feet, "there're still patches of hardened ice up here. I'll bet some spots never melt. Ru, send two men down to spy out the prison."

As soon as the scouts were gone, Anton, Cordon and Ru made detailed plans according to what they saw. Anton was to take ten men and cover the tower on the left, Cordon with ten, the one on the right, and Ru would secure the courtyard with twenty-five.

When the scouts returned, their news was positive, about twenty guards stood on duty, but the mountain was slippery and their descent as well as the subsequent climb back up had proven difficult. The earth was too wet from the warm weather runoff to provide adequate footholds.

"At least the trees held firm," Cordon said with a wan smile.

"Only twenty guards," Ru commented. "The fortress hasn't been attacked for so many years, the sentries have become complacent."

Cordon nodded. "Lepsis thought about a hundred men were stationed here. We'll wait until midnight, when most of the prison is asleep. Luckily, there're no moons. I want to be in and out as quickly as possible. Let's free the prisoners without waking the entire garrison."

At midnight, the Guardians rappelled down the hill. Landing like cats, they spread out, every man to his assignment

Cordon found the head jailer of the eastern tower so drunk he could not stand. "Bind and gag him," Cordon ordered. Grabbing a lit torch and using the jailer's keys, he raced up the tower's winding stairs toward the first of the tiny cells. He and his men found most cubicles empty, but a few held Daenon's enemies. Winding his way to the very top, Cordon freed eighteen tortured and half-starved men. Some of the prisoner's bodies were twisted and mangled; others were missing limbs, eyes, ears and noses. Only six were found whole. Cordon later learned these were scientists whom Daenon needed in one piece. However, even these needed help out of the tower. Cordon's heart pounded while he headed for the last lockup at the very top of the stairs. He wondered if his father was there, and what sort of condition he might be in.

Cordon's hand trembled slightly when he unlocked the metal door. The hinges squeaked loudly as it swung open. Holding his torch high, he stepped into the room.

"Cordon!" a voice rasped. "I thought you were dead. I thought you were dead." A white haired man stumbled toward the door. Cordon let the jailer keys tumble from his fingers. He threw his free arm around the weeping prisoner.

"Ballian. It was Ballian who betrayed us," the captive revealed.

"I know, Dad," Cordon clutched him tightly. "We'll talk later. Right now, we need to move out of here."

Cordon was relieved to see his father walk without assistance. His only thought now was how they were going to transport eighteen crippled men back up the mountain and through the Narrow Passes before the jail break was detected. *I hope Anton doesn't find too many guys in this bad of shape. If he does, we're in real trouble.*

* * *

To Anton's surprise, the tower he entered had no jailer at the base. It seemed completely deserted. No lights, no sounds, no sign of human occupation. One of the men found some torches lying against a wall and lit them. With a flame in hand, Anton led his soldiers up the winding stairs. Making their way from cell to cell, they found no signs of life. Each jail door stood open, with the compartments themselves full of cobwebs and dust. Not even a rat greeted them.

Anton's frustration mounted, but knowing he needed to check each cell to the very top, he and his men pushed on. When they reached the final door at the pinnacle of the tower, to their surprise, it was locked from the outside by a single bolt. Anton slid it back, moving it easily, releasing it with a dull thud. The heavy wooden door groaned when he pulled on it. Torch in hand, he entered the darkened room. It was the largest of the tower chambers. A small table and a single chair were to one side, an armoire stood at the back, and a thin rug partially covered the bare stone floor. The only other furniture in the cell was a bed in the far corner. Starlight poured in from two high windows located near the vaulted ceiling. Anton walked toward the bed, his footsteps echoing in the silence.

"Who's there?" a breathy female voice called out. He did not dare answer. Anton knew he was incapable of whispering. Placing a finger to his lips, he tried a, "Shhhh."

Though he could not see her face in the shadows, he realized she must be someone of great importance to be isolated at the very top of the great, dark tower.

After handing the torch to a Guardian behind him, Anton crossed to the bed and picked a thin, fragile woman up in his arms. She was light as a feather and an odd feeling of familiarity swept over him.

A small squeak came from her when she tried to speak again, but after one more 'shhh' from Anton, she made no further sounds. She seemed to understand she was being rescued because she reached her arms around his neck and held on. Flanked in front and behind by five men, Anton raced down the tower stairs with the woman gently cradled against his chest.

When they exited the prison, Anton motioned to Ru with his head, jerking it toward the waiting ropes at the mountain's side. Ru signaled his men to begin retreating toward the rendezvous spot. Cordon's men were already there, in the process of hauling their rescued prisoners up to the pass. Only the strongest Guardians were capable of making the initial climb, carrying the feeble captives strapped onto their backs.

"We found eighteen," Cordon whispered. "I see you found...What! A woman?"

Anton nodded.

"No more?"

Anton shook his head.

One Guardian offered to take the woman from Anton's arms, but he shook his head, indicating he would take her up himself.

Another odd, squeaky sound escaped the woman's lips, but Anton, his senses straining to detect signs of the enemy, did not take the time to listen to her words.

When he turned to check on how the ascension was progressing, he noticed Gammet in the group of freed men awaiting their turn up the mountain. Stunned, he stared at the famous general. The last time Anton had seen the man, which was only a few months earlier, his hair had been a deep brown color, only beginning to gray at the temples. Now that hair was snow white in color and stood out in sharp contrast against the dark mountain beside them.

With the last of the burdened Guardians beginning the assent, Cordon motioned for Ru and his squad to go up. When the fourth bar and his men ran to the ropes, a cry of alarm came from the far tower where the woman had been imprisoned.

Within seconds, Demarian soldiers came streaming from the barracks.

"Go!" Cordon ordered Anton. He pulled his sword. Ru and his men formed a semi-circle around the dangling ropes with Anton and his charge at the center.

Before Anton could reach for the rigging, the woman twisted out of his hold. Her burst of strength surprised him.

"Help them, Anton," she ordered in a weak, barely audible voice. "You've come for me at last and I will wait for you here." She stepped back against the steep wall and pushed him forward.

He stared at her, surprised that she knew his name. He had not really looked at her face, and now he tried to see her more clearly, but the dark night prevented it. "Who...?"

Before he could finish the question she waved him off. "Help them."

Anton joined Cordon, Gammet, and the remaining thirty Guardians just as the enemy reached them. Nearly one hundred swords came slashing in, but these Guardians were the best of the best that Lyrista had to send, and they stood firm against the onslaught of soldiers gone soft.

Anton heaved his huge sword left and right, downing an adversary with every stroke. Gammet took up a fallen Demarian's weapon and wielded it mercilessly. With each blow he cried out in anger, cursing the jailers and their evil master. Within twenty minutes of the first steel clashing, the few remaining enemy soldiers retreated at a run.

Several Guardians were wounded in the fight, three badly enough they would need to be carried up. The defenders had not moved from their original semi-circle. When they retreated backward to scale the mountain wall, the bodies of the dead Demarian guards marked the perfect half-moon defensive line.

The woman went to Anton. She reached up and caressed his cheek with the back of her hand. "I knew you'd come one day."

He jerked back, as if she had slapped him, and stared at her wide-eyed. By the meager light of the stars, he finally recognized the thin, but still beautiful face of Naydeen, Daenon's mother and Lepsis' older sister. His heart lurched in his chest and he barely stopped himself from crying out. She was the only woman he had ever loved, and for forty-five years he had thought she was dead.

Questions flashed through his mind, but they would have to wait. While she clung to his neck, he carried her up the mountain. He held her once again in his arms while Cordon took lead during the journey back through the Narrow Passes. Not until he was astride his horse, with Naydeen safely tucked against him, did he venture any of his queries.

The first rays of morning light touched the mountains as the band of fifty guardians and eighteen grateful, rescued men followed Cordon eastward through the Snow Peak Range. Anton brought up the rear.

"What happened, Naydeen? I thought ya was gone forever."

"I might as well have been. After Segal died, and you escaped, I was taken to Daenon. He was told I tried to leave with you and that you killed Segal. Daenon knew his father didn't love me; that he never had. I told him the Maronian courts had granted my divorce. I wanted to take him and Lepsis and leave. I tried to explain that Segal attacked you and fell on his own knife when you pushed him away. I begged for my freedom, for Lepsis' freedom, just as I begged Segal earlier, but he only laughed. My boy laughed."

She paused. A weak sob escaped her lips. "You'd think after all these years I'd stop mourning, but he died for me that day. 'If my father refused you freedom, what makes you believe I will grant it?' he said. I asked him if he was going to kill me, but he said he would never be guilty of matricide and sentenced me to life imprisonment in the tower at Snow Peak. For the last forty-five years," she paused, "I never gave up hope you would someday come."

Her tears flowed freely, wetting his shirt while she rested her head against his chest. "When I saw you last night, your large frame in the torchlight…I knew. Only my Anton could 'shhhh' so loudly."

He could hardly believe she was real. Her hair was matted and dirty, but still soft brown in color. She had lost a significant amount of weight during her years of captivity, but her muscles were toned and she was not as weak as some of the men prisoners. "I forced myself on a strict exercise program and ate the food, no matter how bad. My fight for survival was strong because I wanted to see you again."

With half of the horses carrying double loads, the journey back to Verdure was slower going than the ride to Snow Peak. They traveled as swiftly as they could, eating their rations while they rode and stopping only to allow their horses to drink and to redistribute the extra men from one animal to another. Though several offered, including Cordon, Anton never allowed Naydeen to ride with any other soldier.

After three days of nearly non-stop travel, the group met up with Lepsis and a legion of two hundred soldiers. After conversing with Cordon and shaking hands with Gammet, who rode behind his son, Lepsis galloped toward Anton.

"Thought you might need some help, you're behind schedule," Lepsis called out, drawing ever closer to Anton and the lady. "Border's tightened up since you left. Cordon says you found a female pris…" his voice trailed off and his eyes grew wide. He gazed at the fragile woman cradled in Anton's arms. "Naydeen," he mouthed, for no sound came out.

At first she looked at him perplexed, but soon her face lit up. "Lepsis!" she called excitedly. "Oh Lepsis!"

All Lepsis could do was stare in complete astonishment at his sister.

Anton reigned to a stop. Carefully, he handed Naydeen over to her little brother, smiling broadly at the tender reunion. Lepsis silently wept. Naydeen kissed him and wiped his tears with her hands. She finished the trip to Headquarters safely astride her brother's horse, with Anton guarding their backs.

* * *

Gammet had been given a horse by one of Lepsis' men and finished the ride to the Esparian command center beside Cordon. "When you came through that door at the fortress I thought I was looking into the face of a ghost. How did you survive the Dorsett attack?"

Cordon nearly fell off his horse when his father spoke. He had tried several times during their three day journey to talk with the old man, but

Gammet refused to say a word. Now he spoke two complete sentences.

Cordon recounted the details to his father, of how he was covered by the bodies of the dead and wounded and how the Elitet missed him. "Three other men survived in the same manner. Reese was one of them. We alone live to tell the horrors of that battle. What happened to you, Dad?"

Gammet's voice took on a bitter tone. "They surrounded my command, picked off my men one by one. Before I realized they weren't going to kill me, I was captured. I would never have allowed them to take me alive. My weapons were seized and I was taken to a command center. There I saw Ballian, proud of his treachery. From the command post they took me directly to the prison tower at Snow Peak."

"We found out about Ballian a few weeks ago. So much has happened since the battle at Saylon Dorsett that it's difficult for me to know where to begin." Cordon explained about Gayleena, John, and Jessica. He recounted every detail of the last month. They were nearly to Headquarters when he finished bringing his father up to date.

"The Lady Gayleena is here." Gammet's voice was flat. "I would like to meet this son-in-law of hers. He sounds like quite a man."

Cordon was confused at his father's lack of surprise or enthusiasm. Thinking quickly, he hoped his next comment would unleash a spark. "John is. Anyway, *Lyrista* thinks so. I'll send you to him. He's still pretty green and could use all of your help."

When Gammet did not react to the hint of Lyrista's romantic interest, Cordon's confusion turned to worry. During their conversation, he had noticed several changes in Gammet's attitude, but with the absence of curiosity toward Lyrista, the light of their father's life, his son recognized the dark signs of depression. Gammet had spiraled downward, deep within the deadly tentacles of this monstrous disease.

The next day the two men were seated in the command center, awaiting Lepsis. "Are you certain you don't want medical attention, Dad?" Cordon asked.

Gammet shook his head. "My body will mend on its own. I don't want healers poking and prodding at me."

Yeah, Cordon thought sadly, your body will heal, but what about your mind, your spirit?

"Sorry I'm late." Lepsis walked into the tent. "I was looking for Anton, but he wasn't at his campsite."

"He's at the hospital. Hasn't left there since we arrived yesterday." Cordon motioned to the large tent at the center of the base.

"Then I'll see him soon enough. Ready?"

The three men strode to the medical center. Cordon wanted to meet the eighteen freed men. Gammet agreed to accompany him, and Lepsis was along to make the introductions.

Most of the men were scientists Daenon did not want killed. Their stories were similar. Afraid they would defect to Esparia, taking their secrets with them, Daenon imprisoned them. Those who out lived their usefulness were tortured, rather than killed outright. Two of the freed men were the Provincial Regulators of Snow Peak and Palium, retained in case Daenon needed some bargaining tools, and one man was once Segal's leading strategist. Daenon imprisoned him as retribution for his father's death, blaming the man for the Blue Mountain defeat.

Cordon saved their visit to Naydeen for the last. When they approached her room, Anton could be heard. "When I thought ya was dead, I wanted to die too. I stayed alone and shut everyone out, even Larone. I knew I was hurtin' him, but I couldn't tell him I'd killed our brother."

"It wasn't your fault, Anton." Naydeen's voice was soothing. "Segal tried to kill me, then you. You were defending us both when he lunged at you. How were you to know that by sidestepping him, he would slip on the stair and fall on his own knife? It wasn't your fault."

Cordon cleared his throat, then entered the room, followed by Gammet and Lepsis. They found Naydeen sitting up in bed, Anton by her side, holding her hand. Her face radiated happiness. Her light brown hair hung loosely around her shoulders and a soft peach robe complimented the color of her cheeks.

After Lepsis introduced his sister to the two seventh bars, they bowed low.

"I heard of your efforts to warn the Lady Gayleena and her family about the attack on her home fifty years ago," Gammet said. "I was at the Dorsett when your warning came. Lord Graesion was killed then, but the Lady and her little daughter had just enough time to escape. I don't know if you ever knew. I'd like to shake the hand of the bravest women I have ever known. That warning cost you a great deal." He held out his hand and she took it firmly.

Cordon softened at the interaction between Gammet, Lepsis, Anton and Naydeen. He never knew the lady, but seeing her now, the way she looked at Anton and Lepsis, brought a smile to his face. There was unmistakable love there, a familial connection between the three. *John was right,* he thought. *If I survive this war, I'll definitely look toward family life.*

Four days later, Anton galloped at the head of the eighteen freed prisoners, Naydeen, and twenty-five of Lyrista's Guardians toward Ramadine. The other twenty-five Guardians, along with Gammet, and led by Fourth Bar Ru, sped to the Southern headquarters where John was in command. Cordon had planned on giving the freed captives more time to recuperate before sending them to Ramadine, but an urgent, cryptic message had changed everything.

Anton,

Jessica abducted by Elitet. Come now.

Larone

CHAPTER 20

Light Meets Darkness

Jessica had a strange sense of calm about her. She realized that if they wanted to kill her, the Elitet would have done so back in the Colossus Forest. In an odd way, she felt quite important. Daenon must be pretty desperate to send ten Elitet after one girl. The knowledge of them needing her alive, if even for a short time, gave her power.

Escape was foremost on her mind. She kept a sharp watch for any opening to bolt from their circle, but the opportunity never presented itself. Her captors took no chances, keeping her tightly surrounded and not allowing her control of Web's reins.

Following the path of the sun, they rode continually for three days and nights, with only a short break each evening at small pools of water so the horses could eat and drink. At these brief stops the same Elitet would hand Jessica a small pouch filled with shelled nuts, dried fruits and some dried vegetables that tasted remarkably like squash. She was quick to refill her own flasks in the same water that the horses drank from, realizing this liquid should be safe for her as well.

Riding single file, they kept to the wilderness areas. The brutal pace pushed both human and horse to near exhaustion. The first real stop came after three hard days, late into the night. No one spoke to Jessica, but her Elitet threw her a new pouch. This one held a few pieces of dried meat along with the nuts, fruits and vegetables. The men dug into their own packs for the first time and ate. It was the first real nourishment she saw them take, for up until now they had only drunk from their side flagons and eaten what Jessica guessed to be dried biscuits.

Sinking in a heap at Web's feet, she ate the food. "They must really want to get to their deserts," she muttered to the grazing animal. "How are you holding up, boy?"

The picture of a warm stable with plenty of fresh hay and cool water came into her mind. Laughing softly, Jessica stroked the horse's powerful legs. "Yeah, I know exactly how you feel." She drank half the water, then held the container for him to drain the remainder.

The stop was far too short. Jessica felt she just barely closed her eyes when she was pulled to her feet and dumped back into her saddle. Once again, a grueling pace was set as they sped toward the desert lands.

On one occasion Jessica tried speaking with the man whose duty it was to supply her daily food pouch. She had come to think of him as her only semi-friend as his eyes were not as cold as the others. "Could you tell me how many more days until we reach the deserts?" He seemed not to have heard her, so she opened her mouth to ask again, but the query died in her throat. He suddenly glared at her and put a hand to his dagger. The message was clear. *So much for semi-friend* she thought.

It soon became apparent the Elitet rarely spoke to each other. Only their leader, a tall, lean man with cold, gray eyes broke the silence, and when he did, it was to give a brief command. Jessica had the nagging feeling she had seen him somewhere before. With boredom driving her curiosity, she took note of his every action. He dressed as the other Elitet, with the addition of a wide, red sash around his middle. He was a Shield, and she wondered if the width of his sash corresponded with his rank, for the other Shields she had seen wore thin red belts. The commander isolated himself from his men and always rode at the head of the column. When he gave an order, the others quickly executed it. She sensed fear in some of them when he walked by.

With little else to do while she traveled, Jessica worked on her clairvoyant exercises. She began by communicating with Web while they rode. When she first understood him back in Feather Forest, he had whinnied his communication. Now their connection needed to be more telepathic. She had advanced in this area during her drills with Larone, so her goal was to fine tune the ability. She still did not understand her healing gifts, nor how she channeled Edia's power. She hoped to one day understand everything about her heritage, but realized it could take years and the thought scared her. *Years. I need to be realistic, I could die here anytime.* She shuddered, then pushed the reality of her situation aside and concentrated on Web.

Little by little, the environment changed. The dense forests gradually thinned, opening onto filons of short, grassy plain. The further west they rode, the more the grasslands gave way to desert terrain. When Jessica first heard about the Deserts of Demar, she pictured Arabian deserts, with their shifting sands and filons of desolate dunes, but this was more like the Mojave Desert of the Southwestern United States. Large Sonora-type cacti dotted the land as well as smaller, flat pronged cactus plants. Tall, spindly trees and large tumbleweed scrub plants accented the scene. There were a few wild flowers, some bright red and others pale yellow. Many short, spiny bushes were covered in small purple buds. *This place has a stark beauty,* she thought. *I bet that with proper irrigation it would really blossom.*

Once within the desert territory the commander finally slowed the pace. Jessica sensed relief from each of the horses, especially Web.

"How are you doing?" She asked him several times a day, her heart aching because of the strain he was under.

"Do this," he always responded. "For J'ca."

Each night, when unstrapped from the saddle, she would throw her arms around his neck and whisper her gratitude for his strength. "I love you, Web."

She knew he was ready to drop and barely able to keep stride with the others. "Love, J'ca," he replied.

Five days after leaving the Colossus Mountains, the band arrived at a small village. Looking as if it rose up from the desert floor itself, every building was made of adobe brick and brown mud. When they approached, people emerged from the small, sunburned homes. The spectators consisted mostly of ragged women and dirty children--throngs of children, ranging from small toddlers to young teenagers. One, too thin, black haired girl cried out in astonishment, "Ten! There are ten heroes!"

Few men were among the onlookers. Those scattered among the crowd were either grossly maimed or extremely old. Many young ones stared in curiosity and pointed to Jessica's red hair. The older children, however, stared with hate in their eyes. One teenage girl even spat on the ground when she passed by, making her momentarily grateful for the Elitet surrounding her. For the first time since being taken in the Colossus Forest, Jessica felt danger.

At this village they exchanged horses, for the ones they were riding were half dead. Jessica had only a few moments to say good-bye to her beloved Web.

"Find J'ca," he promised and nuzzled her cheek.

"If you can't, then go back to Ramadine. I'll free myself and meet you there," she whispered in his ear. Jessica swallowed hard, forcing back the tears as a stable boy led the trusted animal away. "Take good care of him," she pleaded.

Leaving the squalid village behind, Jessica hid her grief. They won't see me cry, she swore with stern determination. After a while, to replace her gloomy thoughts, she reflected on the differences between Demar and Esparia. The desert people were darker skinned than their eastern brothers. There were no blonds, but hair color ranged from light brown to deep black. Most natives had large, deep-set, ebony eyes, framed by beautiful, long lashes. A few looked at her through gray orbs, encased by shorter, thick, lashes.

Whether black, brown or gray eyed, one common factor stood out, that of the deep affection the women had for their children and the siblings had for each other. The desert people were unashamed to demonstrate their love for one another. Older children cradled younger ones, while mothers embraced them all in protective arms. Tender kisses were exchanged between the groups, even in the presence of Elitet. *If such familial love can exist, then perhaps the people could learn to extend that love to Esparia,* she thought. *But, nothing can be sorted out until Daenon is dead, or at least out of power. His constant diet of hate has scarred these people.*

Each village and hamlet turned out to be the same as the first. Open sewers ran down the streets, children wore rags and many looked malnourished. Garbage lay everywhere, and there were rats, a lot of rats. 'If you see rats in daylight' she remembered her father once saying, 'you know you're in trouble.' Jessica lost count of the many dismal places they rode through.

With civilization now reached, the population increased dramatically the closer they drew to Rendaira, Daenon's estate. The roads were lined with crowds of curious, poverty-stricken natives, many of whom looked as if they wanted her for dinner.

The commander seemed to have an aversion to these small villages. He would increase their speed when they neared one, then gallop through at full speed, regardless of who was in the way. On several occasions Jessica was fearful for the villagers' safety, hoping no one wandered onto the road. In one tiny tiern her fear turned to nightmarish reality when an elderly woman, hampered by her crutch, failed to reach the safety of the roadside. The commander aimed his mount directly for her. As if in slow motion, Jessica saw what was about to occur.

"No!" she screamed.

The woman looked up, surprise on her weathered face. She never had a chance.

Jessica twisted in her saddle to look behind when they passed. A young girl, tears streaming down her face, knelt beside the lifeless body.

The Elitet never slept in the villages. Each evening the commander found an isolated spot away from the road for their campsite. Two men were always dispatched to hunt for food. Fresh snake and a seemingly endless supply of dried biscuits were the usual evening meal. Jessica decided semi-cooked snake wasn't really that bad. She decided that if the men could handle it so could she and forced herself to eat what they gave her. She always refilled her water containers where the horses were allowed to drink.

Nightly rituals consisted of each Elitet meticulously shaving his head, then rubbing an oil-based solution on it. Jessica thought the shiny liquid smelled like vinegar. She would sleep deeply, exhausted by the short nights and long days of travel. Each morning the campers were up and back on the road before dawn.

After four days of feeling like a freak in a zoo, Jessica saw a large city in the distance. She looked inquiringly at her Elitet who was in his usual position at her side. Whether as guard or protector, she hadn't a clue, but she nearly fell off of her mount when he whispered, "Asmoth".

The drab stone buildings peaking above a high, brick and cement fortress-style wall were a stark contrast to the mud huts of the small villages. About a filon from the city, the road leading to it turned from hardened earth to cement. The wooden gates of the citadel wall stood open and the group crossed the entry a little before noontime.

Three and four story sandstone buildings lined the streets. Compared to the structures at Ramadine and in most of Esparia, these smooth, unadorned buildings looked relatively new. From what Jessica could see, shops and small factories occupied the ground levels and residences comprised the upper levels, however few patrons or workers could be seen through the clear glass windows. Though there was no detectable stench of open sewage, garbage lay everywhere and rats ran between the closely constructed buildings.

People on the street gripped their cloth-bound packages close to their bodies, seemingly afraid of the precious parcels being stolen. The shoppers were dressed a little better than those in the villages, their clothing being brighter in color, with a few yellows and greens mixed in with the dull browns and tans. Most of the clothing looked to be made of the same cotton-like material Jessica had seen throughout Esparia.

More men traveled the streets here than previously seen. A few soldiers stood at attention while the Elitet passed, and other small groups of men watched in mild interest. No one smiled, and very few onlookers had any real life in their eyes. Most gazed expressionless at Jessica, with only one or two showing the extreme dislike the villagers had expressed. Many pedestrians were forced to scurry for safety when the Elitet cantered down the center of the street, giving no regard for others on it.

A wave of pity swept through Jessica. If eyes are the windows to the soul, then where is the spark? Where is the passion? It's as if the people of this city were on automatic. The villagers showed complete hatred, but at least they had emotions. She noticed more lightly skinned persons here; they were markedly different from the country people. Side by side, the true desert natives stood out from the rest.

As they drew closer to the center of the tiern, the street became cleaner and the buildings more ornate. At the central square, there was real beauty for the first time since entering the Deserts of Demar. On the border of the main square were many large, elaborate homes. Each of these pink, blue, and green marbled mansions had wrought iron balconies which overlooked a central, statuesque fountain. Several men and women, dressed in bright silks and satins, stood on the balconies. Each person was draped with chains of gold that sparkled in the sunlight. The finery of their apparel made a glaring contrast to the poverty Jessica had seen only an hour or so earlier.

One particularly overweight man leaned over a massive gilded rail and yelled, "Good for you, Commander Addex. This Saylon brat will learn her place." The man's friends laughed, but Commander Addex stared straight ahead, never acknowledging the comment.

Jessica's attention immediately centered on her lead captor. *So this is Addex. I thought I knew him. The guy who killed Haesom and his family.* She shuddered at the memory.

It was dusk when they finally left the city behind and Addex veered off the highway for the night. The sun was long set when he stopped in a field not far from the road. Jessica had just rolled out her blanket when Addex strolled past her.

"Excuse me, Commander Addex," she bravely called, "could you please tell me how much longer it will be before we reach my cousin Daenon's Rendaira?" Every man froze in his tracks. The two Elitet flanking her hardly breathed. Jessica did not flinch, but stared calmly at the commander. *Will he answer me?* She wondered. *He'd be a fool to ignore me.*

Slowly, he turned to face her. She felt a cold shiver run down her spine, but did not waver in meeting his gaze. "Tomorrow," the reply came, then he strode to an isolated spot away from the main group.

She sensed a collective sigh of relief from the men. Three looked at her with momentary admiration. She felt satisfaction when she lay down between her captors. *I'm tired of being on display and feeling helpless.*

A little before noon the following day, a second large city loomed ahead. Once again she looked to her Elitet who rode beside her. "Asmerth", he barely breathed. *No more small towns,* Jessica thought. *Must be a large water source around somewhere.* This city was similar to the one from the previous day, with its high outer wall, sandstone buildings, and the same sad-eyed people in the streets. Faces changed, but the eyes were just as passionless, just as glazed.

The journey through the tiern would have been identical to the one yesterday except for one brief, defining moment. It occurred soon after leaving the central square behind. Jessica, as usual, kept her eyes on the crowd, watching the people going about their daily business when halfway down a side street, a long-haired, bearded man met her gaze. He caught her attention because he was a healthy, native Demarian male in a place where none were seen, but more importantly, he held her attention because his eyes displayed no hate. There was no pity either, but kindness and a smile. He held her stare for a moment then bowing slightly, gave the Salute of Loyalty.

Her column of escorts moved steadily forward, so he was soon beyond her sight. Certain that his actions would have brought on his death, she was grateful none of the Elitet noticed him. They did not look at the people as she did, but kept their eyes riveted on the commander in front. It was a very brave thing this individual had done and she realized if there was one ally in this city, there could possibly be more.

After leaving the metropolis behind, the eternally flat desert land began to change. Ahead of them, like gentle ripples in the desert sea, spread gentle rolling hills. The sun had begun its evening descent when they reached a fork in the main road at the base of the first hillock. On the left, the land was just as arid and barren as a desert usually is, but to the right where wasteland once was, a vibrant garden flourished. Taking the right-hand fork, the band passed under a massive green and purple botanical archway. No one needed to tell Jessica this marked the entrance to Rendaira.

Lush, green lawns framed by tall, weeping-style trees lined the smooth road. Large statues situated atop high points, surrounded by brightly colored flowers punctuated the skyline. One bronze figure stood with his arm outstretched, sword in hand, another sat on a rearing horse, and a third held a bow, pulled back with an arrow locked in it, ready to shoot skyward. Jessica could not see the statue faces clearly yet she was certain each bore a good likeness of Daenon. The ride through the magnificent parks and gardens went for nearly an hour.

This place is beautiful. I was right; the desert can bloom. When the sun at Jessica's back fell below the horizon, the heavens directly ahead glowed as if the sky were on fire.

It took ten more minutes to clear the rising hill, and when they did, a grand mansion, the length of two football fields came into view. Brightly illuminated by scores of torches, the heart of Rendaira shone like a jewel. Jessica was stunned by the opulence of Daenon's palatial compound.

Three structures comprised the main complex, one massive edifice in the foreground with two, smaller ones standing behind it. Forming a perfect triangle, covered walkways connected the three. The main palace rose three full stories. Built of both dark green granite and polished white wood, it boasted a massive front door system. It was perfectly centered and framed in ornately spun gold. Two large windows ascended from ground to roofline on either side of this door. They too were encased in elaborate golden frames. Scores of other windows, trimmed in polished wood, covered the building's facade. Ten sets of French doors, evenly spaced along the building's front, were edged in matching polished timber.

The roofline, supported by ten, triple story high, polished stone columns extended out from the front portico an extra fifty feet. Each column was intricately carved and capped at each end with massive head and base pieces. The drive and pathways were paved with interlocking stones forming geometric patterns of various colors. The stones were leveled so not one bump or seam stood out.

Several other buildings were behind and to the left of the main

223

compound. *Probably the stables and soldier's barracks,* she assumed. When they reached the front portico, only Jessica and Commander Addex dismounted. He led the way into the building, while the other Elitet continued on.

The massive receiving hall matched the grandeur of the palace façade. Large, brightly colored tapestries hung from the walls. The tall, three-story high windows were curtained in layers of cream silk. In the center of the light-green marble floor lay a circular cream-colored rug. A delicately carved table was positioned on top of it. Several plush, finely crafted chairs lined the walls. Ceramic vases that were a head taller than most men were interspersed between them. Smaller matching pots holding tall fern-type plants finished the decor. A large marble staircase, opposite the front door, split to the left and right three-quarters of the way up to the second level. Four hallways, two on the right and two on the left, led from the entry. The room would have been perfect if not for the six black uniformed guards stationed at the hallways and main door.

A man dressed in dark brown pants with a white tailored shirt, and three women, wearing simple brown pants and white peasant blouses, stood at the bottom of the staircase. The man stepped forward, bowing deeply to Addex. Short and grossly overweight, he oozed false charm. "Lord Daenon is waiting for you in his office, sir. The girl is to go directly to her assigned rooms."

Addex walked briskly down one of the hallways to the left. Turning to Jessica, the squat, oily servant motioned for her to go up the stairs. Jessica, taking an instant dislike to the man, looked at him with all the hauteur she could muster. However, feeling drained and not up to a real fight, she slung her saddle pack over her shoulder and climbed the stairs without comment. One of the serving women led the way and the other two followed behind.

Taken through a maze of short hallways to the back of the mansion, Jessica finally reached a luxuriously furnished apartment. It consisted of a main sitting area with two smaller rooms leading from it. One of the smaller chambers was a bedroom with a connecting private bath, the other a mini-library.

"This is a beautifully gilded caged, but it's still a cage," Jessica said to the women. "I can take it from here so goodnight." Jessica waved toward the door. Once alone she cleaned up in the bathroom, changed into fresh clothes from her saddle pack and crawled between warm bed-sheets. She was asleep within minutes.

Jessica had no idea how long she slept before finding herself in a shroud of familiar mist. *Oh, boy,* she mentally sighed. *What now?* Closing her eyes, she stretched her senses in each direction. *Two people, directly ahead.* Running silently, she soon heard a man's voice. *Addex.*

"...had it not been for your orders, I would have killed her immediately."

Jessica heard a brief laugh as the cold crept in. *Daenon.*

"I'm glad you showed restraint, Addex. I'm looking forward to meeting this girl who so bravely confronts my finest shield, but enough of her. I have frustrating news. The prison at Snow Peak has been breached and the prisoners escaped."

"All of them?" Addex's voice held true surprise.

"They were whisked away a week ago, in the middle of the night, while an entire garrison of guards slept. The tower jailer in charge of the scientists, the two provincial regulators and Gammet, was drunk at the time of the attack. The other jailer in control of my 'dear mother'," Daenon said with distinct sarcasm, "was not even at his post. He sounded an alarm, but was too late. Most of the force was killed."

His mother! Jessica thought quickly. Naydeen!

"What have you done with the remaining guards?"

"I saved the two jailers, a little reward for your efforts. They're in shackles at your residence. The others went to the front. They'll be in the first wave that attacks the Esparians."

Jessica shivered. She could only imagine the fate of the two jailers and she realized why hardened Elitet were afraid of Addex.

"Thank you my Lord, I could use some extra amusements."

"We leave at noon tomorrow, Addex. Now that my hostage is here, I want to begin this war. Have fresh horses ready along the way. We must be at the command post by noon, three days hence. We will attack the following dawn. Send the word. I want a well-coordinated assault. I'm sorry I can't give you more time with the jailers. I know how you enjoy prolonging…"

Daenon's words trailed off. Jessica no longer listened. *Well-coordinated assault*, she thought. *Hostage! I was right, that's what I am!* Anger flushed through her body, melting the cold in the pit of her stomach. "Daenon you're a fool," she spat hotly. "You will *never* win this war."

Daenon quit speaking. Jessica did not realize she spoke out loud until after doing so. "Did you hear that Addex?" Daenon sounded stunned.

"Yes, I did."

They heard me? This is great!

"You may win a battle or two, but the war is already lost. You've lost before beginning," Jessica sneered. She wanted to shake them up and hoped she was succeeding.

"Who are you," Daenon cried angrily.

"Remember Daenon, 'Protector new will lead the land, Mercy and kindness from his lips, Upon this course the balance tips'," she quoted. "Your own grandfather foresaw your downfall. You cannot win."

Jessica felt she had done enough and backed off. Daenon said something more, but she did not catch it. When she could no longer hear him, she stopped retreating. *Anger's good, I'm warm. Now to leave, but how?* The mist swirled close and thick. "Well, if I'm awake," she reasoned, "then if I go back to sleep I might end up back in bed. If I'm already asleep, then going to sleep here can do no harm."

So Jessica lay down on the floor she could not see. It was definitely there and it was firm, just obscured by the opaque fog. Her earlier anger dispelled the chill in the air, so now she was neither too cold nor warm and soon fell asleep.

"Mistress. Mistress wake up!" Someone shook her. Jessica slowly came around. One of the young serving women from the previous evening stood over her, her face pensive. Her gray-green eyes darted to the apartment door and back to Jessica. "Please wake up," the woman whispered.

"I'm awake. What's wrong?" Jessica whispered back. The room was still dark except for one small, lit candle on the nightstand.

"You must dress, quickly. Lord Daenon is coming and you must not meet him in your nightclothes. I have brought day clothes. Hurry and meet him with dignity. He comes at this hour to humiliate you."

Jessica did not argue, except to say, "I'm already dressed."

Jessica was barely out of bed and smoothed her hair when the door to the sitting room banged open. Two men, holding bright lamps bustled in. She squinted against the sudden brilliance. A tall, muscular, sandy blond haired man stood in the doorway. He stared at the empty bed, his smug expression turning to dismay and then anger.

She took the few seconds it took him to locate her to size him up. She knew he was her grandmother's first cousin, so was not surprised by the familial resemblance—high cheek bones and thin nose with a strong, square jaw line. It would have been a handsome face, with the well-groomed goatee and short-cropped hair, but his mouth and eyes betrayed the cruelty within.

"Cousin Daenon, at last we meet." Her words were calm, for she had rehearsed the line a hundred times, but her heart pounded and her mouth was dry.

In three strides he crossed the room, stopping only inches from her. His sapphire blue eyes blazed, but she held her ground. His voice was smooth. "I wanted to make certain your accommodations were to your liking. If there is anything you need, within reason, please feel free to tell your servants. You'll notice the windows have no bars. You can go anywhere you please at Rendaira, even to the dine if you're brave enough. There is nowhere to run in Demar, no way to escape the deserts."

She remained silent and for a moment they stared at each other, a contest of who would back down first. Daenon finally said, irritation creeping into his voice, "I will leave you now, but later, you'll join me for breakfast. We have much to discuss." Whipping around, he hurried from the room, the two lamp holders scurrying after him.

"Oh goody," she muttered, "I can hardly wait." She closed the bedroom door. "He's gone."

The serving woman poked her head out of the bathroom door.

"It's safe," Jessica promised. "Come and sit on the bed. I'm wide-awake now and I think you are too. What's your name and how did you know Daenon was coming?"

The woman sunk onto the foot of the comfortable bed. She was smaller than Jessica and very, very thin. *Way too thin*, Jessica thought. Her reddish blond hair, pulled back in a tight ponytail, accentuated her large, sunken eyes, and high, prominent cheekbones. Jessica guessed her to be somewhere in her late twenties.

"My name is Merula. I am the daughter of Tirus, Regulator of Palium," she said proudly, carefully enunciating every syllable of every word she spoke. In a more subdued tone, but just as articulate, she continued, "I have been a slave here for nearly ten years. I knew Daenon was coming because I heard him. I couldn't sleep and was wandering the halls, I often do that." She shrugged her shoulders. "No one cares anymore or pays attention to me. I heard Daenon call for lamp bearers. He has done this before. He likes to surprise his 'guests'. I think it makes him feel in control, more powerful. I assumed it was you he was coming to *surprise* this time so I ran to warn you." A mischievous smile crossed her lips. "I like to see him frustrated."

"Well, I'm in your debt. So, you're from Palium."

"Yes."

"I don't understand. Your province is allied to Daenon, but you're a slave?"

Merula nodded. "Greed and stupidity defeated many of my people, but not everyone fell for Daenon's drug. My father was one. He spoke out against the drug use, but was ignored. We were conquered in just months. I remember the day Daenon's armies marched into our dine. Many citizens of my province fled east, some deserted over to Daenon on their own, but the majority was already dependent on what only Daenon could give them. It took me years to understand they were hopelessly addicted to a powerful drug that had been cunningly introduced."

She looked at Jessica with tears in her eyes. "He's a master at potions, you know. It was so subtle. No one took the threat seriously, or even realized there was a threat until it was too late. The drug was too powerful. Those who used it only once or twice were dependent beyond reason." Merula grunted, "So many stupid people." She shook her head. "Those who fled were the smart ones, the ones who refused to try, even once, something touted as the newest wonderment. I assume they warned the other provinces. That's why Daenon must now fight to conquer the rest of the country. Most of the Palium Regulators refused to be sucked into the drug, so they were killed. I believe they were poisoned. My father was imprisoned at Snow Peak and I was taken into slavery."

"Snow Peak?" Jessica gasped at the name. "But, your father's free. The captives at Snow Peak were rescued a week ago."

Merula looked at Jessica in disbelief. "Are you sure?"

Jessica nodded. "I'm positive. Daenon's furious."

"Daenon's always furious about something. Life here is unspeakable. At least when Lepsis was around, I could bear it. Now that he's gone," she shook her head, "I don't know if I can go on." The pitiful woman began weeping again.

"Lepsis came to us. He commands the Maronian army."

"He's alive!" Merula twisted her hands in the bed covers. "I helped him escape. I didn't know if the Shields had taken him or not. Since there were no wild celebrations, I hoped they hadn't."

"Now that your father's free, you can escape." Jessica's voice became earnest. "Daenon has no leverage over you anymore."

Merula stared wide-eyed at Jessica, her tears ceasing to flow. "The deserts are unforgiving. It would take a great deal of planning and preparation to attempt leaving here alone, but now, at least, I can think about it. I know who you are. Many times this past month Daenon's howled in frustration. You've proved an elusive target. I learned from many years of watching Lepsis, as long as I can help someone, I should try. He did much good with Daenon's never knowing. As long as you're here, I should stay."

Jessica was touched. "Thanks, I could use a friend right now."

"Are you afraid?"

"Yes and no. For the moment, Daenon wants me alive, but that could change at any time."

Light from the morning sun began to filter into the room. Merula blew out the nearly spent candle. "You must finish getting ready. Daenon will be sending someone for you."

She helped Jessica brush out her hair. They just finished when a forceful knock at the sitting room door disturbed their peace. Merula left the bedroom to answer the summons. Following behind, Jessica looked in amusement at the four, black uniformed guards standing in the hall.

"Am I such a threat it takes four armed men to accompany me?" she asked, not expecting an answer. They escorted her through the hallways, down a secondary set of stairs to a large set of double doors, where two more guards stood watch. The doors opened, her escort parted, and Jessica entered the grand dining hall alone.

Daenon was already seated at a large, polished wooden table. He motioned to a place set with silver tableware directly across from him. "I hope you slept well," he said in a silky voice when she sat down.

"Just fine, thank you."

"I also hope you're hungry." He waved his hand over many platters of breads, fruits and meats on the table. He helped himself to much of the food, so she guessed it was probably safe to eat. She was in fact, very hungry and chose several pieces of fruit as well as some fresh, hot pastries.

They ate in silence, then after the meal, he looked at her appraisingly. "You know, you have given me a great deal of trouble."

"I'm flattered," she said dryly. "I didn't know I was worth so much effort."

"Tell me about your father. I hear he is a healer."

"Yes. He tries," was her only response. What kind of game is he playing, being so polite? She thought. I'm not telling him anything, not anything truthful anyway.

Daenon's eyes narrowed at her evasive reply. He rose from his chair, rounded the table and walked up behind her. She did not turn around, but knew he was close...very close.

"I can do terrible things to you," he warned in her ear. "You had better cooperate, little girl."

She slammed both palms down on the table and quickly stood up, ramming her chair back into Daenon, catching him off balance. Yelling, she swung around on him, "Don't threaten me! I've been through more than you could possibly ever know! Ripped from my home, torn from my family and everything familiar, hurled through terrifying blackness and dumped in a place so foreign to me it will never be mine! I've been bruised, beaten, and battered by your lousy thugs for reasons completely irrational. Tied, gagged and dragged across filons of god-forsaken, poverty stricken, rat infested country to a place of such selfish opulence, it makes me want to vomit. I have felt and heard evil of such magnitude it nearly sucked me dry and my senses are on so much overload I can hardly control them. Don't you *dare* threaten me! And don't you ever, *ever* call me little girl!"

Daenon looked totally astounded then his face darkened. He seized her by the arm and dragged her out of the dining hall into an adjacent chamber. Slamming the door shut with his foot, he hurled her onto the floor in front of him. His eyes flashed in fury and little beads of perspiration studded his forehead.

Leaning over her, he hissed, "Talk to me like that again, especially in front of servants, and I will personally cut out your tongue."

She knew he meant it. He dropped the congenial façade and all his evil washed over her. She pushed her hair from her face and looking him square in the eye asked, "What is it you want, Daenon?"

He straightened. His lips curled in a wicked smile. "I will not quit until every man, woman and child swears their allegiance to me."

Slowly she stood upon her feet, not taking her eyes from his face. "Many men have tried and failed to obtain world domination. You are fighting against odds you know nothing about and can never understand— love, liberty, freedom. Even if you succeed for a while, you will never know who your friends are. You will constantly be looking for a dagger in your back. No true Esparian will ever bow to you willingly. You have no authority they will respect so you will be at war for the rest of your life. The people of Demar seem to think you're all right. Why can't you content yourself with this place? Make it into the garden it once was and could be again. That's how you find true satisfaction and peace."

"You truly do amuse me," he laughed. "Satisfaction? Peace? I am well beyond both of those. I'm a God to the desert people. They will do anything I want them to. Why should I quit here when I can control everything, can *be* everything? No, little girl, I do know what I am doing. There is no greater power than to be worshiped."

He started to pace back and forth while rubbing his beard with his hand. "But you have given me something to think about." He stopped and faced her, "You're right when you say the Esparians would never respect my authority." He paused again, his face lighting up. "But, they would respect you."

"What are you talking about?" she asked suspiciously, a familiar nausea creeping into her stomach.

"If you were my wife, I would have the authority necessary to control the country."

"Are you crazy!" she whispered horrified. This was a turn of events she had not anticipated.

"Yes," he mused, half-smiling to himself, "that would work. I planned on killing you when I didn't need you anymore, but this is a much better idea." He walked toward her and brought his face down, very close to hers. Once again she stood her ground. "Don't misunderstand me," he continued, "I will still destroy your father and anyone else who tries to oppose me, but when I return, there will be a wedding and there will be a wedding night. I need an heir."

At this suggestion Jessica backed away. She felt the color drain from her face. "It will never happen." Her voice was barely a whisper.

With a self-satisfied smile on his face, he walked toward the door. "Wait, I've changed my mind," he sneered, turning to look back to her. "I'll capture your father and bring him back here to witness our joyous union. Afterwards, I'll send him to Snow Peak Prison with strict orders he be killed if anything ever happens to me. That should give you incentive to…how did you put it? Oh, yes…watch my back."

When the door slammed closed, Jessica sunk onto the nearest chair. She felt sick to her stomach and needed to catch her breath. *I won't panic,* she thought. She closed her eyes and concentrated on calming her racing pulse.

She sat there for a long time, staring at the wooden floor, absently tracing the lines of its intricate geometric pattern. A sharp rap at the door brought her out of her stupor and up on her feet.

"Yes?"

The door opened and the same chubby butler who met her and Addex the previous night stood in the hallway. "Lord Daenon orders your presence," he said crisply. "Follow me."

What now? She thought in dismay. The portly man led her to the front entrance of the mansion where Daenon was preparing to leave. Five hundred Elitet, with Addex at their head were standing ready to accompany him.

When Jessica appeared at the massive door, Daenon handed the reins of his magnificent mount to a waiting servant and went to her. He swung an arm around her waist and crushing her to him, kissed her hard on the mouth. There was no passion in the embrace, only a brazen show of domination. Jessica stayed limp in his arms. She knew fighting would be useless, as the man was exceptionally strong and she did not want to be any more of a spectacle than she already was.

Her heart pounded when he finally let her go and her face felt as red as her hair. Their eyes locked for an instant and it was then she knew she truly loathed this man.

"When I return..." He swung around and effortlessly mounted his horse.

From the corner of her eye, Jessica noticed movement within the drapery of the tall window beside her. Merula was standing in the silk curtains. Every feature on her face, from the hard line of her mouth to the cold squint of her eyes, screamed hatred. Merula's glare was not aimed at Daenon, she stared directly at Addex.

CHAPTER 21

Unexpected Allies

Centered on the western border of Ramana, just an hour's ride from Palium lay John's command hub. Tens of thousands of troops stretched for filons along this corridor, busying themselves with training and fortifying the surrounding countryside. John did his best to teach his seventh bars the seven ancient Roman attack formations before sending them off to their respective assignments. Ider Hoffle tacticians had come up with four of the battle plans on their own, so John merely supplemented their learning.

Rome was the most powerful and skilled fighting force in the ancient world. Their legions would win, even when dramatically outnumbered. The secret lay in strategy and training. The discipline of the Roman soldier was legendary, as each man understood the formations and never broke from them. John's men also drilled the Testudo, a tactic where shields were held overhead, edge to edge, thereby deflecting even large missile weapons quite effectively.

Since Daenon had not yet attacked, John used his time to familiarize himself with his men and reinforce the lines. He could not understand why the attack was delayed, but the brief reprieve came as a blessing. Had Daenon sent his forces in a week ago, the Esparians would not have been ready.

Thousands of small, four man tents could be seen up and down the border. Nearly half a million Esparian soldiers slept in them, as well as on the ground in the open. Divided into five armies, the men were positioned at strategic roads, bridges and possible border crossings. At night the light of their campfires lit up the sky so brightly, it was impossible to see the stars overhead. Large supply tents, hospital and dining tents, as well as portable, bright Red News Centers, were interspersed throughout the line where they were most needed and accessible to the men. The Message centers were always active, with correspondence birds constantly coming and going.

It was the same in the southwestern cattle province of Kine, where Reese was in command. He proved himself a valiant and savvy soldier in the battle at Saylon Dorsett, so John placed him in charge of nearly three hundred thousand men, divided up into three armies.

John came to appreciate Larone's uncanny ability to foresee need and his swift response as he served as supply commander. Ramadine was made the central coordination point for all men and armaments.

The first John knew about the attack on Snow Peak prison was when Lyrista told him. She rode into his camp with a group of fifty Guardians. Dressed in her blue and silver uniform, her wind tossed blond hair stood out against her deeply tanned skin. Armed with bow, sword, and two knives, she reminded him of an Edian version of Athena, the Greek Goddess of war.

"John," she waved at him, a bright smile on her face. John sidestepped three campfires and avoided several soldiers as he made his way to Lyrista's side. Ready to begin his daily check of supplies and soldiers, he was about to mount Fireguard when she rode up.

"I've come with good news, but I don't want you to be angry," she said while gracefully slipping from her armored horse.

"That sounds strange. Why would you come with good news that would upset me?"

"I received a message two days ago, and came directly here to tell you in person. The prisoners at Snow Peak are free, all of them. My father is going to come here, to offer his services to you. I expect him within the next few days. Cordon was going to let him rest for a bit before sending him."

"That's wonderful news." John was excited. "I could use a great seventh bar like your father. How did he get free?"

"That's the part that could upset you." She crinkled up her forehead, but kept her gaze steady. "I sent a detachment of fifty men to Cordon, who enlisted Anton's help and together, they stormed the prison. None of our men were seriously injured," she quickly added, "and one of the freed prisoners was Daenon's mother, Naydeen."

"Let me understand this. Cordon and Anton led an attack on Snow Peak. Who was left in charge of the army?" John's voice was stern.

"Lepsis."

"What would have happened if Daenon had attacked during their absence?" John felt his blood pressure rise.

Lyrista's voice became passionate, her obstinacy matching his anger. "Look. I know they took a huge risk. They were gone a total of six days. I don't know why Daenon hasn't attacked yet, but I couldn't just sit around doing nothing and neither could Cordon. The risk paid off." She took his arm. "There were scientists, as well as the Palium and Snow Peak Regulators. Once these men have been questioned, we can get valuable information on what Daenon's been working on. Those scientists are among the best in their fields. Consider it an elite operation that was a success. Granted, it was commanded by two of your best seventh bars, but it did work."

"Luckily. Don't ever do anything like that again. Do you understand?" His voice was harsh and he shook his head in disgust. "I'm sending a letter of reprimand to Gordon. I don't know how you do things here, but where I come from that kind of fool-hardy action can get you imprisoned, or drummed out of service, or even executed."

Dropping her hand to her side, she nodded. "It has serious repercussions here also."

"Then why was I not consulted?" John's anger flared again.

"It could have been a disaster. I know that...I know that." Her tone became soft. "But, if Cordon and Anton had felt it an unworthy undertaking, they would never have gone."

"I don't know about that." John began to calm down. "Cordon wanted nothing more than to free your father and Anton, well, he's Anton. He likes nothing better than a good, hearty challenge. Fortunately, the operation was a success, so Snow Peak is one less thing to worry about. Maybe now your brother can focus."

Lyrista's eyes flashed at the comment. "Hey, he was focused. He would never have left had anything been lacking in preparations. He..."

John held up his hand for her to stop. "All right," he cut in. "I look forward to meeting Gammet."

Lyrista opened her mouth to make a reply, but a large, winged shadow passed over them, causing the words to die in her throat. An enormous carrier bird swooped low over the troops before it came to a landing on the Red News Center.

"That's the biggest bird I've seen yet." John felt awed by its size.

Lyrista sounded worried. "That bird is known for its swiftness, so this can mean only one thing, urgent news, and urgent news is almost always bad news."

Together they ran to the Message Center, nearly colliding with a young soldier running out of it. "Protector John," the young man sputtered. "A message...from Healer Larone." He handed John a rolled up note.

John tore the sealing ribbon off. Once read, he handed Lyrista the paper and stood motionless, staring up at Ragus.

Jessica taken three days ago by Elitet in Colossus Forest. Unforgivable mistake. Thought giants wanted meeting, clever trick. Sent for Anton and Varnack, best trackers. Sorry. So sorry.

Larone

"Oh, John," Lyrista gasped.

He shook his head. "Well, it's happened." He looked at her. "Walk with me."

For many minutes they wandered through the individual campsites, neither one speaking. Not until they reached the edge of the defensive line did John break the silence. "Ever since we arrived here, I've been worried something like this would happen." His voice was full of grief. "Not that she'd be captured, but that she'd be in a situation where no one could help her. There's nothing I can do."

"John, I'm so sorry." Lyrista's face reflected the compassion of her words. John felt a surge of warmth when he looked into her concerned face. "Anton and Varnack will find her. Daenon's probably having her taken to Rendaira. Maybe we should attack now and go after her? I could send a regiment of Guardians."

John considered the idea, then shook his head. "No. I won't jeopardize the lives of good men by sending them on a fool's errand and we cannot attack first. As Larone said, it would prove disastrous. The only thing we can do right now is wait and be patient."

"But what if he…I mean, what if Daenon hurts Jessica," Lyrista barely whispered, "tortures or kills her."

John closed his eyes and fought the rising panic, for Lyrista vocalized his own morbid fears. *Jess!* His anguished thoughts reached out for her, then he took stern hold of his emotions. "No!" he snapped and his eyes flew open. "If Daenon wanted her dead, he would have killed her long before now. He wants her alive and in one piece or he wouldn't have gone to all this trouble. I don't know what his plans are, but I do know they don't include her death."

Lyrista relaxed and nodded. "You're right."

They continued their walk, meandering along the perimeter of the encampment. After several minutes of silence, John gave a little laugh. "It's ironic. Now I understand why you and Cordon couldn't sit by and do nothing about your father, especially when Cordon was so close to Snow Peak. I don't condone the action, it was highly dangerous, but I do understand it."

Lyrista reached up and brushed the back of her hand against John's cheek. "You've taught your daughter well, John. Jessica is a resourceful young woman, with unique and powerful gifts." She put her arm through his and smiled reassuringly. "I think Daenon is going to find it quite difficult, if not impossible to hold her for long."

John took Lyrista's hand. "This is why he hasn't attacked yet. He was waiting for Jessica."

* * *

Three days later, Fourth Bar Ru rode into camp with his twenty-five Guardians and Gammet. John had just returned from the southern end of his defensive line when the tired, dirty travelers rode in. He knew immediately who they were. The two in the lead made a striking combination. One sat quite tall with a crown of snow-white hair, the other was an entire head shorter with shiny black hair and matching mustache-goatee. Each of the Guardians, except Ru, were large men, some of the largest John had yet seen in Esparia.

John approached the dusty newcomers. He was immediately struck by the remarkable resemblance Gammet had to Cordon. The man looked every bit as one would think a seventh bar should look. His head was held high and his entire manner demanded respect, but even from several feet away, John saw something haunting and a deep sadness in the older man's eyes.

Once dismounted, Ru went directly to John. He held out his hand and John took it firmly. "Protector John? I am Fourth Bar Ru. Our orders are to serve as your personal guard." He turned his head toward Gammet, who just walked up. "This is Seventh Bar Gammet, commander of the Dorsett brigade."

"I know the men of this campaign will want to see you, sir, but why don't you come with me to the command tent and rest first. I'll send for Lyrista and have food brought. Join us Ru, I'd like your explanation of the Snow Peak rescue."

The sparsely furnished command tent was slightly larger than the surrounding structures. Four stools, a large wooden table, and two candle lamps were its only amenities. The floor was the grassy meadow.

The three men barely began their lunch meal of warm stew and fresh brown bread, when Lyrista burst in. "Dad!" Her breath came in gasps.

"Lyrista!" Gammet caught her up when she ran to him. John and Ru quietly exited the tent, giving them a few minutes alone.

Waiting outside, John reflected on the last hour. When Fourth Bar Ru rode into the camp with Gammet and the twenty-five Guardians, they made quite a stir. The men recognized Gammet and though Ru was not the physical presence the seventh bar was, he cut no less a commanding figure. Strong and confident, when he spoke, he did so with authority and purpose. For what he lacked in size, John found Ru made up for in strength, skill and knowledge. John was at once impressed with Ru and seeing the manner in which the Guardians respected him, only served to reinforce this good opinion.

"Protector John," Ru pulled him from his thoughts. "I have a message for you from Seventh Bar Cordon. I was to give it to you when we were not within Seventh Bar Gammet's presence."

John opened the sealed paper.

236

John,

I am sorry about Jessica. By now Lyrista has told you about our little adventure. I hope you have forgiven us. I am sending Fourth Bar Ru with half of his Guardians to be at your personal command. The other half is with Anton, on their way to Ramadine with the rest of the Snow Peak prisoners. Once there, they will team up with Varnack and go in search of your daughter. I am sending my father to you. He is still a great warrior, but is not the same man he once was. I hope you can help him. We are prepared for Daenon's attack. Lepsis is a skillful drillmaster and strategist and the men become more expert with each passing day. Our advance scouts provide daily updates on enemy movements so they will not take us by surprise.

Cordon

Lyrista called from the tent door. "John, you can come back in." She smiled sheepishly. When he and Ru walked by her, she whispered, "Thank you."

"Don't go." He took her arm. "I'm going to show your father and Fourth Bar Ru the latest updates on the enemy troop positions as well as our counter positions. I expect Daenon will attack sometime within the next five to six days."

"You're right." She followed him to the wooden table. "From the maps Lepsis gave us, Rendaira is a good three days away." She pointed to an open map and followed an imaginary route with her finger. "It would take his men at least six days to take Jessica from the Colossus Forest to his estate."

The front flap to the tent opened and several men walked in, the first of twelve, high-ranking officers. The men looked pleased to see Gammet. John had called this meeting after learning the seventh bar was free and coming to him. He felt the experienced soldier would have invaluable advice and wanted a last minute pep talk and tactical session with his leaders. Within a half hour, each one of the summoned men arrived, with Reese being among the last.

"Grandfather," he cried on seeing him and ran to the older man. They warmly embraced, neither one able to speak. The others in the tent politely turned their backs and tried to continue with non-essential matters. John would have liked nothing better than to give the family members time together, but the reunion needed to be cut short by the business at hand.

"We've received another shipment of armor and shields from the province of Ironton. We have both chain mail armor and solid steel armor." John began. "Have your supply masters requisition what you need. I want every soldier outfitted with the best we can offer. Now, report."

One by one, the men gave an accounting of their preparations. Positioned throughout the entire line were packhorses loaded down with extra arrows for the archers, more stones for the slings and hundreds of javelins. Each combatant in the army and horse in the cavalry was protected by high quality armor. Discipline was strict and the men were training non-stop since advancing to the front lines. The consequences of defeat were drilled into each soldier.

When the reports were given and the necessary adjustments made, John came to the last item of business. "Three days ago I received a message from Healer Larone telling me my daughter has been captured by Elitet."

The men looked at him, some with pity and some with horror. Reese let out an involuntary, "No!"

"We now understand the reason for the attack's delay. Daenon was waiting for a special hostage, and now he has her, but this turn of events makes no difference to me. I won't fight any differently, and I will not let this cloud my judgment. I assume the attack will come within the next five to six days. I want our troops to advance into Palium and Snow Peak. It's time to make them free.

"Make sure each tiern is secure before moving on. I don't want stupid mistakes made with people's lives. I have been in contact with several underground groups who are waiting for us. I want strict orders given to leave the women and children unmolested and the farms intact. We have good supply lines that are heavily guarded, so I don't want to leave the local populace devastated. Remember, the people were once part of Esparia, but through stupid choices lost their freedom. We are rescuers, not conquerors."

Every man nodded in agreement. John knew this would be the easy part. *Now for the hard part,* he thought. "Once Palium and Snow Peak are secure, we will advance into the Deserts of Demar."

Lyrista smiled, they all smiled. "Demar needs to be annexed to Esparia as a new province, or several new provinces," John continued. "Our attitude is one of liberation. The same orders go for the women, children, farms and tierns of Demar as for those of Palium and Snow Peak. Let's not give the desert people extra reasons to hate us. I'm not waging a war for vengeance, but for justice. There *is* a difference. Does anyone have a problem with that?"

There were no objections. "If any soldier is caught looting, burning, or in the least way harming civilians, he will be immediately and harshly dealt with as a criminal," John warned.

238

"Seventh Bar Gammet," he turned to the distinguished man, "I'd appreciate it if you would come with me to inspect the troops today and tomorrow. The word of your escape has spread throughout the camps and the sight of you will greatly inspire the men. Then, I need you to take command of a fresh division being sent from Ramadine. The soldiers should be here in three days and will need an experienced leader. I want your men to be ready to move at a moment's notice to where ever they may be needed."

"Thank you," Gammet said with a nod toward John. "You can count on me."

Ru was studying the maps while John gave his last orders. He ran his finger along the dotted line representing the Demar-Palium border. "Small groups of native Demarian resistance fighters are located here and here," he said, pointing to two dashes on the map about an inch apart. "I was sheltered by this group here," he indicated the more northern dash, "while assessing the Demarian strengths a month ago. They call themselves Ghost Walkers and are led by a man named Farin. He said he would help us, but not until we are fifty filons from his border. He wants to make sure we are within striking distance before he shows his hand and allows Daenon to learn his whereabouts."

"It's good to know not all the Demarians have been taken in by Daenon," John commented. "Ghost Walkers, huh. Why that particular name?"

"I don't know, but if Farin knew of your daughter's abduction, he might be willing to help her."

John grasped at the possibility. "Do you have a way of getting a message to him?"

"Not right now, but once inside Palium, I could contact him through the Second Older of Rown, the dine located here, just inside the province," he pointed to a medium-sized dot about twenty filons inside Palium.

"I'll leave it to you then."

When the meeting was over, John held Lyrista back. "I need thirty of your best scouts. I want Daenon's lines penetrated by at least forty filons. I want to know how many reserve troops he has and where they are. Only an idiot would have all his men bunched up at the front with nothing in reserve, and someone on Daenon's team is no idiot."

* * *

Daenon, Addex and their escort made it to the front in record time. The seventh bars were at attention when Daenon rode into his headquarters. The Demarian command tent was as different from the Esparian as Rendaira was from Ramadine. A sprawling tent, it consisted of five well furnished rooms with thick, woven rugs covering the ground. The main chamber held soft chairs and a couch with silk pillows, as well as a large table in the center and ten polished silver candle stands around the perimeter.

Daenon began giving orders as soon as he entered it. "I want updated maps and information on last minute troop movements. I also want to know the exact position of John Ernshaw. I will give one thousand silver coins to the men who catch him alive and bring him to me." He looked at the map in front of him and pointed to a starred point in the center of Ramana. "Ramadine is finally within reach. I want it leveled to the ground, with Larone put in chains." He smiled at the mental picture, then hit the table with his fist. "Spread the word. We attack at dawn."

It was a well-coordinated attack. Daenon set a precise timetable, and as one his Northern army, Southern army and Hentan army mounted an all-out assault. He counted on a swift victory.

* * *

Ophir worked day and night to prepare the people of Galland for war. He was gratified to see how vigorously they responded to his efforts and the passion the people had for their independence. Bolstered by the hundred thousand troops John had sent and the tons of weapons, armor and supplies from Larone, he was optimistic. He commanded a force of over two hundred fifty thousand foot soldiers and forty thousand cavalry.

He divided his men in groups of twenty thousand, with three thousand cavalry each, and numbered them one through ten. He spaced his armies along the western border according to his spies' information, only two filons from the Hentan army. The farms, tierns, and cities within fifty filons of the front line were evacuated and the fields burned. Ophir wanted nothing left for the Hentans to pillage or take as booty. The cities beyond the fifty-filon line were well fortified. Ophir was as ready as he could be.

He received John's communication giving the calculated timetable for the attack. It came as predicted, at the rising of the sun on the fifteenth of the month, a hot, cloudless day. When the first rays of morning sun peeked over the horizon, the Hentan forces, bolstered by one hundred thousand Demarian regulars, streamed over the Gallish border.

Galland was a heavily wooded country. Only three highways connected Hent and Galland, one in the north, one in the south and one in the very center. Thick forests covered the rest of the border, providing good coverage for Ophir's archers. Thousands of men hid in the tops of the trees lining the three main roads and thousands more in the surrounding woodlands. Protective blinds were built and camouflaged in the larger treetops, with three to five archers assigned to each. Extra ropes were rigged high up in the branches so the men could swing from tree to tree as a means of escape. Two filons of forest that lay between the Hentan and Gallish armies were prepared in this manner. Ophir and his seventh bars had barely enough time to secure the bowmen in place, with the last man being hidden the night before the assault. Had Daenon attacked sooner, or had John ordered his forces to begin the fighting, Galland would not have been ready.

The foot soldiers stood three men deep, with the slingers in front and cavalry protecting the flanks. They were positioned on deforested farmland up and down the border, ready to receive the enemy. The ten divisions were clumped into three groups and assigned to the three main highways. Advance scouts and runners informed the Gallish seventh bars where the enemy points of penetration were located and the divisions were deployed accordingly.

Galland was outnumbered two to one. Ophir hoped the intensive training each man had gone through in the few short weeks he had commanded them would be sufficient to carry them through. He personally took command of the fourth, fifth, sixth and seventh divisions in the center of the country, at the middle highway.

The first reports coming from the woods were encouraging. When the first line of Hentan brown uniforms marched across the Gallish border, the archers let fly their shower of arrows. Many found their mark in exposed arms, legs, necks and faces as well as striking at skewed angles under metal breastplates. The human wave of heavily armored men momentarily faltered under the assault. Many archers pulled their bows at close quarters, thus making certain their prey would never leave the forest.

The sound of snapping bowstrings and whistling arrows hitting their marks reverberated through the woodlands. Thousands of enemy soldiers fell to unseen attackers. Soon the main highway leading into Galland was filled with dead and wounded Hentans, rendering the road impassable. The foot soldiers were forced to detour through the surrounding forests where more hidden archers waited.

The tree forts were well placed, providing ample protection for the lightly clad occupants. Ophir dressed his men in colors resembling the forest around them. They wore no cumbersome armor, as they needed to move freely among the sturdy treetops. When a fort was compromised, the Galland archers grabbed the escape ropes, swinging out of the forests in organized retreats. Not every archer made it out, but the vast majority did. They inflicted great damage on the enemy.

The Hentan cavalry fell behind the advancing foot soldiers, their horses stumbling over the bodies littering the roads. The enemy emerged from the forests disorganized and without cavalry backup. They had not expected such resistance from Galland. When the Hentan officers tried to shout orders to their confused men, Ophir ordered the Gallish slingers and spearmen into action. Being men of great strength, the slingers hurled four and five-pound weights. The Hentan helmets were of little protection against these crashing meteorites. Needle sharp, metal tipped javelins replaced arrows as highflying projectiles, easily piercing the enemy armor. The Hentan soldiers fell by the thousands, but still they pressed forward, a seemingly innumerable army, being urged on by the Demarian troops.

Astride his loyal stallion, Ophir positioned himself at the head of the Gallish army. "The blue flags," he ordered. Up and down the long line of troops, blue flags waved to signal the cavalry advance. With a roar, the horsemen galloped forward, their bright swords flashing in the sunlight. Slashing left and right, they cut down huge pockets of the enemy, but were soon hard pressed by the sea of advancing men. Slowly retreating, they led the Hentans to the waiting Gallish infantry.

"Horns!" Ophir shouted. With blasts from scores of deep-throated horns, the foot soldiers charged in. The dreadful battle raged throughout the day and long into the night. The Gallish soldiers fought valiantly, moving with precision at each command Ophir gave, their long hours of preparation showing in their discipline. They made the Hentan army pay dearly for every foot of ground it advanced.

All along the Gallish border the clash of swords and the agonizing cries of men and horses could be heard. By midnight, the enemy at last retreated back into the forests. What was at first a death trap now became a refuge for them. Hent had won the first few filons of land within the Gallish border, but at a terrible price.

"Everyone knows his duty," Ophir instructed his commanders. "The enemy has withdrawn for the night. It's time for our medical people to retrieve the wounded. Remember, I want anyone alive to be attended to, be he friend or foe." When the work of clearing the living from the muddy, blood stained farmland commenced, Ophir began reorganizing his shattered divisions. By morning, he was ready to receive Hent.

The rising sun brought the enemy once again, advancing on the Gallish army, however, they were not nearly as numerous as they had once been. Galland had lost thousands of men, but Hent had lost tens of thousands.

They battled the entire day and little by little, the Gallish troops were forced back. They were overwhelmed by the superior numbers of the Hent enemy. Each night the two armies would retreat a bit while the wounded were cleared from the field, and each morning the fighting would resume.

By nightfall of the sixth day, Galland had retreated fifty filons; past the abandoned tierns and charred fields, to the first fortified cities. No tents were set up, no fires lit. The exhausted men crumpled where they stood. The retreat was so rapid, their food and supplies were left behind. They were hard pressed to safely transport all of the wounded.

"I have received communications from both our northern and southern armies," Ophir told his officers later that night. "They are in the same situation as we. Their troops are exhausted, but determined to fight on. We know Hent has suffered severe losses, however. From what I can gather from our spies, we are still outnumbered. The odds are improving, but the cost in human life is tremendous." He shook his head. "I'm still confident we can defeat the enemy, but I'm beginning to wonder if the price is worth it."

Ophir had come to love the people of Galland, and to see them fall around him was heart-wrenching. "I am sending word to your Olders of the situation, asking for any and all reserve troops to be sent to the three fronts. I realize none of you have slept much these last few days. You've fought as valiantly as an Ider warrior and I'm honored to serve with you. Remind your men the reason they fight. Freedom can be costly, but worth it in the end. Hent seeks to destroy your nation and enslave your people. Go now, my friends, and try to sleep. It will be light soon." The Gallish commanders filed out of the tent. They were a grim lot, but showed fierce loyalty to Ophir. They had life-oathed to him. If he felt the war was winnable, they would fight to the bitter end beside him.

On the morning of the seventh day, the Hentan troops did not attack, but a Hent envoy rode into the Gallish camp under a flag of truce. He carried a letter to Ophir from the Hentan commander. Summoning the closest Gallish governmental leaders, Ophir read the letter out loud.

To Commander Ophir, leader of the Gallish forces,

My compliments to you and your valiant men. You have proved a worthy adversary and we salute you. This loss of life is so unnecessary. Let the battles end now and surrender to us. We will allow you and your Esparian soldiers to return to your homeland in peace. This is not your fight and you cannot win. Your situation is hopeless, for you are so outnumbered, you will never stop us. I promise Galland will be dealt with in an equitable manner. Their leaders are fools and we have come to bring true order to their country. Unconditional surrender is all I require. I will allow you and your men to go. Stay and we will destroy you.

I am Commander Radan, leader of the supreme forces of Hent

Ophir felt astonishment, amusement, and finally anger at the boldness of Radan. "I would never surrender to such a criminal as this," he told the Gallish leaders. "But, you tell me what you want to do and I will do it."

The ranking Gallish political leader, Vice-Premier Grodin spoke up, "Let us read this ultimatum to the troops. Let the people decide the matter."

So it was done. The troops were assembled, the letter read, and the choice left in the hands of the courageous men of Galland. No debate was given, no words spoken to sway the opinions one way or the other. The vote was taken by a show of hands. First Vice-Premier Grodin asked for those who wished to surrender to make it known. To Ophir's astonishment, not one hand went up, then the Vice-Premier asked for those who would continue the fight. Not only did hands go up, but swords and javelins as well. The vote was unanimous, not one soldier would surrender.

Ophir composed the reply to Radan's letter with Vice-Premier Grodin looking on in agreement.

To Commander Radan,

Our fight is just. We will not surrender.

I am Commander Ophir, leader of the free Gallish

With the letter sealed, Ophir personally delivered it to the Hentan envoy, who was then safely escorted out of camp. "This letter means there will be war again tomorrow," Ophir sighed to Grodin.

"We will be forever in your debt, Lord Ophir," the Vice-Premier said. "Whatever the outcome this war may have, no one will ever forget the courage you have shown, nor the love you have displayed for our people."

That evening, a fresh division of young soldiers, barely fifteen and sixteen years old, marched into the Gallish camp. Their leader saluted Ophir. "We've answered the call from our leaders and are here to aid in the cause of freedom. There are eight thousand of us. A similar force has been sent to reinforce your northern and southern camps."

Ophir appraised the lad from head to foot. "How old are you?"

"Seventeen, sir."

"Is there no one older who can come and fight this war?"

"No one sir. All of the men are here, or in your other two camps. Even the olders have taken up arms, and as we speak, ride to your northern army. This is our homeland, and we've trained hard for this day. Please, give us a chance."

Ophir smiled kindly at the youth. "Your courage will inspire fresh hope in your tired comrades. We're proud to have you with us."

The following morning dawned clear and bright, a cloudless sky with temperatures rapidly inducing sweat from the soldier's bodies. Ophir and his men rose early to complete their preparations for receiving the Hentans.

They clutched their swords and held their shields high. Archers, slingers and javelin throwers stood combat ready. This was a crucial day. If they lost any more ground, they could lose the fortified cities and women and children would then be in mortal danger.

Ophir was about to give the command for the arrows, stones and javelins to be sent eastward, when the resonance of distant, rhythmic thunder came to his ears. Bit by bit, the sound increased in intensity and volume.

"What the…" he looked around. Other soldiers, on both sides of the battlefield, seemed to have also heard the unusual noise, as their astonished murmurs drifted in the still air. Eyes turned skyward in an effort to locate the deep sonic source. Growing ever louder, Ophir finally identified the rumble as coming from the north.

Ophir squinted, his hand shading his eyes, as he searched the northern horizon for the cause of the strange sound. To his utter and complete astonishment, an immense, dark mass appeared. At first it was just a dark wall, but gained in height and breadth as it approached.

The thunderous noise became clearer; it was the sound of loud drums pounding a marching beat. After several minutes, Ophir could make out enormous forms, and when they reached the northern end of the Gallish army, his men cheered.

"Come on boy," he spurred his horse forward. "Let's find out what this is about." Riding swiftly to meet the approaching mass, he reined to a stop when only halfway there. He too cheered when he realized the advancing wall was made up of thousands of giants marching his way. Flying before them, proudly displayed from a grand flagstaff, was a great Banner of Freedom.

CHAPTER 22

The Fight for Esparia
The North

Cordon received the communiqué from John warning of an attack on either the fifteenth or sixteenth of the month, so he and Lepsis hurriedly finished their preparations. The armies assembled along the provincial border separating Verdure and Snow Peak, a flat, lightly wooded area. To the north lay the Snow Peak Mountains, running the full length of the Snow Peak and Marone border, as well as a full third of the Verdure-Marone boundary.

Where the land was not cleared for farming, tall, spindly evergreens grew. These scraggy trees did not give the protection the trees of the deep southeast did, so hiding in the tops was not an option, but dense shrubbery thrived, much of it large enough to provide adequate cover. This thinly forested wilderness sprawled eastward about two filons into Verdure from Snow Peak, before the farming lands began.

Thirty thousand allied Maronian and Esparian archers, strategically positioned along the lengthy border, hid in the woodlands behind the thickest bushes. These well prepared men carried enough arrows to bring down scores of Demarian soldiers. They wore, from head to toe, lightweight, tightly woven palium chain mail. The escape routes were thoroughly pre-planned.

Every civilian within fifty filons of the border had evacuated, fleeing to the safety of Esparia's interior. As per John's instructions, Cordon, like Ophir, had fortified the cities beyond the evacuation line. Thick, cemented stone walls, reinforced by local timber, were built up around the major tierns with battle turrets designed into them every hundred feet. Twelve foot deep, V-shaped ditches, eight feet wide at the base, increasing to twenty feet wide at the top, surrounded the walls. The evacuated earth from these trenches was deposited thirty feet beyond the city wall, making a continuous ridge eight feet high that served as the first obstacle an enemy would need to cross. Men, women, and children had worked non-stop to create these defenses.

Lepsis and Cordon had nearly five hundred thousand foot soldiers, twenty-five thousand slingers and one hundred thousand cavalry between them. Not completely certain of the enemy force, they hoped they had enough men and supplies to beat back the Demarians and retake Snow Peak.

Cordon split the army in two, giving Lepsis full command of the north. Each army was further broken down into legions of thirty-five thousand and labeled Maronian and Esparian one through ten, with cavalry divided into groups of ten thousand, numbered one through ten. All of these were further subdivided into manageable fighting divisions. Each division consisted of light infantry, archers, slingers and javelin throwers, heavily armored infantry, and cavalry to protect their flanks.

Located in front of the foot soldiers, the spearmen and slingers' job was to take out as many of the enemy as possible, then fall back, with swords drawn, behind the regular army. Cordon and Ophir were trained in the same school and so, given similar terrain, their battle plans, as well as equipment, were basically identical.

Lepsis, however, had a few tricks up his sleeve and tried to convince Cordon to try something new. His men dug trenches, just large enough to hide in, then covered them with planks and camouflage. This was accomplished under cover of darkness to avoid the prying eyes of Demarian spies, of whom quite a few had been caught over the last several weeks. Lepsis secreted a full one fourth of his men in the earth. These were his best warriors, and were instructed to listen for the sound of the shrill battle horns. The bellowing trumpets would signal the hidden men to rise up, thereby attacking the enemy's rear and effectively surrounding him. Cordon, conservative and from the old school, opted not to try this innovative measure, but wished Lepsis luck.

On the evening of the fourteenth, Cordon held a last meeting inside one of the large dining tents. His command center was too small to accommodate the large company of upper level officers assembled for this historic moment. Cordon personally arranged all of the wooden stools in neat rows as well as oil lamps along the sides and back of the room. When the somber men gathered at the appointed hour, the tent was ablaze in light, an optimistic welcome in this time of dark foreboding.

Cordon, smartly dressed in polished boots and a crisply pressed uniform stood to address his men. "As we speak, the advance archers are taking their places where we believe the enemy will cross our borders. Be prepared to give them cover once their missions are completed. After the archers have cleared the field, have your slingers and spearmen ready, I fully expect the Demarians to be close behind. I want the enemy reeling before they march twenty paces from the woods."

"This is not a war of our making, but we will not run from it. Remember Saylon Dorsett, remember Protector Haesom, Protectoress Lila and their innocent sons, remember one thousand dead soldiers. Do not let the men forget."

Cordon reached into his pocket. "I have here a message from Protector John." He held a small paper for them to see. "It reads,"

To Cordon and all valiant men,

Greetings. We stand on the threshold of history. Tomorrow and the tomorrows beyond will determine the fate of this great nation. Remember who you are and what you fight for; your wives, your children, your heritage, your liberty. In all your battles, remember mercy, always giving your enemy the option of surrender. We are not murderers, we are not here to plunder or pillage. Fare well, my friends, until we meet again.

Your brother-in-arms, John Ernshaw of the House of Saylon, High Protector of Esparia

* * *

The morning of the fifteenth dawned cloudy and overcast. A light drizzle cooled the gloomy summer day. At the first hint of morning the Demarian army, eight hundred thousand strong, marched over the Verdure border. When the first enemy soldier stepped onto Verdure soil, the archers opened up. Runners kept Cordon informed of the various battles' progress. There were four points of penetration, and the fighting was fierce.

Well supplied and fast on their feet, the bowmen hit the enemy hard. They shot at close range, taking the Demarians by surprise. The wave of advancing troops faltered slightly, but being well protected with armor, many of the arrows bounced off them with little damage done. The archers pulled their bows with speed and accuracy, while the enemy pressed forward. A volley of Demarian arrows flew in answer to the Esparians. For a while it was archer against archer, a deadly contest of hide and seek. The Esparian bowmen closest to the border began to retreat, with the others soon following. Periodically they stopped their withdrawal long enough to send more deadly volleys at the encroaching enemy.

Cordon, sitting on his horse at the front of his foot soldiers, watched while the first of the archers emerged from the light forest onto the cleared farmland where his vast army waited. He knew this same scene was being played out for filons to the north and south, all along Verdure, and he steeled himself for the coming day.

The slingers and javelin throwers were set to aid the retreating archers. At Cordon's command, these troops inflicted the greatest damage to the

248

invading enemy. Arms and legs snapped like twigs when a well-aimed stone crashed down on it. Skulls imploded inside dented helmets. The javelins were thrown with such force, the armored target was gored clear through. The ghastly work of death caused the Demarians to waver.

The cavalry charged next, making short work of the first enemy wave, but then the Demarian Dragoons met them. At the appearance of the black clothed horsemen, Cordon commanded his foot soldiers to charge in. Cavalry fought cavalry, soldier fought soldier, and the two armies raged on nearly equal terms. Daenon's men had suffered losses in the forests at the hands of the allied archers, but worse were their losses on the grasslands by the slingers and spearmen. Their wounded were trampled by the battling horsemen, their dead strewn everywhere on the fields.

Cordon fought throughout that day, wielding his sword like a man possessed. His chance for vengeance had come, and his only thought was to repay death for every comrade who had fallen at the Saylon Dorsett massacre. He knew this was not a war of vengeance, but his anger poured out in the heat of battle. He lost track of time. His expertise as a swordsman had earned him a reputation in Esparia, but now the Demarians too witnessed his mastery in action. As the day drew to a close, Cordon saw terror in the eyes of those whom he opposed. Both armies had stood their ground throughout the day, neither advancing nor retreating.

When nightfall came, the enemy quickly withdrew into the forests. Deciding not to follow, Cordon held his men and had them prepare for the morrow. He gathered the many prisoners they had captured and forced them to retrieve the wounded from the blood soaked plain.

Alberod, John's friend from Ider Hoffle, having finished his training at Ramadine, had swiftly risen in the ranks of leadership, and was in command of the surgical units interspersed along the northern allied lines. He and Cordon were friends from long ago, so Cordon felt relieved to have someone he trusted in charge of the wounded. Alberod came into Cordon's command tent where Cordon was meeting with his seventh bars. Without saying a word, the physician quietly set to work. He pulled sutures and bandages from his medical kit, then stepped to the nearest seventh bar. One by one, Alberod stitched and bound the men in the tent, coming last of all to Cordon when the meeting ended.

"I thought you might need some attention," Alberod said when Cordon sat wearily on his makeshift bed.

"I'm not hurt," Cordon said, his voice devoid of emotion.

"Oh, really? Then why is your side covered in blood?"

"Alberod, I'm covered head to toe in blood and gore."

"Just sit still and let me do my job."

Before Cordon could protest further, Alberod pulled his friend's shirt open. "You need mending here and here and here."

Cordon looked at where Alberod pointed. To his genuine surprise, his flesh was indeed sliced open, three nasty looking gashes to his torso and several smaller ones in his arms and face.

"Huh! You're right." Cordon heaved a deep sigh. "How bad were our losses?"

"Not as terrible as they could have been. I have some very fine healers working with me. They've saved many lives today. Now clamp your teeth, this is going to hurt."

Alberod poured a disinfecting liquid into a seven-inch cut in Cordon's side, then a numbing powder. Threading a fresh needle from his bag, he quickly stitched the torn muscle.

"I knew you would never come to a healing tent for help. Your seventh bars are as bad as you are," he chided. "These wounds don't heal well by themselves. They need tending."

"Vengeance is hollow, Alberod," Cordon said and he shook his head.

"Cordon?"

"I've waited so long for this day, to avenge my brothers from the Dorsett, but now…"

"It's understandable, Cordon." Alberod began disinfecting the wounds on his friend's arm. "Not one man was left alive at Saylon. You're not the only one who wanted revenge for that, but at least you've come to understand that nothing good comes from it."

Cordon nodded. "There's a prophecy, made by Larone's father. In it, he warns that vengeance would plunge this land into numberless years of darkness. I understand that now. I saw terror in the eyes of my enemies today."

"I've seen you fight, Cordon and I never want to face the sharp end of your sword. I can imagine the fear the Demarians felt. What you need to do now is use that fear, that terror, to bring a quick end to this bloodshed. John was right, we need to give more opportunity for Demarian surrender." Alberod finished the last stitch in Cordon's scalp. "Now try and take at least an hour or two of sleep. If you can't think clearly, then you can't command coherently."

Three more days of battle went much as the first. The Demarians would attack, and as soon as they stepped out of the forest onto the bloody meadow, the Esparian archers, slingers and spearmen would cut down thousands. Cordon did his best to take as many prisoners as possible, an all-out slaughter was not something he wanted. After surrounding pockets of soldiers, the Esparian officers took to heart John's orders and offered them their lives if they would only throw down their weapons. Fighting for a higher cause, the Esparians found the edge they needed to hold their ground and win.

Throughout the battle, many black uniformed men yielded their scimitars, swords and spears, taking advantage of the Esperians' mercy. Soon the ranks of enemy prisoners grew to tens of thousands.

On the fourth day, about three hours before dawn, the Demarians struck with deadly force. A volley of fiery arrows, stones, and javelins crashed through the tents of the sleeping Esparians. Cordon barely managed to exit his tent before it collapsed in flames. The entire camp was ablaze. Men fought the fires while trying to protect themselves from the deadly projectiles. Others ran, seemingly in circles, trying to escape the hail of death.

"Leave the tents!" Cordon yelled. "To your ranks! Shields! Shields!" He ran among his men, shouting orders to assemble and counter strike. The weeks of disciplined training showed as the men rallied. After the initial panic of ambush wore off, the troops fell into combat formation at the first order.

During these days of conflict, Cordon had instructed the men to sleep in full armor with their weapons by their sides. They charged the Demarians. The fighting continued for hours with Cordon's men slowly pushing the enemy back. When the sun settled in the western horizon, for the first time, the Demarian ranks broke. By hundreds, then thousands, the enemy surrendered, and many more fled, leaderless, back into the woods.

It was nearly midnight when Cordon met once again in the command tent with his remaining officers. They were in the process of reassigning legions when Alberod, medical bag in hand, walked in on them. He looked at the injured men and shook his head, a disgusted look on his face. "None of you leave until I've had a chance to piece you back together," he interrupted.

One by one, the healer tended the wounded officers, for none had escaped without several sword wounds or burns. When he came last of all to Cordon, he frowned at the dried blood plastering his friend's brow. The meeting was at a close, and the freshly bandaged officers left Cordon in Alberod's care.

"Cordon," Alberod began in a lecturing tone, "what did I tell you about letting these wounds fester?"

Before Cordon could defend himself, two of the advance scouts staggered in, completely out of breath. Fearing the worst, Cordon jumped to his feet.

"No sir," a scout quickly said. "You misunderstand our haste. We bring heartening news; the Demarians are on the run. They are retreating back into Snow Peak, heading for Lansterdine, the provincial capitol."

* * *

In the far north, it took the Demarian army an entire day to traverse the few filons of thin forests, as the Maronian archers kept them from any rapid advancement. It was nearly noon of the second day when Lepsis finally saw the enemy break through the forested death trap.

"Here they come," he yelled when the first black uniforms came into view. "Slingers...spearmen...do your damage."

Taking aim, the human ballistae launchers hurled their projectiles. When the deadly missiles found their marks, men screamed out in agony. Demarian counter measures came flying back. Anticipating these, the Maronian shields were thick and forged of the purest, strongest palium steel, thus providing the best protection possible.

"Hornmen," Lepsis addressed those who sounded the short bugles, "blow the signal for retreat." *It is time to spring our little trap.* A rush of adrenaline coursed through his veins. When the horns blasted out the short, staccato retreat warning, the cavalry and footmen fell back, without ever engaging the enemy on a hand-to-hand level. The plan was to draw the Demarians well away from the line of hidden, underground Maronians. To Lepsis' gratification, the enemy charged forward, following their prey. The overcast and gloomy weather aided in the concealment of Lepsis's men when the enemy crossed over the hidden burrows.

"It's working!" Lepsis tensed as he closely monitored the action. "The last enemy has cleared our hidden rows of men. Now hornmen! Blow the assault signal!"

At the long, sustained blasts of the horns, the ground erupted, and up from the depths of Edia came the hidden Maronians. These were mighty men, the best warriors Marone could offer. Ferociously, they fell on the enemy's rear, causing nearly the entire Demarian army to stop its pursuit of Lepsis and turn to fight.

Lepsis led his frontline soldiers directly into the fray, his cavalry assaulting the northern and southern flanks. Unable to hold their position under the cavalry onslaught, the fringe Demarians were splintered into small units, many of which fled the battlefield. The ring around the enemy closed.

In the end, they could not hold against the determined Maronians, whose leaders continuously reminded their men of their reasons for fighting, and the men responded with astounding vigor. After twenty exhausting hours, the tide of battle turned irreversibly in favor of the Maronians. The enemy as a whole could not retreat, though many individuals escaped back into the woods, and they could not move forward. Their leaders tried to slash their way to freedom, with many troops succeeding during the night, but for the most part, Lepsis, with his unfaltering Maronians, stood firm.

By morning, with the victory undisputedly his, Lepsis called for a halt to the killing. "Sound the 'cease all action' call." When the horns rang out, two short blasts followed by one long note, the clashing of steel stopped. The Maronians stepped several paces back from their foes.

Since much of the battle had raged by the light of two moons, Lepsis was unaware of the extent of the carnage about him. Now, in the increasing light of a new sunrise, the destruction appeared obscene. Thousands of bodies stretched for as far as he could see, their spilt blood mixing with the dry earth to create a sticky, foul mud. The twisted corpses, many limbless and headless, were further disfigured by the trampling feet of living combatants. The acrid smell of blood hung so thick in the air he could taste it with every breath he took.

"Men of Demar, I am Lepsis, prince of Marone," he shouted for all to hear. "Look about you and see the death of your people. We do not delight in your slaughter. Many of your comrades have already surrendered. Throw down your weapons and cease this useless struggle."

From deep within the enemy ranks a tired voice rang out. "We are not Demarians. We are natives of Palium and Snow Peak. The Demarians escaped hours ago."

A murmur of surprise rose from the Maronians. "Then why do you fight us?" A soldier asked.

In response, a man stumbled from the main body of defeated men. He threw down his sword and unbuckled his armor. Tottering on his feet he cried out, "For the drug! It is the drug that compels us," then he crumbled to his knees.

Another man came forward, adding his armor and sword to that of the first. "Before the battle began, we filled with that cursed drug. It clouds our minds, but now its effects are gone and we're left empty."

"Help us, brothers!" another agonized voice pleaded.

"Throw down your weapons," Lepsis called. "I swear to you, what help we can give, we will."

Visibly shaking from withdrawal, the remaining combatants dropped their weapons. The few who did not were forced into submission by their comrades.

Lepsis openly wept. Tens of thousands of bodies lay piled for as far as he could see. The ground was soaked in blood and gore, the stench drifting with the morning wind.

"We'll burn the dead, then secure this region. Once done, we liberate Snow Peak," he ordered.

CHAPTER 23

The Fight for Esparia
The South

With more men marching into camp every day, John accumulated an army of seven hundred thousand spread out over several hundred filons of the Palium border. His defenses consisted of one hundred thousand cavalry, one hundred thousand archers, one hundred thousand slingers and spearmen and four hundred thousand foot soldiers.

Because the Palium border stretched twice as far as the Snow Peak border, John was uncertain where the entire enemy was located, so the troop positions constantly fluctuated with his best guesses. Even though he had the updated advance scout reports, there was a nagging feeling Daenon was somehow hiding a large portion of his army.

The Palium-Ramana border consisted of flat grassland with a few gently rolling hills. John took personal command of this region. The Palium-Kine border was more wooded, and Reese commanded there. John had given Reese, with his seventh bars, free rein to do what they felt was best in their region. Reese was young and smart, but more importantly, besides John, Cordon, Ophir and Gammet, the only Esparian leader to have been in a real battle. The few active military officers who participated in the Battle at Blue Mountain fifty years earlier were killed in the Saylon Dorsett massacre. Reese's combat experience was invaluable, and he was a natural leader. John felt confidence in the youthful seventh bar's abilities.

By the fourteenth, none of Lyrista's thirty specialized scouts were heard from. Their mission was to penetrate fifty filons past the Demarian line at the Palium border and send word about enemy reserve strength. Since there was no communication with these men for over a week, John feared the worst.

With the palpable certainty of war hanging over the camp, John held his final council meeting. No real measurement of the enemy strength could be given, so they did their best to finalize troop positions and supply lines. When the meeting ended, the grim faced seventh bars and upper ranking officers filed from the command tent. Lyrista hung back.

"I'm worried about my scouts, at least one should be back by now." Lyrista's face was lined with concern.

254

"I know, but there's nothing we can do. They knew the dangers." John tried to sound comforting.

"I hand picked them, they would never have turned the assignment down." She laced her fingers behind her neck and looked up at the tent ceiling. "This is real. This is war. It's one thing to teach about it at the defense academy, but it's another to live it. People are going to die, people I care about." She dropped her hands and bit her lip. "Everyone's supposed to live a hundred and eighty years, not die in their youth." Tears stung her eyes and one slipped down her cheek.

John wiped it away with his finger. "Yes, this is real life and people you know are going to die. I don't like it any more than you do. Why do you think I hesitated so long before agreeing to this position? I've seen war, seen its horrors, but I'm committed. Whatever it takes, I'm going to see this thing through."

"What about Jessica? What if Daenon uses her to get to you?" Lyrista put into words the thoughts John tried to avoid. Her face reflected the anguish he felt.

He shook his head. "It makes no difference. If it comes down to it, she'll understand." He said no more, but his message was clear.

Lyrista swallowed hard and wiped at her eyes. "I won't fall apart, John. You can count on me."

He gave her a drawn smile. "Are the civilians evacuated?"

"Yes. The last left yesterday. Seventy filons are free of innocents and those remaining are fortifying the major dines to your specifications. They're well stocked with provisions and weapons in case of a siege."

"You've done a great job."

"Keeping busy helps me focus."

"Good, because I have another job for you. I need you to take charge of the wounded. They'll need transporting from the battlefield to the hospitals. I've given orders to the third battalion that they're under your command for this very purpose."

"You don't believe in giving much notice, do you?"

"Well, I've seen you work best under pressure."

She smiled and light replaced the sadness in her eyes.

When midnight approached, John was filled with nervous energy. Since sleep seemed impossible, he decided to make one last walking tour through the individual camps closest to his tent. Only a few minutes into his stroll, he spotted a figure moving ghostlike between the small fires. It was Gammet.

The seventh bar's presence helped inspire the troops, so John was grateful to have the aging warrior with him, but he noticed the man looked drawn and tired all the time. He had difficulty focusing on details in their tactical meetings, his mind never fully on the matters at hand. He never smiled, never joked and only once volunteered his opinion. Just as now, he wandered the camps at night, a lone figure going from fire to fire, never actually talking with anyone. Recognizing the signs of deep depression, John tried to keep the man busy with training young recruits and assigning supplies to the various divisions.

John made certain each of his men had full armor, from rock-hard steel helmets to specialized leg gear, with the option of chain mail or solid metal covering their vital organs. When Anton ordered arms from Ironton, it was made clear that only the finest materials were to be used. The life of every soldier depended on quality equipment.

Each man carried a shield and trained hard to properly use it. The rectangular plates were weapons in and of themselves. Each one had a sharp, spear-style point built into it extending outward eight inches from the center.

John commanded his archers and slingers to practice on horseback. They became expert at guiding their mounts with only their knees at full gallop, leaving their hands free to shoot at any target. In the open ranges, this ability could provide the difference between victory and defeat.

As expected, the attack came at dawn on the fifteenth and John's men stood ready. Foot soldier formation was three men deep and the cavalry was interspersed in groups of six thousand. The archers, slingers and spearmen were placed in front of the foot soldiers, along with hundreds of pack horses loaded with extra arrows, stones and javelins.

When the enemy came into view the Esparians watched while their frontline of mounted archers and throwers swung into action. First arrows, then stones and javelins flew westward. A similar volley flew eastward from the enemy lines and the soldiers used their shields testudo style for protection against the deadly projectiles.

Before him lay an endless sea of humanity and John felt sick at the knowledge of what was ahead of them. The battle was ferocious, lasting the entire day. Men and horses fell dead and wounded, and the ground ran red with their blood. John led his troops, with shield in one hand and the Sword of Judgment in the other. Having mastered the sword's cut and feint techniques, his skill saved the life of many a man by heroic leaps and well-aimed thrusts. All day his arm cut, slashed and stabbed at the well-armored enemy around him. Fortunately, John's peripheral vision was excellent and many times he saw, from the corner of his eye, an enemy strike. With a quick turn of his shield he protected not only himself, but also men around him. He suffered several wounds, but nothing that could not be quickly bandaged.

John was vaguely aware of his other leaders; thankful they knew their duty and performed it with precision. Twice he noticed Gammet positioned on the highest location, sunlight glistening off his polished armor, directing the reserves where they were needed the most. Many times during the battle he witnessed Lyrista's profound fighting talents while she protected those who transported the wounded. She inflicted her share of damage to the Demarian army, never flinching or backing away. All day long her battalion protected the medics and transport personnel from the makeshift hospitals. More than once Lyrista herself wielded her sword as guardian while a surgeon bound one of John's deeper wounds.

Finally, at the setting of the sun, as if on cue, the soldiers separated to their respective camps. The day ended in a draw, with neither army gaining ground. Meals were prepared, the wounded cleared from the battlefield, and the men tried to sleep. John, astride Fireguard, rode the length of the camp, trying to assess the damage. He found three of his seventh bars dead and many lesser officers out of commission. Knowing he needed to replace these men, his first thought was of Ru. It did not take him long to locate the fourth bar, rearming his men and organizing others around him.

"Ru," John called. "You are no longer a fourth bar. I'm promoting you directly to seventh bar. You're the seventh bar in charge of the fourth, fifth and sixth legions."

Ru looked thunderstruck. "Sir," he exclaimed, "I prefer to lead the Guardians at your side, as I have done this day."

"Sorry Ru, but I've seen your leadership and tactical abilities. You're better used as a commander of thousands than a leader of hundreds." The man nodded, visibly not happy about the promotion. "I have one more promotion to make and then I'm calling a council in my tent. Be there in an hour."

Ru, Gammet, Lyrista, and four other seventh bars, met with John in the command headquarters. "I've combined the sixth and seventh light infantry divisions," John began. "You seventh bars are in charge of reorganizing your divisions and appointing your replacement officers. By now you've had a chance to assess what needs to be done. Lyrista, we need…"

"I've already begun shipping more supplies to the archers, slingers, and spearmen," she said.

For the first time that day, he smiled. "I can always count on you." He held up two small pieces of paper. "I've received communiqué's from Reese and Cordon. Reese's day went even worse than ours, he's lost several filons of ground. There's little I can do to help him, and it's frustrating. I can't spare a single man, so I've sent a note to Larone asking him to send reinforcements south. Cordon gives me cause to be grateful, he's holding his own and feels victory is in the air. No news from Lepsis or Ophir yet. If there're no questions, then we'll adjourn now, you have much to do before dawn."

Finding himself alone and unable to sleep, John headed for one of the field hospitals. *At least I can do some good in surgery.*

Just before dawn a runner burst through the surgery doors. Catching John's eye, he stammered, out of breath, "Protector, the enemy comes!"

"I'm on my way," John said while he finished the last stitch on a soldier's chest. He raced from the hospital to his own tent, with scarcely enough time to throw on his armor, grab his sword and shield, and race to the front of his troops before the fighting began anew.

The second and third days of conflict went much like the first, except the Esparians lost ground--a great deal of ground. During the second day, the battle line was slowly pushed back by constant pressure from the enemy, but on the third day the Demarian heavy cavalry pressed hard on John's southern flank. Before Gammet could send reinforcements, the men broke under the stress. Running, they retreated by thousands, causing a domino effect down the entire Esparian line. It was well into the evening before John and his seventh bars could reorganize the men, and with the help of the archers and slingers, temporarily repulse the pursuing Demarians.

John slept little during the next two days, his nights being spent in conferences with Gammet and Ru and what other officers were still on their feet. Legions were reorganized and assignments given. There was high praise for the archery and slinger companies. They were remarkable on their mounts and had saved many comrades from certain death. Lyrista had her hands full with protecting and transporting the wounded.

The reports sent from Ophir and Reese were grim. Both were being slowly pushed back, but their men bravely stood up to the enemy. They knew the cost of defeat. On the fifth day, John's men held strong, so he decided to send thirty thousand troops south to aid Reese, who was pushed back to the evacuation line, then he sent a message to Cordon asking for any troops he could spare.

At around midnight, one of Lyrista's thirty missing scouts stumbled, half dead, into camp. John had just lain down to catch some precious sleep when he was summoned, and he came at a run. He found the man in Ru's arms, being carried to the field hospital.

The poor man had been tortured and could barely talk. "Rebels...Farin...freed me," he said haltingly. He took a deep breath. "Daenon...thousands and thousands and thousands...fresh troops...tomorrow." They reached the hospital where Ru gave the scout up to the very capable healers.

John moaned inside as the message sunk in. "This explains why Lepsis and Cordon are having victories, Daenon obviously misjudged the strength of the Maronian army and didn't send enough troops northward," he commented to Ru when they walked back to the command tent. "If he had sent those reserves north, our troops there would be in big trouble now."

Ru nodded. "I don't think we can hold against that many fresh soldiers."

John looked at the two moons, one full and the other nearly there. "We'll have to, that's all there is to it. I'll send an emergency message to Larone, but I've already told him to send reinforcements to Reese; I don't know how many more men he has to deploy. Hopefully Lepsis and Cordon can spare troops, but they won't be here for several days."

The sixth day of fighting proved disastrous. With the Demarians reinforced by nearly three hundred thousand fresh troops, the Esparians retreated time and time again. They were out-numbered and exhausted and could not hold, though they never again ran. Their cavalry were reduced by half, the enemy archers and spearmen having slaughtered thousands of horses. By the end of the day they were pushed back so far, the line of fortified cities lay within walking distance.

In the late afternoon, John answered a call to the Northern line of battle where most of his upper level officers were either dead or so severely wounded they were unable to command. Leaving Ru at the center, John raced to reorganize the north.

He found Garrett desperately trying to rally the men. The young man wore the insignia of a third bar officer and yelled his orders in a loud clear voice. "Stay in formation men, shoulder to shoulder. Use the shields, the shields! Don't let them get around our flank."

John quickly appointed new leaders. "Keep the men in formation," he ordered, "then fall back in an orderly fashion. Cavalry should be here soon."

John jumped from his horse and ran into the melee. He hacked his way to Garrett's side, saving him just as an enemy soldier jabbed from behind.

"Good to see you, Protector," Garrett said. "It's been touch and go here for quite some time. I sent three messengers to find you in hopes at least one would get through. We..."

"Garrett, my friend," John yelled as he swung his sword. "Shut up!"

They fought side-by-side for nearly an hour, shouting orders while they slowly fell back, foot by foot. Eventide fast approached, and with it, John hoped the end of fighting for the day. All of a sudden, a concentration of nearly two hundred Demarian troops came out of nowhere. They managed to push through the tight Esparian line to the left and to the right of where John fought, trapping him in a circle with only Garrett and eight other Esparian soldiers. Pressing on every side, they methodically killed the Esparian defenders one by one, until just Garrett and John remained. Garrett fought with a strength and stamina John had seldom seen in any man. They struggled back to back, their swords inflicting death with every stroke. Just when John realized they were dead men, Gammet, astride a large gray stallion, came flying over the heads of the Demarian troops, his sword dripping red.

"John," Gammet yelled above the din, and with superhuman effort, reached down, grabbed the Protector, and hoisted him up. "The Demarians want *you!*"

Before John could react, Gammet spurred his horse and plowed out of the deadly circle. "They were doing to you what they did to me."

"Garrett!" John screamed, twisting on the horse.

"He's dead whether you go back or not!" The old seventh bar tightened his already iron grip on John's bloody arm.

John's last glimpse of Garrett was of him swinging his sword with both hands, completely surrounded by enemy troops.

Gammet headed for a small hill further north, while the enemy pursued them from the south. Reaching the hill as darkness fell, the two men dashed up it and took cover among a grouping of rocks.

"I don't think they'll attack until morning," Gammet said and settled into the hillside.

John panted for breath. He sheathed the Sword of Judgment, then turned on the old man. "I don't want to stay here to find out. I've got to get back to my men. You killed Garrett."

"No, the Demarians killed him. Haven't you heard anything I said? From my vantage point I saw what was happening. As soon as they realized you'd moved to the northern line, they rushed a full division to grab you. I saw them push through your lines and splinter off your small group. It's just what they did to me. Didn't you wonder why your men were being targeted by their swords and not you? Garrett was the last to stand. After they killed him, what would you have done? They would have captured you; taken you to Daenon."

John listened, his anger slowly melting to frustration.

"With you captured," Gammet continued, "who would have led our men?"

"You."

Gammet shook his head. He looked particularly old in the twilight. "My time is past."

John opened his mouth to protest, then decided it was not worth it. What was done was done and no amount of argument could change that fact, so he focused on the present. "There must be some way out of this. We need to go up and over the hill, then circle around back to our own men."

Gammet remained silent, so John took that as agreement.

"I should have died at the Dorsett with my men," Gammet mumbled.

It took John a few seconds to process what the seventh bar had just said. When he did, he understood where Gammet's depression came from. "That's nonsense!" His voice was sharp. "Your life is valuable, not only as a seventh bar, but to Cordon and Lyrista. You've been a tremendous help here. Stop thinking that way."

Gammet shook his head. "I can't keep myself from wondering, *why me?* I wasn't even wounded!"

"Gammet, listen to me!" John shook the old man roughly. He suddenly wished he had an arsenal of anti-depressants at hand, but the only thing he could do was try and talk sense to the seventh bar. "The Esparians need you, and more importantly Lyrista and Reese need you. Cordon risked his life to rescue you. Hold onto these thoughts."

John felt closed in. Their little groove in the rocks provided them protection, but was not a good location for scanning the surrounding terrain. In order to have a better idea of the hill's height and topography, John would have to crawl out onto a more exposed ledge.

"Lyrista and Reese," Gammet thought out loud. "Reese has become a man, and I'm very proud of him. He's my only grandchild, but no longer a boy. Now Lyrista..." His voice trailed off in thought and John was at a loss for words. He crawled out onto a flat rock beside them, checking the hillside above.

"I've been watching you, John Ernshaw," the elder man spoke clearly. "You're a good man, and I'm glad I've had the opportunity to know you." The night was as dark as it was going to be, as light from the first moon would soon illuminate their position. John resumed his place beside Gammet, for the gloomy tone in his voice concerned him.

"We have a lot of years of good friendship ahead."

"Promise me something."

"What do you want?" John was wary.

"Promise me you'll take care of my Lyrista. I've seen how her eyes light up when you're around. She loves you, and I'd be proud to have you as a son-in-law." Gammet was serious.

John tried to read the seventh bar's face, but in the shadowy darkness, all he could see were sad, haunted eyes. "I'll do my best."

"I also want you to take care of my country," Gammet continued. "You're not here by chance, my boy. Your destiny lies with us. I knew the moment I saw you."

John did not know what to say. He had committed himself to these people for the duration of the war, but Gammet referred to something more, something permanent. A small rock fell from above just when he opened his mouth to respond. Both men sprang to their feet. The hair on John's neck prickled when he realized they were most likely surrounded. Gammet drew his weapon. John pulled the Sword of Judgment.

"Your capture would be a catastrophe," Gammet hissed. "On three, we'll rush out of here and go up, cutting our way to the top if we have to. Once there, you run down the other side and don't stop until you're well within the protection of your own men."

Before John could argue Gammet yelled, "Three!"

Scrambling out from their protective crevice, they managed to take a score of soldiers by surprise. Slashing left and hacking right, Gammet fought like a man possessed. John had never seen anyone fight so viciously. When they reached the top, Gammet pushed him down the other side. "Remember your promises," he yelled as he turned to face the enemy.

Knowing the Demarians were close on his heels, John hesitated only a moment before bolting down the hill. Behind him he could hear the clashing of steel. Gammet was a dead man, whether John stayed or not, and understanding his own capture would be a terrible blow to the Esparians, he ran. Gammet was giving his life so John could escape. He would never forget the selfless act.

John ran and hid, then ran and hid some more. The enemy patrolled everywhere, but he managed to elude capture. Zigzagging across the grassland, he slowly made his way to friendly troops.

Stumbling unexpectedly into the northern most Esparian guard camp, John was nearly slain by his own startled men. With swords drawn, two of them jumped at the intruder.

"I'm Protector John Ernshaw!" he managed to say in the few seconds it took him to duck and parry three blows.

Hesitating, but with swords raised, the men regarded him suspiciously. "Come closer to the fire," one ordered. Dropping his sword to his side, John complied.

"If you don't believe me, then bind me and take me to Seventh Bar Ru."

A soldier from across the fire let out a low gasp. "Lord John," he exclaimed and in two bounds stood beside him. It took John a few seconds to recognize the young man.

"Mica!"

"Lower your weapons," Mica said to his comrades. "This is truly Lord John. I know him well, as I rode with him from Ider Hoffle to Ramadine, many long weeks ago."

"You don't know how glad I am to see you." John felt relief. "I didn't want a skirmish here. Is there a horse I can use? I've got to get to headquarters."

"Take mine," Mica offered and ran to retrieve the animal.

After John swung onto the mount, he said, "What of Garrett?"

Mica's reply was steady, but in the firelight, John saw the young man's shoulders droop and grief enter his eyes. "I found his body at sunset, surrounded by many Demarian dead."

John had clung onto hope that Garrett had somehow survived, but now his heart sank. "I'm sorry, Mica."

Mica nodded. "He died bravely, a true Ider warrior."

While John turned the horse, he called over his shoulder, "I'll return your animal as soon as I reach my camp." Then he galloped away.

It was nearly sunrise before John rode into headquarters. Seventh Bar Ru was there, issuing orders in John's absence. When John rode up, the seventh bar gave a short cry. "John!" His look of joy faded into concern when John neared the torches outside the command tent. "Run and bring a healer," Ru ordered an aid.

Ru held the horse while John dismounted. "I thought you were dead."

"I should be." John handed the reins of his mount to a soldier standing nearby. "Send this horse immediately to Third Bar Mica of Ider Hoffle. He is the officer in charge of our most northern guard camp." The soldier saluted.

Getting right to business, John said, "Well Ru, what do you have for me?"

Before Ru could answer, a slight commotion came from several tents away. John turned in time to see Lyrista plowing through two sentries at a full run. "John!" she cried.

Without a word he darted toward her and caught her up.

"When Fireguard came back without you, I was worried out of my mind," she whispered. "I sent a full company out searching the battlefield for your body."

"Your dad saved my life. He gave his, so I could live."

Through tears she looked up at him. "He was never the same after the Dorsett. I think he always felt he should have died there."

"I promise, his actions will always be remembered. He'll be honored as a hero."

In a swift, surprising move that caught him completely off guard, Lyrista reached up and pulled his face to hers. She gave him a passionate kiss. Then, just as abruptly, she pushed him away, and brushing the tears from her cheeks, walked in the direction of the hospital tent.

"All is ready, Protector," Ru said from behind. "I don't know how much longer we can hang on, but the men are determined to fight."

With a burning in his chest, John turned to his faithful seventh bar. He nodded, as much to catch his wind as to respond to Ru's comment. He knew they were in a tight spot.

"I'm going up there," he said, pointing to a small hillock at the back of the camp. "I can see our situation better and maybe scrape together an idea or two." He swung up on the nearest horse, then took off at a gallop. Of necessity, John had become an expert horseman in the last several weeks and he no longer feared any animal.

He rode to the highest point, surveying the land around him. The night sky was fast fading into morning light. It would be only a short time before the sun cleared the eastern horizon and the day's battle would begin.

John could see for filons. To the west were the endless rows of smoldering enemy campfires. The black uniformed soldiers were breaking camp and preparing to attack. Behind him, to either side, were the fortified cities, where women and children streamed out by thousands, trying to flee further east before the Demarians overran them. His own men were slowly assembling into battle formation.

John looked at the overcast sky; his mood matched the gloominess of the approaching day. Shaking his head, he thought, *how can we stand against so many?* Finally, he looked south. Thick clouds rose from the earth, reaching up to meet their gray brethren in the sky. It was an unusual optical illusion and it held his attention. *Clouds of dust?* He watched for nearly a minute. *They're coming closer!* The distant sound of thunder came to his ears.

Ru galloped up, joining the hilltop surveillance. "How does it look?" He scanned the enemy to the west. "They are so many."

"Ru," John continued to stare southward. "What do you make of that? Is it a dust storm coming our way?"

Looking to where the protector pointed, Ru let out a low whistle. "I have no idea! I've never seen anything like it." He paused and listened. "Thunder?" The two men stared at each other, then back at the rapidly advancing storm. The deep sound grew louder.

"Forget the south. Daenon's coming," John said, then kicked his horse into a run.

The two men rode hard to arrive at the front lines in time to lead their men into battle. The deep, thunderous sound from the south drew ever closer, ever louder, but the soldiers ignored it as the warfare began.

They fought for nearly half an hour when John, who was at the front of his men, heard a faint cheer rise from behind. He did not dare to look, as the enemy pressed on every side. There was a flash to his right and many of the enemy soldiers he fought looked up in surprise. John sensed, rather than saw, a large mass move in beside him.

How much time elapsed, no one knew. In the bitter contest of warfare, time seems to stand still. Only the gradual loss of strength and the slowing of reflexes measure the passing of the day. However, it was after several hours of intense fighting that the Demarian soldiers began to give way. Only then did John dare to take a good look at the mammoth figure fighting by his side. There, in full armor and looking like a demon from a child's horror story, was a giant.

John recognized him as the one he had spoken to weeks before in the Colossus forest. To his surprise, the man wore a small Banner of Freedom tied around his forehead. It held his long, flowing hair back and out of his face.   Glancing around, John saw hundreds of giants interspersed throughout his men, each one sporting a similar Banner of Freedom. He later learned thousands had joined in the battle. The Demarian army fell back under the new onslaught, and by early evening was in full retreat. The giants had won the day.

"Let them run.   We won't pursue the enemy today," John commanded. "There'll be time enough for that later. For now, I want every man to rest and gather his strength." No one argued.

Led by Lyrista, the medics fanned out through the wounded, worn out men. Many had fainted from loss of blood while others tottered on their feet. The giants helped once again, by carrying wounded men to the field hospitals.

With his men cared for, John finally took the time to understand the day's events. He looked in wonder at the battle weary, armor-clad giant, still at his side. The ten-foot-high man looked as John remembered him, long, thick, white-blond hair and creamy complexion with not a hint of facial hair. He had many questions for his new companion while they walked to camp.

"You came," John said gratefully. "Why?"

The soft-spoken giant explained. "My name is Prince Tor. Some weeks ago, I was in my forest and heard a woman scream. There were men dressed in black, and a girl, bound and gagged…their prisoner. I was too late to help." He shook his head. "No one enters the Colossus forest without my knowing, but they did. I found this." He reached into a pocket and handed John a folded piece of thick, yellow paper. "I assumed the girl dropped it." John opened the paper and read the simple message.

It took him a few seconds to decipher the writing.   John was no longer surprised by his ability to understand foreign tongues. "'Meet again, John'," he read out loud. "This is written in your language, not Esparian."

"Yes," the giant nodded. "But, I did not send this. I don't know who did, but I will find out. This is our writing material, and the message is in our tongue. I am certain it was bait for a trap, set up by the men in black. For this trap to work however, they must have had assistance by one or more of my people. They did not hurt the female. I assumed she was your kin, you look much alike."

This statement surprised John. He always thought Jessica looked just like her mother. He felt a surge of fatherly pride to think a stranger could see a resemblance between them. He also felt intense relief to know that Jessica had not been harmed.

"She's my daughter, and I've been worried sick about her."

The large man put a hand on John's shoulder. "I am ashamed that one of my people would help with this plot. I decided we could no longer watch evil happen and do nothing."   Dropping the hand, Tor looked around the camp. "It was time for action, for helping. I had to convince the Olders of this. There are some who oppose our interfering with the outside world. Showing this note, I argued someone had already interfered. I may be a prince, but I need the support of our council to wage war. Fortunately, the majority of my people agreed with me and we came as quickly as we could."

John's thoughts ran to the other battlefronts. "To the south, my men are being badly beaten."

"Yes, I know. My trackers informed me and I sent half of my men to their aid before coming here."

"I also have an army on the Hent-Galland border," John said hopefully.

"Men were being gathered to send there when I left," Tor assured him. "I came here with the warriors who were ready. My brother, Wix, was leading the force to Galland. They were not prepared to go when I left six days ago, but should be marching to your men's aid by now. Galland is a gentle country and many volunteered to help."

When they reached the camp, John paused to look around. His exhausted men collapsed at their tent doors, not bothering to remove their armor. Hardly a single man did not suffer from several wounds. The giants were busy transporting the injured and many tended the less severe cuts and gashes of their smaller allies. Some giants were even going from man to man, offering food and water from their own rations.

"Your people are remarkably compassionate, Tor." John swallowed a lump in his throat. "My men need to rest for a few days, but we will follow the Demarian army into the province of Palium. It needs to be freed. Will you join us?"

"I will speak with my comrades, but that should be possible. We have committed ourselves to your aid. Also, we have seldom ventured out of our mountains and many of us wish to see this country. It is most intriguing."

After helping with the worn out Esparians, the Giants set up their own camp on the grassy plain. John made his way to where they unloaded their supplies and stared in amazement at their odd looking mounts. He knew they were horses of a sort, for Tor indicated his men rode to the battle, however these animals looked more like bearded oxen than horses. Mammoth in size, these creatures were olive green in color, smeared with patches of chocolate brown, and each sported a deadly pair of bull-style horns. John later learned the animal's coloring aided in their blending into the foliage of the Colossus Forest and the horns were readily used as weapons.

After making sure the needs of the giants were met, John went to find Ru. He finally located him at one of the field hospitals, helping Lyrista with the wounded. "I've spoken to Tor, the giant's leader. They'll march with us into Palium."

"Oh John, that's wonderful," Lyrista exclaimed, relief showing on her strained face. Ru smiled and nodded in agreement.

"We'll free these people," John continued, "then we'll march on, into the Deserts of Demar."

CHAPTER 24

The Sword of Mercy

After watching Daenon and his soldiers gallop at full speed down Rendaira's road and disappear over the small hill next to the mansion, Jessica's thoughts turned to Merula. Leaving the front portico, she walked back into the lavish entry hall and straight to her new friend, who stood staring out from the large, ornate window adjacent to the front door. Her fists were clenched so tightly that blood trickled from where her nails were digging into her palms. Merula, so engrossed in her own thoughts, did not notice Jessica and jumped when she spoke.

"Come with me," Jessica ordered, taking firm hold of Merula's thin arm. "We both need some fresh air and you need your hands tended to." They walked straight to an outside fountain, where Jessica plunged Merula's hands into the cold water. The cuts were not very deep and clotted with a little applied pressure. They crossed four acres of front lawn and climbed the first hill in silence. When they reached the statue of Daenon shooting a bow, Merula let out a deep breath. Only, then did Jessica speak again. "I saw the look on your face. Your hate for Addex is unreal."

"I have every right to hate him," Merula said vehemently. "He was a Junior Older in my father's government. It was he who introduced the drug that destroyed my people. He was the one who poisoned the Regulators. He would have poisoned my father, but my mother drank the glass by mistake. I was only fifteen years old, Jessica. I had two brothers, one twelve and the other sixteen. Addex murdered them in front of me. Have you any idea what sort of impact that has on a child? He said if I ever tried to escape, he would kill my father also. He's butchered several of my friends here as well." She paused, her body shaking. "Hate! Hate is the only thing keeping me alive!" Tears rolled down her gaunt cheeks, but her eyes shone defiantly.

A surge of compassion swept through Jessica, but she had no words of comfort. For a few moments they wept together in silence, then placing her hand on Merula's arm, Jessica managed a sincere, "I'm so sorry." There was nothing more she could give, but she meant every word.

"When everything comes crashing in, when I think I'm going to go mad with the pain of existing," Merula whispered, "I do this." She pulled up her long sleeves to her elbows and held out her forearms. Long, fresh slash marks, healing cuts and older scars marred her skin. "The pain from cutting releases the pain in my soul."

Jessica was nauseated. She swallowed hard against the rising bile in her throat. "Merula, I'm here and you can trust me. I can only imagine how hard it must be for you to show this to me."

"The only other person who knows is Cook Stratin. She's all I have left."

"I'm here too." Jessica gently rolled the sleeves back over the broken flesh. "When you feel compelled to do this, please, please, *please* come find me. You can talk it out, scream it out. I'll listen and do my best to *just* listen, not give advice, not judge. Hate can keep you going, but it can also destroy." Jessica realized hate was not the only thing giving Merula life. She had seen the look in her eyes when Lepsis' name was mentioned, but hate definitely drove her now.

Merula took another deep breath and roughly brushed her tears away. "Let's not talk about it anymore. What can I do to help you?"

"Me? You ask what *I* need."

"I keep busy, Jessica. It numbs the pain."

Jessica stared in bewilderment at Merula. "All right...well...I want to know everything about this place. I want to know who is friend and who is foe. I don't plan on being here when Daenon returns. One way or another, I will leave and I want you to come with me."

"I'll think about it," Merula promised. "Come. We'll begin your tour with the stable."

The stable was located about three hundred yards behind the house, off to one side. A large, two-story rectangular structure, it was capable of accommodating two hundred and fifty horses, but now housed only twenty. Painted a muted green color, it paled into near obscurity next to the brilliance of the main mansion. Inside the building, Jessica marveled at how spotless it was kept. Each stall was scrubbed clean, with a bound bale of fresh hay in the corner.

"I've never seen anything so clean," Jessica exclaimed.

"Six of the servant-slaves work here full time. Daenon is a neatness fanatic, with a strong aversion to dirt."

Outside were three large, empty corrals, just as tidy as the barn. The white fences surrounding them looked freshly painted. Beautifully groomed, the soft earth was raked smooth, with not a single foot or hoof print in the dust. Walking between the corrals and stable, the women came to a second barn-like structure, the same height and general shape as the stable. It was painted the same dull green color, but from the window placements in the building, Jessica could tell the interior was divided into three levels.

"This is the barracks. It can house up to three hundred men. Don't let the outside fool you. It's incredibly plush in there and each Elitet has his own room. Daenon keeps a small army here," Merula explained. "Three more barracks are just like this, one on the northern end of the property, one on the southern end, and another, way over there, on the eastern side of Rendaira." She waved her arm in the general direction.

"Wow! Talk about paranoid. Any idea how many men are left here?"

Merula shook her head. "I'll try and find out. There's a stable and set of corrals located next to every barracks, the same size as what you see here. We can begin our soldier count by investigating those, but that'll have to wait until tomorrow. It's getting late and we wouldn't make it back before dark. Any servant-slave out after the sun goes down is automatically whipped, no questions asked. I remember once a maid showed up, only a minute or so late in returning from the dine. Daenon had her bound, then with all of us watching, slit her throat. Not even the slightest infraction of his rules is tolerated. Now, let me show you the servant's quarters."

Merula had shown no emotion during her narrative. Jessica felt revulsion at the story and was amazed at how this woman could, after her emotional outburst only a short time before, so quickly stifle her feelings now.

They made their way towards the mansion, to the first of the two identical buildings situated behind it. On the exterior, these buildings were mini versions of Daenon's opulent home. Jessica judged each building to be around fifty thousand square feet. Both were located a hundred yards directly behind each end of the mansion. A sprawling, well-tended garden covered the space between the two buildings and ornately roofed walkways connected each structure to the palace.

"The building over there," Merula pointed to the far edifice "is a guest house of sorts. It used to belong to Lepsis, but now it is Addex's. We will not go in there."

Jessica nodded in agreement. She imagined all sorts of torture equipment and body parts and had no desire to confirm her thoughts.

"This building is the servant's housing." Merula led the way through the main door.

A blend of dormitory layout with prison-like security, the interior of the servant's quarters was depressing. Being three stories high, the building had a central meeting room, from which a staircase led upwards to the other levels. Positioned on either side of this gathering room was a long, narrow hallway from which diminutive, hotel-style sleeping quarters could be accessed. Levels two and three consisted of the same, small, side-by-side rooms opening onto a slender corridor. Each room contained a bed, a small armoire, and a desk. Six communal bathrooms, two on each level completed the building's design. All windows had bars on them, and each entrance to the six halls was secured with thick, metal prison doors. A jailer kept each door.

"Most of the servants," Merula explained, "are slaves. Several, however, are not--the six well paid jailers Daenon has positioned on each floor, and the head butler, Chak. A few of the grounds keepers and maintenance personnel are also free men who work here willingly."

Jessica said in a bare whisper, "Do you think the slaves would revolt, if the opportunity came?"

Merula shrugged. "You must understand, Jessica, these people have lived so many years in total fear, many of them are either broken or nearly there. The last person who tried escaping was given to Addex, and that was two years ago."

Chak was the short, corpulent head-butler who had greeted Jessica and Addex when they first arrived. Normally in charge of the household staff, he was placed in command of the entire compound while Daenon was gone. Merula made sure she and Jessica stayed well out of his path while they explored Rendaira over the next several days.

It took an entire morning and half an afternoon to make the trek to the outpost on the northern end of the estate. Jessica could have done it in better time, but Merula was not strong. Since Lepsis left, she confessed her will to live had diminished and she was half-heartedly trying to starve herself. It was due to Lepsis' constant care she had survived her captivity this long.

When they reached the post, everything was as Merula described; the buildings looked identical to the ones close to the mansion. Even the dull green paint was the same. Jessica neither saw nor heard another soul around. The grounds were completely deserted and looked as if they had been that way for some time. Cobwebs hung in the crooks and crannies of the stable and weeds grew tall inside the corrals. The women stayed but a short time. Fortunately, the days were quite long, for they barely made it back to the mansion before the sun passed beyond sight.

The southern Elitet compound had the same desolate appearance. The barracks and stable to the far east of the mansion were also deserted.

"Daenon must have sent all of the troops to the front," Merula commented. "There are only forty left at the house, and none of them are Elitet, only regular troops."

Like a haunting spirit, Merula had roamed the mansion for ten years, thus she knew every room, every secret passage, and every person there. In the three days it took Merula to give an abbreviated tour of the mansion, Jessica counted eighty-five guest rooms, six dining halls, two grand ballrooms, and twelve conference chambers, two libraries, four laboratories, two billiards rooms, six swimming pools (three indoor and three outdoor), and a massive receiving room which would rival the throne rooms of ancient Egypt. Daenon's personal apartment complex was located in back of the mansion. It overlooked the beautiful gardens separating the two mini-palaces. Two large kitchens were also located in the rear of the massive building.

One of Jessica's favorite rooms was a sewing chamber. Bolts of satins, linens, cottons and wools, sorted by color, were stored on large wooden frames stretching from the floor to the ceiling. A smaller frame held spools of thread, assorted needles in cushions, and a few pairs of scissors.

"I can sew. Well...I can sew a little bit." Jessica said while she ran her hand over a bolt of pale green satin. "I'm going to make myself some new clothes. I'll make some for you too, if you'd like."

"Thank you, but it would not be wise...for me that is. You're welcome to use whatever is here as Daenon took the tailor with him, however, I must keep to my own uniform."

"Is that what you call this?" Jessica fingered the sleeve of her friend's tunic. "I'm really not into fashion, but there has to be something better. You're falling apart."

Merula gave a weak smile. "It will do."

"All right, suit yourself. Just remember, I did offer."

Late into the third night of touring, Jessica awoke to see Merula standing over her. "Good heavens, Merula!" she nearly shouted, "Do you want to give me a heart attack?"

"Shhhh," Merula put a finger to her lips. "There is one last room I must show you and now is the only time." Her voice was scarcely a whisper.

"All right, but shake me next time. My heart's still pounding."

In nightgown and bare feet, Jessica followed while Merula crept out of the bedroom and down the dark hallway. They tiptoed to where a six-foot high ceramic urn marked the corridor's end. Merula bent to a kneeling position and wiggled behind the vase, then disappeared. Jessica crouched down to peer behind the tall pot, but in the dark, she could see nothing. Slowly inching herself forward, she reached out to the wall and patted around. To her surprise, she found a small opening.

"Hurry," came a whisper from the dark.

Wiggling like a snake, Jessica squeezed through the open trap door. Merula took her arm and helped her up.

"Don't move," she warned.

Jessica heard Merula secure the trap door, then reach for something. An instant later, a spark flashed and Merula held a small fire brand in her hand.

"I keep a supply there," she motioned with her head to three other torches lying beside the closed hatch.

In the flickering light, Jessica saw they stood at the top of a narrow, winding staircase made completely of stone.

"Wow! It's a good thing you stopped me from stepping forward, I could have broken my neck."

Merula quietly laughed. "I nearly did the first time I found this passage." Holding the torch high, she led the way. "Be careful, these steps aren't very wide." They descended at least three levels before coming to a narrow hallway. "We're on the lowest level of the mansion," Merula whispered.

Built of precisely fitted stone blocks, the secret hall was not only a passageway, but a part of the mansion's foundation. There were several side channels, but Merula stayed on a straight course until the fourth passage to the right. Here, they turned and followed it to the end. Reaching up, she pressed on a stone where the dead end wall met the ceiling. A small door magically appeared in the wall. She pushed it opened and went through, with Jessica right behind.

"Daenon spends hours in this room," Merula said. "It's his Treasure room." She held the torch high. "About a year ago, very late at night, I was in here admiring these things, when I heard someone unlocking the main door. I dove for this hidden passage and only just made it out without being detected. Daenon would have killed me on the spot if he'd caught me."

"You like living on the edge." Jessica shook her head.

The size of the Treasure room amazed Jessica. High-ceilinged and windowless, it was filled with every type of priceless object. The light from the torch's flame revealed delicate marble sculptures directly in front of them and many paintings on the walls. There were four long rows of gleaming treasure and slowly, the pair walked up and down the slender aisles. Jessica inspected golden artifacts of every sort: goblets, jewelry, coins, and vases. There was a crown imbedded with polished rubies and emeralds, an elegant scepter, and matching ceremonial shield. She caressed intricately carved jade statues of birds and animals, many of which were accented with jewels. Daenon had accumulated polished and uncut gems of every description, both precious and semi-precious stones, as well as shoebox-sized chests of rubies, emeralds, diamonds and topaz. Strands of pearls and ornaments of silver, copper and bronze lay neatly displayed on satin-covered racks. There were bolts of rich, velvet cloth and many pieces of gilded mirrors and fancy furniture.

"This place looks like a pirate's den," Jessica exclaimed.

"More like a den of thieves," Merula corrected. "This is the accumulation of years of preying on the people. In here are the art treasures from the Palium Provincial Art Gallery and the Snow Peak Museum of Art. There are jewels from the wealthy families who tried to buy their freedom and ended up in slavery anyway. He has plundered and robbed his entire life. I'll wager his father was just as bad."

While Merula walked around the room she described some of the different artifacts and the circumstances surrounding their acquisition. "This golden platter belonged to a drug dealer who was caught keeping some of the profits. In fact, this entire set of eating ware used to be his. It's solid gold. Addex took care of him. Now this little trinket," she held up a delicate locket studded with tiny diamonds and rubies, "is new. It was brought here about a month ago. I think it belonged to your Aunt Illa, Protector Haesom's wife."

Jessica took the offered necklace and opened it. Inside, were two tiny drawings. Gasping, she recognized the same stoic young men from her vision so many weeks earlier. These were her cousins and tears stung her eyes. She placed the chain around her own neck, then hid the locket portion under her gown.

"I come here often, when I want to be alone," Merula said. "I don't know if Daenon knows about the secret passage. It's so well-crafted into the wall behind the urn that it's invisible. It was pure chance I found it while hiding from Chak when I was younger."

"Did you have to hide a lot?"

"Chak fancied me; he forces all the new female slaves."

Jessica's stomach turned. "Merula…"

"Lepsis put a stop to it when he found out."

"But Lepsis is gone now."

"Yes, but I'm no longer a child and Chak knows I'd kill him if he touched me again." Her tone sent a shiver down Jessica's spine.

"What about the other women here, are they safe?"

Merula cast her eyes toward the ground then shrugged.

Jessica turned her attention back to the spotlessly clean room with its neatly ordered rows. "Daenon sure is a neatness freak."

This brought a laugh from Merula. "You don't know the half of it. Now come and look at this," she motioned. "This is one of the more interesting trophies I know nothing about, but wish I did. It was here before I came. It's the most beautiful thing I've ever seen." She pointed to a glass case, set off from the rows of glittering objects, at the very front of the chamber.

When Jessica walked to the case, she let out a low whistle. There, lying on a red satin cloth was the Sword of Mercy. She would have known it anywhere. It perfectly fit Anton's description. Stunning in its simplicity, the blade was not as thick or as wide as the Sword of Judgment, that sword was forged for battle. This one was obviously ceremonial.

The hilt was covered in pearl dust, with the delicate hand guard being encircled by a spiraling cord of spun gold. The metal was twisted as it cooled and then wrapped in a web-like pattern around the elongated handle to form a filigree sphere. A clear, round ball, of what looked to be glass or crystal, crowned the end of the hilt. Anton had said the blade was sprinkled in diamond dust after being forged, but in reality, Jessica saw it was studded in thousands of one and two point diamonds. In the gleaming torchlight, the entire piece seemed to come alive. Torchlight reflected from every facet of the blade and Jessica was certain the clear ball on the end of the handle pulsated. She had a nearly overpowering urge to take it.

"This sword belongs to my family," she told Merula. "It was my great-grandfathers. It's called the Sword of Mercy. It has a sister sword my father now owns, the Sword of Judgment."

"Then this is yours. What was it used for anyway? It's not strong enough for battle."

"I was told it's a ceremonial sword. You're right though, when you say it's mine. I can almost feel it in my hand, but not now. I'll know when the time is right."

Jessica looked up. Directly opposite the glass case was a large wooden door reinforced with bands of steel. Pointing to the door she asked, "Where does that lead?"

"Oh, that's the only real door in and out of this room. Daenon keeps it locked."

"You said this is the last room to show me? There are no more?"

"None of consequence."

"Well, I've been looking for a room with two old men in it, scientists I think. It's heavily guarded and there's a green crystal ball about this big," Jessica held her fingers together, forming them into the shape of a softball, "on a pedestal this high," she held her hand at waist level, "in the center of it."

Merula looked perplexed and shook her head. "There's no such chamber here and I've never seen two scientists, but Daenon has another retreat. More than once, servants were transferred there, but they never return. I've heard terrible experiments are done. How do you know about such things?"

"You'd never believe me, but trust me when I say Daenon's working on a lot of stuff. War is the mother of invention and I have a feeling my cousin is inventing some terrible weapons, or at least trying to. I just hope he doesn't succeed in time to use anything against the Esparians."

"We'd better go now. I don't want anyone to miss us."

They left the room by the secret passage and retraced their way to the bedchambers, narrowly escaping detection by a guard doing his nightly rounds. Back in her bed, Jessica lay staring at the ceiling, unable to sleep. Thoughts of the magical sword burned in her mind.

In the morning, Chak put Merula on a clean-up project in Daenon's quarters. It was to take several days, so, left to herself, Jessica decided to do some cross-country running. For four days, from sun up to sun down, she ran over the grounds of Rendaira. It did not take long to become familiar with the layout. Because Daenon had mastered irrigation, the rolling hills abounded with green life. Manicured grass accented with colorful gardens made Rendaira a visual paradise. In the desert climate, where few trees could normally grow, Daenon produced several forested areas of firs and hardwoods. Jessica wondered if it resembled the lush land Demar had been millennia earlier when Bree was alive.

Merula had said she thought the Palium border was three to four days of hard riding to the east. Jessica figured the war probably began on the fifteenth or sixteenth, a little over a week ago. She did not know how the war was going, but optimistically hoped no news was good news.

To keep her mind from worry, she kept herself busy, spending her evenings in the sewing room until exhaustion drove her to bed. Having no patterns, she used her jeans and ingenuity to make new clothing. Drawstring cotton pants and capris with a few simple silk blouses soon complimented her wardrobe.

Many nights, when sleep was impossible, she stole through the secret passage behind the vase and went to the Treasure room to gaze at the beautiful sword. Whenever she drew close to the case, the crystal ball at the hilt's end would glow. It did not reflect light from her torch, but pulsed with a power of its own. When she would back away, the glowing ceased.

After a week and a half, Jessica became bolder. She asked a guard for a horse to go riding. The man ignored her, which came as no surprise, so she walked into the stable and chose one herself, a beautiful chestnut mare.

"I won't hurt you," Jessica told the animal. "I just want to explore the land." The horse agreed to the outing. When they rode past the mansion, no one tried to stop them.

In the beginning, Jessica stayed well away from the main roads leading to Rendaira and explored the countryside around the estate. She found Daenon's irrigation source, a small river dammed up to make a lake. It was an abnormal oasis in the barren ecosystem, with flourishing plant life of natural desert flora and tall, thickly twisted desert trees growing at the edges. Mountains lay in the distant north and Jessica reasoned the source of the water to be there.

The desert of Demar was typical of most arid lands, little variation in vegetation, mostly cacti and small scrub plants. Due to the heat of the day there was no sign of animal life, but Jessica knew better and carefully guided the horse so as to avoid disturbing any snakes or poisonous bugs. For the most part, the land outside of the estate was level. Daenon had chosen his parcel well, picking the most interesting property with its few hills and intermittent flat lands.

After a few days of inspecting desert land, Jessica decided it was time to check out the nearby city. The head chef, Cook Stratin, told her the tiern was called Asmerth. After Merula, this woman was Jessica's most trusted friend. A short, muscular lady, Cook Stratin was not rotund, as one would expect a cook to be, but pleasantly plump. She had green eyes that sparkled when she spoke, and a high-pitched voice which, when angered, became harsh on the ears, much like fingernails scratching on a chalkboard.

Jessica distinctly remembered passing through Asmerth. She especially remembered the brave man who had saluted her. She decided to try and find him again. She remembered a large sign with a loaf of bread on it marked the side street where she had last seen him.

Before leaving the estate, she tied a large, homemade scarf around her hair to hide the color. Unsure of who might recognize her as a Protector, and wanting no trouble, she felt this thin disguise was necessary. It took her four and a half hours to reach the city, and if she was going to make it back to the estate by sundown, she could only stay about an hour. Traveling the road to Asmerth, Jessica encountered few travelers. Those she did see were all women. Some had wares to sell, others were there, she assumed, to do some shopping. No one paid any attention to her.

Asmerth appeared just as she remembered, dingy and dirty. Following the main road, she made her way to the central plaza. As the afternoon wore on, the streets became more and more deserted, for the oppressive afternoon heat drove the people indoors. Stopping at a fountain, Jessica let the horse drink her fill while she herself downed a small flask of water. The undersized flask was the only thing she was allowed to take on her ride. This was Chak's way of making certain she did not travel too far from Rendaira. She was forced to return there each night for food and more water.

Jessica planned to retrace her journey through the tiern, scouring each side street until she found the one with the bread sign. After the water break, she started the trip back out of the city, taking the same route her captors had taken two weeks earlier. After about thirty-five minutes she spotted the sign. With her time quickly running out, she marked the place in her memory. She would have to return the following day.

Jessica arrived at Rendaira just as the sun was going down. After caring for the horse, she ran for the mansion. Chak, the household general, awaited her at the door.

"Where did you go today?"

"To the dine." It was best to tell as much truth as possible. "I'm exceptionally bored here and thought there might be something in there to amuse me, but it's so far away I could only stay a short time."

Chak seemed to be satisfied with her answer. "Perhaps tomorrow you will be more successful."

"Yes, perhaps."

As soon as morning broke, Jessica rode to Asmerth, straight to the sign with the loaf of bread on it. No customers patronized the small bakery. She followed the narrow side street and quickly found herself in a residential district. Two and three story sandstone homes lined the long, straight, narrow road. She rode to its end, exploring all alleyways as she went. The smell of cooking fat drifted in the still air, but the only sounds were those of her horse's muted steps in the sandy earth. Every door was closed and each window shuttered against the afternoon sun.

She had no idea what she was looking for; just anything out of the ordinary. She was not very confident in her success, but when she reached the end road's dead end, with no sign of her man, she felt disappointment none-the-less.

Turning her horse to go back to the main thoroughfare, she scanned the immediate row of homes once again, and this time something caught her eye. A bright red scarf poked through the shutters of a second story window, two houses down. It had not been there a few moments earlier. She stared at the odd pennant. If someone wanted to get her attention, they had succeeded.

Dismounting, she walked to the door below the red scarf. She knocked softly and glanced around, but the street remained empty. When no one answered, she knocked again. This time the door opened.

"Please stay here," she told the mare. The animal nodded. Taking a deep breath, she walked in. The door quickly closed behind her.

A rush of cool air washed over her, a relief to the stifling temperature outside. The room was darker than the alley had been, making it difficult to see. She sensed others in the room. Slowly her eyes adjusted. A wooden table with three chairs around it was in the center of the small room, and what looked like a wooden couch covered in pillows against the far wall. The floor of the home was made of stone with several tan, braided rugs thrown about, but the walls were bare. Through a doorway to her right was a kitchen, and on her left was a staircase against the wall leading to the upper level.

She removed the scarf covering her hair.

"I told you she was the one," a man said from behind.

Startled, she jumped with a yelp and spun around. Dressed in dusty, dark brown clothing, four long-haired, bearded men stood staring at her. One of them was the man she was looking for.

She had anticipated this moment, but now was not quite sure what to say. "I, uh, I was looking for you." With no nauseous warnings disturbing her stomach, she took courage and ventured, "I'm Jessica, granddaughter of Graesion and Gayleena of the house of Saylon."

"I know who you are." The man did not smile, but his eyes were warm and friendly.

"A war has begun," she continued. "Do you have any news? My father, John Ernshaw the Healer, leads our army."

He motioned toward the table. Jessica, followed by the men, sat on an offered chair. "My name is Farin. I am the leader of the Demarian freemen in this portion of Demar."

He motioned for his comrades to sit also. "Doran here," he indicated the middle of the three men who were now seating themselves cross-legged on the floor in front of her, "just returned last night from Palium and can give you news."

Doran, a man with sad, gray eyes, cleared his throat. He sat very rigid and spoke softly. With a report devoid of detail, he told her significant facts. "At first, the war went against your army. When it looked the worst, a large group of giants arrived and turned the battle to their favor."

Jessica gasped. "So the giants came! I'll bet Daenon was furious!"

"No doubt," Farin said dryly.

"That was a week ago," Doran continued. "Now the army marches toward Palium. A northern army is already in Snow Peak. Daenon's men are on the run."

"We are called Ghost Walkers," Farin added. "We are native Demarians who hate Daenon. He and his father before him have plundered our land and robbed us of our natural resources. He uses our own water as leverage against us and many of our people are no longer enchanted by his ways of ruling. Protector John has ordered an invasion of the Deserts of Demar. That is why we are here now, to finish gathering our forces and be ready to help when he comes."

"This is great news!" Jessica was relieved. She now knew her father had not been captured and he would soon come to free her. "Thank you. I should go now. I don't want you in danger by staying here too long, but I've one request. If it's possible, could you help free the men and women who are held slaves at Rendaira?"

"When the time is right, someone will be there," Farin promised. "If you need to contact us, give a message to Cook Stratin. Every other day, a fresh delivery of dairy products is made to Rendaira. She will give the note to the deliveryman and he will give it to me. We are leaving this house tonight, so you will not find us here again."

"I understand," Jessica nodded. "Good luck and be ready. If I know my father, he'll be here sooner than you think." She stood up and the men did too. She shook each man's hand, beginning with Farin's. "If your other men are anything like you four, then Daenon doesn't stand a chance."

They saluted.

When she reached the estate that evening, Jessica forced herself to be calm. She needed to hide her news, especially from Chak, who again waited for her at the front door. "Any amusements today?" his voice was haughty and condescending.

"No," Jessica snapped. "The dine is dingy and dirty and the people are like zombies. It's more depressing there than here. I won't be going again."

Jessica was forced to sit on her news for an entire day before she managed to whisk Merula away from her duties at the mansion. In the back garden, with only the flowers to overhear, Jessica told about the adventure in Asmerth and how freedom loomed, at last, within site.

"The northern army is in Snow Peak right now. That means Lepsis is on his way, too," she reminded Merula. "Spread the word so the staff'll be ready. I don't know what to expect. I'm sure there'll be a battle, but at least it will be a battle that can be won."

Jessica had never taken notice of the deliveries before, but now she intently watched for each one. When the dairy delivery came, she was sitting in the kitchen, helping to peel vegetables. She had no message to give, but wanted to see the person who was her link to hope.

A small, bearded man with bright eyes and long hair pulled back in a braid, the dairyman brought in several tall urns of milk and large rounds of cheese. He joked with Cook Stratin and the other servants as they helped him unload his wagon. He gave a slight bow to Jessica just before he left. Jessica later learned the men of the underground vowed to never cut their hair until Demar was free from Daenon's tyrannical rule.

Nearly two months crept by with no news about the war. The few soldiers left at Rendaira were showing signs of strain. With hair trigger tempers, beatings were more and more common. Though no one ever dared to touch Jessica, she was no longer allowed to take a horse, and her movements were restricted to the grounds immediately surrounding the mansion.

Finally, the dairyman came with a note. The cook slipped it to Merula, and Merula gave it to Jessica late at night when everyone else had gone to bed. By the light of a small candle she read it aloud.

Palium and Snow Peak are free. Esparian forces moved into Demar two days ago.

Jessica burned the note. Merula's eyes shone with excitement. "Finally, I can go home."

"Hopefully it will be soon," Jessica added. "But I think some of the hardest fighting is ahead. The border may be only a few days away, but this is Demar, and the native people won't allow Esparia in without putting up a fight."

CHAPTER 25

The Battle for the Deserts of Demar

Addex stood at attention inside Daenon's opulent tent. It was the first lodging to be set up after the Demarian retreat, and the last of the support stakes had, only minutes before, been pounded into place. An angry and frustrated Daenon was pacing like a caged tiger. "Victory should have been swift! The strategy was so well prepared, battle plans carefully developed and everything laid out in detail." He shook a fist above his head. "I made a mistake, not invading immediately after destroying Haesom. Ballian's information piqued my interest and I wanted to capture Graesion's heir." He ran his fingers through his short hair. "My hesitation gave them too much time to prepare. I will *never* make that mistake again." He stopped pacing and faced Addex. "But the giants, the giants have taken me by surprise. They've always stayed to themselves, not venturing from their mountains. Didn't our ally assure you he could keep them out of this war?"

"Yes," Addex was thoughtful. "I don't know why he failed. He led me to believe he had enough power to influence any debate to our favor."

"Obviously, he over-estimated himself. These fools," Daenon waved his arm in the general direction of the open tent door, where soldiers could be seen setting up camp, "they ran...**they ran**! So here we are, pushed back nearly thirty filons from where we were yesterday."

"Our spies tell me the Esparians are not in pursuit. They rest," Addex ventured.

"A small reprieve. I never anticipated defeat, so we have no resorts of protection. No one sleeps. I want the men to spend day and night throwing up walls and digging traps. Let's see how well the Esparian army does when the earth caves in underneath them."

So the command was carried out. Pits were dug and imbedded with knife-sharp spikes. They did not have to be deep, only unseen and deadly. The weight of a man tripping into one would be enough to impale him. The Demarians were careful to conceal their traps with small branches covered with tufts of grass.

Once this was done and the Esparians were seen advancing, Daenon called Addex to him again. "Now I want you to organize a force of two thousand Elitet. Arrange them in groups of one hundred and send them into Palium. I want the land swept clean of everything; a scorched earth campaign. I want your Elitet to round up the people. Anyone too old, too young or too sick to march will be left to starve, or executed, you decide. As we follow, we'll seize anything of value and burn the rest. Nothing will be left for the advancing Esparians, not one person, animal, or stalk of grain. Any men you find, those between the ages of twelve and one hundred twenty, will join my army.

"I want hostages," he finished. "Women and small children as they are the most sympathetic. Also the very elderly who can travel. Anyone unable, just kill them."

* * *

With the giants as allies, and three days of rest, John's Esparians were ready to fight with renewed vigor. Reese sent word of the giant's timely arrival in his camp and renewed troop morale. The time had come to advance on Palium.

John never realized Daenon's men would be able to rig so many deadly traps in so short a time as three days. Innumerable and well hidden, the pits proved to be effective and deadly. Hundreds of front-line Esparian soldiers fell to their deaths before John even knew what had happened. He himself missed a trap by only inches.

Slowing their advance, they now spent time clearing the fields before them. The concealed death pits enraged the Esparians and John fanned the anger. When his men finally reached the Demarians, they hit them with such force, they broke the enemy ranks within hours. Following close behind the retreating enemy, John found massive destruction, the dead, and the suffering. His men spent a great deal of time extinguishing the burning fields to salvage at least some of the summer crops. The homes, barns, and buildings made of wood were smoldering ashes by the time he reached them, and those made of stone or brick were smashed beyond repair. A full division was put to gathering, then burying the dead, both human and animal. How many were killed though, no one was certain, as they soon discovered the burned buildings also contained the remains of partially cremated bodies. The few living persons found hiding in ponds and rock crevices were shown extraordinary kindness. It was from them John learned of the hostages.

Never before had he felt such anger. With every step that led him further into Palium, his outrage grew. Daenon was leaving behind a message, and John wanted to shove it back down the man's throat. He would be glad when this monster was taken out of power. Reese's reports were filled with tidings of the same appalling brutalities. Only twenty filons into Palium, John called a meeting. Tor, Ru and Lyrista, along with several other officers, were gathered. "Our advance scouts report the Demarians are fortifying the major dines, concentrating their forces. House-to-house fighting would be grueling, as well as costly in lives. There must be a better way. Suggestions?" He hoped for several good ideas.

Tor came up with a plan. "Your enemy has taken all living things with him, including livestock. We can assume he has left nothing in these dines. His men then, would be dependent upon supply lines for their sustenance. If we can destroy these supply lines, cutting the armies off, it would be only a matter of time before those left in the dines run out of food. Without supplies, they would have to give up or starve."

"We'll need to keep our men in tight formation," Ru observed. "Daenon will no doubt have quick strike units trying to pick off our outlying camps."

"All right," John nodded. "But I won't divide my army. We'll do this dine by dine. Reese will start with the most southern, Tratetiern," he pointed at the map, "and we'll begin here, in the center of the province, with Jornell."

The plan was a good one, but worked only twice, at Tratetiern and Jornell. After those two dines, the Demarians would quickly retreat from the other cities before further strangleholds could be completed. They left each tiern in ruins and it took John's men weeks of careful advancement to clear all the traps.

After nearly two months of fighting and running, Daenon abandoned Palium to the Esparians. John's spies reported the enemy retreat ended at the Demarian border. A note came from Cordon informing John the enemy troops were leaving Snow Peak as well.

John was alone in the command tent, going over maps when Lyrista appeared in the open doorway. "More of our advance scouts have reported," she said.

John smiled at her. "Come on in."

She looked at the maps. "Daenon's going to make a stand on his own land. What do you think he'll do with all the innocents he's gathered?"

"Human shields."

"Just when I wonder how things can get any worse…" She shook her head. "The scouts estimate he's got at least fifty thousand women and children, probably more."

John put his arm around her shoulders. "How are you holding up?"

"I told you I wouldn't fall apart and I'm keeping my promise."

"But?"

She took a deep breath. "But at night, when I close my eyes…" A single tear slid down her cheek.

He gently wiped it away with a finger. "I know. I hear the same screams, see the same ravaged bodies, feel the same sorrow."

"The sooner this war is over, the better. I'm tired of death, John."

"The worst is still to come," he sighed. "Demarians fighting on Demarian soil."

She turned into him, burying her face in his chest. He held her close, allowing her to let the pain out, if only for a few minutes.

* * *

John made camp about twenty-five filons from the desert border. His first concern was for the thousands of captives. "I've sent for Reese," he told Ru. "It'll take him two days to travel here."

"I look forward to meeting this young seventh bar I've heard so much about."

"You'll like him." John looked west, toward the border. "I want more scouts sent out. We need to find where the hostages are being held. Hopefully they'll return with some news for us before Reese arrives."

"Consider it done."

The evening that Reese rode into camp with his small accompaniment of soldiers, Lyrista, Ru and Tor were sent for. The four advisors met with John in the sparsely furnished command tent. John was not a pretentious man, so he was quite specific as to what he required in a command center. He had the necessary equipment, a large wooden table covered in maps and several tall candle stands for lighting, however the tent itself resembled each of the other army tents in camp, save it was just a little larger.

Every tent was made of tightly woven cotton and sheep's hair, making it lightweight and breathable. Only four wooden stools were brought in for the night's meeting as Tor sat cross legged on the ground. His large frame took up half the tent space. His head grazed the top of the canopy. The five strategists had barely begun their conference when a longhaired, bearded man with sad gray eyes suddenly appeared from nowhere. He was thin and dressed in dark brown, dusty clothing. His long brown hair was pulled back into a thick braid.

No one had heard nor seen him enter and he startled the group when he spoke.

"Protector John?" Three swords came quickly from their sheaths and Tor leaned forward menacingly. Only John seemed unruffled by the salutation.

"Lower your weapons." The man raised his hands to show he was unarmed. "I come in peace and as a friend. My name is Doran. I am a Ghost Walker. I come from the desert to offer you the services of three hundred men."

"A Ghost Walker," Ru exclaimed while he sized up the man. "Who's your commander?"

"Farin," the man replied.

Ru sheathed his sword.

"What's a Ghost Walker and just who exactly is Farin?" Reese asked, his sword still ready. John saw the distrust on his face and for the first time it struck him how much the young man had aged in the last couple months.

"The desert free men," Ru explained. "A group of Demarians who want Daenon out of power even more than we do. Farin is their leader. They're called Ghost Walkers because they slip in and out of places virtually unseen. Only their work is left behind as proof they were there."

"We are not many, a few thousand, but we are ready to help you," Doran offered. "Farin sent me to represent him."

Reese put his sword away, but Lyrista retained hers. John eyed the man carefully. "If Jess were here, I'd know for certain if he were honest, but since she isn't, I'll go by my own instincts." He placed his hand on her arm. "Put your sword up. We'll trust him."

She hesitated, but finally did as requested, though she never took her eyes off of him and stayed close to John.

"I'm honored to have the Ghost Walkers as part of the offensive," John said when he shook the man's hand. At the table, John pulled open one of the maps. "We have an urgent matter your people could help with. Daenon took many of our countrymen, mostly women and children, as he left Palium. I don't know his full intentions, but I think he plans on using them as shields. We cannot attack the deserts until the hostages are freed, but first, we need to find them." John's hand swept the open map. "Many of my scouts have not returned. Those that have say the enemy line is unsettled and the prisoners are still being moved. I want to know what sort of guard is on them and where they're headed."

"You will know within two days," Doran promised and he left as silently as he came.

True to his word, just after sundown two days later Doran arrived with the necessary information. John was in meeting again when Doran appeared inside the command tent.

"Protector John, I have the knowledge you requested," Doran quietly announced, and for a second time startled everyone present.

"You've got to teach me that," John said.

Doran smiled, a glint of humor lit up his sad eyes. "It takes years of practice and concentration. Most of us learned the technique as children. It was a game."

"Well, Larone considers me still a child," John smiled back. "So what of the hostages?"

"They're in large groups, being held in five different locations along the border. There are a few older men, but, as you said, most are women and children, thousands of people. They are guarded, but not so heavily a rescue attempt would fail." He pointed out the five locations on the map.

"Would your people be willing to help us free them?" John asked.

"Yes," Doran replied. "My commander, Farin, is coming with three hundred men. We're to meet at the Great Rock," Doran pointed to a spot on the map just inside the Demarian border. "When would you like to free your people?"

"As soon as possible."

"Have one thousand of your Guardians ready by midnight. They'll need to cross the border in small groups and meet us at the Great Rock by morning. There we'll divide into five companies of two hundred guardians with sixty Ghost Walkers. The furthest camps are a day away. We'll go in at night and rescue your people. Give us three days to get them back here."

"What do you think, Ru?" John asked his advisor.

Ru nodded his head. "It's a good plan. With stealth and luck it could work. Doran has shown us the stealth part, so we're already halfway there."

"It's settled then," John decided. "Doran, our men will be ready, and thank you."

Doran smiled broadly and this time a row of brilliant white teeth showed through his scraggly beard. He slipped out without making a sound.

"Lyrista," John began, but before he could finish, she cut in.

"I know, I know." She sighed, raising a hand to her forehead and rubbing it. "You need a thousand Guardians by midnight. I'll work on it." She walked out of the tent still rubbing her forehead.

"I'll go too," Reese announced. "We'll need to prepare to receive the hostages that come from the south."

John shook the young man's hand. "If everything goes as planned, we'll attack Demar in five days."

"I'll be ready."

Ru stood beside John while they watched Reese and his men ride south. "You were right, John. I do like that boy." With a gleam in his eye he asked, "Do you think he'd be willing to meet my oldest daughter?"

* * *

The next three days were spent preparing for the hostages and neutralizing Demarian spies. After a day John sent twenty groups of fifty soldiers westward to aid in bringing the hostages home. He sent Ru north with a similar force to receive hostages there.

By late afternoon on the third day, the advance scouts rode into camp with the report of thousands of worn out women and children trudging toward the Esparian lines. John rushed his men forward.

The people were half starved, and John's army reached them just in time, as many were ready to collapse. The Ghost walker leading the rag-tag group held three children on his horse with him. The Guardians and underground soldiers were also carrying as many children as they could. It pleased John to see the compassion his men showed these poor souls and how quick they were to offer their own rations. Lyrista directed the freed prisoners to shelters, set up behind the lines.

John went to the leader and held out his hand. "I'm John Ernshaw, Protector of Esparia."

The man took the offered hand in a firm grip. "I'm Farin, leader of the Ghost Walkers."

"How many men did we lose?" John asked.

"Not as many as I thought we would. I have no knowledge of the other four groups, but in ours, we lost two Ghost Walkers and fifteen Guardians. We were able to take the Demarians by surprise. There were some Elitet among the guards and they were our worst foes. We've been moving without break for nearly two days. I don't know if the enemy is in pursuit. If they are, they'll not be far behind. I'm glad you advanced your men to meet us. These people have made a super-human effort just to journey this far."

John readied his men, but no pursuing troops materialized. With positive reports coming in from the four other hostage centers, John knew the time had come for giving the order to advance, but first, he reminded the men about his no-exceptions rule of leaving the land and the inhabitants untouched.

"This is a campaign of liberation, not revenge," John told Farin. "We'll show the Demarians we're here to help them, not destroy them. Even though their armies ravaged Palium, they did it under orders and their leaders will be held responsible. All enemy troops will be allowed to surrender and eventually go back to their homes, but only after taking a life-oath of peace."

Farin looked pleased. "Demar is my homeland. I think many of the simpler people will surrender if given a chance to return to their homes without fear of retaliation."

"I hope so," John sighed.

"Your daughter told me you'd be here soon. I'm amazed at how swiftly you liberated Palium and Snow Peak."

John was stunned. "Jessica?" His heart skipped a beat. "You've seen her? Is she okay?"

"Yes. She's being held at Rendaira, Daenon's private garden, but she's well. I have a man keeping an eye on things there. She asked if I'd help free the slaves."

John smiled in relief. "Yes, that's Jess." He looked at Farin and squared his shoulders. "Let's free them together."

287

Once John felt satisfied that every soldier thoroughly understood his orders, he gave the command to press ahead. The sun had just reached the eleventh hour in the sky when the men of Esparia, accompanied by giants mounted on their massive ox-horses, set their sights on Demar. With the Ghost Walkers leading the way, a mighty host comprised of cavalry, foot soldiers, supply wagons, hospital coaches and healers moved forward. An immense cloud of dust rolled up toward the sky as the thousands of marching feet displaced the dry earth beneath. Deep in thought, John rode next to Farin. The heartland of Demar lay before them and he knew the fighting would be the fiercest they had yet encountered.

* * *

Daenon was in his lavish, five room headquarters when word came his hostages were gone and nearly one hundred of his Elitet dead. He jumped from his leather chair and howled in frustration. The poor messenger who had come with the news cowered in terror. "I am surrounded by incompetents!" he screamed, his face red with rage. "Can't anyone follow through on one single order?"

He paced back and forth for several minutes. The cape of his black satin uniform swished at every turn he made, the only sound in the deathly quiet room. Many of his fifth, sixth and seventh bars were there, at strict attention. They were meeting to determine how to distribute the captives when the news came. Daenon finally stopped his pacing and spoke to his leaders. "I will allow no man to surrender. No one. Do you understand me? We will stand as one and defend our deserts. Let every man fight to the death. If someone tries to surrender, kill him."

Daenon pointed to one of the Elitet commanders, a muscular man of average height, with a droopy mustache and thin beard. "You, Corter."

The man quickly saluted. "Yes sir?" His brown eyes gleamed.

"Take one hundred Elitet and capture John Ernshaw. I want him dead or alive. It doesn't matter. I just want him." Corter bowed low and left the room.

"Now go," Daenon commanded his leaders, "and remember, if anyone even talks of surrender...kill him."

Each of the officers saluted, then quickly left. Daenon flopped onto a velvet couch. "Addex!" he called. Addex quickly appeared at the tent door, he was never far from Daenon's side. "Take twenty men with you and fetch Jessica. It's time I use my insurance." Addex saluted and left without a word.

* * *

Corter handpicked the best Elitet he could find. They rode north and, under cover of night, slipped between Ru and John's armies, stealthily riding behind the Esparian lines. The Ghost Walkers were not the only Demarians to have mastered the silent skills. Daenon's orders were clear: dead or alive. Corter secretly hoped the Protector would resist capture. The thought of killing John made his palms itch.

* * *

Two days after the hostages were freed, the Esparians and Demarians clashed on the Palium-Demar border. Never, in the known history of the people, had fighting been so vicious and brutal. Even the giants were hard pressed.

After the slaughter caused by flying arrows, stones, and javelins, the hand-to-hand combat began. Already thousands of bodies littered the field and men tripped over them as the two sides came together. The normally parched desert earth combined with the blood of the wounded, becoming a treacherous, slippery sea of red mud. The howling of men combined with the screams of horses rent the air. Metal scraped on metal, bones snapped, and flesh ripped.

Astride Fireguard, John spearheaded a group of four thousand horsemen at the center of the onslaught. The rest of his cavalry pressed hard on the right flank and the giants were positioned to the far left. Foot soldiers battled in between. John cut through the enemy around him. In the din of battle, words were useless, so he inspired his men with his actions, his courage and stamina. For three days the fighting continued, with only a small respite at night for the men to sleep in their armor with swords by their sides.

Anticipating the horrific battle, John asked Larone to send a plea throughout the country for more healers. Volunteers had poured into Ramadine from all over the country, with a group of nearly four hundred young men and women from the province of Florio responding. Larone was able to send over two thousand fresh medical personnel to the front. Five hundred arrived at John's camp the day before the hostages were freed, the other fifteen hundred were divided between Reese's camp, Ru's camp, and Cordon's. Countless more men would have died if these healers and assistants had not shown up when they did.

At the end of each battle day, John rounded at the various hospitals. When he visited the ones manned by the Florio healers, he was especially impressed with their skill. Though young, they were well trained in surgical methods. They stitched wounds and repaired arteries with remarkable skill. These extraordinary specialists saved limbs that would normally have been amputated.

Catching one surgeon between operations, he asked, "Where did you learn your art? Who trained you?"

The young man smiled with pride. "I was taught by Orin, the great healer of Florio."

It was nearly midnight on the evening of the third battle day when Lyrista found John exiting the surgical center of the hospital tent closest to his command hub. She firmly took hold of his arm. "Come on John." She pulled him from the medical tent. "You've got to catch some sleep. You cannot fight throughout the day, then operate throughout the night. Daenon will attack early again tomorrow and you need a clear head."

"I know, I've got competent healers, but I hate the night and this makes it go faster."

They wound their way through tents of resting soldiers and circles of waning campfires towards John's own sleeping quarters. "I think you're so exhausted, you won't dream."

"Well, that was never the problem."

"So tell me."

"Things are so critical right now, that I'm afraid if I stop and rest, something might happen that I can't react to fast enough."

"Your reflexes won't be any good to you if you're half asleep on your feet."

When they neared John's small, one-man tent, the hair on the back of Lyrista's neck prickled and stood on end. She searched his face, but he seemed not to register any danger. "Do you trust me, John?"

"With my life," he smiled at her. They had reached his quarters. Lyrista pulled the flap aside and helped John down, onto a thin cushion. When his head hit a small pillow he began to lightly snore.

Kneeling beside him, she ran her hand over his dirty, matted hair. It had grown quite a bit since she first met him. She touched the three day beard growth on his cheek, then leaned down and softly kissed his lips.

As soon as Lyrista stepped from John's doorway, the sense of danger tugged at her again. Being a warrior and having generations of warrior breeding in her, she had learned long ago to trust her instincts. She pulled both her daggers. The camp lay dark and quiet. Only the crackle of embers and the snoring of men sleeping came to her ears, yet her uneasiness grew.

Spotting a lone soldier kneeling two fires away, Lyrista raced to gain his aid. "You must help me," she addressed him.

"Commander Lyrista!" The startled man jumped at her sudden appearance.

"I have a unit of Guardians over there," she motioned to a tight grouping of tents circled around a blazing campfire, the only fire to flame so brightly at this late hour. "Alert them in my name, the Protector's in danger. Tell them to make a sweep of the camp. Something's not right."

Without a word the man flew from his fire and ran for the Guardians. Lyrista circled John's tent, every muscle in her body tense, her nerves on edge.

Her Guardians silently spread out, fifty men in all. The lone soldier, a sword in his hand, returned to join Lyrista at her vigil. Neither spoke, but she was grateful to have him. After several tense moments, Lyrista heard a dull thud, then several dull thuds. Suddenly, the nearly imperceptible sound of a footfall directly behind, caused her to whirl around.

With her dagger, she barely deflected the deadly thrust of an Elitet's short blade. The assassin lunged again, but she nimbly sprang to one side, cutting upwards with her own weapon and slicing the man's arm. A second Elitet sprang toward her, but the soldier who stood guard with her threw a well-aimed knife.

Three more black clothed invaders appeared from the dark and Lyrista, along with her companion, fought them down. While Lyrista side kicked one man, she sliced at another. Her razor sharp knives drew blood with each twist of her hands. Two more Elitet flew at her from an angle. One managed to slash her forearm, hitting her bone with his blade, the other cut into the side of John's tent. In a flash, Lyrista realized John would be dead in two breaths and she could not save him. Another Elitet was on her and she rotated away from him, still jabbing with both weapons.

The lone soldier roared at the killer entering John's tent. He threw his sword, javelin style, felling the man where he stood. Seeing her new friend unarmed, Lyrista tossed a dagger to him. He caught it in a rolling leap which brought him in front of the gaping hole at the side of John's tent. An Elitet charged him, but the soldier parried the sword with Lyrista's knife, then wrapped his arm around the attacker's neck and twisted. It was over.

Esparian soldiers came running from every direction. A high pitched whistle, not too far from the tent, rent the air, and a state of confusion ensued for the next several minutes. Lyrista ignored the commotion around her. Clamping her lacerated arm closed, she crossed to her comrade. He put a supporting arm around her waist when she stepped through the ripped tent to check on John, who had just jumped through the front flap, sword in hand.

"What is going on?" he yelled above the din. "Everyone quiet." His authoritative voice rang over the disorder and brought a measure of calm.

"John," Lyrista called. In the dark, she could feel her wound spurt with every beat of her heart. "Elitet were here. I don't know how many."

He rounded the tent, stepping over two bodies to get to her. "If it weren't for this soldier," she nodded to the man who continued to support her, "you and I would both be dead right now." Suddenly, Lyrista felt light headed. "My arm..." Her knees buckled. The soldier picked Lyrista up in his arms.

"My Lord Protector, the commander's badly wounded," he said.

John put his sword away and called for light. Three torches immediately appeared as well as a young healer from the nearby hospital.

"I heard the yelling and grabbed some supplies," the physician said, shouldering his way through the growing crowd. He pulled a purple fern from his pocket when the soldier laid Lyrista on the ground.

With the magical sap numbing the wound, Lyrista tried to think more clearly. "Have the Guardians returned?"

"Yes, Commander," a voice came from behind. A tall Guardian, the leader of Lyrista's reserve band, came around and knelt beside her. The crowd quieted when the man spoke. "We're all accounted for."

"What did you find?" she asked. John and the young healer worked together to stitch her severed artery and muscle.

"Elitet, though I don't know how many. We took them by surprise and killed quite a few. Others committed suicide rather than surrender. Someone whistled for them to leave, so I'm not certain how many escaped. My men are gathering the bodies."

"You can have these too," John said dryly, looking at the bodies scattered around his tent.

"I'm dizzy," Lyrista said in a weak voice.

"You know, it only takes a few minutes to bleed to death," John said grimly. "Were you trying to set a record?"

"Didn't know I was hurt that bad."

"Don't worry, Commander Lyrista," the young healer said, a note of satisfaction in his voice, "we got to you in time. You'll be good as new in a couple of days."

John shook his head. "Never ceases to amaze me, how fast Edians heal," he whispered to Lyrista.

She inspected her arm. A three inch line of tiny, neat stitches were all that remained of the nasty cut. "You're from Florio, aren't you?" she said to the healer. "A student of Orin?"

"Yes," he answered, a proud smile on his face.

"We really need to find out who this Orin guy is," John said.

Lyrista nodded. "Help me up." With John at her side, she looked to the soldier who was such a tremendous help. "Are you hurt?"

"Only a few marks. They'll heal soon enough."

"I owe you my thanks," John said, offering the man his hand. "I'm sorry, I don't know your name."

"I am called Brayon of Vorgen Hoffle, and you owe me nothing." He shook John's hand. "I've searched for a way to repay my life debt to your daughter, Lady Jessica, and now I've found it. I was all but dead, and through her Salupathic Gift, she healed my body and brought back my life."

After nearly a week of fighting, Daenon's line broke and began to retreat. His death ultimatum achieved its purpose. It took only a few brutal executions to convince his troops to never consider surrender.

Finally realizing his men were spread too thin, Daenon decided to consolidate. "Send orders to every officer to retreat to Twin Hills," he ordered his communications men. "We will regroup there and crush these Esparians. Send word to each hoffle. I want every man, woman and child who can hold a weapon to join us."

Where is Addex when I need him? He thought angrily. *I sent him to fetch Jessica six days ago. What could be keeping him?*

* * *

The warm morning found Jessica under one of the many beautiful shade trees that graced the front lawn at Rendaira. She lay on her stomach with her chin resting on her hands, intently watching the main drive. The dairy deliveryman had not come in nearly a week.

Her mind wandered while she observed a short, fat bee gather pollen from a nearby flower. The days had flown away, but she guessed she had been on Edia three or four months. It felt like years. *On Earth, it would be sometime in late August or September,* she thought to herself. *School begins soon. I wonder if Sophia told Rachel where I am. I wonder how Thomas is doing in Europe.* "Thomas," she said out loud. "Oh, what's the use? Earth is light-years away." She rolled over to stare at Ragus, hanging like a specter in the cloudless sky.

A snapping twig, then Merula sitting beside her brought reality back. "If the deliveryman doesn't come today," Jessica said, "then I'll take the Sword of Mercy."

Merula nodded, a gleam in her eyes. "It's time. I'll tell the others, tonight Rendaira is ours."

"Be careful. The guards may not be Elitet, but they're still well trained."

"Don't worry. We know what we're doing."

Jessica waited out on the lawn until dusk. The deliveryman never came. "Well, that's it. It's time." She jumped to her feet.

When she reached the mansion's front entrance, a distant rumble caught her attention. She gazed down the long drive toward the sound. "Horses!" she breathed. Her heart beat faster. "Dad?" She strained to look. In the twilight, she found it difficult to make out the uniforms, but, then they registered. "Black!" To her horror, she recognized Elitet! And

293

Addex led the pack.

She threw the mansion door open and ran for the kitchens. The battle for Rendaira had already begun. She hurdled the bodies of four palace guards before bursting into the first kitchen. Most of the staff was there. They were arming themselves with knives and many held swords, two dripped with fresh blood.

"Elitet," Jessica yelled. "And Addex is leading them."

Cook Stratin looked at those around her, then rested her eyes on Merula. Everyone looked to Merula. "How many Elitet?" Merula asked.

Jessica had not stopped to count them. "I don't know, about twenty or thirty maybe."

"We outnumber them and we have surprise on our side." Merula gazed at her friends. "We've already taken care of most of Rendaira's guard, and I say we attack."

"I agree," Cook Stratin said.

"Go, Jessica," Merula commanded. Turning her back on her friend, she began giving orders to her people. "Spread out throughout the house and grounds. We..." her voice trailed off as Jessica bolted for the back stairs and ran for the secret passage. The sounds of fighting filtered up from the entry hall. She squeezed through the tiny opening, lit a torch, and scampered down the stairwell. She flew through the narrow passageways to the Treasure room.

After entering the dark chamber, she picked up a small, golden statue. When she reached the glass case the crystal at the end of the sword's hilt glowed brightly. "You know, don't you?" She felt an odd sense of oneness with the beautiful weapon. She extinguished, then discarded the small fire brand, its light a pathetic glow to the brilliant effulgence radiating from within the glass box.

With both hands Jessica raised the statue above her head, and with all her strength brought it straight down. The case imploded under the force of the blow. Gingerly reaching in, she took the sword. As soon as her fingers curled around it, the glow of the crystal ball increased tenfold, bathing the entire room with bright light. The hilt felt cool to her touch and the sword itself was unexpectedly lightweight. Turning the sword over in her hand, she could only stare at it in amazement. "So much power."

Without warning, the main door burst open.

"What are you doing in here?"

She did not have to look up to know the voice behind the question belonged to Addex.

"Just retrieving something that belongs to me." She said coolly, meeting the Shield's stony stare. "Why have you come back without Daenon? Deserted?"

The nausea started churning in the pit of her stomach. Slowly, she

294

walked backwards, edging her way towards the hidden passage. He smelled of blood and breathed heavily. In one hand he held a torch and in the other his crimson covered sword. He slid the torch into a holder just inside the door. Jessica felt bile rise in her throat. He sheathed his sword and pulled his dagger. She knew she was in trouble.

"Do you see this?" He waved the dagger before her. "This is the weapon I used to kill your Uncle Haesom with. I also used it to kill your aunt and your two cousins."

"No," Jessica hissed, trying to stifle the queasiness. "You killed my Uncle with your sword. I was there. I saw you do it."

Addex wavered for an instant, surprise registering on his face, but it was briefly lived. Continuing his advance, an evil smile twitched at his lips.

Anger flooded through her, sweeping away the paralyzing nausea. "Addex, you're a coward!" she seethed. "In a truly fair fight you'd never win. You prey on women and children and you never take on a real man by yourself, you always have an army behind you."

He stopped, his face turned scarlet and his hand shook. "If I had more time, I'd show you what I am capable of."

"You can't kill me," she taunted, forcing her voice to remain calm. "Your master wouldn't like it."

"I have no intentions of killing you. But a woman without sight is much easier to control than one with it."

The nausea came shooting back. Her grip tightened around the sword. The delicate blade may not have been forged for battle, but it was the only weapon she had and she decided to use it. Instantly, the nauseous feeling vanished, as strange warmth crept through her sword arm. She glanced at her hand. The magnificent blade pulsated with an electric energy which traveled through her fingers, upward into her body.

As soon as she broke eye contact, Addex lunged, reaching for Jessica's hair with his left hand while he held his knife in his right. From the corner of her eye, she saw the movement. She readied to thrust the sword forward, but Addex suddenly gasped and stumbled. Jessica spun away from him. A queer, thunderstruck look crossed his face as he jerked upright. When he turned around, a large butcher knife protruded out from between his shoulder blades. It was plunged in up to the handle, and from its angle, Jessica could tell it pierced his heart.

"That's for my mother." Merula's voice echoed. "And this is for my brothers."

The sound of metal ripping into flesh was heard again and the tip of a sword slide out through Addex's lower back. He lurched forward, reaching for his assailant, but his knees buckled. With his blood pooling around him he looked up at Merula. "You!" he choked as blood spilled from his mouth. He fell forward, rose briefly on his hands, then dropped back down, a look of shock forever engraved on his ashen face.

Jessica stared open mouthed. Her eyes darted from Addex's lifeless form to Merula and back again. "Th…Th..Thanks."

"Go!" Merula hissed, then standing aside, she pointed to the massive open door. White faced, she shook uncontrollably. The sporadic sounds of battle could be heard in the silence of the treasure room. An occasional yell, then brief metal on metal, let Jessica know the fight for Rendaira was still going on.

"Don't worry about us. Just go! Raise your sword and bring freedom to this land!" Merula cried.

Jessica ran from the scene of Addex's death straight to her bedchambers. She passed several Elitet and servants lying lifeless in the hallways. Chak's body lay sprawled upside down on the marble staircase, a meat cleaver imbedded in his chest.

With trembling hands, Jessica changed into the pants and shirt she had made especially for her escape. Blue satin, drawstring pants, a white peasant blouse she had tried to embroider with silver thread, and a red waist sash for accent was as much of an Esparian uniform as she could manufacture on her own. Grabbing a small box from under her bed, she reverently pulled out her aunt's precious locket and placed it around her neck.

Before she left Rendaira, the servant-slaves took the jailers and Elitet prisoner. While obtaining the Sword of Mercy, she missed most of the action, but the slashed, lifeless bodies of servants and soldiers, as well as the many wounded, gave testimony of the bitter, brief conflict.

Having been stripped of their weapons, the Elitet were being marched to the servant's quarters to be locked up. Cook Stratin gave Jessica a knapsack of food and large container of water. The stableman brought her favorite mare, and with the Sword of Mercy strapped firmly to her side she galloped eastward to find her father and the armies of Esparia.

CHAPTER 26

The Protectors of Esparia

With both moons in their new stages, the night seemed much darker than usual. Stars glistened overhead, but their meager light gave little illumination to the desert terrain. Once beyond Rendaira's borders, Jessica passed several riderless horses. She asked two for news of the war, but they were of little help. Anxious to find her father, but not accustomed to navigating by unfamiliar constellations, she determined after only a few hours of travel, rather than become further disoriented, she would stop until morning. While the mare grazed on meager desert flora, Jessica curled up in a shallow ditch and fell into a light sleep.

A footstep brought her around. Motionless, she listened, her heart pounding in her ears. She felt no nausea, but that did little to calm her overactive imagination. Slowly the steps drew closer to where she lay. *Why didn't I grab a real weapon?* She chided herself. *I can be so stupid sometimes. Go away, please just go away!*

"J'ca?" Jessica felt the words form in her head. "J'ca?"

"Web? Is that you?"

A joyful whinny came in answer. Jessica sprang from the ditch and threw her arms around the horse's neck. Tears stung her eyes and she choked back the rising flood. A feeling of warmth washed over her as her faithful friend nuzzled her cheek.

"How did you find me?"

"Many days, ran away. Brother, carried Elitet, saw you. Surprised human speak. Search."

"An Elitet's horse? You weren't afraid of the animal?"

"No. Brother's no war. Rules, order. No war."

"You have no idea how glad I am to see you. Are you thirsty? I have water."

Jessica gave Web a drink, then set the mare from Rendaira free. When the animal trotted off, Jessica settled down for the rest of the night. With Web standing guard, she felt safe for the first time in many weeks.

For six days Jessica and Web rode due east. The desert seemed to be one, never changing land of rock, sagebrush and cacti. They never encountered another human soul, however two more riderless horses were able to give them information on the whereabouts of the gathering armies.

At last they caught a glimpse of the Demarian forces in the distance. "We need to hide now," Jessica said. "We'll continue on after the sun goes down."

Taking shelter behind a small clump of rocks and thick, scraggly bushes, Jessica waited until midnight to continue the final phase of her journey. Without a sound, Web trotted to the enemy line, his stealth surprising Jessica. They followed the line of campfires for nearly two hours before finding an opening to squeeze through. Jessica leaned forward and flattened herself against the horse's neck while they galloped, unnoticed, into the no-man's land between the two opposing armies.

"Wow," Jessica whispered, "where did you learn to walk and gallop so noiselessly? I didn't think a horse could be so quiet."

"Brother carried Ghost Walker. Teach."

"Impressive! Right now we need to find a high spot somewhere, and we need to find it before the sun rises. I have a plan."

The armies were aligned to the east and to the west, both camps stretching for nearly a filon. Jessica realized she and Web were on the southern end of the camps. Fires on both sides blazed as far north as she could see. She and Web traveled down the pitch dark center of the soon-to-be battlefield, trying to find some high point, but the land lay utterly flat.

Jessica desperately needed a high point and her anxiety began to mount. At last, the land under Web's feet rose. She urged him forward and within minutes they stood atop a small hillock. It would have to do. The almost imperceptible outline of another small knoll about five hundred yards further north caught her attention. She later learned these were the Twin Hills, and the only high points in the surrounding desert for filons. They were located in the very center of the battlefield.

After assuring Web she did indeed have a good plan, Jessica sent him to the Esparian line. She pulled the Sword of Mercy from its cloth wrapping and sat down to await the sun's first rays. Sleep had fled long ago. Her heart pounded, uncontrolled, inside her chest. *I hope this works. If the sword is half as impressive as I think it will be, then maybe I can put some fear into the Demarians.* From the Demarian line, the brief clashing of swords drifted up to where she sat. She peered southward, down the enemy ranks, trying to locate the source and thought she heard some muffled cries. One of the flickering campfires shining at the end of the line went out. *What's going on down there? Fighting within the ranks?* She shrugged. *Curious.*

The surrounding landscape slowly turned from black nothingness to gray shades, and with the increasing light, the gray shades started to take on muted color. The opposing armies were waking. Clinking metal and marching feet filled the air when the soldiers on each side entered battle formation.

I hope this works. Jessica stood to her full height, and taking the sword in both hands she raised it high above her head. *If this battle begins before the sun rises, I'm doomed.* Hundreds of thousands lined up on both sides of her, as far north and south as she could see; an ocean of humanity, seemingly innumerable. The giants stood out on the Esparian line and they held a slight advantage with the morning light to their backs. *This'll be a blood bath if I'm not successful.*

The horizon steadily brightened and Jessica gripped the sword. Facing north, she focused straight ahead when, to her amazement, a lone figure rose up to stand at the very top of the twin hill in front of her. *Was he there all night, waiting like I was?* The man was dressed in full plate armor, it having been polished to a high gloss. There was a familiarity in the soldier's stance, the way he held his body. With sudden recognition, she gasped. *Oh my gosh…Dad!*

Unhurriedly, he turned in a circle. When he spotted Jessica atop her hill he stopped. A soft breeze blew, swirling her long red hair gently about her face. Slowly, he raised his right arm directly above his head. In his hand was the Sword of Judgment. Father and daughter faced each other, their two sister swords held high.

The first rays of sunlight flooded over the plain, hitting John and Jessica at the same moment. The tip of the Sword of Mercy caught the rays which bounced from diamond facet to diamond facet, multiplying a thousand times. The hilt of Jessica's sword quickly heated up in her hands. The warmth spread down her arms and through her body to the tips of her toes. She looked up. The crystal ball at the end of the handle glowed with a pure, white light. The glow quickly increased in intensity, finally forcing her to avert her eyes. The handle never became hot, but the warmth continued to radiate down through her. The sword shone with a brilliance that dazzled both armies into complete silence. The powerful light pulsed in rhythm to Jessica's heartbeat.

"Listen to me, people of Edia," Jessica shouted into the profound stillness. "This war will have no winners. Throw down your weapons of destruction and live in peace. I am Protector Jessica Ernshaw, granddaughter of Protectors Graesion and Gayleena Saylon. I am the daughter of John Ernshaw Saylon, the High Protector of Esparia."

When Jessica finished her short speech, she knelt on one knee and pointed her sword at her father on the opposite hill. The Sword of Mercy surged into power, completely encompassing Jessica in a cocoon of brilliant white. In seconds, the light gathered around her and rolled upward to the sword. An arc of pure energy, later described as hundreds of lightning bolts, jumped from the tip of the Sword of Mercy to the tip of the Sword of Judgment. It traveled down the blade, enveloping John in a radiance that momentarily blinded everyone looking at him, including Jessica.

"Desert people of Demar, Esparians and Giants," John's voice boomed out, as if a microphone were amplifying his words. "I have come from far away to heal this land. This world and I have become one. I do not come in vengeance. I do not come in anger. I come with peace. I come with justice. Lower your weapons and return to your lands. Your farms have not been destroyed, your homes still stand, ready to welcome you back. Let hate rule you no more, but live with us in peace."

Murmurs rippled throughout the Demarian line as Jessica and John's messages spread to those who did not hear them. The air was still, for the breeze had died away and everyone waited in silence. Jessica expected Daenon to give the command to attack at any moment, but it did not come. Yet on one knee, she lowered her sword, still warm and faintly pulsating with captured light, to her side. John lowered his sword and the glow around him slightly diminished.

The Esparian ranks opened and a lone rider came onto the field. The man rode directly between the twin hills, stopping on the Demarian side of them.

"I am Lepsis," the rider called to the Demarians. At the mention of his name a buzz rose throughout the entire army. He raised his hand for silence. "You know me. I have willingly given this protector my allegiance." He pointed up at John. "He is an honorable man. Throw down your weapons. Go home. Take your wives and your children with you and live in peace."

Jessica held her breath. *Where is Daenon?* She thought. *I can hardly believe he hasn't said or done anything against us.* She looked at her father. The light surrounding him was slowly fading.

For a full ten minutes no one spoke and not a soul moved. *What could they be thinking?* Jessica wondered. *Is death so preferable to peace, they must take so much time to think about it?* A skirmish broke out towards the northern tip of the Demarian line. Jessica stood, but could not see exactly what was happening. John stood at attention, he too watched the fighting. "Jessica," he whirled around to face her. "Send me another lightning bolt."

"Another lightning bolt?" she questioned. *I don't know how I made the first one.* Raising the sword above her head and gripping it tightly in both hands, she held her breath. *Another lightning bolt, huh?* Nothing happened.

The clash of steel grew louder, as the skirmish had spread to other sections of the Demarian line. Screams of women and children could be heard above the ringing of metal on metal. "Come on Jessica!" her father yelled. "I need that power now!"

Looking up at the blade in her grasp, Jessica concentrated on the clear ball at its end. She turned toward the sun, its rays full in her face. Closing her eyes, she imagined Edia, bathed in the sun's life giving light. She 'saw' the planet, felt her pain at the loss of nearly a million of her children.

"Bree...Bree...Bree." She whispered. As if in response, a flash of fire shot from the soles of Jessica's feet upward through her body. It poured from her hands into the Sword of Mercy. She opened her eyes. The crystal ball pulsed once again with power. Focusing on the clear sphere, she willed it to burst into flame. She became a human conduit, with energy traveling from the ground she stood on to steel clutched in her hands. With a mighty effort, she swung around and pointed the sword at her father. The arc of lightning he needed shot to the waiting Sword of Judgment.

John caught the force without flinching. With the Sword of Judgment now alive in his hand he turned toward the fighting Demarians. He raised the weapon above his head and, as if casting a fishing rod, he threw an energy bolt directly in front of the deadly chaos. An enormous explosion hammered the dry earth. Tons of sand shot up and rained down upon the stunned Demarians. A crater, nearly twenty feet wide and five feet deep was created.

"People of Demar, stop this fighting now!" John roared, his voice filled with authority. "Throw down your weapons. If you do not, I will obliterate you with the next bolt of power."

Jessica collapsed after sending her light to John. She now had a much better understanding of the relationship between the sister swords. When her father threatened the warring desert people, her heart sank. *He can't be serious. I don't have enough energy to stand, let alone conjure up another bomb.*

John did not speak again. It took nearly a half hour for anyone on the field to move. At last, a Demarian commander stepped from the line of soldiers and walked to Lepsis. Jessica could see the two conversing, but she could not hear their words. At length, the officer stepped back, unsheathed his weapons and dropped them at Lepsis' feet. Turning to face John, he bowed slightly, then returned to his troops. After several more long minutes, a few Demarian men followed his example, then gradually, by tens and twenties, then hundreds, soldiers stepped forward and threw their weapons on the ground. Jessica rose to her feet, remaining upon her hill during this ceremony. Her father never moved an inch.

To her amazement, not only men come forward, but also women and many children. Not all the Demarians surrendered however. Many shouted curses and obscenities at those who opted for peace. Jessica learned these were mostly Elitet, and they fled westward before they could be stopped or captured.

Lepsis later reported the gist of his brief conversation with the Demarian commander. Without Daenon screaming at them and feeding their hate, the desert people, tired of death and war, decided for themselves to try the path of peace. The battling in the northern ranks broke out because the Elitet would rather have seen the people dead than surrender.

An hour after the Demarians began dispersing, John descended the hill. Lepsis dismounted and the two men clasped arms. "You have amazing timing, Lepsis," John grinned. "Without you we'd be knee deep in bodies right now."

"I knew you'd never attack without giving the desert people a chance to walk away with dignity. I thought I might be able to help, but it was the display of fire that convinced most of them."

"And that would never have been possible without Jessica," John stated.

"Dad!" Jessica came tearing down her little hill.

"Jess!" John ran toward his daughter. He caught her up and swung her around. "I was so worried. I could hardly believe my eyes when I saw you on that hill. Are you all right?"

"I'm fine, Dad. Look what I found, the Sword of Mercy!" She held it out to him and he reverently took it.

"I've never seen anything like it." He turned it over in his hand. Giving it back to her he said, "It's yours now. You've learned its secrets."

"I've got a feeling I've only scratched the surface," she said, and slipped the blade through the sash at her middle. "When you asked for that second bolt of power, I felt a little like She-ra calling on the powers of Grayskull."

John smiled. "That was your favorite cartoon growing up."

Slipping her arm through her father's and grabbing Lepsis with her other, Jessica walked to the Esparian line amid wild cheers. A handsome, white-blond giant stood out from the rejoicing soldiers. He approached the trio and bowed low to Jessica. John made the introductions in fluent Giant.

"Prince Tor of the Colossus Mountains, I would like to present my daughter, Protectoress Jessica Ernshaw of the house of Saylon."

"How do you do," Jessica said, holding out her hand to the giant. He gingerly took, then kissed the offered hand, a move which impressed her. She didn't realize she was speaking Giant

Speaking slowly, in simple, carefully chosen words, he explained to her what happened with the note and how he had seen the Elitet seize her in the Colossus forest. It seemed important to him that she understand a rogue giant assisted with the trap.

Jessica reached up and placed her hand on the giant's thick arm. "I understand. I don't hold you responsible."

Tor smiled. "Thank you." To John he said, "We will go home now. I must find the guilty one who aided the Elitet. If you ever need us, we're at your service."

"And we are forever in your debt," John bowed to the giant prince. "If we can ever repay you, please allow us to do so." It did not take long for the giants to load their tents and supplies on their exotic ox-horses. They sang as they toiled, their words rising up in a strange tongue. Jessica tried to comprehend the words, they seemed so close to her understanding, but they eluded her.

"Tor, what song is this? The tune is so lively, but the words, I ..."

"It is ancient Esparian, a dead language. We no longer speak it, but there are some of my people who have been appointed to be the keepers of all that once was. They teach us the meaning of the past, so we never lose the future. This song tells of our beloved mountains, the meadows, and the streams. We have been gone a long time and my men are eager to return. Our aid in this war has been a worthy venture, but our hearts yearn for the sweet smell of our woods, the familiar faces of our friends, and the love of our families. It is time to go home."

Without warning, Jessica felt an intense yearning for the same thing and tears stung her eyes. "Home," she whispered.

It was an incredible spectacle to see the giants mount their strange looking beasts and head eastward. "I'm going to miss them." John stood beside Jessica, watching the receding goliaths. "They take with them the ashes and personal effects of all their fallen brothers. Like us, they never leave a man behind."

John sighed. "Did you realize you've been speaking Giant?"

"What?" Jessica was stunned. I was speaking English.

John smiled. "No dear daughter, you were speaking Giant. And I think right now we are both speaking Esparian."

"What are you talking about?" she laughed. "We're speaking English."

"Larone told me that we both picked up a little something on our trip here. After my time with Tor my Giant's quite fluent now. It seems that The Expanse of Gonta gives gifts. Don't worry," he patted her shoulder, "you'll get the hang of it. I finally did."

Before Jessica could question further she heard a familiar female voice call from the distance. "Jessica!"

Both John and Jessica turned. "Lyrista!" Jessica called back and ran to embrace her friend.

"Well, let me look at you," Lyrista said, a broad smile on her face. "You're beautiful Jessica; the most wonderful sight I've seen in months." She hugged the girl once again.

"Come on you two," John walked up, grinning from ear to ear. "Lepsis and I want to hear all about Jessica's time at Rendaira."

Settled in the command tent, Jessica spent the next several hours telling her father, Lyrista, and Lepsis about her last few months. She noticed Lepsis paid particular attention when Merula was mentioned. He looked quite grim when Jessica described how Merula had saved her life by killing Addex.

No one interrupted Jessica's monologue. She had a gift for storytelling, and with her true-life adventures being more bizarre than fiction, her audience sat spellbound. The only items she failed to include were Daenon's threat of marriage and parting kiss. The incident still made her skin crawl and she preferred to forget the entire matter.

"So what do you think happened to Daenon?" Jessica asked, signaling the end of her story. "He obviously was not with his troops or they would never have surrendered."

Lepsis shrugged his shoulders. "It's a mystery to me. It's not like Daenon to just leave, not when he has an army in front of him the size he had there today. He would never give up until every last soldier, be it man, woman or child were dead around him. The only life he cares about is his own."

"Dad, we need to go to Rendaira before returning to Ramadine," Jessica said. "You must see this land as I've seen it."

"I agree," John nodded. "Lepsis, will you come with us?"

"Yes. I've some unfinished business at Rendaira."

Late afternoon found the four leaders seated in one of the many large dining tents, celebrating with the men the end to the brutal war. A feast of roasted meats from Kine, boiled vegetables from Verdure, and fresh fruits from Uberty was spread for all to enjoy. Many soldiers, with tears in their eyes, expressed gratitude and admiration to both John and Jessica for the incredible way they staved off the dreaded confrontation. Lepsis received many heartfelt thanks as well for his influence in the Demarian surrender.

"There's someone I think you'll be happy to see, Jessica," John said as he motioned his head toward a group of Guardians who had just entered the crowded tent. "I'll be right back." He left the table and went to the group. A moment later, one of the soldiers left his companions and followed John back to the table.

Jessica caught her breath. "Brayon!"

Smiling, the tall man knelt before her.

"He saved my life, and Lyrista's," John said.

"I joined this war not only to defend my country, but to repay my debt to you, My Lady," Brayon said. "I'm now a Guardian, in the service of your father."

Jessica sat speechless, her eyes glistened with moisture. She reached out and placed her hand on the kneeling man's shoulder. Finally, she controlled her emotions. "You're my one and only Salupathic healing, and I still don't know what I did that day. I only know I couldn't let you die. I couldn't have used that power on a better man. Thanks Brayon."

When the meal was nearly finished, a flushed second bar officer ran into the tent. Spotting John, he yelled, "Sirs, come quickly. You must see this! Everyone hurry."

Diners dropped their forks and rushed out through the wide tent opening. Additional soldiers streamed to the area from surrounding campsites. Horns blew and the excited bass and tenor voices of men filled the air. It took a minute for Jessica to locate the cause of all the fuss. A group of rugged looking Guardians, led by an even more rugged looking Anton, came riding up the center of camp.

"Varnack!" Jessica squealed and set off toward the incoming procession at a run. The large Trigal Hound let out a yelp, then bounded from Anton's side and bowled Jessica over.

"Safe. You're safe. Worried." His words came into her mind. When he licked her face several times, she did not wipe it off, but kissed his furry forehead in return.

At the head of twenty-two Guardians, Anton grinned from ear to ear. "Jessi," he boomed over the din, "yer a sight from heaven. Yer hair looks great, too."

Jessica laughed. He's never going to let me live that down.

In the midst of the Guardians, bound by several ropes sat a black uniformed man. A cloth sack covered his head. Three horses were led at the back of the group, their lifeless riders draped crosswise over the saddles. While the impressive group made their way through the throngs of curious soldiers, Jessica and Varnack walked back to where John, Lepsis, and Lyrista stood.

Jessica thought Anton looked the most disheveled that she had ever seen him. His uniform was blood-stained, filthy, and torn while his hair lay matted with several twigs sticking out, but the huge grin on his face was infectious. Coming to a stop in front of John, Anton reached down and shook the Protector's hand.

"Brought ya a little present, John." Anton's deep voice roared out. "Bring 'im up boys." He waved to the two Guardians who flanked the hooded man. Once level with him, Anton reached over and pulled the hood from the man's face.

Jessica gasped, while Lepsis chuckled.

"This here's my nephew, Daenon," Anton announced. "Daenon, yer lookin' at the High Protector of Esparia."

Daenon sat on his horse with sparks flying from his eyes. The gag in his mouth stopped him from making any intelligible sounds and Jessica was glad for it. She could just imagine what he would say if allowed.

"Well, we were wondering what happened to him," John said lightly.

"Me and my boys here rode in from Rendaira way last night. We'd been all over the place searchin' for Jessi. A couple of hours before sunrise, we found ourselves just west of Daenon's camp, so I decided it was time to pay my nephew a little visit. It wasn't too hard to spot his tent, it being the biggest and best. Most of the sentries were patrollin' the front of the camp. I guess they didn't figure on anyone sneakin' up from behind. We had to handle some of the guards, and I will admit, Daenoboy put up quite a fight, but he was no match fer us. We got a gag on him and covered his face, then wrapped him up in some of his own sheets, like a dead body. Getting' out of camp was a bit tricky. We had a little skirmish with a southern guard post, couple of the boys here are hurt, but we managed to steal away without upsettin' the whole army."

"We'll have your men tended to right away," John promised.

"So where do ya want him?" Anton asked.

"The sooner we lock him out of the way, the better," Lyrista said. She stared at Daenon, her mouth set in a hard line.

Jessica looked around. Lyrista was not the only soldier looking at Daenon with cold hatred.

John must have also noticed the sudden change in atmosphere for he turned to Lyrista and said, "I'm tired of blood and death. I now understand why Graesion did not have Segal killed those many years ago. It must stop somewhere; let it stop here, with us." He looked at Anton. "I think your father was right. Rash anger and vengeance would only plunge this country into darkness."

John raised his voice so it rang out loud and clear. "I will not order Daenon's death. He will be tried for his crimes in a court duly appointed by the laws of this country. His final fate will be determined at that time."

John turned to Lepsis. "You know this land better than anyone. Where do you suggest we put him?"

Without hesitating Lepsis answered, "Snow Peak Prison. He can await trial there."

"That's so anti-climactic," Jessica commented. Daenon struggled in his saddle. "I'm sure everyone here would like to see him drawn and quartered."

"Even the butchers of World War II had a fair trial, Jess. Daenon will die, rest assured of that, but not until his own people understand just what a monster he truly is. A trial will bring his evil into the open for all to see. Kill him now and the Demarian people will make him a martyr."

Raising his voice again John announced, "The prisoner goes to Snow Peak Prison until such time as a war crimes court can be convened. We will find and try all the Demarian leaders who ravaged Palium and Snow Peak. Justice will be meted out."

To Lyrista he asked, "Will you gather a volunteer group of a hundred men to escort this man to the prison? We'll be adding other inmates as we root out those who've committed atrocities. No guard will serve duty longer than six months at Snow Peak. I won't make it an outcast's outpost."

Jessica kept an eye on Anton throughout this entire exchange. Relief cross his face when John promised a trial would be required before deciding Daenon's fate. She reached up and patted his hand. She realized how difficult it would have been for him to watch his nephew executed on the spot, especially since he was the one who brought him in for judgment.

"That sounds fair." Jessica heard Lyrista say. "I would wish duty at Snow Peak on no man. I'm certain you'll have your volunteers. They can leave in the morning. Until then, I suggest you send Daenon to the Red News Center. Let him rant and rave to the birds."

* * *

While eating his portion of the celebration meal, Anton described the mayhem at Ramadine after Jeema returned without Jessica. He and his men were little help in describing what happened in the Colossus forest. By the time any of them had their horses under control and found their way back to the scene of the kidnapping, the Elitet were long gone. Realizing he was out of his league, Jeema returned to Ramadine.

Varnack never made it to his tribe. He told Jessica, who translated for the others, he felt an unusual feeling of dread and made it back to Ramadine just in time to join Anton and the Guardians.

Since no one had any idea of where Jessica was taken, the search was begun in the Colossus Mountains. The trail had not been difficult to pick up, as the Elitet seemed to be more concerned with speed than stealth. The search went without incident until Anton and company reached the first Demarian desert village. The trouble there was mostly a war of words with the women, but they decided they could not afford bad publicity, so they avoided each population center, while trying to keep hot on the trail. They ran into several bands of Demarian soldiers, losing time in skirmishes and small battles.

"It seemed like every time we'd make progress toward Rendaira, we'd hit another group of Elitet or army regulars. We finally started ridin' at night, just to avoid bein' seen. It took weeks to make the trip. I'm sorry, Jessi. We tried to go faster."

"I understand. It's okay."

"A couple of filons from Rendaira we ran into a fella named Farin. He told us where Jessi was and about the big ta-do brewin' at Twin Hills. We rode into Rendaira only minutes after Jessi left," Anton explained. "It was a good thin' we did too, 'cause the Elitet doogeroots had gotten free and we came just in time to round 'em back up."

"No!" Jessica gasped.

"Yer friends are fine. A lady in charge, her name was Merula, sent us off in the direction ya took."

Anton grabbed another apple and between munches finished his story. "We rode fast as we could to the battle line and reached the Demarians just before dawn. Ya should've seen Daenon's face when I walked in his tent.

It took us a while to ride back here 'cause we cut a wide path round the retreatin' Demarians. We didn't want any more trouble."

"I saw your fight," Jessica said. "When I was up on the hill, I heard swords and saw a campfire go out on the southern end."

"Yeah, I threw a couple of Elitet onto it. Snuffed it right out."

Jessica regarded him suspiciously. "You're leaving quite a bit out, aren't you, Uncle? Daenon is no fool, and he's as paranoid as they come. He probably had fifty body guards…"

"Fifty-five." Anton interjected.

"And," Jessica continued, "I can see the blood on what's left of your uniform is caked so thick it still isn't completely dry."

"Look, Jessi," Anton's voice took on a stern tone, one that truly surprised her. "I'll admit it was tough goin'. I lost some good men there, but we managed to do the job. Without Deanon's venom poisonin' 'em, the Demarian people chose peace. That's all I'm goin' to say on the matter," he shot an unyielding look to John and Lepsis, "to anyone."

It was well into the night when the narrative came to an end. Jessica, stifling a yawn, was having a difficult time staying awake. Beginning long before sunrise, the day had been physically and emotionally exhausting.

"What a day this has been," Lyrista said. "We have much to be grateful for. Anton, tomorrow we're going back to Rendaira. Jessica has some friends she wants us to meet and places to show her father."

"Yes," Jessica nodded and stifled another yawn. "Will you come with us?"

"Yeah, I'd like that. There's a lot a country I haven't seen yet. I was too busy trackin' and fightin' to stop and appreciate it."

"We'll be leaving early," Lyrista explained, "so I'll take Jessica now and show her where she can sleep." She stood gracefully, and with an arm around Jessica's shoulders, bid the men goodnight.

Morning came quickly for Jessica. Lyrista woke her with a hot breakfast. Within an hour, a group of three hundred Guardians accompanied John, Jessica, Lyrista, Lepsis, Anton, and Varnack to Rendaira. It took eight days of easy traveling to make the journey. They took their time. John explained he wanted to give Reese and Ru, who were given charge of the occupation, time to secure the roads and cities.

The afternoon they entered Rendaira's borders, the sun ruled a cloudless sky, but a cooling breeze blew from the north. While they rode up the main road, Jessica noticed the grand statues of Daenon were no longer standing.

'It's absolutely beautiful here," Lyrista said. "Almost as beautiful as Ramadine."

"Shows what can be done with good irrigation," Jessica pointed out. "Daenon dammed a small river north of here. That dam could be made larger and the water put to greater use."

When they came over the last hill, the entire troupe stopped. The elegant mansion gleamed in the bright sunlight.

"Oh, my," Lyrista breathed.

"Wait till you see inside," Jessica said enthusiastically. Lepsis smiled at the animated girl.

When the travelers rode down the smooth, stone road leading to the covered portico, Rendaira staff, smiling and waving, streamed from the front door. Cook Stratin sported fresh bandages and a sling she did not have when Jessica left a week ago.

Merula, wearing a dress for the first time since Jessica knew her, acted as head greeter. She sent the Guardians to the barracks behind the mansion, then gave Jessica a big hug. An unmistakable light shown in her eyes when she looked at Lepsis.

Bowing to Anton she said, "I'm pleased you've returned so we can repay you for everything you did, Lord Anton." She turned to the others and explained, "This man came to our rescue when prisoners we thought were secured had attacked. Twenty-three of our number are dead and many more wounded, but it could have been much worse."

Jessica gave her uncle a questioning stare. "I didn't want ya to worry, Jessi."

"Let me look at the wounded, I'm a healer," John offered.

"Merula, this is my Dad, John Ernshaw," Jessica introduced him, "and this is Lyrista, daughter of Seventh Bar Gammet."

Merula nodded to them both. "Your help would be welcome. We have done the best we could, but five men barely cling to life." Merula turned to a young girl standing nearby. "Take the Healer to the wounded." The girl nodded, and John, accompanied by Lyrista, followed her.

"Let's go to the central dining hall," Merula suggested. "The kitchen staff will have something prepared soon, and it's pleasant in there."

While they walked through the mansion, Jessica noticed that every door stood open. "Quite a change here, I must say."

"There will be no more secrets at this place," Merula promised. "No more terror behind closed doors." She turned to Lepsis who was deep in thought beside her. "Lepsis, I've saved everything. There are those who wanted to burn anything belonging to Daenon, but I insisted it be saved until you had a chance to look at it. You should be the one to determine what is destroyed and what is not. I knew you would come back."

Lepsis nodded. "I'll go through the office papers first. The most useful information should be there. Hopefully we can find out what happened to so many good people."

They reached the dining room where the smell of roasting meat filled the air. "The poor kitchen staff," Jessica said, "I'm sure we took you by

309

surprise. Showing up with three hundred guardians must have given Cook Stratin quite a shock."

"Oh, you know how well she works under pressure," Merula laughed. "You wait, she'll have a wonderful meal in no time."

Merula's words were prophetic. Toward the end of the simple, yet delicious meal of baked bread covered in thinly sliced meat and milk gravy, John and Lyrista came in. Plenty of food still lay on the table, and with no one in a hurry to leave the table, they had pleasant company while they ate.

"How is everyone, Dad?" Jessica asked.

"Your friends are good healers," he said. "Most of the wounded were already well cared for, but there was one or two things I was able to do. As long as they keep getting the care they currently have, I think they'll pull through."

"Merula hasn't touched Daenon's personal things, they're just as he left them," Lepsis told John. "If his files are anything like he is, they'll be in perfect order. When you're finished eating, I think you should come with me."

"I'm finished now," John said grabbing an extra apple-like fruit. "Let's get to it."

The two men strolled from the dining room. Jessica did not envy them any. "I'll bet Daenon had a lot of dirty little secrets," she commented to Lyrista. "I wouldn't want to go through his stuff."

"Well," Anton yawned, rubbing the back of his frizzy head, "I've eaten a fine meal and had a long day. Ma'am," he addressed Merula, "if ya could show me to a bed, I'll be out of yer hair."

"Of course," Merula smiled.

"We'll go with you," Jessica offered. "I'm sure Lyrista would like to see more of the mansion. Come on Varnack, let's take a walk."

Merula led the way up the servant's back stairs to one of the spacious guest rooms. "See ya in the mornin'," Anton said, yawning as he closed the bedroom door.

With Varnack at their side, the three women walked through the rest of that section of the mansion. They looked into several of the guest rooms, the sewing room and a library on the upper level. On the main floor they wandered through three of the enormous dining halls, the smallest of which they had just eaten in, a beautiful grand ballroom, Daenon's ornate throne room and one of the kitchens.

In the kitchen Merula grabbed a torch. She led the way to a set of stairs close to Daenon's private quarters and descended them to the palace's sub-level.

"Have I been here before?" Jessica asked.

"Once, but you were in such a hurry you wouldn't remember," Merula said. "This is the only real passage leading to the treasure chamber."

"I guess I was running pretty fast. All I could think about was getting out of there."

The hallway was made of polished stone and their shoes echoed with each step. Halfway down this lower passageway they came to a junction. To the left lay another set of stone stairs, but they passed on by, keeping to the straight path.

"Those steps lead to three torture rooms and thirty prison cells," Merula explained. "I thought I knew every inch of this place, but even I didn't realize they were there until after we took the mansion. We found some pretty terrible things. We're still trying to clean everything up. It's a little difficult, considering one wants to throw up soon after entering. I'm going to have the entrance to those stairs sealed so no one will ever go down there again."

When they reached the Treasure room, Jessica was surprised to see the large oak door still locked. Merula handed her the torch and produced a bright gold key from her skirt pocket.

"I thought no more secrets," Jessica said.

"This room is just too tempting. The things in here should be returned to their rightful owners, and what is left over, well...Lepsis will know what to do with it all."

"Wow," Lyrista breathed when she entered the windowless chamber.

Jessica saw the broken sword case was untouched, shards of glass still scattered on the carpeted floor. Blood stained the ground where Addex had fallen. The three women walked through the room in silence. Every few paces Lyrista would reach out and touch a statue or a painting. Eventually, she stopped in front of a gold framed portrait of a handsome young man dressed in a blue and silver military uniform. He had a kind smile on his face and looked about eighteen years of age.

"Jessica, do you know who this man is?"

"No. Why?"

"This is your grandfather, Graesion Saylon."

"Grandfather!" Jessica held the torch higher and gazed into the young face. Light green eyes stared down through waves of soft brown hair, but the painter had captured more than physical beauty. There was warmth in the eyes and gentleness around the mouth.

"I see why Grandma fell in love with him," Jessica whispered. "My Grandma would love to see this."

When they left the Treasure room, Jessica took one more look at the portrait hanging on the far wall. She had never noticed it before and now she wondered how she could have ever missed it.

"Merula, where are Daenon's quarters?" Lyrista asked.

"I'll take you there. It's on the main floor, behind the grand ballroom. He liked his privacy and his rooms are tucked at the back of the house.

They overlook the large gardens behind the mansion."

It took a few minutes to climb the stairs and weave through the hallways to Daenon's rooms. "One could become lost here," Lyrista commented. "It's like a maze."

"Segal built this place and made it maze-like on purpose," Merula explained.

Daenon's main sitting area was a two story, high-ceilinged room paneled from top to bottom in polished, maroon wood. The intricately carved paneling was hand pieced to flow together seamlessly. A massive stone fireplace stood in the center of the wall opposite the door. Flanking it on either side were three-foot wide windows running from floor to ceiling. All of the furnishings, from draperies to floor rugs, were the muted color of green sage. The room overlooked the back gardens, and if it had been daylight they would have had a spectacular view.

Jessica had seen the room before, when she first arrived and was taken on tour by Merula, but it was dark then, and late at night. Now the room was brightly lit by dozens of thick candles. Taxidermy animals packed the open spaces, with heads of various beasts mounted on walls as well as whole bodies arranged in woodland settings in the corners. A large, stuffed bird of prey in flight was suspended from the ceiling. Before she really took it all in, Jessica heard her father's voice from down a connecting hall.

"I can hardly believe this!" he sounded exasperated. "Everything is so well documented. It's as if he were going to publish his memoirs or something."

"Hey, Dad," Jessica yelled. "Where are you?"

"In here," he stuck his head out of a side room.

Daenon's office bureau looked as if a hurricane had hit it. Paneled in the same wood as the sitting room, the den was brightly lit by silver candle stands in each corner. Papers lay strewn all over the floor. Cupboard and file drawers stood wide open. Sitting in a black leather chair behind a long desk, Lepsis thumbed through a ledger while John rummaged through an armoire against the wall.

"Daenon kept detailed diaries and records of everything he did," John said, looking up when Jessica walked into the room. "So he wanted to marry you, huh? You're not the only one to leave out certain details of your adventures."

"He thought he could rule more legitimately," she shrugged. "It was not a pleasant prospect."

"What's all this?" Lyrista gave her light, gentle laugh, as she picked up several of the discarded papers.

"Mostly garbage." John sounded disgusted. He tossed another couple of documents on the pile. "The important things are on the desk, but this stuff," He indicated the mess on the floor, "is all trash, the rantings of a truly deranged mind."

"It'll take us a couple of days to go through everything," Lepsis warned. "So don't expect to see us any time soon."

It was a gentle dismissal, but a dismissal none-the-less. Merula showed Lyrista to a guest room identical to the one Jessica was in, and Jessica, with Varnack still by her side, settled into the one she had occupied for over two months. Her things were still in their drawers, and a fresh candle sat by her bedside.

Varnack curled up on a rug beside the bed.

"Varnack, do you miss your family?"

"Sometimes."

"I'm sorry."

"Larone and Anton family now."

"And me."

"Yes. And you."

In the morning, John and Lepsis made a late appearance at breakfast. After they took some nourishment, Merula suggested the time had come to show the men the Treasure chamber.

"My, oh my!" John exclaimed when he walked in. "It looks like a king's ransom!"

"I assume this is where Addex met his end," Lepsis said dryly, looking at the large bloodstain on the carpet.

"Yes, thanks to Merula I'm still in one piece," Jessica said. Merula remained silent.

"Daenon used to talk about this room, but I never once saw it in all my years of living here," Lepsis said.

Jessica pointed to the painting of her grandfather. "Dad, this is Lord Graesion."

"I haven't seen that picture in more than fifty years." Anton's loud voice echoed in the room. "Looks just like the lad. He was as fine a man as I ever knew. Ya remind me a lot of him, John." Anton affectionately slapped him on the back. "Haesom always wondered what happened to that paintin'. Now we know."

After looking everything over, they exited the room. Merula locked the door and handed the key to Lepsis. "Here. It belongs to you now."

He looked at her in surprise. "She's right," John agreed. "You are the rightful regulator of this province. It's been your home, and the people trust you. Who better to head a transition government? Use the money Daenon so selfishly accumulated and transform this desert. I'm sure you'll have willing hands ready to give you whatever help you may need." John smiled at Merula and she smiled back.

For four days Jessica barely saw her father. When she did, he was busy sorting through Daenon's papers, sending directives, and answering messages from Reese, Cordon and Ru. As far as she knew, the occupation was going smoothly. John mentioned only one village that actually took up arms against the Esparians, and they were quickly subdued. Lepsis sent riders to all corners of Demar, trying to consolidate power and guarantee freedoms.

John published a standing offer of amnesty to any Elitet willing to take an oath of peace, but from the small number of assassins Jessica had known, she felt few, if any, would accept it. Reports came in concerning one Corter, a Shield trying to gather Daenon's remaining loyal troops.

Anton roamed the countryside with Varnack, and Jessica contented herself with showing Lyrista around Rendaira, inside and out. Lepsis moved back into his house and a major renovation project on the servants' quarters was planned.

"Hopefully we can stem Corter's flow of support by proving to the desert people we mean to rule in mercy and justice," John said one night at dinner. "In two days we'll set off on our desert tour and begin putting actions to my words of clemency."

"I've prepared a route for us to follow," Lepsis said. "It'll take about two weeks to complete the scheduled stops."

On the night before they were to leave, Cook Stratin prepared a sumptuous meal of herbed meat, sweetened fruit compote, braised greens and leavened whole grain breads. The servants, the three hundred Guardians, and the honored guests all assembled in the grand ballroom.

When the meal came to an end, Lepsis stood and raised his hand for silence. He formally bowed to John and Jessica, then held his hand out for Merula. She wore a soft pink gown, and her curled hair glowed in the candlelight. Jessica saw her blush when she took the outstretched hand, but standing beside her gallant hero, her eyes glistened with love.

"My friends," Lepsis began, "I...no...we have an announcement." He placed his arm around Merula and continued. "I will make the tour of Demar with the Protectors, and upon my return here to Rendaira, Merula and I are to be wed."

A collective gasp rose from the crowd, but within a second the servants erupted in wild applause and cheers. Jessica ran to Merula and hugged her.

"I knew it, I just knew it!" she gushed. "Merula, I'm so happy for you!"

"I sent word to my father at Ramadine," Merula said. "He should be here in time to perform the ceremony. Until elections are held, he is still the Regulator of Palium."

John shook Lepsis' hand. "I'd like you to come to the wedding, if you can," Lepsis said hopefully. His eyes glanced over at Lyrista. "Everyone is invited."

314

"I wouldn't miss it for anything," John grinned.

"I sent a message to my family in Marone, and to my sister, Naydeen at Ramadine this morning," Lepsis emphasized Naydeen's name. "I hope they will be here by the time we return from our journey. I've also taken the liberty of inviting Lady Gayleena and Healer Larone."

Anton perked up at the mention of Naydeen. Lepsis slipped from Merula's side and moved smoothly to where Anton was seated. Being only a chair away from them, Jessica overheard what Lepsis proposed.

"Anton, I'm going to speak boldly. I want you to carefully consider what I'm about to say." He sat on an empty chair next to the large man. "I have loved Merula for many years now, but because of circumstances I could never control, I couldn't do anything about that love until now. I've come to realize, in these last few months of fighting and seeing death all around me, that it's never too late to grasp happiness. Anton, I may not know much, but I saw my sister when she looked at you. She loves you. Forty years of her life have been wasted away in a prison. It's time to take life and live it while you can. It's up to you, of course, but I'd be honored to make this a double wedding."

Anton sat speechless. Lepsis squeezed his shoulder and left him to his thoughts. Jessica considered his words and found she completely agreed with him. Lyrista's gentle laughter drifted over to her. She was in an animated conversation with John. *I wonder if Lepsis could talk some sense into my Dad.*

"Uncle Anton," Jessica turned around to him. "Uncle Anton," she tapped him on his shoulder. "**Uncle Anton**," she called a little louder.

"Huh? What?" he looked blankly at her. At last, the light of recognition came into his eyes, "Oh, Jessi! What can I do for ya?"

"I'm sorry to interrupt, but I have a favor to ask."

"Go ahead. Ask away."

"Well, I know my Grandma will want to come to this wedding, and I'm a little worried about her traveling here without a good guide or escort. I was wondering if you could take some of your Guardians and go to Ramadine and...hmmm...make sure she gets here safely. If it worked out, Merula's father, Uncle Larone and Lady *Naydeen* could go with her too." Jessica also emphasized Naydeen's name.

Anton stared at her for a moment, digesting what she had just asked of him. The corners of his mouth twitched and a small smile appeared on his lips. It grew larger and larger until he grinned broadly. Jessica noticed for the first time how deep the smile wrinkles were around his eyes and mouth. His tanned face accented his white teeth, and he looked quite handsome at that moment.

"Jessi, m'dear, that's a terrific idea. I'll go give the orders right now." He pushed his chair back and almost ran over to where his group of

Guardians sat. With contagious enthusiasm, Jessica watched Anton tell his buddies they were going back on the road.

"What's Anton so excited about," Jessica recognized her father's voice in her ear.

"Oh, Dad, we may have a double wedding." And she told him what Lepsis had suggested to Anton. Swallowing hard, she decided to take a plunge. "Dad, I bet they would love to have a triple wedding."

"And who are you planning to marry?" He did not crack a smile.

"C'mon dad, don't play dumb. You know exactly what I'm talking about."

"Don't go there, Jess," he warned. "I'm not ready yet." John turned away from his daughter and walked from the ballroom. She knew she had upset him, but someone needed to prod him along, and this was a first step.

"What was that about?" Lyrista asked walking over to Jessica. "His mood seemed to change so quickly."

"Denial," was the only explanation Jessica gave. She walked out of the ballroom with Varnack romping after her.

Anton left in the morning with his twenty-five Guardians. Before he rode out, Jessica saw him talking with Lepsis, and Lepsis looked very happy.

CHAPTER 27

John's Dream

"This is the tiern where I first met Farin, I wonder if he's returned to Asmerth?" Jessica said to Lepsis. They slowly approached the large city. The highway teemed with people, not just women and children, but men as well, many men. The accompaniment of fifty Guardians kept their weapons close and Jessica saw the distrust on each soldier's face, but she felt no premonitions of danger, so enjoyed the humanity around her. Varnack too seemed content to be on the road again while he romped up and down the line, teasing the horses.

At one point Web whinnied his frustration and Jessica had to scold him. "You're driving the horses crazy, Varnack. Will you please calm down?"

"Good fun," he replied.

"Fun, huh? Well don't come crying to me when one of these mounts gives you a swift kick."

Lepsis rode at the head of the procession, with Jessica beside him. John and Lyrista followed directly behind, while the fifty Guardians rode three abreast in a neat column after them. Unusually quiet, John seemed to be troubled. Lyrista tried several times to engage him in conversation. Inwardly Jessica cringed after each of her father's cryptic responses.

"What is bothering you?" Lyrista finally asked, a frustrated look on her face.

"Nothing.

"Oh, please. You've got a black cloud the size of Ragus hanging over your head."

"I just need some space."

Her mouth dropped open and her eyes bulged in astonishment. "Fine, enjoy your solitude." Lyrista reined her horse so it slowed, and the Guardians split to allow her to join their ranks.

Jessica felt terrible. She looked at Varnack. "Any advice for the love sick?"

He shook his shaggy head. "Human problems. Human solutions."

John trotted up and fell into step beside Lepsis. "Farin's a good man," Lepsis said to John. "I want to make contact. He would be invaluable as an advisor in the new government."

"He comes and goes with an uncanny quiet," John commented. "'Ghost Walker' is an appropriate title. I wouldn't be surprised if we were to run into him when we least expected it."

"You have him measured quite well," Lepsis agreed.

Jessica showed them the house where she first encountered Farin and his men. He was not there, but Lepsis left a note, certain the Ghost Walker would eventually receive it.

When out of Asmerth, John finally snapped out of his mood and began bouncing ideas off of Lepsis for improving the villages and the desert land.

Realizing Lyrista was still back with her men, Jessica turned to look at her. The woman's emotions played across her face, alternating between confusion, hurt, and anger.

A slight pause in the conversation between John and Lepsis gave Jessica an opening to chide her father.

"Dad, please don't take this the wrong way, but you can really be a jerk sometimes."

"What!" He looked astounded. Lepsis laughed.

"Lyrista? Remember her?"

The startled look on his face did not change.

"Men!" Jessica felt frustrated and pulled Web to slow him down. She maneuvered next to Lyrista.

"Don't let my dad upset you," Jessica blurted out. "He's got a lot on his mind."

Lyrista said nothing.

"I know he loves you, Lyrista. I've seen it in his eyes. He just can't seem to let go of my mom."

"I know." Her body language said the brief conversation was terminated.

Jessica reflected on her friend. When she had first met Lyrista, Jessica felt a little overwhelmed, but now, she felt every bit the woman's equal. Lyrista certainly treated her like an equal. There was a bond with Lyrista, and it came without a great deal of effort. Jessica was determined to have another chat with her dad.

The countryside was just as she remembered, barren, but with its own kind of stark beauty. This time, she enjoyed her trip through the desert. The temperatures were dropping as the autumn days approached. They only stopped to eat, sleep in the open, and purchase supplies in the small villages. Four days went by, and they traveled southwest about a hundred and fifty filons. Jessica noticed the further west they rode, the more distrusting the desert people seemed to be of them and the more arid the land became. The ground slowly changed from hard, barren earth to crumbling, dry, sandy soil. Gazing westward across the vast wasteland before her, Jessica saw vast dunes of hot, dry sand.

The Deserts of Demar were of a dual nature. The eastern half, or Eastern Desert, was inhabitable, with small water sources allowing for some farming. The western half, or Western Desert, was utterly parched.

The Esparian troops had penetrated all of the inhabited areas of the Eastern Desert to the line of civilization along the Western Desert. As per John's orders, the occupation troops paid for their own supplies and remained busy by helping the locals where opportunity arose.

The far western lands were forbidding to all but the truly foolish. There was no water for filons on end and invisible sand traps lurked throughout the barren regions. The traps were like dry quicksand, they blended in with the normal sand until anything over ten pounds happened to cross, then the object was quickly ensnared and sucked under. The greater part of the desert people completely avoided the west.

After two hundred filons, Lepsis turned due north. They followed the imaginary line between the eastern and western deserts. "I want you to see the border settlements," he explained to John. "I think it's important you show the border people you care enough about them to travel to their bleak hoffles."

In the larger tierns they stopped long enough to meet the local leaders and hear their concerns. Everywhere it was the same, food and water. The task of bringing water to these desert parts emerged as the single most important endeavor the Esparians could undertake to win the trust of the Demarian people. As it turned out, that was how Segal originally won them over. He found untapped water sources and brought the precious liquid to the masses, thereby allowing for larger cities and greater prosperity.

They had braved the dust and heat of the invisible western border for five days when Lepsis announced the end of the journey. "We'll be at our last stop, Jorton Hoffle, tomorrow afternoon. This is the last tiern along the western border that I want you to see, then we'll turn southeast and head for Rendaira. Jorton Hoffle is unusual in that it's a tiny green haven in this barren, desolate land. I've never been able to figure out their water source. About twenty years ago, Daenon had me thoroughly explore this region, but I found nothing. The Olders are quite good at evading questions about their water supply. If Daenon were with me, he would have ordered the people tortured to extract the information. Luckily, I was able to divert his attentions from Jorton after the underground spring near Rendaira was discovered. He only wanted Jorton's water source for himself, not the general good of the people, so when he dammed his own private lake, his interest in this little hoffle disappeared. There's still much more of Demar, but I think you have seen enough to have a good idea of what the desert is like. To the north are mountains. It would take several more days to reach them and many more after that to see the tierns. The people there are less wary and more open to Esparia. In the past, they've had good associations with the citizens of Snow Peak."

"I'd like to see maps of that area when we return to Rendaira," John said. "Perhaps there is a way to bring the water from the north to the deserts in the south."

"That's a tremendous undertaking, John."

"Well, I'm up to a good challenge, Lepsis. We'll see just how good the Esparian engineers are." When the conversation turned to the ever-present water problems in Demar, Lyrista, spurred her horse flush with the two men. She had a few ideas to interject on the subject and wanted more information on Jorton Hoffle. Jessica and Varnack were left as lone companions, traveling behind the three leaders and ahead of the Guardians in the rear. During their journey, Brayon was the only Guardian who spoke with Jessica. The others never interacted with either her or Varnack. They were respectful and kind enough, but she knew most of the men viewed her as little more than a child. As for Varnack, Trigal Hounds were creatures of myth and legend, so many of the men regarded him with wary respect.

"Well Varnack, how are you holding up? The sand isn't too hot for your feet I hope."

"No," came the telepathic reply. "Anton made boots before, but this sand cool."

"I'm glad to hear that. You..." Before she could finish her sentence the beginning twinges of nausea crept into her stomach.

"Varnack!" she barely whispered.

He growled in response, immediately on his guard. She did not need to express in words her anxiety, for her telepathic terror reached him immediately after her stomach lurched. Web, as well as each of the other horses, also felt the warning communication and as one, reduced their pace. The sudden, unbidden slow down alarmed the riders and they murmured their surprise.

"Guardians!" Jessica yelled, "ahead...on the right...those boulders." She pointed at the location. Looking forward, she knew she had only seconds to save the three leading the column. Understanding her thoughts as soon as she had them, Web sprang into action, galloping toward John and Lyrista, while Varnack ran at Lepsis. Web squeezed between Fireguard and Lyrista's mare while Jessica, in a swift, powerful motion driven by adrenaline's strength, thrust her arms outward at each side, pushing her loved ones off their mounts. Varnack, jumping up, slammed sideways into Lepsis, unseating him from this horse. Just as the three riders crashed to the ground, a volley of arrows barely missed them. Two, however, hit Jessica, one in her right arm and another in her right leg.

The Guardians, only seconds behind Jessica, galloped toward the hidden attackers, their own arrows filling the sky. A whistle was heard, then moments later a band of Elitet left the boulders and escaped into the western desert.

Lepsis, up on his feet and recovered from the fall, yelled to the Guardians. "Do not pursue them. The western deserts are suicide to anyone who doesn't know the sand-trap secrets."

As if to prove the truthfulness of his statement, the scream of a terrified horse rent the air. The Guardians pulled to a halt and everyone, including a pain-racked Jessica, watched in horror as an Elitet and his unfortunate mount sank quickly into a deadly sand trap.

Web stopped as soon as Jessica was hit. A weak sob from her broke the gloomy quiet. "Dad." He was instantly at her side.

"Jess, I'm sorry. I didn't know you were hit." Gingerly, he pulled her off Web and laid her on the ground. Lepsis and Lyrista ran to his side. The arrow in her arm passed completely through, grazing the bone as it went. Lepsis broke the feathers and finished pulling it through the wound. Lyrista pulled her dagger out and ripped Jessica's pants at the second puncture site. John grabbed his ever-present emergency bag.

"Do you have some of that wonderful purple fern?" Jessica asked weakly.

"I don't, Jess. I'm sorry."

"Here," Brayon said from behind them, "I have some. I found this when I traveled to Ider Hoffle to enlist. I've carried the magical leaf with me throughout these many battles. One never knows when it may be needed." He handed a small piece of the precious plant to John. Breaking it in three pieces, John bound two of them to the entry and exit wounds in his daughter's arm with some cloth bandages. He winced when he turned to the leg.

"I'm sorry Jess, but we're going to have to dig this one out."

She nodded. Lepsis offered her his hands and she gripped them tightly. "Go ahead," she whispered.

Working quickly, John and Lyrista cut and pulled the arrow out at the same angle it had entered. The entire operation took only seconds, but Jessica screamed, one short agonized cry, then bit her lip so hard it bled. Placing the rest of the fern over the fresh wound, John tightly bound it.

"We'll spend the night here," Lepsis said. "Then tomorrow we'll head back to Rendaira."

"No." Jessica was already feeling the soothing pain relief from the fern. "You said it was important for Dad to go to Jorton Hoffle. It's less than a day away, so let's keep to our schedule. You take Dad on. Lyrista and Varnack can stay here with me." She turned to her father. "It's important for you to be the Protector, Dad. I'll be all right."

Brayon stepped forward. "I would be honored to stay here and protect the Lady Jessica." Many other Guardians also offered to stay.

Lyrista took tender care of Jessica while John was away. Varnack tried to cheer her up by telling her some jokes, but she laughed more at his offbeat wit than at the gags themselves. Trigal Hound humor did not translate well into human thought.

It was late into the night following the ambush when John and Lepsis returned to the campsite. Neither man said much about the visit. Jessica knew her father well enough to recognize his 'ask me no questions, I'll tell you no lies' look. Lyrista too was becoming adept at understanding John's more subtle signals.

Jessica waited until the camp bedded down before searching her father out for a heart to heart talk. Hearing the even, deep breathing of sleep come from Lyrista, who always lay beside her, Jessica rose up and hobbled to where John sat.

Still awake, he had separated himself from the others and now gazed up at the foreign sky. She silently watched him for a few minutes. To her, he looked very lonely. "Dad, we need to talk."

"I know, Jess."

"I can't…no…I don't want to stay here forever. The war is over now. I've done my part. I have a life on Earth and I want to go back and see how it plays out, besides, I really need to shave my legs."

John laughed. He reached for his daughter and brought her to sit on his knee. He held his arms around her while they both watched the two moons. It was a beautiful night. A light breeze blew and a night bird whistled from far away. A shooting star sailed across their line of vision.

After a long while, he said quietly, "I understand. You have school. It should be starting about now. And you have friends who mean a lot to you."

"What about you, Dad? What are you going to do? What do you *want* to do?"

"I don't know. I honestly don't know. My job at the hospital would be gone by now and my post at Whitworth College should be filled by someone else. I could do a lot of good here."

"You know I love you very much, but you need to decide what's best for you. Just remember, I'm a big girl. I'll be fine whatever your decision." She kissed him on the cheek and left him alone with his thoughts.

* * *

"John," A soft voice came from far away. "John," The voice came closer. "John, open your eyes."

He never knew if he was dreaming, or how to accurately describe what happened next, but when he opened his eyes, John saw his wife, Shallenon, standing before him. Hovering above the ground and surrounded by soft light, she wore a long, flowing white dress. A breeze he could not feel gently tossed her shoulder length red hair and her sapphire blue eyes sparkled when she smiled at him. She looked just as beautiful as he always remembered.

"John, it's time you move on with your life."

"Shallenon? Is it really you?"

"Yes, my love. I've come to thank you for everything you've done for my people. I've never been prouder of you or our daughter."

"I miss you so much." He sat up on his blanket, wanting a better look at her.

"I know, John. I feel your pain. We are connected, you and I. Nothing can ever break our bond, not even death, but it's time to move on. You have been alone too long. I want you to be happy. I'm not far away and I've always been there when you needed me," she smiled, "though, you never knew it."

"Where have you been all these years? How do you know what's been happening?"

"Do you truly think death is the end? Just because I'm on a different plane, it doesn't mean I'm completely disconnected from this one."

"I've met someone."

Shallenon smiled. "I like her, John. Follow your heart. You've always done the right thing. You've been a wonderful father and you're a good man. When your heart and your head agree, you can't go wrong."

The light slowly gathered around her and John sat speechless. She faded back into the night. The last he saw were her eyes shining brightly and her words echoed in his mind. "Follow your heart."

It only took him a second to leap up and race to where Lyrista slept. He jumped over four sleeping men and skirted the fire to reach her. Jessica was in a deep sleep beside her. They both looked angelic, and Lyrista was especially beautiful with the moonlight dancing on her face.

"Lyrista," he shook her shoulder. "Lyrista, wake up. I must talk to you and I can't wait until morning."

"John," she said groggily. "What's wrong?"

He knelt on one knee. "Lyrista, marry me. Marry me as soon as possible. I've come to realize that life is short, so when you find someone as perfect as you are for me, I can't let minutes waste away. Say you'll marry me...please."

Her face registered complete surprise, then she relaxed and a smile spread across her lips. "John, you're crazy. Of course I'll marry you." She gracefully sat up, wrapped her arms around his neck and passionately kissed him. When she was done, she pushed him away and said with a gleam in her eye, "Now go to sleep, I'll see you in the morning." She lay back down and closed her eyes.

John felt wide-awake, but he tiptoed back to his bedroll. He chuckled to himself. *She'll certainly keep me on my toes.*

"So, will it be a triple wedding?" Lepsis asked him.

John propped himself on one elbow, surprised to see his friend awake, but he grinned and said, "Looks that way buddy…looks that way."

In the morning Jessica squealed with joy when John and Lyrista told her their news. It didn't take long before the entire group of Guardians had congratulated the happy couple. During the ride back to Rendaira John told Jessica about his dream.

"When she disappeared," he said, "my pain disappeared too. It was as if a burden was lifted off my shoulders and I was free to live again. Your mom always knew just what to say to make things all right. She hasn't lost her touch."

* * *

Brightly colored banners of red, yellow, green and blue lined Rendaira's road, and the usually quiet thoroughfare was alive with wedding guests in summer buggies and delivery men driving wagons of food. When Jessica and company rode over the last hill leading into the heart of Rendaira, a welcoming sight greeted them. A Banner of Freedom flew from a newly erected pole directly in front of the mansion. The sound of laughter floated up from the many individuals who lounged on the front lawn in the late afternoon sun.

Lepsis seemed to know everyone, as he pointed to and named the various dignitaries, among whom were his extended family members from Marone. Even his cousin, the king of Marone was there.

After dismounting, John and Lyrista followed Lepsis to his family. Varnack trotted to a shade tree and plopped down under it. Jessica wanted to clean up a bit and find her grandmother. Limping into the mansion, she nearly collided with Merula who was running out of it. Merula looked beautiful in a long yellow dress, a purple sash complementing a purple ribbon in her hair. In the two weeks since Jessica last saw her, the woman had gained a bit of weight, thus helping to round out her far too thin frame.

"Merula, is my Grandma here yet?"

"Oh yes. She's been wonderful. I couldn't have organized everything without her. She's in the Grand Ballroom right now, supervising the final touches on the decorations."

The ballroom had been transformed into a sea of white and gold. Two large crystal chandeliers hung from the ceiling suspended by heavy golden chains. They were loaded with scores of small, white candles, ready to be lit. The walls were draped with white satin and accented with six large, green and gold wreaths. Jessica recognized many of the golden and crystal statues from Daenon's treasures scattered throughout the room. A thousand chairs were set up, lined in two columns, a wide aisle between them. Each chair was draped in white fabric and accented with a green, leafy vine secured by golden ribbon.

Sunlight streamed into the room through high, tall and wide windows. It hit the crystal in the chandeliers and where it did, split into rainbows of color that danced off the walls.

"Pretty spectacular, isn't it?" Gaylee commented from behind her granddaughter.

"Grandma, it's breathtaking!" Jessica exclaimed. She hugged her tightly with her good arm. "I've missed you so much."

"I've missed you too, child."

"Have you seen the portrait of Graesion in the Treasure chamber?"

"I have," she smiled wistfully and looked up at the chandelier. "It was painted just before we were married. It's a perfect likeness."

"Grandma, Dad, and Lyrista are engaged. Dad finally proposed three days ago. I think they want to be part of this wedding ceremony."

"Good for them. Your Uncle Anton finally asked Naydeen to marry him too, so I think it'll be a triple wedding."

"I have something for you." Jessica took the locket, hidden under her blouse, from around her neck. When she handed it to Gaylee she explained, "I found this in Daenon's treasure room the first time I was in it. It belonged to Illa, Haesom's wife."

Gaylee took the locket, opened it and stared at the two tiny drawings inside. "Those are your grandson's," Jessica said.

Tears welled in Gaylee's eyes and a sad smile touched her lips. "Thank you, Jessica." Her voice was a whisper. She blinked the tears away, then truly smiled. "Now you run along and clean up." She touched the streaked dirt on Jessica's face then noticed the bandaged arm. "What happened?"

"We were attacked by Elitet and I got the worst end of the deal. I'm doing fine though. Honestly. One of the Guardians had some of the purple fern and I'm healing ten times faster than I would ever heal on Earth. Dad's amazed I can walk without a cane, though I'm not running yet."

"You were hurt in the leg too?" Gaylee stepped back and took a good look at the leg, an even more worried expression on her face.

"Yeah, but really, I'm fine. You need to go tell Cook Stratin, she'll have to make another cake."

"Jess?"

"Grandma, go. I need to clean up and change out of these filthy clothes."

Gaylee closed the locket and slipped it around her neck. "All right, but send someone for me if you need help."

"I promise, I will. Oh, wait, is Uncle Larone here?"

"Yes, you just missed him. He went to the front lawn."

Within fifteen minutes, Jessica was cleaned up and making her way back to the front lawns. She wanted to meet Naydeen and see Larone again. There was so much to be done and so little time to do it in. She began to feel the pressure of not having enough hours left.

Spotting Anton with little trouble, Jessica admired the lady by his side. A delicate, older woman, Naydeen was still very beautiful. Her soft brown hair was lightly streaked with gray and swept back into a French knot behind her head. She held onto Anton's arm and spoke animatedly with John and Lyrista. Anton looked like a new man. The mats were gone from his hair, and it was cut from shoulder length to the nape of his neck, though it was still quite frizzy. His beard had also been trimmed closer to his face, so the whiskers did not stick out every which way. Larone stood with them, dressed in his usual gray robes.

Jessica strolled over to the group. She quietly slipped her arm through Larone's and squeezed it. Larone smiled down at her and patted her arm affectionately.

"And of course, I said yes," Naydeen said.

"Well, Jessi," Anton's low voice rumbled across the lawn, "sorry I wasn't there this time to pick ya up. Ya doin okay? That purple fern's great stuff."

Jessica blushed. "You missed out on a unique battle experience Uncle Anton. It was over before it actually even started."

"Lady Naydeen, may I introduce my daughter, Jessica Ernshaw," John said formally.

Before Jessica could offer her hand to shake the woman's, Naydeen bowed to her. "I'm honored to meet you, Protectoress Jessica. I owe my freedom and my happiness to you. It was you who brought my Anton back from his loneliness, and because of you, Demar is finally free."

"I, uh... think I had quite a bit of help," Jessica sputtered, blushing once again. "You honor me too much, Lady Naydeen."

"Don't worry 'bout it, Jessi," Anton said with a grin, "If ya start gettin' too big a head, I'll just tell everyone about the brush thing."

"Thanks, Uncle. I feel so much better," Jessica laughed. Larone gave her arm another gentle pat.

"Oh, Uncle Larone, I've figured out how to overcome the nausea," Jessica blurted out the thought. She was suddenly embarrassed yet again, when she realized how silly that must have sounded to anyone who did not understand her unique gifts. Sure enough, everyone laughed, but Larone looked at her seriously.

"How would that be?" he asked with genuine interest.

"Well," she looked around. Everyone had stopped laughing and listened for her answer. "If I become angry, the feeling goes away and I'm able to function more clearly. Addex made me mad, super mad, and the nausea vanished."

"That is fine, Jessica," Larone commented, but his brow was furrowed. "However, you will find anger takes a great deal of energy to maintain. It can also cloud your judgment, so you may wish to keep exploring other ways of controlling your gift."

"Jessica!" A call caught her attention.

Merula stood with Lepsis on the opposite end of the lawn. An elderly, frail looking man sat on a bench under a large shade tree in front of them. Merula waved for Jessica to join them. The older man wore a long, purple robe trimmed in black. His thick silver hair was cut short and he had a thin silver mustache. A cane rested next to him.

"Oh, Jessica," Merula grabbed her hand. "Meet my father, Regulator Tirus."

Jessica scarcely managed to contain her shock. She had assumed the man was her grandfather. "If it weren't for Merula, I wouldn't be here today. I owe her my life."

The old man smiled with pride. "She is everything I have ever hoped for and more," he said in a strong clear voice that did not match the feebleness of his body. "It was the thought of her that helped me stay alive those terrible years." He gave several little coughs.

"Come Father," Merula said tenderly, "let's take you out of this heat."

He nodded in agreement. Grasping his cane in one hand and holding to Lepsis with the other, the three made their way into the mansion. Jessica was left staring after them.

"It's sad, isn't it?" John said behind her. "He can't be older than Anton, and yet the years in prison almost broke him. Larone's done everything possible for him. I couldn't have done more myself."

"Lepsis seems very good to him. At least his last years should be happy ones."

The pounding of horse's hooves on the drive interrupted their conversation. They turned to see Cordon and Ophir riding up together, dusty and dirty. John ran to meet them. Ophir dismounted first and as soon as he did, John grabbed him in a tight bear hug. Ophir stood rigid in the embrace, a look of bewilderment on his bearded face. John let him go only to grab Cordon in the same tight squeeze, however Cordon hugged him back. It was like two brothers reuniting after years of separation.

Ophir smiled. "I left Galland as soon as I received your note about Lepsis and Anton's wedding plans. To see Anton married after all these years, and to Naydeen at that, is an event I would never miss. I met up with Cordon by chance at the Twin Hills."

Cordon grinned from ear to ear at John. "I see you don't have too many scars to tell me about. My lessons on swordsmanship finally paid off."

John grinned back. "I have a lot to tell you. But first, there's an important matter we need to discuss. Where I come from, it's customary for a man to ask permission of his lady's family to marry her. So Cordon, as Lyrista's older brother, I'm asking you for her hand in marriage."

Cordon looked thunderstruck and Jessica was momentarily afraid her dad's friend would actually say no, but then tears welled up in Cordon's eyes and he thickly said, "She said yes?"

John nodded.

"Finally." Cordon grinned and threw his arms around John in a huge bear hug.

CHAPTER 28

Going Home

The triple wedding was held five days after the touring group returned to Rendaira from their desert explorations. Dignitaries from throughout the country arrived during those days, and Rendaira was filled to capacity. Even one of the barracks had to be made into a guest hall. The ballroom overflowed, with each of the thousand chairs occupied and soldiers standing in every available space.

The grooms, all three of them, were dressed in their finest clothes. Lepsis wore traditional Maronian attire of deep purple and cream satin robes. He had a thick gold cord draped around his neck that touched the floor on both ends. His head was bare and his long hair pulled back, secured by a golden clamp.

Anton dressed in traditional Esparian clothing consisting of deep blue velvet pants and a white silk shirt elaborately embroidered in silver. He wore several long, heavy silver chains, and a broad silver band adorned his right middle finger. It was obvious someone had tried to help him with his hair, but it was a lost cause, still frizzing out on the ends.

John chose his blue and silver military uniform with the Sword of Judgment polished and strapped to his side. The coat lay unbuttoned revealing a white satin shirt and a deep red satin sash, much like a cumber bun, around his middle. Jessica had made the shirt and the sash. She wanted him to wear the colors of their native country. Nobody would understand the red, white and blue other than Gaylee and themselves, but the red added a pleasant accent to the uniform.

A full orchestra assembled for the occasion, and when the music began, the brides came walking down the aisle, one by one. Escorted by a clean-shaven, short haired Farin, and dressed in a white, flowing gown, Merula was the first to come. A golden tiara belonging to her mother adorned her head. Jessica smiled at Cook Stratin, who cried tears of happiness, while the other staff members beamed with pride and joy.

Naydeen came next, escorted by Larone. A simple, elegant gown of ivory silk fit her like a glove. The hem of the gown and the end of the long sleeves were embroidered in gold thread with many of the same designs matching those on Anton's shirt. On her head swirled a garland of tiny pink rose buds held together by gold ribbon. Her eyes sparkled, and when Larone gave her hand into his brother's, he kissed each of them on the cheek.

Finally Lyrista, accompanied by Cordon, walked in. She wore her best blue and silver military uniform. Jessica had given her the Sword of Mercy to wear, and it was tied to her side by a thick red cord. Her face shone just as brilliantly as the fabled sword. Her head was bare, but her soft blond hair, which had grown out a bit since Jessica first met her, was actually curled and softly framed her face. Upon her entering the hall, every soldier snapped to attention and smartly touched their left fists to their foreheads, and then struck their left breasts smartly, saluting her in honor.

Jessica sat on the front row of chairs along with Gaylee, Ophir, and Reese. Varnack lay positioned at her feet. Before leaving for the two-week tour of Demar, Jessica had given her makeshift uniform, which she had worked so hard to sew, to Merula with the request it be cleaned for the upcoming wedding. When Merula returned it to her the night she returned to Rendaira, Jessica was amazed at the transformation the clothing had undergone. Someone had lovingly re-embroidered the blouse, covering it in silver and gold patterns. The pants were embroidered down each side seam and around the cuffs to match the blouse. Jessica complemented the ensemble with a thin, dark red satin belt. Her curled red hair cascaded around her shoulders, and for the first time since arriving on Edia, she felt truly beautiful.

Merula's father, Regulator Tirus, stood at the front of the room. He wore the silver ceremonial robes of Palium High Regulator. With the aid of his cane, he stood straight and tall, beaming at each couple when they came to kneel before him. His body may have been broken, but his voice rang out strong and vibrant as ever. No one strained to hear his words as he performed each marriage with solemnity.

All three husbands turned to their respective wives and kissed them, while the wedding guests erupted into deafening applause. Good food, good drinks, and fine music marked the party that followed. There were no fewer than twelve long tables set up with food of every type and description. A wide variety of drinks were offered at a large booth set up beside the tables, and the orchestra played non-stop.

Jessica's wounds had healed at a phenomenal pace and no longer gave her pain. After the weddings, she congratulated each of the couples. It was a bittersweet time for her as she attended the celebration with mixed feelings.

She noticed how easily her Grandmother mingled with every group in attendance. Gaylee spent the evening gliding from Maronian and Esparian dignitaries to units of soldiers and servants. Envying the older lady's grace and talent, Jessica felt out of place. She tried to follow her Grandmother's example, but soon ran out of things to say. Larone rescued her once by asking her to dance. Farin also gave her a turn on the floor, leaving her breathless from the spins and twirls.

As the night wore on, Jessica saw the newly married couples disappear one by one from the ballroom. Lepsis and Merula went to the guest house, Anton and Naydeen to a deluxe guest suite, while John and Lyrista retired to Daenon's former quarters, Gaylee having redecorated the entire apartment.

Giving up on socializing, Jessica finally went for the food. She had a mouth full of crème pudding when Reese walked up. "The wedding was...nice," he said awkwardly.

"Yes, it was. I hope they'll each be very happy." She reached for a square pastry filled with a purple mystery fruit and sprinkled with sugar.

"I heard about what happened to you at the Colossus Forest," he shook his head. "Jeema was such a fool. It was his first big assignment and he let it go to his head. He didn't take any precautions. I've seen him and he feels pretty bad."

Jessica took a bite of the pastry and was pleasantly surprised by the cherry taste. "Did he tell you I tried to warn him...three times? You should try this," she pointed to the pastry in her hand, "it's wonderful."

Reese shifted his feet nervously. "Lepsis has asked me to head the security forces here in Demar. It's an offer of a lifetime."

Jessica set the pastry down and took a good look at Reese. He was tall by Ider standards, dark, and handsome. A neatly trimmed beard added to his already attractive features. He had an endearing boyish shyness and was a good person at heart.

"Reese, I think that's great," she said honestly. "I can't think of a better man for the job."

He smiled and slightly relaxed.

"I want you to be the first to know I will not be staying here much longer." Jessica spoke softly, but Reese looked thunderstruck.

"Where are you going?"

"Home, back to Earth. I have a whole different life there. I want to go to school and be with my best friend, Rachel, again. She's going to be my roommate and I can't let her down. I want to see where it all takes me."

Reese sighed and Jessica saw several different emotions travel over his face. Finally he asked, "Will you come back?"

"I don't know. I truly don't, but if I can, I will. My Dad is here as are many people I've come to care a great deal about."

He nodded, then he held his hand out. She shook it and smiled warmly at him. "Good luck, Jessica. I hope your life is full and everything you want it to be."

"Thanks, Reese. You take care of yourself and always watch your back."

"Hey, Reese." Someone calling from behind him interrupted their goodbyes. Jessica saw Jeema beckoning him over. At the sight of Jessica, Jeema turned deep red, worry crossing his face.

"Go," Jessica smiled. "Tell him not to worry, he's forgiven. I'll see you later." She watched him for a few minutes after he fell into easy conversation with his friend. Jeema seemed to relax, then turning toward Jessica, he bowed.

Scanning the crowds of people, Jessica spotted her Grandmother talking with Regulator Tirus. She was about to join the two when Ophir walked toward them, his eyes fixed on Gaylee. Bowing low, he offered her his arm to lead her to the dance floor. Surprised by his grace and polish, Jessica smiled. All at once, she felt very tired. She did not belong there.

Desiring the safety of her chambers, Jessica turned to leave. "I have been watching you. You seem lost." Larone fell into step beside her. He held his arm for her, then led her to the back of the mansion. They strolled through the waist high hedges of the beautiful garden. The distant sound of laughter and music drifted to where they walked. Two moons and numerous stars showed down, illuminating the paths in their soft, mellow light.

"Uncle Larone, show me the star that's my sun." He pointed to a faint grouping in the northern sky. "My role here is finished now," she sighed. "It's time for me to go back."

"I thought this is what was on your mind. Have you discussed it with your father?"

"Yes, I've told him."

"Then I will talk to Anton at the first opportunity," he promised. "You can leave as early as tomorrow if you wish."

She was astonished. "You mean it?"

"Yes, I do."

"Oh Uncle Larone!" Jessica threw her arms around his neck and hugged him tightly. "I might still make the first day of classes! And I can see Rachel, and I can see *Thomas*!"

"Thomas?" His eyebrows went up, but he smiled knowingly. "I understand," he nodded. "Jessica, you have done everything required of you and more. I am proud of you. You can count on going back tomorrow. Everything will be ready, but I am afraid I will miss you very much."

Jessica went to bed that night with clashing feelings. On the one hand she felt excited to go home, and on the other she was sad about leaving her newfound family and her father. She could not guess what her grandmother would do, but in the morning she would find out.

Breakfast consisted of leftovers from the celebration. Not feeling hungry, Jessica grabbed one of the cherry-like pastries and set out to find her grandmother, finally locating her in the kitchen.

"Grandma, I'm going home today," she announced. There was no easy way of saying it, so she felt the direct approach was best. "Uncle Larone promised to have everything ready."

Gaylee was sorting through fresh herbs, and at Jessica's news her hands stopped in mid-air. "I knew this was coming." She turned to face her granddaughter. "I've wondered how I would react when you told me, and now I know." She sighed, "I'm going with you."

"With me? Honestly?"

"Yes. I could live here as an honored woman, but I would always be just an honored woman. On Earth I have friends, people who care about me, Gaylee, not Lady Saylon. It's been a good visit, but I want to go back too."

* * *

Larone was sitting outside on a bench under the same shade tree where Jessica had met Merula's father when his two nieces located him. Gaylee told him of her desire to accompany Jessica.

"I anticipated this. Perhaps someday, you will come back and wish to stay."

Jessica wondered if anything ever surprised her all-knowing uncle.

"So there ya are," Anton thundered from the front door. "I've been searchin' all over this place for ya." In a grand mood, he nearly skipped over to where they were. "So ya want to go back, do ya?" he addressed Jessica.

"It's hard to leave, Uncle, but…yes I do."

"We'll miss ya, Jessi. But I know yer young and ya need to spread yer wings." He looked at Gaylee. "And ya need to go with her, huh?"

Gaylee nodded. It seemed Anton had anticipated this decision as easily as Larone.

"All right," he smiled. "I'll have everythin' ready in a couple of hours. I'll send ya back to yer door. Once yer there, the hole'll dissolve and not activate again."

He looked around at the other guests roaming the yard. "We don't need an audience for this. I guess I'll set it up so's you'll enter the hole from Daenon's office. That work?"

"It will be fine," Gaylee affirmed. And so it was settled. Anton went back to his rooms to finish his calculations. Larone excused himself and disappeared around the side of the mansion. Gaylee said she needed to write a few letters, so left to find paper and writing equipment, and Jessica wanted to find her father.

She found him with Lyrista in the back garden, meandering around knee high, thornless rose bushes. "Dad and Lyrista!" Jessica ran up to meet them.

"Jess, we were just about to go look for you," John said.

She laughed. "Look Dad, this is your time together. You don't need to worry about me. Honestly. I'm so proud to have Lyrista as my new mom." She hugged them both, then stepped back, a sad smile on her face. "I've come to tell you--Grandma and I are going back home in a couple of hours. Uncle Anton is setting it up as we speak."

"So soon?" John was startled.

"Oh, Jessica. I would never want to drive you away," Lyrista said worriedly.

"No, no. You don't understand," Jessica quickly explained. "I've already talked to dad about this. I told him nearly a week ago I wanted to go back. It has nothing to do with you, Lyrista...well...actually that's not true. Now that I know how happy he is, it makes it that much easier for me to leave. I won't worry, knowing he'll be happy with you."

"I'll bring the Sword of Mercy," Lyrista offered, but Jessica held her hand to stop her.

"No. It needs to stay here with the Sword of Judgment. You keep it safe. If I ever return, I'll claim it. Until then, you'll keep it safe."

John looked at her tenderly. "It's hard letting you go, but I understand."

Jessica hugged each one again. "I love both of you," she choked. "I'm going to find Merula now and tell her." She ran off, wiping away the tears that stung her eyes.

Spotting Merula walking along the covered path leading from Lepsis' house to the mansion, Jessica yelled, then waved while she ran across the garden. Merula looked relaxed and Jessica saw the pain of so many years gone from her gray-green eyes; they actually sparkled.

"Jess, I was looking for you," Merula called. "I wonder if you would come to dinner tonight. There's a very nice kitchen in Lepsis' home and I thought I'd try my hand at cooking."

Jessica stopped in front of her friend. Without a word, she threw her arms around her and squeezed her tightly. She would miss Merula later as much as she missed Rachel now.

"What's wrong?" Merula asked in alarm.

"Merula..." Jessica began, but could not finish. The words would not come. She hated goodbyes more than anything else and could not say one more.

"You're leaving, aren't you?" Merula's voice was soft. "I can see it in your eyes."

"I have a life beyond here."

"I understand. So I guess dinner is out."

Jessica nodded. "I leave in a few hours. I wanted you and Lepsis to come and be there. When I go back, my Grandma's coming with me."

"I'll tell Lepsis. Do you need help packing, getting the horses ready?"

"Oh, Merula," Jessica smiled. "I almost forgot, you don't know."

Merula looked confused. "Uncle Anton said he'd have everything ready in a couple of hours. Just don't go anywhere and I'll come and get you when it's time. Be prepared for a shock though, and tell Lepsis to be prepared. After I'm gone, my dad can answer any question you might have."

Four hours later a small group gathered in the large mahogany room that used to be Daenon's. The living space was miraculously transformed. Gone were the taxidermy animals and weapons of destruction, and in their places were the statues and beautiful paintings from the Treasure room. Cream curtains replaced the green. Two pastel floral tapestries hung from opposing walls, a bright contrast to the dark wood paneling.

Furniture was moved from the center of the room off to one side. A long, thin, flat stone lay on the bare tiled floor where a couch had been. A blue rock, the size of a robin's egg, balanced on top of it.

Anton stood behind Naydeen, his hands resting gently on her shoulders. Lepsis and Merula were holding hands, looking thoroughly confused, and John had his arm around Lyrista. Cordon, Ophir and Reese stood solemnly in a row, while Jessica and Gaylee were in the center of the room, standing next to the flat stone. Jessica wore her jeans and a simple Demarian blouse. In her hands, she held her embroidered uniform, wrapped in a neat package; it was the only thing she wanted to take with her. A hush came over the group while they waited patiently for Larone and Varnack.

"Sorry I am late," Larone said breathlessly when he entered the room. Varnack trotted at his side. "It took longer than I thought it would to form this." He held out his open hand to show everyone what was in it. A small, marble sized, clear white ball rested on his palm. He offered it to Jessica. "This is for you, a parting gift."

She gingerly took the velvety smooth sphere from him. "It looks like the same crystal ball that's on the end of the Sword of Mercy," she commented.

"It is made of the same material," he explained, "White Persite."

All of the native Esparians gasped, including Gaylee. "Some still exists?" she asked in awe.

"What exactly is persite?" John said.

"It's a very rare mineral," Anton explained. "Blue is much more common than white, and then there's green, but we won't talk 'bout that stuff. It's evil and nearly impossible to unlock. I was able to gather some of the white in my travels over the years. It's found in tiny pockets way up north."

"Persite's mentioned in ancient writings," Lyrista explained. "It has magical qualities, but I never believed it truly existed."

"This substance has many qualities I do not as yet understand. This blue crystalline rock here is blue persite," Larone indicated the small stone on the thin rock slab. "It powers the Transmirian spiral. White, however is more than just a power source, it seems to have strong magic that connects to certain life compositions. Anyone can use blue, but only someone very special can wield white. One of the capacities white has is to act much like an amplifier. Hold it in your hand, Jessica, and concentrate. Your energies flow through the persite and are made greater...stronger. You can connect with it. It was with a piece much like this that I was able to locate you on Earth. I thought about you and reached out with my mind. My telepathic powers were greatly enhanced to the point where I was able to find you. It is this increased energy that causes the Sword of Mercy to gather such great power from your life force."

Jessica walked around the room holding the piece in her open palm so everyone could have a good look at it.

Larone continued his explanation. "Your natural gifts will be amplified if you use this. I have hesitated to give it to you, but once I heard about what happened on the Twin Hills, I knew it was the right thing to do. Persite is very powerful, and since I do not fully understand how it works, it could be dangerous, but I feel you will be able to master it. Your powers are not as pronounced on Earth as they are here, and so Earth is the safest place for you to learn how to use this magic."

Jessica stuffed the ball into her front jean pocket. "Thank you, Uncle Larone. I'll work at it, I promise."

"I have a gift of my own," Gaylee smiled and walked over to John and Lyrista. "I've spent much of these last two months at my old home, Saylon Dorsett. Larone gave me sufficient funds to completely restore it. Larone knows of all the improvements and will show you everything. I give the estate to you, for your children and for your children's children."

John smiled. "You're quite a lady, Gaylee. Thanks for everything." He leaned forward and kissed her cheek.

Lyrista timidly wrapped her arms around the older woman and squeezed. "Thank you."

Gaylee hugged her back then turned to rejoin Jessica, but before she took two steps Ophir called to her. "Gaylee," he said clearly. It was the first time he had used her informal name and Jessica was surprised by it. He walked over to her, took her hand, and gently kissed it. "Do not wait another fifty years before returning to us." The two gazed at each other for a long moment.

With a jolt, Jessica realized that Ophir was in love with her. Warmth began to radiate from her front pocket where the ball of persite was hidden and it quickly spread throughout her body. When Gaylee turned from Ophir, her face was a mask of calm, but as her eyes briefly met Jessica's, a wave of emotion flooded from them.

Instantly, with the help of the persite, Jessica read her Grandmother's thoughts and felt her frustration. *Ophir! Why now? Why only now, when it's too late, do you let your feelings show?*

"It's time," Anton merrily announced. "You do good at school, Jessi. Make us proud."

The persite's warmth immediately ceased. "I will," Jessica said with a lump in her throat. She ran and gave one last hug to her father and Lyrista, while Ophir retook his place next to Cordon. When Jessica walked to the center of the room, she saw nothing but sad faces, except for Varnack, Larone and Anton. The two men were smiling and the Trigal Hound waged his tail.

Anton pulled a small vial of green liquid from a pocket in his leather vest. He walked over to the blue rock in the center of the room. While he poured the vial on it, he explained, "Daenon isn't the only one who can conjure potions. This green stuff here unlocks the persite's power." He began to chant. "By the voice of T'Aalin, through the Expanse of Gonta, I call on the powers of Bree, to open this passage, by the winds of Malana, I call the Transmirian key. Open a channel, through the portal of black, terrene four, two, one arc line six, two track. By the voice of T'Aalin, through the Expanse of Gonta…"

Softly repeating the words, he hurried back to Naydeen. The rock commenced to smoke and the air above it started to swirl. A low-pitched rushing noise hissed from the swirling air and it quickly increased in intensity. Each of the spectators took an involuntary step backwards, including Jessica and Gaylee.

"Uncle Larone," Jessica yelled above the noise.

"What is it Jessica?" he yelled back.

"Why are you and Uncle Anton smiling, and Varnack so happy?"

"Why should we be sad when we know you will be coming back to us?"

"What do you mean?" Jessica could hardly be heard above the noise.

"The prophecy, Jessi," Anton boomed. "Ya gotta return to finish fulfillin' it."

Those were the last words Jessica heard, for just then the spiral reached full force and she and Gaylee were sucked in.

The trip home was as bad as the trip to Edia. Jessica closed her eyes to the rush and concentrated on relaxing. She tightly clutched the package. After what seemed like forever, she hit the hard tile floor of her kitchen and skidded across it. The package went flying when she slammed into a wall and her forward momentum was abruptly stopped. Gaylee landed right after her and skidded to the same point, smashing into Jessica.

Jessica's first thought was for Gaylee, but blackness threatened to envelope her. She fought against it. Warmth from her front pant pocket gave her an unexpected shock and she reached for the small ball. Holding it tightly, she thought about staying conscious. A second jolt ran from her hand, coursing throughout her body. She jerked fully awake, then fisting her hand over the crystal, jumped to Gaylee's side.

"Grandma!"

Gaylee did not move. She barely breathed. Jessica placed her free hand, palm down on Gaylee's forehead. Closing her eyes, she concentrated on making Gaylee conscious. The little ball sparked to life and heat ran from Jessica's fist, through her chest, directly to her open palm on Gaylee's brow. Within moments, she moaned and slowly opened her eyes.

Hearing footsteps, Jessica slid the ball back into her pocket. Jacob and Sophia rushed into the kitchen.

"Gaylee! Jessica!" Sophia shrieked. "You're home, oh, you're home!"

She threw her short arms around both of them. She tried to talk further, but could only whimper through her tears of joy. Jacob walked over and helped Gaylee to her feet.

"We were upstairs when we heard the rush of wind. I'm very glad to see you back, Gaylee. Are you all right?" he sounded concerned.

"I'm pretty dizzy," she said haltingly. He helped her to a chair, then turned to Jessica who was already on her feet and helping a sobbing, yet smiling Sophia to the chair next to Gaylee.

"I feel fine," Jessica told him. She was surprised at how true that was. She found her package and set it on the table.

"Oh, Jessica dear," Sophia managed to say. "You came back just in time. Rachel left a week ago for the university. She drove your car. I packed all your things and sent them with her. I was hoping you'd come home in time to go, and here you are!"

She turned to her husband, who had just given Gaylee a drink of cool water. "Jacob, you need to call the airlines and see if we can purchase a flight for Seattle tonight. I hope it's not too late. Even first class will do, if there's no coach left."

"Tonight!" Jessica exclaimed. "When does school begin?"

"Last week, dear," Sophia said a little more evenly. "We must fly you there before you miss more classes." Focusing on Jessica arriving at the university helped a great deal to calm her down. "As I said, I sent your things with Rachel. She doesn't know about your adventure this summer, I thought it best for you to tell her."

"That was very wise," Gaylee gave a thin smile. By degrees, the color was returning to her cheeks.

"Where's Sneakers?" Jessica asked Jacob.

"Oh, I put him out a couple of hours ago. He's got us on a schedule."

Jessica laughed. "What?"

"Don't ask," Jacob held up his hand. "Suffice it to say, Sophia spoils him rotten, caters to his every whim, or I should say, meow."

"He'll be back soon, dear," Sophia said. "He always returns this time of night."

"Grandma," Jessica could hold back no longer. "Ophir…" But, before she could finish her sentence, Gaylee cut her off.

"That was worlds away."

"Gaylee, I'm so glad you're back," Sophia repeated. "I did nothing but worry about you this entire summer."

"I can testify to that," Jacob said dryly after he hung up the phone. "There's a flight out in three hours. I guess you're all set, Jessica."

"Wow, this is so fast," Jessica felt a little light headed. "What's the date anyway?"

"It's October second," Sophia replied.

Jessica shook her head. "I can't believe only four months have passed. It seems like a lifetime."

Gaylee placed her hand on Jessica's shoulder. "For you, it has been. Your friends are going to find you've changed. Be prepared for that."

"I'll call Rachel and have her meet you at SeaTac," Jacob offered.

A meow at the door brought a lump to Jessica's throat. She raced to open it and scooped Sneakers up into her arms. "I missed you soooo much," she whispered.

Sneakers squirmed out of her grasp and scampered out of the kitchen. Surprised, she followed after him. He ran down the hallway, up the stairs and disappeared.

"Sneakers!" She followed him up to her room. Once through her bedroom door, Jessica stopped dead in her tracks. It was barren of nearly everything, including the books on her shelves and the pencils on her desk. Sophia had sent everything last thing Jessica owned to her apartment in Seattle.

Looking to the stripped down bed, Jessica spotted a ball of calico fur. "Sneakers!" He was curled up in the middle of her mattress. He twitched his ears. She plopped down beside him and stroked his fur. He looked at her blankly then closed his eyes. "Sneakers, what's wrong?"

A warm sensation spread down her leg from her front pant pocket. She took the ball of persite in her hand, it softly glowed.

"You left me." The words formed in her mind.

"I didn't mean to leave you. I wasn't given a choice, but I'm back now and I missed you more than you can ever know." She put her face close to his. "I don't blame you for being angry. I'm truly sorry."

From under his ribs, she felt a shallow vibration. The purr grew stronger as she continued to pet him. "I forgive you." He said, then licked her arm.

She spent well over an hour explaining to him where she had been and the things she had done. He stopped purring at the first mention of Varnack, but purred again at her reassuring touch.

"I'm leaving again," she finally said, "but I won't be gone long. I'm off to college, but I'll be back in soon for the holiday. Grandma's here and she'll take care of you now."

He licked her arm again. "Like Grandma."

"All right," she smiled. "I love you, Sneakers. I'll bring you a toy." At that, his tail twitched. She picked him up and gave him a gentle squeeze, then placed him back where he had been lying. When she walked out the bedroom door, his loud purring wished her a sweet farewell.

Jessica said good-bye to Gaylee and Sophia at home. It was an easy parting as Thanksgiving vacation was just around the corner, so she would not be gone from them for long. "Take good care of Sneakers for me, Grandma. He likes you."

"Don't worry Jess, I'll give him lots of love."

With her package from Edia as her only luggage, Jessica stood ready to go. Jacob drove her to the airport and they reached the security gate with only a few minutes to spare. "Here, this is for you." He reached into his coat pocket and handed her a thick envelope. "This has money and your school documents in it. We've already paid your tuition and rent. Your Grandma will put your finances in order now that she's back."

"Thanks, Jacob. You're awesome." She threw her free arm around his neck, giving him a big hug.

"Good luck," he said kindly and waved goodbye when she passed through the metal detectors.

The flight left on time and Jessica found herself seated next to a window. The city lights grew smaller and smaller as the plane climbed into the night sky. Within minutes of leaving Spokane, her view of the earth below as well as the stars above became obscured by thickening clouds. With nothing of interest to see, she wiggled into a comfortable position and drifted off to sleep.

Within minutes, the mists outside the high flying aircraft invaded her dreams and she found herself surrounded by them. She knew enough about this type of dream to close her eyes and stretch her mind. Off to one side she felt a gentle pull. She had not traveled for very long when a distant, rhythmic thumping came to her ears. One, two, three, swish, someone paced.

"I can't believe this is happening to me," a deep voice grumbled.

Daenon! Jessica was shocked.

"I thought I had grandfather's prophecy beaten."

She wondered who he was talking to.

"Locked in my mother's cell. I'll bet they think that's quite poetic, but I'm not defeated yet. That prophecy gives me another chance, and I won't make the same mistakes twice. Grandfather, always the poet. 'Dark succeeds to twice arise, with army fierce in strength and size.' They don't know the meaning of fierce. When I'm free again, there will be a cry of death the likes of which have never been heard before."

Jessica was stunned. She had given little thought to Anton's parting comment, but now the words of the prophecy came clearly into her mind. 'When light returns with allies strong, keep justice true, do not go wrong.' She would be going back.

A distant voice interrupted her thoughts. "The captain has turned on the seatbelt sign. We are making our final approach to SeaTac airport."

Jessica opened her eyes. The plane was nearly to Seattle. Looking out the window, the lights of the city grew ever brighter as the plane descended below the cloud cover. Seattle weather looked overcast, but there was no fog and it was dry.

After disembarking the plane, she followed the other passengers up the concourse to where she hoped Rachel would be waiting. Crossing the security barrier, she looked over a sea of unfamiliar faces.

A good-sized crowd milled about, people waiting for friends and loved ones to come from the planes, but Rachel was not among them. Finally, Jessica spied someone she knew, a tall, handsome young man who made her heart beat faster.

"Thomas," she breathed. He walked toward her, a little hesitantly.

"I hope you don't mind, but when Rachel told me you were on your way I asked if I could pick you up."

"No, I don't mind at all."

He was just as she remembered him. Soft, kind eyes, and a smile that made her go weak in the knees. The look on his face when he saw her was enough to convince her she had made the right decision to come back.

"I brought you this from my trip to Europe." He reached inside his coat pocket and pulled a bar of fine chocolate. "Last time we met you said you wanted about a pound."

She was amazed he had remembered. "Ohhh….a pound sounds really good." She took the bar from him.

He took her free hand firmly in his. "I missed you," he said. "How was your summer?"

Jessica gazed up at him. *Should I tell the truth?* She thought. *He'll never believe me.* The ball of persite pulsated warmly in her front jean pocket while she searched his face. *Then again, maybe he would.*

341

About the author

Lisa Wilson is a registered nurse who has seven great children.
She loves Doctor Who and the Sci-fi Channel.

Other Books by Dragon Scale Publishing

www.ingramcontent.com/pod-product-compliance
Lightning Source LLC
Chambersburg PA
CBHW020827180626
46814CB00001B/130